NOTHING
but the
BLOOD

J. MATTHEW SAUNDERS

SAINT GEORGE'S PRESS

Saint George's Press
York, S.C.
www.saintgeorgespress.com

Beware of false prophets, which come to you in sheep's clothing, but inwardly they are ravening wolves.

— MATTHEW 7:15

1

WEDNESDAY, AUGUST 15, 1962

Jamie sat in the bed of the broken-down pickup truck, smoking a cigarette and talking to ghosts. "Five nights in a row now. Same bad dream. Wish I knew why I keep having it."

It was coming up on three in the morning, and though he knew better, Jamie imagined himself the only person awake in all of Avalon, South Carolina. The light of the full moon threw long shadows across the yard. Somewhere close by, an owl called out. *Who cooks for you? Who cooks for you all?* The crickets, the cicadas, and the frogs all added their voices to the chorus wafting on the thick, stagnant air. The humidity made Jamie's t-shirt stick to his back.

"I remember the lullaby you used to sing to me to put me to sleep when I was little." He hummed a few notes. "I wish it still worked."

He clutched an old, creased photograph of a man and a woman standing by a tree in a garden. The scribbled date in the corner said *May 13, 1927* in faded, brown ink. The man, tall and lanky with a mess of blond hair, had his arm around the woman. She was a good head shorter, her dark hair pulled back in a severe bun. Neither of them smiled or seemed particularly happy to be there, even though the picture was taken the day after their wedding.

A light came on inside the house. Ginny must have woken up.

Jamie sighed. "I'm going to be in trouble soon, though I guess I can't complain much. She just worries. Rather have that problem than the opposite."

The light in the kitchen switched on. Ginny was probably checking to make sure he didn't get into the leftover pot roast.

"I wish you had the chance to meet her. You'd like her."

Another light flickered on, this one in his daughter's room. He was really going to be in hot water now. Ginny must have woken her up looking for him.

"I wish you had the chance to meet Amy Lynn, too. You'd love her as much as I do, I know. She's one of a kind, that's for sure."

The light in Amy Lynn's room went out again. Time to leave the ghosts behind.

"I better go. I miss you both. I wish we could talk for real. I have a lot of questions I need answering, but I guess this will have to do." Jamie ran a finger over the faces of the man and the woman. "Good bye for now. Love you, Mom. Love you, Dad."

Jamie stuffed the photograph into his pocket and stubbed the cigarette out. He swung one leg over the side of the truck but froze with the other leg midair when a noise like nothing he had ever heard before boomed from the direction of the woods. Jamie had trouble describing it, but if pressed, he might say it sounded like something between a dying car horn and an old coon dog baying.

The tree line at the edge of the yard stood out in the light of the moon. Jamie squinted and peered into the woods. The owls, the crickets, the cicadas, and the frogs had all gone silent. Jamie held his breath and waited. The seconds ticked by. Fifteen. Thirty. Almost a minute. Nothing happened.

Then something crashed through the underbrush making all kinds of racket. Jamie's heart pounded in his chest as a black shape rose up and then receded back into the darkness. He couldn't make out what it was, only that it was big.

The back door opened. Ginny stood in the doorway wearing her bathrobe over her nightgown. Jamie couldn't see her face, but he felt her frown. He waved at her sheepishly as he finished climbing out of the truck bed. But as he ambled toward the house, he couldn't stop from glancing over his shoulder at the black trees outlined against the indigo sky.

———

THE NEXT MORNING Ginny was finishing up with the scrambled eggs when Jamie came downstairs.

"Sorry about last night," he mumbled as he sat down at the table.

She put a plate of eggs and sausage in front of him. "You know, most people just toss and turn when they can't sleep. Sometimes they read a book."

"I didn't want to bother you."

"And we both know how that worked out. Anything you want to talk about?"

"Not really. Just couldn't sleep. That's all."

Ginny pursed her lips. She didn't believe him, but she wasn't going to push. Not yet. "Well, if you change your mind, you can let me know."

Ginny knew about the wrinkled photo in Jamie's pants pocket, of course, having saved it from the washing machine more times than she could count. He missed his parents, even after all this time, and especially at this time of year.

But Jamie acted like the world rested on his shoulders, and he was as hard-headed as they came. It wouldn't do any good trying to get him to talk if he didn't want to.

Jamie moved his eggs around on his plate with his fork. "Did ... did you hear anything strange last night?"

She shook her head. "No. Why?"

"There was something in the woods. I couldn't see what it was. It moved too fast, but it sure did make a row."

Ginny shrugged. "Probably a deer."

"Too big to be a deer."

Ginny grinned. "A big deer then."

Jamie looked like he had more to say, but their conversation was cut short by Amy Lynn, who bounded down the stairs. As usual, she had a book tucked under her arm. Everyone always said she was a miniature version of Ginny, with dark brown hair and bright blue eyes. Jamie joked the only thing about her that came from him was her stubborn streak. Ginny couldn't really argue about that part.

"Good morning, sweetie," Ginny said. "Come have some breakfast."

Amy Lynn clambered into her chair. As soon as Ginny slid a plate in front of her, she grabbed a fork and scooped a heap of scrambled eggs in her mouth. Then she set her book down on the table and opened it to where she'd marked her place.

Jamie gently placed a hand on top of the book. "Now, Amy Lynn, what have we told you about reading at the table?"

"Sorry, Daddy, I was trying to finish my book, but I got hungry." She made a go at looking regretful as she closed the book, but she wasn't fooling anyone.

Jamie may have been right. Reading at the table was bad manners, but Ginny didn't want to completely discourage her. "What are you reading about?" she asked.

"The moon," Amy Lynn replied.

Jamie scrunched up his face. "What's so interesting about the moon?"

Amy Lynn's eyes lit up. "Everything. Did you know the moon has seas and oceans even though there isn't any water up there? And the same side of the moon is always facing us? No one knows what the other side of the moon looks like. There could even be aliens living there."

Jamie leaned in close and asked with all the earnestness in his voice, "Well if there are aliens up there, why haven't they come to visit? Not very neighborly of them."

Amy Lynn ignored the joke. "There was a full moon last night. Did you know every full moon has a different name? My book says the full moon in August is called the Red Moon, but it has other names, too. Sometimes it's called the Sturgeon Moon or the Green Corn Moon. Do you know why people call it those things?"

"I didn't know they called it any of those," Jamie said.

Amy Lynn turned to her mother. "Do you think Grandma knows?"

"Why don't you ask her when you see her on Sunday?" Ginny pointed to Amy Lynn's plate. "Now finish your breakfast before it gets cold."

"Yes, ma'am." She cleaned her plate in four gulps, then snatched up her book and hopped off her chair.

"You know you only got five more days before school starts back up again," Jamie said. "Why don't you go outside and enjoy the sunshine?"

Amy Lynn groaned and rolled her eyes. It was not the first time she'd heard that speech.

"And don't spend all your time reading, either," Jamie continued. "Take your bike to one of your friends' houses."

"Yes, sir." Amy Lynn's shoulders slumped as she headed for the door.

"You know she's going to go sit under the oak tree and read that book, right?" Ginny said after the screen door banged shut.

"Yeah, but I had to try."

"She's already read all the fourth- and fifth-grade books. They're not going to have any books to give her this year at school."

Jamie finished the last bite of his own breakfast and pushed away from the table. "Smart as a whip. She must get that from you."

Ginny swatted at him with a dishrag. "Now come on. You're smart, too. In your own way." Jamie went to grab hold of her, but she dodged him. "You should get going before the boys set something on fire at the garage."

"Now you know that only happened once."

He put his arms around her and gave her a kiss.

"Don't be too late," she said.

"I won't."

She let him get about halfway to the door before she called after

5

him. "Mr. Peterson asked about buying that old truck again. Maybe you can talk to him."

He didn't answer. They both knew he wasn't going to sell that old truck. He swore he'd restore the '33 Chevy to good as new someday, but as Ginny liked to point out, the truck had been sitting in the back yard for going on ten years, almost as long as they'd been married.

He just never had the time, he told her. The shop was always busy. He spent all day fixing everyone else's cars. There weren't enough hours left to work on his own.

Ginny suspected he'd gotten used to sitting in the back of it, late at night, thinking he could get away from the bad dreams when they came. She knew better. You can't run from your nightmares. She hadn't told Jamie about her own bad dreams, that they had woken her up in the middle of the night. Dreams about him. Dreams she planned to fight.

———

JAMIE STEPPED OUTSIDE to face another scorcher of a day. As he walked to his actual working pickup truck, he passed by Amy Lynn sitting under the oak tree with her book. He opened his mouth to say something, but thought better of it. Whatever he said, it wouldn't do any good. He'd told her to ride her bike to one of her friends' houses, but truth be told, she didn't seem to have any friends.

Jamie worried for her. Why did she seem to prefer books to people? She was a good girl. She got straight A's in school. She did her chores. For the most part she minded him and her mother, and she usually remembered to say "please" and "thank you." Ginny said she'd come into her own in time. He hoped so, for her sake. Some problems in the world couldn't be solved with good grades and good manners.

———

No one set the garage on fire before Jamie got there, but they came close. Bartholomew Avery's shiny red Ford Galaxie stuck halfway out of one of the bays while Mr. Avery, red faced, screamed at one of his assistant mechanics.

After getting Mr. Avery calmed down, Jamie turned to Eddie, the mechanic at the receiving end of Mr. Avery's verbal tirade. As Eddie explained it, he had broken the news to Mr. Avery that something was wrong with the Galaxie's drivetrain, which wasn't a cheap fix.

"It's highway robbery is what it is," Mr. Avery yelled, his cheeks burning red again. "I honestly don't know how you get away with charging so much. I don't have that kind of money."

Of course, he did have that kind of money, seeing as how he was a vice president at the bank, but Jamie had the common sense not to argue with him.

Jamie took Eddie off to the side, leaving Mr. Avery to stew. "Why do you think it's the drivetrain, Eddie?"

The mechanic jabbed a finger at the Ford. "You try to drive that car and tell me what else the godawful noise could be."

"Lots of things make godawful noises." Jamie surveyed the sedan. "Did you check for a loose hose?"

Eddie glanced down at the ground. "No."

He patted Eddie on the shoulder. "Why don't you do that before you get Mr. Avery so worked up he blows a gasket, okay?"

Eddie nodded. "Sure thing, Jamie."

Jamie shook his head as he walked toward his office. Eddie was a good kid. He'd make a good mechanic someday, but he was only nineteen, and sometimes he was a little on the dense side. Of course, Jamie could have said the same thing about himself at that age. When he was nineteen, he didn't have a clue what he wanted to do with his life, but then the army came along and soon he found himself on the other side of the world, fixing jeeps while dodging North Korean shells.

Come to find out he actually liked fixing jeeps. When he got out of the army, he came straight back home to Avalon and got a job as an assistant mechanic at Old Carl Hutchins' garage. Jamie worked his way up to manager in no time at all, and when it came time for Old Carl to retire, he'd offered Jamie the garage.

Jamie jumped at the chance. He was paying off Old Carl a little bit at a time. A few more years and the garage would be his free and clear.

Jamie dug into the mountain of invoices and parts orders on his desk but didn't get very far before Bobby Rawlins, another one of his mechanics, knocked on his door.

"Hey, Jamie," he said. "We need you out here for a second."

Jamie glanced at the pile of paperwork. "Can it wait?"

Bobby made a face. "Not really."

With some exasperated muttering, Jamie went outside to find a sheriff's patrol car pulled up to the garage alongside a tow truck. The tow truck had another car hanging off the back, a fancy one, too—a silver Chrysler.

Jamie met the sheriff's deputy as he was climbing out of his car. "Good morning, Rick. What's this you got here for me?"

Rick Burke, a middle-aged man with thinning hair and a thick build, shook Jamie's hand. "Need a place to stow this car for a little while until we figure out what to do with it."

Jamie cocked an eyebrow. "What's wrong with parking it at the sheriff's station?"

"Nothing." He winked at Jamie. "But I thought I might let you in on the fun. Sam Murphy and his son found this car in a ditch this morning on Dry Creek Road. No sign of any other vehicles involved in the accident and no sign of the driver either. We're trying to figure out what happened, and frankly we're stumped. I thought you might take a look, maybe see if you can help us out."

The hair on the back of Jamie's neck stood on end. Dry Creek Road was only about a mile from Jamie's house as the crow flies, directly through the woods.

"Do you know who it belongs to?" Jamie asked.

"Not a clue," the sheriff's deputy replied. "License plate's been ripped off. We got the vehicle identification number off the chassis, but it's going to take a few days to get an answer back on that."

Jamie surveyed the Chrysler. "The license plate was ripped off? That's weird."

"That's not the only thing. The damage ... well we've never seen anything quite like it. I thought your expertise might come in handy. What do you say?"

Jamie glanced at the garage. Of the three bays, two of them were already occupied. "I don't know. We're pretty busy right now."

Rick put his hands together. "As a favor? A car that nice, someone's going to come looking for it eventually. We'd at least like to be able to tell them what happened to it."

Jamie sighed. "Okay, but only for a few days."

Rick grinned. "Thanks, Jamie. I'm sure we won't need longer than that."

He got back in his car and drove off while the tow truck driver eased the Chrysler into the garage's third bay. With the car settled in its new home, Jamie was able to take a closer look. It turned out to be a 1959 300E, a very nice car. Someone paid a pretty penny for it.

A lot of the damage Jamie could safely assume happened when the car landed in the ditch. The front bumper was mangled. The front axle was broken, and both the front wheels were bent. Rick was right, though. The other damage was like nothing Jamie had ever seen. The driver's side door was dented in, with four enormous parallel gouges running all the way from front to back.

The driver's window was shattered, too. That could have happened when the car slid into the ditch, but something didn't fit. The cracks radiated out from a single point, like something hit the window hard.

Jamie walked around to the back of the car and knelt down to take a look where the license plate should have been. The screws holding it in place were sheared clean off. Jamie frowned. He couldn't think of anything with enough strength to do that.

He got his biggest surprise, though, when he wrenched open the passenger's side door. There was blood smeared inside, where the hinges connected to the body of the car. Based on the damage, Jamie couldn't imagine the driver came away uninjured. But if he was hurt badly, where did he go? Why didn't he knock on someone's door to ask for help? Jamie figured he should probably tell Rick about the noise he heard the night before. It had to be related to the car crash, but what he saw in the woods hadn't been any injured driver, he was sure of that.

2

WEDNESDAY, AUGUST 15, 1962

The Black students always got the leftovers and the hand-me-downs. That was just how it worked. Addie didn't know why she expected anything different for the new school year. As she stared down at the pitiful collection of pencils on the desk in front of her, she sighed. It looked like her students would have to share again. Maybe she could pull together some money to buy more pencils and more paper, too, but she wouldn't be able to do that until she got paid, which wasn't until the end of September.

The textbooks were another matter. She couldn't really do much about them. She counted exactly four fully intact U.S. history books. They'd have to cobble together something usable from the rest of them. Never mind the flag on the cover had only forty-eight stars.

She'd figure out a way to make it all work.

Again.

Addie spent the morning getting her classroom set up as best she could. As she was leaving a little after noon, she passed by the principal's office. The door was cracked open. Inside he was talking with someone. Addie didn't mean to eavesdrop, but they weren't keeping their voices down.

"Now, Viola," the principal said, "I know it's hard, but please reconsider. We need you."

Viola Crawford, one of the other third- and fourth-grade teachers, was a year or two younger than Addie. She was only in her second year teaching. Addie liked Viola well enough, but she acted like she was afraid of her own shadow.

Viola sounded like she was on the verge of tears. "I have five English grammar books and thirty kids, Mr. Deakins. There isn't even any chalk for my blackboard. How do you expect me to teach? I can't do it."

"Look, I know we have too many kids and not enough supplies, but we all just have to make do."

Martin Deakins had been the principal of Ezekiel's Mill Elementary School for as long as Addie had been teaching there. She heard the frustration in his voice. He agreed with Viola, but he couldn't tell her that.

"Not all of us have to 'make do,'" Viola retorted. "The teachers in Avalon aren't fighting over crayons. What good did it do sending our kids over to their schools last year? We're not one step closer to integrating than we were before."

A year before, twelve students from Ezekiel's Mill, the mostly black community near Avalon, had been chosen to attend the all-white Avalon schools. It turned out to be a big deal, with news reporters coming in from places like Charleston and Columbia, even as far away as Raleigh and Greenville. Of course, not everyone was happy with the decision. There were protests and hellfire sermons and threats, but in the end, no one had to call up the National Guard like they did in some places. Tensions died down, and people went on with their lives.

No one really wanted to rile things up again.

Mr. Deakins' tone became a bit more pointed. "What did you expect? You know they're not going to let our kids into their schools without a fight."

"But the fight's already been fought," Viola argued. "They lost."

"That doesn't mean they're going to do anything, not without someone breathing down their necks. Besides, have you thought of the fact that you might not have a job at all if we actually did integrate?"

"What do you mean?" Viola asked quietly.

"You know exactly what I mean," Mr. Deakins snapped. "How many white folks do you think are going to be happy with a black woman teaching their kids? Viola, we need you. You can't quit."

Addie didn't hear the rest of the conversation. She moved away before they could catch her listening. If Viola quit, it would mean more students in her own third- and fourth-grade combined class. She fought back the tears that came. No use in crying. Like Mr. Deakins said, she'd figure out a way to make it work. She always did.

Always looking at the bright side. That's what her grandmother said about her. Never a frown on her face.

But these days she didn't feel much like smiling.

Unfortunately, the day didn't get any better. On her way out the door, she ran into Rose Ellison. Rose taught a fifth- and sixth-grade combined class. She and Addie didn't get along, and Addie didn't know why. She heard through the grapevine that Rose had her eye on Mr. Deakins and thought Addie did, too. Of course, that couldn't have been further from the truth, but Rose had apparently made up her mind.

"Is everything okay, Addie?" she asked, her voice sweet as honey.

Addie did her best to wipe her tears away. "Yes, Rose. I was just leaving for the day."

Rose raised an eyebrow. "So soon? Do you have your room in order?"

Rose's room was always perfect—desks in straight rows, books organized neatly on the shelves, cursive alphabet hung with care above the pristine blackboard. Her kids always got the top grades and won all the prizes. Addie tried to focus on her own classroom, but that was hard when Rose was there to constantly remind everyone.

"Almost, Rose." Addie tried to hide her annoyance. She wasn't entirely successful.

Rose put a hand on Addie's arm. "Well, good luck getting everything together before the kids come next week."

Addie bit her tongue and smiled. "Oh, don't you worry about me. I'll get it done." She gently shrugged off Rose's touch. "Listen, I'd love to chat a little bit longer, but I don't want to hold you up, and I should be on my way. Good luck with your classroom, too."

Rose's expression could have frozen Hell itself, or even South Carolina on an August afternoon. "You take care, now, Addie."

Addie nodded, still smiling. "You, too, Rose."

Addie didn't live very far from the school, but the walk back home was hot and sticky. She guessed it had to be at least a hundred degrees. Normally she didn't mind the heat, but she found herself wishing for some sort of relief, if only a cool breeze. Idly, she began to whistle, random notes at first, but then a melody came to her. It seemed familiar, though she couldn't recall hearing it before. Out of nowhere, a cool breeze fluttered her dress and took the edge off the heat, for a moment at least.

Exactly what she'd been wishing for.

———

DAVID DOWNED the glass of bourbon and immediately poured himself another two fingers. He wiped the sweat off his forehead and adjusted the electric fan before he surveyed the line of photographs tacked to the wall, each one labeled neatly with a date and a place. The oldest was taken on April 28, 1943, in Munich, Germany, the latest on July 11, 1952, in New York City. Every photo was of the same man, and right then they were all mocking him.

So close. He was so close, and yet David managed to let the man slip through his fingers again. His contact was supposed to give him all the information he needed—the name the man had been living under and enough evidence to nail his ass to the wall, right next to all the pictures.

But David's contact didn't show, which left him with nothing at all.

"Don't act so smug," he slurred at the photos. "I'll find you. You're going to make a mistake one day, and when you do, I'm going to be right there ready with a bullet."

The pictures didn't reply.

David swore. *Useless,* he told himself. All useless. He could be hiding as anyone at all in this nothing, middle-of-nowhere town. And why here? Why Avalon, South Carolina? What could possibly be here for him? It was the perfect place if you wanted to disappear, but David knew better.

He wagged an unsteady finger at the wall of photos. "I'll figure out your game. You didn't come here to retire. What are you up to?"

The pictures were silent.

———

JAMIE DIDN'T GET HOME from the garage until after seven o'clock, despite his promise he wouldn't be late. Bartholomew Avery turned out to be the easy customer of the day, and having one of the garage bays down because of Rick's mystery car didn't help.

Ginny was waiting at the door. He gave her a quick peck as he came inside. "I'm sorry. Crazy day. You aren't going to believe everything that happened."

She smiled faintly. "You can tell me about all of it over dinner. I kept it warm for you."

Jamie glanced down at his coverall. He normally came home covered in grease and sweat, but that day he seemed to be covered in an extra layer of grime. "Let me get changed first. Where's Amy Lynn?"

Ginny crossed her arms and cocked her head to the side. "Where do you think she is?"

Where she always is.

"Up in her room reading?"

"You should check on her before you come back down."

Upstairs, Jamie threw his dirty coverall on the floor and picked out a clean shirt and pair of pants. Before he went back down, he stopped by Amy Lynn's room and pushed her door open a crack. Sure enough, she sat on her bed cross-legged, a book open in her lap, surrounded by her stuffed animals and dolls. He watched her for a minute or so. She didn't notice him, too enchanted by whatever she was reading. He pulled the door to and went back downstairs.

Jamie sat down at the kitchen table and spent the next ten minutes moving his mashed potatoes and meatloaf around on his plate. He couldn't get the silver Chrysler out of his head. He'd seen cars damaged in a lot of creative ways, especially back in the army, but he didn't have a clue what could have made the giant gouges in the side of the car or sheared off the license plate. Maybe there was another car, despite what Rick said.

"So, are you going to tell me about this crazy day of yours or what?" Ginny asked.

Her question jolted Jamie back to reality. "Sorry. Just trying to sort through some things in my head. You know Bartholomew Avery, right?"

Ginny grimaced. "The blowhard who works at the bank? I've met him a time or two."

Jamie told her about Bartholomew's shiny red Ford and about Dotty Green, who brought in her Caddy saying her windshield wipers came on every time she tried to use her left turn signal. Eddie spent a good hour explaining to her that she was, in fact, flipping on her wipers and not her turn signal, but Jamie didn't know if he ever got through to her.

Eventually, he got around to the accident on Dry Creek Road and the car Rick brought to the garage. He told her about the strange damage and the blood he'd found on the inside of the door.

"I'm sure the sound I heard last night had something to do with that accident," he said. "Maybe tomorrow I'll head over to Dry Creek Road and take a look at where the car went into the ditch, you know to see it for myself."

Ginny inhaled sharply. "Maybe you should just let the sheriff do his job."

He held up a hand. "I know, I know, but I can't stop thinking about this car. Rick said he wanted me to take a look at it, to see if I could find anything that might explain why it ran off the road, but I can't shake the feeling he wasn't telling me something, like there was some other reason he wanted me to look at it."

"You want to know what I think?"

"What's that?"

She grinned. "I think you've been watching too many of those detective shows on TV."

Jamie grunted. "Maybe you're right."

Ginny's smile faded. "You do what the sheriff asked, but that's it. Leave the detective work to them, okay?"

Jamie slumped down like a scolded child. "Okay, fine. I promise I won't go poking around places I shouldn't."

"Now you think you might want to ask me about my day?" Ginny prompted.

"I'm sorry," Jamie said. "How was your day?"

"I got a telephone call from Amy Lynn's school."

Jamie frowned. "Something wrong?"

Ginny shook her head. "Not at all. In fact, she scored so well on her tests last year they want her to skip a grade."

Jamie shot her a dubious look. "Skip a grade? But school starts next week. That means she'd be going into the fifth grade. Do you think that's a good idea?"

"I asked her. She wants to do it."

"What about her friends? She wouldn't be in class with them anymore."

Ginny drew her mouth into a thin line. "You and I both know she doesn't really have any friends. Maybe this will be a good thing for her. A new start."

Jamie nodded, but he wasn't entirely convinced. Maybe he would have argued more, if his day hadn't taken so much out of him. He definitely would have argued more if he had known everything the next full moon would bring.

———

ADDIE SAT on the porch listening to the crickets sing as the sun set. All the small things she had to do before school started on Monday ran through her head. Too many things and not enough time.

What she was really doing was distracting herself. August, in a lot of ways, was a difficult month.

Nine years earlier, her favorite aunt Gloria, who was only ten years older, was hit by a car while walking down the road in broad daylight. The driver of the car was three sheets to the wind, but he was a white man, a preacher even. He didn't get any time in jail because the judge felt sorry for him.

He just made one mistake.

Is that really worth ruining his life over?

He cried and thanked the judge. He said he had already asked God to forgive him, and then he had the audacity to ask them to forgive him, too. Her mother looked him in the eye and told him no. Never mind Gloria's life. She didn't get a second chance. Her life had been ruined forever. Why did he get a free pass?

Addie never forgot the look in the man's eye when her mother rejected his plea. No remorse. No self-pity. Only hatred and anger. Anger at being denied something he felt he was entitled to, by her of all people.

And then only four years later, on the night of August 10, 1957, her little sister disappeared. She went to a friend's house and didn't come back. The police searched the area. They questioned her and her parents as well as her sister's friends, but after a few days, they gave up. Her sister was an adult after all. She could have disappeared on purpose.

Of course, that was bullshit. Cora would never have put her family through the pain they all still carried. At least with her aunt there was a funeral. There was a gravestone. With Cora, they had nothing. They never had a chance to say good-bye.

"Addie," her mother called from inside the house, "are you still out there on the porch? Feel free to come in here and help me with the rest of these dishes."

Addie sighed and turned to go back inside, but before she did, she heard a sound, quiet and distant, almost blending in with the night noises. She couldn't even be sure she really heard it. She stood still, closed her eyes, and concentrated.

Music.

Someone hummed the same melody she'd whistled on her walk home when she conjured up the breeze. *No, that's silly.* She didn't conjure up anything. It was a coincidence. And yet, the music drifted on the balmy night air.

Addie went down the steps into the yard to see if she could hear better. She closed her eyes again and listened, but she couldn't figure out where the music was coming from. She couldn't even tell if the person humming was a man or a woman.

"Who's there?" she asked, almost in a whisper so her mother wouldn't overhear.

As if in response, the humming grew louder. Addie scanned the yard but couldn't see anyone in the dying light.

"Look, I don't know who you are, or what you're trying to do, but you'd better cut this out right now."

The humming stopped.

Standing out in the yard in the dark, Addie suddenly felt alone and exposed. Things moved in the shadows around her, waiting for their time. She retreated to the porch as fast as she could. *No one's out there,* she told herself as her eyes roved the darkness. *It's just nerves. Just nerves.*

When Addie came into the kitchen, her mother looked at her sideways. "You get lost on the way here?"

"Sorry, I just got a lot on my mind." Addie grabbed a dishrag and started drying off the pan her mother handed to her. In the living room, her father snored in his recliner.

"What's bothering you?" her mother asked.

"Thinking about school starting." Addie sighed. "I've got a full classroom and not enough books to go around, not to mention pencils or notebooks. Plus, it's going to be like an oven in this heat. One fan doesn't cut it. And do you know that every time it rains, I have to put a trash can in the middle of the floor to catch the water dripping from the ceiling? I'm not sure what I'm going to do."

Her mother handed her a plate. "You're going to do the best you can."

"Another teacher quit this morning." Addie half-heartedly passed the dishrag over the plate and put it in the drying rack. "It's hard."

"Everything is hard. No sense complaining." Her mother passed her another plate.

"I just wish someone cared about the kids in this community."

Her mother paused and looked at her, smiling faintly. "Someone does. You."

The two of them continued in silence for a few minutes. Addie hummed the melody that had come to her earlier in the day, the one she heard outside in the yard.

"Your grandmother used to sing that song," her mother said.

Addie stiffened. That's where she heard the song before. Grandma Zee. Though, she couldn't recall any specific memories of her grandmother singing it. "What's the name of it?"

Her mother shook her head. "I don't remember. I don't really even remember the words, if there were any. I just recognize the melody."

Grandma Zee was always singing or humming some tune or another. She preferred gospel hymns. Addie ran through the melody in her head again, and this time she gradually prized out a memory. Addie must have been eight or nine years old. She was in her grandmother's kitchen, watching her cook. Grandma Zee was humming the same melody while her giant cookbook rested open on the counter. She occasionally glanced over at Addie and smiled while she dumped ingredients into a bowl.

Something was off, though. Her grandmother's cookbook, the one she always used and the one her mother still had on display, had a blue cover. The cookbook in her memory had a red cover.

"When Grandma Zee passed, what happened to her cookbooks?" Addie asked.

Her mother narrowed her eyes. "You know what happened. We have the big family cookbook sitting over there." She pointed to a shelf that held a few old church cookbooks and a big, thick, blue notebook stuffed with loose papers.

"But is that it? Did she have any others?"

"Why do you ask?" Her mother's expression got serious, like she just heard about a death in the family.

"Well, it's hard to believe one book could hold all her recipes," Addie said. "She was 102, and she cooked Sunday dinner for all of us the day before she died."

"If there are any more, I don't know about them." The tone in her mother's voice was sharp enough to cut grits. "That book's got enough recipes in it you could make something different every day for a year and not repeat. Can you think of anything she ever made for us that's not in there?"

Addie shook her head. A stupid question. Of course, there wasn't another cookbook. "Never mind. I'm just tired. I thought I remembered a different cookbook, but I must not be recalling things right."

Her mother took her hand and held it. "Look. I know this is a hard time right now for all of us, but you got to remember that life goes on. You can't get down, especially not with all those kids that need you come Monday. Now why don't you get some rest."

Addie nodded. "You're right. I think maybe I'll try to turn in a little early tonight. Tell Dad I'll see him in the morning."

That night Addie's dreams were filled with her grandmother's singing and the unfamiliar aromas of things made from recipes in the red cookbook.

3

THURSDAY, AUGUST 16, 1962

The giant rotating clock on the roof welcomed David to the Tick-Tock Diner, the oldest eating establishment in picturesque downtown Avalon. At least that's what the sign said. David felt eyes on him as soon as the bell on the door jingled. That kind of attention would've normally made him uneasy, but today he wanted to see who exactly was paying attention to the stranger in town. He made his way past the chrome and red vinyl booths toward the counter and chose a seat where he could see the door.

The waitress, a middle-aged woman with dyed red hair and a superficial smile, came over and threw a menu down in front of him. "Coffee?" she asked.

David hadn't bothered to take off his sunglasses since they hid his bloodshot eyes. "Yes, please."

"Cream and sugar?"

"No, thanks—" He squinted to read her name tag. "—Peggy."

She gave him a knowing look and left him to look over the menu. She came back with his coffee a few minutes later. "Know what you want?"

David pointed to the menu. "I'll have two eggs, poached, and hashbrowns, please."

Peggy raised an eyebrow. "No bacon?"

He smiled. "No thanks."

"You sure? It's the cook's specialty. Comes straight from Will Aiken's farm, not even ten minutes from here."

"No, that's okay. Allergies."

She gave a little shrug. "Suit yourself."

She took his menu and walked away. As David sat sipping his coffee, he took a quick survey of the other patrons. The breakfast crowd was mostly older, a lot of them farmers judging by the way they were dressed. He frowned. This was going to be harder than he thought.

Peggy came back with his food and a refill for his coffee. The poached eggs were bearable, and the hashbrowns were edible, if cold. While he ate, he read the copy of the paper he'd picked up from the stand outside. He wasn't particularly surprised by anything he found. Updates on the 4-H Club. Recaps of the recent Rotary Club and Junior League meetings. Recipes. A schedule of church services. An editorial about taxes being too high and another one railing against the integration of the local schools. A couple of novel-length obituaries. A few national news stories pulled from the wires. The two movies advertised at the local theater were *Ben-Hur* and *G.I. Blues.* Both were two years old.

But one ad caught his attention. Tucked into the back page with the rest of the classifieds, the small ad began with a single large word in all capital letters. MISSING. It described a woman who had disappeared a few months before. The family was begging for anyone who had any information about what might have happened to her to contact the police. Something else for David's wall.

Two men walked in and took places at the counter not far from him. They both looked like they were in their mid-fifties. One of them was tall and wiry while the other was shorter and stockier. In his head, David named them Jim Bob and Joe Bob.

Peggy had a genuine smile ready for them when she brought them coffee. David pretended to read the paper while he listened in on their conversation. They both ordered eggs and biscuits with gravy, and bacon of course. They flirted a little with Peggy. She laughed at their dumb jokes. Cozy. Happy. Familiar. David wondered what that was like.

When their food came they both dug in and the conversation stopped for a few minutes.

"Had a pretty unusual call yesterday," Jim Bob said after a while.

"Oh, yeah?" Joe Bob replied. "How so?"

"I had to go pull a car out of a ditch over on Dry Creek Road. Sam Murphy and his son found it."

Joe Bob chuckled. "Are you sure he didn't put his own car in the ditch?"

Jim Bob joined in the laugh. "No, this one was nicer than any car Sam could ever afford. A pretty silver Chrysler."

"So, what was so unusual about it?" Joe Bob asked.

"The car looked like it went into the ditch on its own," Jim Bob explained. "There weren't any other tire marks on the road that might belong to another car. And there wasn't any sign of the driver either."

"Something could've been wrong with the car," Joe Bob offered.

"I'd think that, too, but there was some other damage, big gouges on the driver's side door. If I didn't know better, I'd say the car was attacked by a wild animal."

Joe Bob looked askance at Jim Bob as he stuffed half a gravy-soaked biscuit in his mouth. "There aren't a whole lot of wild animals that can shove a car into a ditch, at least not around here."

"I know, but hear me out." Jim Bob glanced around the diner before he continued. David barely avoided making eye contact with him. "About five or six years ago. I had a call to come tow a car over off of Sumter Highway. It was late on a Saturday night, and when I drove out there, I came up on a group of about seven or eight teenagers. One car, a pretty blue Chevy Bel Air, was in the ditch while another car was pulled over by the side of the road. Of course, I thought the two had gotten into an accident, but they all swore that wasn't the case. They didn't want to say what they were all doing out there, but when I promised I wasn't going to snitch on them to their parents, they admitted they were coming back from a drag race. They said some kind of animal attacked the Bel Air and made it go off the road. Whatever it was ran away when the second car came up. The Bel Air had the same kind of damage, big gouges on the side."

Joe Bob still didn't seem convinced. "Do they know whose car it is?"

Jim Bob shook his head. "No, they can't figure that out."

"What did you do with it?" Joe Bob asked.

Jim Bob took a giant swig of coffee. "Sheriff had me take it over to Jamie Fletcher's garage."

Joe Bob grunted. "Well, if anyone can figure out what happened, it'll be Jamie."

Peggy brought David's check. David stood and threw some money on the counter. He tucked the newspaper under his arm and exited the diner, still well aware of those looking at him. Outside, he took a walk down Assembly Street, Avalon's main drag it would seem. Aside from the diner, there wasn't much to see. An antique shop. A barber shop. A drug store. A feed and seed. A five and dime. *Why here? What's so special about this place?* The questions ate at David. And now he had another. David was all but certain the driver of that silver Chrysler was his missing contact. *But what happened to him?*

"Hey, Cole, Coach wants to talk to you."

Cole Carter pulled his shirt over his head and looked up to see his buddy Andy standing in the door of the locker room.

"Sure thing. I'll be there in a minute." He slipped on his shoes, threw his gym bag over his shoulder, and met Andy outside.

"Boy, Coach sure put us through the wringer at practice today," Andy said as they walked. "It was so hot I thought I was going to pass out."

Cole shrugged. "Seemed like any other practice to me. Don't be such a pansy."

Andy looked at him sideways. "Man, you are so full of it. I saw you panting out there, too."

"Well, I'm not going to admit it like a pansy."

Andy punched him in the arm. "Watch it or this pansy's going to give you a black eye. That wouldn't be so great for the date with Mary Beth I heard you got tonight."

"Yeah, we'll see if I can make it past second base this time."

Andy chuckled. "You mean you haven't already?"

Cole turned and poked him in the chest with a finger. "Hey, it's just a matter of time. We're seniors this year. All the girls are going to want us. They'll be beating a path. Just you wait."

"Maybe they will for you, Mr. Starting Quarterback."

"Oh, come on." Cole gave a lopsided grin. "I'll make sure there's plenty for you, too. A nice sister. Or a lonely best friend."

Andy punched him in the arm again, harder.

Cole clutched his arm. "Hey, watch it."

"I swear, Cole, one day that mouth of yours is going to get you in a lot of trouble."

By then they'd reached Coach's office.

"Any idea what Coach wanted to talk to me about?" Cole asked.

Andy shook his head. "No, he just told me he wanted to see you. He had a big frown on his face, though."

"Coach always has a frown on his face," Cole retorted.

"That's true. Good luck in there, and good luck tonight, too." Andy made to punch Cole in the arm again but stopped short. "See you tomorrow."

Cole gave a salute as Andy walked away. Then he opened the door to Coach's office and poked his head inside. Coach was sitting at his desk, studying the team's playbook, a pencil tucked behind his ear.

He waved Cole in. "Hi, Cole. Have a seat."

Cole did what he was told. "Sure Coach, what's this about?"

Coach glanced up from the playbook, a somber look on his face. He steepled his fingers, took in a deep breath, and let it out slowly. "I needed to let you know, I've decided to have Marcus start a few of the games this year."

Cole felt as if he had been punched in the stomach. "But I'm supposed to be the starting quarterback. This is my year."

"And you're still the starting quarterback for most of the games." Coach held up a calming hand. "No one's replacing you. I only want to start Marcus for a few games to see how it goes."

Cole wasn't in the mood to calm down, though. "See how it goes? That sure sounds like you're replacing me."

"Even you have to admit Marcus has an arm on him. Since he joined the team, we have a really good shot at going to the state championships."

"We don't need him to get there," Cole said through clenched teeth. "I can take us there."

Coach leaned back in his chair and tapped the playbook with his finger. "Maybe you can, but I like to hedge my bets."

This wasn't how his senior year was supposed to be. Cole saw his whole future slipping away. "But I'm supposed to play football for USC next year. You're ruining my chances."

The Coach laughed. "That's ridiculous, Cole. You'll make it to USC. You're going to have plenty of opportunities to show off. Don't you worry."

Cole stood up, fists clenched at his sides. "This isn't fair. He shouldn't even be at this school. I've been waiting for four years for this and you're telling me he's going to waltz in a take it all away?"

Marcus Jones was one of the kids they brought over from Ezekiel's Mill High School. He and Cole weren't friends, but Cole never saw much reason to go out of his way to be mean either. Cole had watched Marcus get shoved, called names, even get spit on. Sometimes, he thought about saying something, but didn't want everyone turning on him, too.

Coach raised his voice. "Now, Cole—"

"No, this isn't right. What do I have to do to get you to change your mind? I'll stay longer at practice. I'll even come to extra practices. Whatever it takes, I'll do it."

"Cole, I appreciate the dedication, but I've made up my mind." Coach's voice had a hard edge to it. "You still get to start our first game tomorrow, but Marcus is starting the one after that. Now go get some rest and I'll see you tomorrow."

Cole stood there for a moment, wondering how much more he could say without getting into major trouble. Remembering what Andy told him, he decided arguing any further would only dig him a deeper hole. "Okay, Coach," he said, seething. "See you tomorrow."

Cole stormed out of Coach's office only to run into the last person he wanted to see at that moment.

"Hey, Cole, how's it going?" Marcus asked.

"Shut up," Cole spat. "Why don't you go back where you came from?"

He kept walking.

"Cole," Marcus called after him.

Cole didn't answer.

———

THE GARAGE WAS SO busy Jamie didn't have time to turn around, much less take a closer look at the silver Chrysler. He was exhausted, and at the end of the day, nothing sounded better than going home, having some dinner, and relaxing a little before collapsing into bed. When he left the garage, though, he didn't turn his truck toward home. Instead, he turned in the direction of Dry Creek Road.

He'd promised Ginny he'd let the sheriff do his job, but that silver Chrysler sat in its garage bay taunting him all day long, and he let his curiosity get the better of him. He wanted to see the site of the accident for himself. Ginny didn't have to know about the detour.

Dry Creek Road meandered through farmland. On both sides, split-rail fences and cow pastures alternated with patches of woods and old farmhouses that had been in the same families for generations. Jamie knew most of the people who lived along the road, though not well. He considered knocking on a couple of doors and asking if anyone had heard anything strange the night before last, but he decided against it, figuring they'd probably all think he was crazy.

The place where the car went into the ditch wasn't hard to find.

Tire marks crisscrossed the asphalt, narrow ones from the car and fatter ones from the tow truck that pulled it out. Jamie pulled his truck over as far as he could and climbed out to survey the scene. The ditch was overgrown with a summer's worth of weeds, except in the spot where the car came to rest. There the weeds were crushed, and the smell of gasoline and oil still lingered in the air. Nothing too surprising there.

What Jamie didn't expect was the smaller trail of trampled vegetation leading away from the car, into the woods, the same patch of woods that backed up to his house. The Jordan farm was directly across the street. If the driver was hurt, why did he go into the woods instead of there?

On the other hand, surely someone must have heard the crash. Why didn't they come outside to offer help or at least to see what happened? And why didn't they call the sheriff?

After glancing down the road in both directions and seeing no one, Jamie climbed down into the ditch, picking his way carefully through the tangle of weeds. He slipped once, getting red mud all over his coverall. He swore. Ginny would get on him for that unless he could come up with a good enough story.

He reached the bottom and scrambled up the other side. Once there, he picked up the trail he had seen and followed it into the woods. He didn't even get ten feet before he found the first blood smear across the trunk of a pine tree, dried to a dark reddish brown. A few feet away, he found four parallel slashes across the trunk of another pine tree, exactly like in the door of the car. They were deep, at least an inch. If Jamie didn't know better, he would've said they were claw marks.

Jamie pursued the trail deeper into the woods. He found more trees with slash marks across the trunks and another patch of dried blood on the ground underneath a large oak tree. He expected he'd come across the body of the unfortunate driver at any moment. He didn't see how anyone could survive losing that much blood, but there was no sign of the driver anywhere, and soon Jamie lost the trail in the thick underbrush. He didn't understand. He asked himself again, if the driver was hurt, why didn't he go across the street to get help at the Jordan farm? Why run into the woods?

Unless he was running away from something.

The sudden thought sent a chill up Jamie's spine, despite the heat. All at once, the forest seemed darker and quieter. Jamie became aware of every crunch the leaves made under his feet, every twig that snapped as he moved. The sun dipped rapidly. The shadows grew and multiplied. It was already getting too dark to see.

He snapped his head around at a noise to his right. It might have been the wind. Or it might have been a deer. Or it might have been neither of those things. Something lurked in the darkness where the light failed to reach, something that made those gashes in the trees. He glanced back in the direction of the road and realized how far away he was. If it were to leap out at him, he wasn't sure he'd be able to reach his truck in time.

His heart thrummed.

He held his breath.

He waited.

Then he shook his head and laughed at himself. It was only a little wooded patch between a bunch of farms. What was going to leap out at him there? A bear? He turned and walked back to his truck. As he emerged into the orange light of the setting sun, he glanced over his shoulder. Nothing in the woods could hurt him, he told himself again.

But there was the blood. And the missing driver. And the feeling of being watched.

No, not watched.

Stalked.

4

FRIDAY, AUGUST 17, 1962

M cGill's Bar wasn't going to win any points for style, which is why Jamie liked it. Wood paneling covered the walls. Dark green carpet covered the floor. Old, rusted tin signs and license plates passed for decor. Mismatched chairs were arranged around a few tables, and equally mismatched stools lined the bar. Jamie went to McGill's every Friday night after work to unwind a little. Sometimes he met up with some of the other guys. Sometimes he had a few beers alone. That night he felt like being by himself.

Jamie took a deep breath as soon as he entered. It smelled like cigarette smoke and beer—exactly like it should. The bar was dark and cool, a relief from the stifling heat outside. Ceiling fans turned lazily overhead, moving the air around so it wouldn't get stale.

Jamie's good spirits were short-lived, though, as he soon discovered his regular seat was taken. The guy was big, easily six-foot-three, with muscles that strained his t-shirt. Over the t-shirt he wore a leather vest. A lit cigarette dangled from his lips. At least a day's worth of stubble covered his face. A pair of leather motorcycle gloves poked out of the back pocket of his jeans, which were tucked into heavy black boots. Jamie flashed to the Harley he'd seen in the parking lot.

Jamie sat down at the other end of the bar. Mack, the bartender on duty that night, brought him over a beer right away.

Jamie thanked him and took a swig. "So, who's the guy in my chair?"

Mack shrugged. "Don't know. Never seen him before. Says he's in town for a few days 'on business.' What kind of business I'm not sure, and honestly, I'm a little afraid to ask."

The biker threw his head back and let out a laugh at something the man next to him said.

Jamie took another swig of his beer. "His night seems to be going better than mine."

Mack raised an eyebrow. "Rough day?"

"Rough week."

Someone flagged Mack from across the bar.

"Hey, at least it's over." He pointed at Jamie's beer. "Let me know if you need another, okay?"

Jamie nodded. "Will do."

Things at the garage had been frantic all day again. Jamie never got a chance to catch his breath, much less check out the silver Chrysler. He'd promised Rick he'd take a look at it, but at the rate things were going, it would be 1963 first. He also wasn't sure if he should say anything about his trip into the woods. Maybe Ginny was right and he should've left well enough alone. Maybe they'd searched the area and already knew about the blood and the slashed trees. Maybe the sheriff had tracked down the name of the driver from the vehicle identification number and already contacted the family. Maybe they'd come get the car on Monday and he wouldn't have to worry about it anymore.

Wishful thinking. He was never that lucky.

Two men entered the bar and grabbed chairs at one of the tables. They waved to Jamie. He saluted them with his beer. Hank Porter and Wade Tucker both worked at the same factory where Jamie's father-in-law was a shift manager. They were good enough guys, but from the stories his father-in-law told, it was a wonder either of them still had a job.

Once they got beers of their own, Hank walked over to the jukebox and studied the selections for a minute or two. Then he tossed in a nickel and punched some buttons. "Your Cheatin' Heart" by Hank Williams started playing. He looked over at Wade and grinned as he walked back to their table, obviously very satisfied with himself.

For whatever reason, this grated on the new guy. He seethed as the song played. When it was almost over, Hank got up again to put on another song, but the man jumped up from his stool and shoved Hank out of the way of the jukebox. Hank staggered backwards and fell over a chair. Wade stood, fists up, ready to defend his friend, despite the biker being twice his size. Everyone close by cleared out of the way, expecting a fight.

"Hey," Jamie called in a voice that boomed through the small space.

Everyone stopped what they were doing and turned toward him.

"This is a neighborhood establishment," he said. "Let's make an effort to keep it neighborly, okay?"

The biker looked Jamie up and down. Jamie wasn't big, but the job at the garage kept him in shape. He still weighed the same as he did in the army, and he knew how to throw a punch. He glared, but Jamie looked him in the eye and didn't flinch. Finally, the biker smiled, scooped up his glass, and finished his drink in one gulp. Then he dug into his pocket, pulled out a few wrinkled bills, and threw them on the bar before he turned around and left.

Mack shot Jamie a grateful look.

Everyone went back to their own business, including Jamie, who had almost reached the bottom of his beer. He was about to ask Mack for another when a shadow darkened the stool to his right. He looked over to see Jasper Cordell sitting next to him.

"Pretty brave of you there," Jasper said. "That guy could have come after you."

"I can't stand bullies," Jamie replied. "Never have."

"Still, I'm not sure the odds would have been in your favor, there."

Jamie finished off his beer. "I don't know. I think my chances might have been pretty good."

Jasper clapped him on the back. "I knew you had some spunk in you. Wish more people did."

"How's business down at the store?" Jamie asked.

Jasper was the manager of the five and dime. He could usually be found there, distinctive with his red hair and beard, stocking shelves or running the cash register or working the soda fountain. Amy Lynn thought he made the best root beer floats and insisted on having him personally make hers whenever they visited the store. He always gave her an extra cherry.

"Can't complain," Jasper said. "How's business for you?"

"Same," Jamie answered, "but I do wish things would slow down a bit so I could at least catch a breath. I swear no one in this town knows how to take care of an automobile."

Jasper grunted. "That's true about a lot of things. People used to take care of their belongings, and they lasted forever. Now everything is disposable."

"Good for the store, though, right?"

Jasper stared into his own empty glass. "I suppose so. Sometimes I just wish things were the way they used to be."

Jamie laughed. "You sound like Ginny's dad."

"Maybe he's onto something."

Jamie started to laugh again but noticed that Jasper was serious. "Maybe, but change isn't always bad. Like the way they changed the body of the Corvette. See, it used to be a lot boxier in the back, but with the '61 models, they completely redid everything. They smoothed it out, added the duck tail and the round taillights, made it a whole lot more streamlined. It looks a lot cooler now than it did before ..."

Jamie trailed off as he watched Jasper's eyes glaze over. That happened a lot when Jamie talked about cars. He'd learned not to go into too much detail with most people, including Ginny. Neither of them said anything else until Mack turned on the radio behind the bar. He fiddled with the dial before a man's voice trickled out, talking about that night's high school football game.

"Headed to the game tonight?" Jasper asked.

Jamie shook his head. "Nah, I'm going home after this."

"You're missing out. It's supposed to be a good one. We're playing Camden High School."

"Maybe next week," Jamie offered halfheartedly.

Jasper stood. "I should be on my way. Don't want to miss the kick-off. You stop by the store soon, and bring Amy Lynn. It's been forever since I've seen her. I'm sure she's growing like a weed."

"Don't I know it. But you're going to have to make her a root beer float."

Jasper winked. "I'll be sure to give her an extra cherry."

———

THEY WON.

It was the season opener, a home game on top of that. They played a much bigger school. They were the underdogs. And they won.

But Cole wasn't happy.

With five minutes to go in the third quarter, he let himself get sacked on the third down. They had to punt the ball away, and Camden ran it back for a touchdown. That put Camden only three points behind. Thankfully, they never caught up, but it didn't change the fact that Cole screwed up. He got distracted. He didn't see the defensive lineman barreling at him. Coach chewed him out for it on the sidelines in front of everyone, including Marcus. Cole imagined him secretly gloating.

It didn't help that Marcus was the one who distracted him. Just a glimpse of him sitting on the bench, and all those feelings Cole had during his meeting with Coach came back up. His anger literally blinded him, and he didn't know what to do about it.

A bad ending to a bad week.

Cole's date with Mary Beth hadn't gone the way he wanted it to go either. He took her to the diner for burgers and then to see a movie. She wouldn't let him touch her the whole evening, not even when he tried to put his arm around her during the chariot race in *Ben-Hur*. When he suggested they go for a little drive after the movie, she flatly said no. Defeated, he'd driven her home.

There were plenty of other girls. Mary Beth wasn't special. But her refusal irked him. He was smart, good-looking. He was the starting quarterback, at least most of the time. Who was she to tell him no?

He was one of the last to leave the locker room. He trudged across the almost empty parking lot to his car and tossed his stuff in the trunk. As he opened the door to get in, though, he heard a voice behind him.

———

"HEY, GREAT GAME TONIGHT."

Startled, the boy spun around. "Huh? What?"

"I said great game tonight," he repeated.

The boy relaxed. "Oh, sorry, I didn't hear you come up behind me. Uh, thanks."

He turned to get in his car.

"You don't seem so excited."

Cole paused. "No, I'm happy we won and all, but I didn't play my best."

"Well, we all make mistakes. I'm sure you'll do better next week."

"I'm not playing next week," Cole muttered.

"What was that?" He'd heard perfectly, but he wanted Cole to say it himself. Rumors spread quickly in a small town, and this rumor was one he intended to take advantage of, if it was true.

"I said I'm not playing next week."

He feigned surprise. "Really? Why?"

Cole clinched his jaw. "Because Coach wants to start Marcus Jones."

"Marcus Jones. Isn't he the kid from Ezekiel's Mill?" Of course, he knew exactly who Marcus Jones was.

"Yeah. He's ... only been here a year." The bitterness shone brightly in Cole's eyes.

"Well, that hardly seems fair." He glanced to each side and then leaned in closer. "You must be a much better quarterback than he is."

Cole shrugged. "I know I am, but it's Coach's decision. You can't argue with it."

"That's a horrible attitude to have." He spoke with a small amount of authority in his voice, something he knew Cole would respond to.

"What do you mean?" the boy asked.

"I mean you don't want to give up, do you?" He took in Cole's black hair and blue eyes. Perfect, really. "A good-looking, smart guy like you? You don't seem like a quitter to me."

"No, sir. I'm not."

"Of course, you aren't."

"I just don't want to rock the boat, that's all," Cole said with a pained expression.

He took a step forward, pressing Cole against his car. "If you want something, you should go and take it. That's how the real world works. You shouldn't worry about stupid things like rocking the boat. Besides, I'm sure you're not the only one unhappy about your coach's decision."

"No one knows except for the other guys on the team."

And everyone else they told.

"But what about all the other people at the game?" he pressed. "What about the other students, all the parents and teachers, all the people in the community? How happy are they going to be when they see a ... kid from Ezekiel's Mill starting and not you?"

"I hadn't thought about it that way."

"You know, I think I know a way you can fix it." As if the idea had suddenly dawned on him.

"How?" Cole asked, frowning.

"It wouldn't be easy. It would take some time and effort."

Cole threw up his hands. "I already told Coach I'd come to extra practices. It didn't work."

He almost laughed at the naïveté. "What I'm thinking of would be done off the field."

Cole shook his head. "I don't know."

"Well, I'm easy to find if you want to talk."

He walked away, leaving Cole with a confused look on his face. The boy wasn't quite ready yet, but the more he thought about things, the angrier and more resentful he was going to get. Cole would come by to talk soon, and he planned to feed that anger and that resentment until it all boiled over.

5

SUNDAY, AUGUST 19, 1962

"Good morning, Mr. Fletcher," Fred Peterson bellowed as Jamie entered the church with Ginny and Amy Lynn.

"Morning, Mr. Peterson," Jamie replied, shaking his hand.

After Mr. Peterson greeted Ginny, he bent down to talk to Amy Lynn. "And Miss Amy Lynn. Just as pretty as your mother. I hope you're having a fine Sunday."

Amy Lynn did her best to hide behind her mother's dress.

"Say, 'Thank you,' Amy Lynn," Ginny told her.

"Thank you," Amy Lynn mumbled.

Mr. Peterson chuckled. "You've got yourself a shy one there."

Watching Amy Lynn literally try to disappear, Jamie couldn't say he didn't sympathize. Sometimes he felt like disappearing himself. The church vestibule buzzed with conversation as everyone greeted one another before the service started. Trinity United Methodist Church wasn't the biggest church in town. That was Good Shepherd Episcopal next door, where the "old money" went. But Jamie liked to think it was the loudest. The pastor didn't know how to talk without yelling, and the music minister had a curious idea of what it meant to make a "joyful noise" unto the Lord. Jamie threatened every week to bring ear plugs, earning him a glare from Ginny or a punch in the arm if she wasn't feeling charitable.

Across the room, he spotted Ginny's parents talking to Don and Betty Evans. He gave a curt nod to his father-in-law.

"I wanted to talk to you about that truck of yours, Mr. Fletcher," Mr. Peterson said. "It's a fine one you have there."

Inwardly, Jamie cringed. "You mean the one in my back yard?"

"Yes, sir. That's the one. The '33 Chevy."

"But it doesn't even have an engine that works."

Mr. Peterson waved a hand dismissively. "That's an easy thing to take care of."

Jamie shook his head. "I'm sorry, Mr. Peterson, but it's not for sale. I'm going to fix it up."

He looked to Ginny for help, but Ginny was talking to Harriet Paige. Amy Lynn fidgeted beside her mother. She wasn't allowed to bring any other books into the church service besides her Bible. Not anymore.

Mr. Peterson deflated. "Well, if you ever change your mind ..."

"You'll be the first one I call," Jamie assured him.

Inside the church sanctuary, Charlotte Lloyd, the church pianist, banged out the opening bars of "Love Divine, All Love Excelling," meaning it was time for everyone to stop gossiping and find their seats. Inside, Jamie, Ginny, and Amy Lynn took their customary pew near the back on the right side, next to Ginny's parents. No sooner had the final notes of the hymn faded away than Charlotte started in on "God of Grace and God of Glory," hammering the piano keys harder to set a more dignified tone. The choir proceeded in with the pastor, the assistant pastor, and the music minister.

Already the heat was almost unbearable, even with the windows open. A bead of sweat ran down Jamie's face. He wiped it away with his handkerchief.

Wayne Preston, the music minister, came to the podium flashing a toothy grin. "Good morning, everyone. Let's greet the Lord in song on this beautiful Sunday He has made. If everyone will please stand and turn to hymn number 292 in your hymnals."

The whole congregation dutifully did as they were told. What followed was a racket loud enough to wake the dead. Jamie always said what Methodists lacked in pitch they made up for in enthusiasm. The one exception was Ginny. She had a beautiful singing voice. She declined multiple invitations to join the choir. Amy Lynn had a good voice, too, when she remembered to sing.

The rest of the service dragged on, through the doxology, the offertory, the announcements, and the prayer requests, and by the time the Reverend Earl Griggs stood to give his sermon, Jamie's shirt was soaking wet.

"Now I have a few points to make in today's sermon," Pastor Earl said, "so if you all will bear with me. I might get you to your lunch a little late, but I promise you I'll get you there."

Jamie sighed loud enough for several people to turn and look at him. He smiled sheepishly and pretended to study the church bulletin.

"Today, I'm going to talk about evil," Pastor Earl began, "because evil is real, and it is all around us. Paul said in his letter to the Ephesians, 'Finally, my brethren, be strong in the Lord, and in the power of his might. Put on the whole armor of God, that ye may be able to stand against the wiles of the devil. For we wrestle not against flesh and blood, but against principalities, against powers, against the rulers of the darkness of this world, against spiritual wickedness in high places.' Remember that. When we stand up against evil in this world, we are not fighting other people, flesh and blood. We are fighting against demonic forces."

Jamie was certain he nodded off a few times before Pastor Earl came to his fourth point, something about how evil can get inside you without your even noticing. Jamie wasn't so sure. Right was right and wrong was wrong. He believed he had a pretty good handle on the difference.

His train of thought was cut off when a young woman near the front of the church leapt out of her seat and started shouting. Jamie recognized her as Sarah Jordan. She yelled out complete gibberish while she threw her arms out and spun around in some strange dance. Several of the men around her tried to restrain her, but she pushed them away as if they were nothing.

"She's speaking in tongues," Ginny said.

Pastor Earl, for his part, looked stricken. Nothing like that had ever happened before at Trinity United Methodist Church. This wasn't *that kind* of Methodist church, after all. He quoted scripture to drown her out—Matthew 16:23, James 4:7, Romans 16:20, even 1 Peter 5:8—but she only got louder, waving her arms frantically, spinning faster and faster, until finally she stopped and collapsed to the ground. Two of her brothers lifted her up and carried her out. Pastor Earl, still clearly shaken, immediately said a prayer for her and her family and then dismissed the congregation.

Nobody really felt like being social as they left the sanctuary. Outside, Sarah Jordan sat in the back of a car surrounded by her four brothers. Jamie accidentally made eye contact with one of the brothers and immediately looked away, embarrassed to be caught staring. He risked another glance a few moments later, though, and found all five of them, Sarah included, staring at him.

———

ADDIE BREEZED into the vestibule of the Emmanuel AME Church with her parents an astounding ten minutes before service was supposed to start. Normally they made it right as the ushers were shutting the doors. No matter how much poking and prodding her mother did, Addie's father always took his sweet time drinking his morning coffee, eating his breakfast, shaving, putting on his suit, tying his shoes. He almost always made them late. They encountered more than a few shocked stares from people as they walked in. Addie's mother flashed everyone a self-satisfied grin.

Addie groaned inwardly as she spotted Rose Ellison coming toward her in a pink dress and a matching pink hat, looking every bit like a giant bottle of Pepto-Bismol.

"Why Addie, so nice to see you early this week," she declared loud enough for everyone in the room to hear.

"You mean rather than shuffling in at the very last second?" Addie dropped her voice to a whisper. "My mother set my father's watch ten minutes fast."

Rose laughed, but Addie hadn't made a joke.

"That's a lovely hat, Rose," Addie said, "very pink."

"Thank you. I got it at a little boutique in Sumter a few weeks ago. I saw it and I just had to have it." She did a little spin right there in the vestibule of the church. "Doesn't it match this dress perfectly?"

"Perfectly," Addie agreed.

Perfectly nauseating.

Rose pointed to Addie's hat. "Your hat is nice, too."

Addie was wearing a small navy-blue pillbox hat with a cream-colored satin lily. "Thank you. It belonged to my grandmother."

Rose's smile could have curdled milk. "Well, aren't you fortunate you're able to have a few nice things because of her."

"I suppose I am," Addie replied, too addled to say anything else.

Rose glanced toward the sanctuary as the piano started. "I'd best be off to my seat. Nice chatting with you, Addie. Maybe I'll see you after the service."

Addie seethed as Rose walked off. Why did the woman go out of her way to give such backhanded compliments? What exactly did Addie do to her? What would it take to make her stop?

Inside the sanctuary, Addie and her parents found a pew to squeeze into. Everyone was seated hip-to-hip. Fans fluttered throughout the congregation, trying and failing to battle the stifling heat. Addie didn't pay much attention to the service. The choir sang a few hymns. One of the elders made announcements. Another elder led everyone in prayer for the sick and the shut-ins.

Addie put away Rose and her petty little insults. Her grandmother's melody still ran through her head, and she hadn't stopped thinking about the red cookbook. If the book was real, then one of her aunts likely had it. She could always ask them, but then she'd have to come up with some excuse as to why, and she was a terrible liar.

She was still working through that quandary when the Reverend

Elijah Edwards took the podium to deliver his sermon. "Today I want to draw your attention to the matter of evil," the preacher said. "Evil is real. Evil is in this world. The Apostle Peter says, 'Be sober, be vigilant; because your adversary the devil, as a roaring lion, walketh about, seeking whom he may devour.' The Devil has a plan for you and your life, and let me tell you right now, it ain't good."

A ripple of "amens" and "hallelujahs" went through the sanctuary as Preacher Edwards spoke. Addie, though, suddenly felt uneasy. When he warned against engaging in "occult practices," he looked directly at her, or so she thought.

"The Devil knows you," he continued. "He knows what your heart desires, and he offers it to you with a smile on his face. He'll tell you you don't need God. You can find knowledge and power in other places, by other means. But there is a price to pay, and let me tell you right now, that price is too high."

Another round of "amens" echoed through the room.

Addie's sense of unease only grew, but during the final part of Preacher Edwards' sermon, things took a turn for the truly strange. The image of Addie's grandmother came to her mind. Only she was much younger than Addie ever remembered her being, maybe even Addie's own age. She was somewhere dark, surrounded by candles. Spinning, arms waving, earth underneath her bare feet, she screamed words Addie couldn't make out, but somehow, Addie knew what she was saying.

She recited some kind of chant, or prayer. She was asking for protection. Or was it a protector? She was praying for God to send a protector for the community. Or maybe not God. Maybe the gods, or the spirits, or the universe. Then all at once, Addie was somewhere else. Some other church. A white woman was saying the same prayer, spinning and dancing like her grandmother. For a moment, she fixated on a man in the congregation with dirty blond hair and blue eyes, sitting between a woman and a girl of about nine or ten. Then she collapsed to the floor.

Addie came back to the present with her mother poking her. Preacher Edwards had finished his sermon. The music minister was at the podium again. Everyone was standing up except for her. She jumped to her feet and fumbled with her hymnal until she found her place. She didn't know what she'd seen, but she knew it really happened.

———

EVERY SUNDAY AFTER CHURCH JAMIE, Ginny, and Amy Lynn had dinner with Ginny's parents. George and Evelyn Owens lived in a small, neat house not too far out of town, surrounded by a white picket fence with big oak trees that shaded the yard. As soon as Jamie pulled the truck into the driveway, Amy Lynn jumped out and ran into the house to find Bo, their old blue tick hound. Jamie sometimes thought she loved that dog more than them.

"When are you gonna get that girl a dog of her own?" Ginny's father asked.

"Why do I need to?" Jamie responded. "She can play with Bo any time she wants, and I don't have to take care of him."

His father-in-law laughed and slapped him on the back as they walked toward the house, even though Jamie told the same joke at least every other week. Inside, Ginny's mother was busy setting the table while Ginny helped. Amy Lynn came running into the dining room.

"You go wash your hands after you've been playing with that dog," Ginny told her.

Crestfallen, Amy Lynn left.

"And I'd better hear the water running," Ginny called after her.

Once they were all seated around the table, George said Grace, and they passed plates of food—fried chicken, mashed potatoes, green beans, rolls. The conversation turned on the same subjects as it always did—the weather, the business at the garage, baseball, the church gossip. Inevitably what happened with Sarah Jordan at the service came up.

"A mental breakdown," Evelyn said. "I've said for a while there's something not quite right about that girl. Even when she was little, she was always talking to herself and saying the oddest things. I feel sorry for her parents."

Jamie cleared his throat. "Speaking of her parents, has anyone actually seen them in a while? Sarah always comes to church with her brothers, and I run into one of the brothers from time to time in town, but I can't remember the last time I saw either of their parents."

"What are you trying to say?" Evelyn asked.

Jamie shook his head. "Not sure. I just think it's strange. That's all."

"That whole family's strange if you ask me," George interjected.

Amy Lynn tapped her grandmother on the arm. "Grandma, Momma said she was speaking in tongues. What's that?"

Evelyn eyed Ginny, a sour look on her face. She placed a hand on top of Amy Lynn's. "Honey, that's when you're so filled with the Holy Spirit, you kind of lose your senses, but I'm not sure that's what happened today."

"You know what it reminded me of?" Jamie said. "Last time I took a trip down to Charleston, I heard some folks talking what sounded like English, but not any kind I'd ever heard before, not even around here. I asked someone, and they said it was their own language they'd been speaking for hundreds of years."

Evelyn pursed her lips. "Well, clearly Sarah Jordan wouldn't know anything about that. Her parents should have gotten her help before now, but you know how some people are. Afraid of being talked about. Afraid of what everyone might say."

An awkward silence followed. Finally, Ginny cleared her throat. "Amy Lynn, why don't you ask Grandma the question you wanted to ask, you know, about the moon."

Amy Lynn's face lit up. "Oh, right. Grandma, I was reading a book, and it said the full moon in August is called the Red Moon or the Green Corn Moon or the Sturgeon Moon. Where do those names come from?"

Evelyn frowned and crinkled her nose. "Well, the only one of those I've ever heard of is the Red Moon, and I'm not exactly sure why it's called that. Maybe because the moon looks big and red when it rises this time of year."

Amy Lynn seemed disappointed by that answer. "So, it's not because of anything magical?"

"Why would you think that?" her grandmother asked.

Amy Lynn pushed her uneaten green beans around her plate with her fork. "I thought maybe there was a story of an Indian princess and an evil magician and a handsome hunter who has to come and save her."

George chuckled.

Evelyn put on an indulgent smile. "Where do you get such wild ideas, Amy Lynn?"

"Why don't you write a story then?" Ginny glared at her parents. "I'm sure Grandma and Grandpa would love to read it."

Evelyn patted Amy Lynn's hand. "I'd certainly try."

Dessert was peach cobbler with vanilla ice cream. After that Amy Lynn went to play with Bo some more while Ginny and her mother cleared the table and carried the dishes to the kitchen. That left Jamie and George.

Ginny's father lit a cigarette and fell down into his recliner in the living room. He tuned on the radio and fiddled with the dials, trying to find a baseball game. He settled on the Los Angeles Dodgers playing the Cincinnati Reds. They sat and listened for a while before George spoke up.

"So, business is doing good?"

"Yes, sir," Jamie replied. "Never better."

"That's good to hear. How many guys you got working for you now?"

"Two full time. Eddie works three days a week, and when we get really busy, I can call in Carl. He's supposedly retired, but he never turns me down. I think he misses working."

George laughed. "I think you might be right there." Then his face got serious. "You know, I might be able to help you get even busier. Maybe expand even."

Jamie raised an eyebrow. His father-in-law had never expressed an interest in the garage like that. "What do you mean?"

"You doing anything this coming Friday night?" George asked.

"Not that I'm aware."

George took a long drag on his cigarette. "I've got some friends I'd like you to talk to. What do you say? You interested?"

Jamie couldn't think of who those friends might be. Ginny's parents didn't really socialize outside the church. They knew all the same people.

"Sure," he said, equal parts curious and confused. "I'm in."

George smiled. "Great. I'll call you later in the week to give you the details."

The announcer's voice on the radio rose to a shout. Frank Howard hit a home run for the Dodgers, tying the game. George went back to listening, leaving Jamie to wonder about this mysterious meeting.

———

ADDIE WAITED until her mother left to go visit Addie's aunt. Her father was asleep in his recliner again. She pulled down the trap door to the attic as quietly as she could, which wasn't really quiet at all. The old springs groaned and squealed as the door came down. Still, her father kept snoring. She climbed up the rickety ladder, wincing every time it creaked, but thankfully her father didn't wake up.

At the top of the ladder, the heat was overwhelming. Sweat trickled down Addie's back after only a few steps. She reached up and pulled the chain to turn on the bare light bulb. Dozens of boxes surrounded her, and her heart sank. She didn't know where to start. Grandma Zee had been gone for so long. She remembered her mother bringing home several boxes of her grandmother's things, but she didn't remember what they looked like or what happened to them.

She almost turned around and went back down the ladder, but she knew she'd regret not trying at least to find the red cookbook. Addie moved toward the back of the attic. The boxes there looked older. She picked one at random, but when she opened it, she found it full of some of her mother's old clothes. Three other boxes yielded the same thing.

The next box, though, was different. She opened it, and immediately the tears welled up in her eyes. It was her sister's things from her room. The books and little ceramic figurines from her shelves, her pictures, her records. Addie went through the box one item at a time. Each one had some memory of her sister attached to it.

Reluctantly, Addie moved on, but after nothing interesting turned up in the next few boxes, she was ready to give up. She decided to look through one more box, and that was when her luck changed. As soon as she opened it the smell of her grandmother's house hit her nose. It took her back there, to summers spent sitting on the porch breaking beans and shelling peas, to winter mornings huddled in bed underneath piles of quilts, to Thanksgivings and sweet potato pies fresh out of the oven.

Most of the box was full of clothes, but at the very bottom Addie found a book. Her heart skipped a beat as she picked it up. It had a tattered red leather cover, and the pages were yellow and falling out. On the inside, she discovered a note inscribed in her grandmother's handwriting.

Hello, Addie. About time you found this book. You be sure to read it from cover to cover. We've got a lot to go over and not much time to do it.

This was the red cookbook from her memory, though as she leafed through it, she wondered if it was a cookbook at all. Even more, she wondered how she was supposed to read it. Much of it wasn't written in English, at least not any English she'd ever seen. While many of the words were recognizable, a lot of them had different spellings, and the order they were in wasn't normal. On top of that, a good many of the pages had strange diagrams drawn on them, circles with stars and crosses, surrounded by symbols and letters and numbers.

Before she could study the book anymore, a noise came from

downstairs. Her father must have woken up. She tucked the book under her arm and scrambled to the trap door. She climbed down as fast as she could, folded the ladder up, and lifted the door back into the ceiling. No sooner was the door closed than her father rounded the corner into the hallway.

"Addie? What are you doing?" he asked.

She hid the book behind her back. "Nothing, Dad. I was just going to my room to make sure I had everything ready for school tomorrow."

Her dad eyed her, but nodded. "I thought I heard a noise. I hope we don't have animals up in the attic again."

Her dad had spent months that spring trying to get squirrels out of the attic. They became his obsession.

"I'm sure it's not that. Maybe you heard something outside."

"Maybe."

He went back to his chair in the living room. Addie hurried to her room and shut the door. She opened the book on her bed and reread the note from her grandmother. It seemed like Grandma Zee had written the note to her yesterday. Two things were certain. She wanted Addie to find the book, and she wanted her to use it, but Addie didn't know what she meant by not having much time. As she stared at the book, the clock next to her bed ticked by the seconds.

6

MONDAY, AUGUST 20, 1962

J amie got to the shop a little early on Monday morning, hoping to finally get a chance to take a look at that silver Chrysler. He stood at the entry to the bay for a good long time, just staring. Only about six hundred 300Es were ever made. In the places the car wasn't dented up, the silver paint still shined like a mirror. Jamie imagined the car flying down the Interstate like a lightning bolt, or slipping around backroads like a ghost, hugging the curves and growling like a panther.

The first thing he did was kneel down to really examine the gouge marks on the side. The metal was crinkled and ripped, as if a giant claw had torn through the car. The driver's side door wouldn't even work, the gouges were so deep. Nothing about the car's trip into the ditch could explain where they came from. They had to have been made before the accident.

Jamie moved to the front of the car and swore under his breath when he popped the hood. Someone had managed to cram a V-10 engine into the space where a V-8 should have been. That kind of work was impressive. Jamie wasn't sure he could have done anything like that. The engine itself looked pretty much intact. There were some busted and loose hoses and a crack in the radiator, but all that could have happened in the crash. Everything else seemed fairly normal.

Next, Jamie circled around and opened the trunk, which was empty other than a tire iron and the spare tire. Out of curiosity, he picked up the tire iron. One of the ends was off-color, but he told himself it was only rust. He shut the trunk and took a look again at where the license plate should have been. Nothing about the crash could explain how the screws were all sheared in two, or why no one found the license plate at the site of the accident. Inside, Jamie opened the glove box, but didn't find anything interesting there.

When he jacked the car up to look underneath, he found more modifications. The car had a heavy-duty suspension it definitely didn't come out of the factory with, and the gas tank was larger than standard. Jamie slid out from under the car, sat up, and scratched his head. Nothing he found would explain why the car went off the road, and the mystery just seemed to get deeper and deeper. Who would get an expensive car like this and then go to the trouble to modify it? What was the point?

He sat and stared at the car for a minute or two more. Even in its current state, he couldn't help but stop to admire its sleek stream-lined form. For the 1959 model they made the back of the car a little longer so the tail fins flared out more.

Then something occurred to him. He hopped up and went around to the trunk again. He opened it and shined a flashlight into the very back corner. Sure enough, it wasn't as deep as it should have been, given the length of the car. He climbed into the back seat and probed all around the leather cushion with his hand, until he found what he was looking for, a latch. With a click, the entire back cushion came loose. There was a hidden compartment.

A chill ran down Jamie's spine as things started to add up. This was a bootlegger's car. Whoever owned it ran moonshine. All the modifications were common ones bootleggers did so their cars could outrun the police. But that was mostly way back during Prohibition, when bootlegging meant big money. No one had that sophisticated an outfit anymore, not even the Hawkins brothers, and even if they had a souped-up car, it would never be this fancy.

The compartment didn't have any jugs of moonshine in it, but it wasn't empty either. Jamie reached in and retrieved an envelope. Inside were old documents, beginning to yellow. None of them were in English, though Jamie didn't have to guess too hard at the language. At the top of every page was a symbol that set Jamie's hair on end—a swastika. He thought he ought to let Rick know. He wasn't sure what the sheriff would do with a stack of Nazi documents that somehow found their way to the middle of South Carolina, but he'd at least know who to contact about them, surely.

Jamie heard a car door slam. He stuffed the papers back into the envelope and tucked it under his arm. At that moment, Bobby came into the garage bay.

"What are you doing here so early?" he asked Jamie.

"Thought I'd get a head start today," Jamie answered.

Bobby looked toward the silver Chrysler. "Figure out what made the car go into that ditch?"

Jamie shook his head. "Not yet. Honestly, I was thinking of asking Rick to come and get it and find another place to put it if they can't figure out who it belongs to."

Bobby nodded. "Good idea. We're awfully busy to have one whole bay down to store a car as a favor, even if it is for the sheriff."

A horn honked. Jamie and Bobby peered out of the garage bay to see Bartholomew Avery back with his red Ford. He didn't look happy.

"So," Jamie said, "I've got some paperwork I've been putting off. Let me know if you have any problems while you're assisting Mr. Avery."

Bobby gave a mock salute. "Will do."

Back in his office, Jamie stuffed the envelope in the top drawer of his desk and almost forgot about it. Things only went downhill following Bartholomew Avery and his lemon of a Ford. Jamie spent the whole day dealing with impatient and, on occasion, confused customers. There were routine oil changes that didn't go routine, mystery noises that insisted on remaining mysteries, and a stuck convertible top it took three of them to get unstuck.

Jamie didn't have a chance to even think about the papers he'd found again until late that afternoon when there was finally a lull in the customers. He went to his office and shut the door. He pulled the envelope out of the desk drawer and spread all the papers out on top. Of course, he still couldn't understand what any of them said. Everything was in German, but one word, repeated over and over, stood out from all the rest. Jamie didn't need it translated.

Werwolf.

———

DAVID TOSSED the bag with the hamburger and fries down on the bench next to the boy. Sitting at the Tick Tock Diner eavesdropping on random conversations was a good way to take the pulse of the community, but not the greatest for the kind of information David needed. For that he had to find an informant.

He'd found Mick on his second visit to the diner. The boy was sitting alone in a booth in the corner. White t-shirt, greased hair. Not exactly the clean-cut all-American type. Perfect for David. He went up and introduced himself as a reporter from New York City and offered to pay for Mick's meal if he'd talk. The boy was more than happy to oblige. Turns out he was a senior in high school, and he was skipping that day. David learned a lot about the town of Avalon and it's mostly white, blue-collar residents—mainly that they were a bunch of lying hypocrites, at least according to Mick, who may have brought some biases to the table. David also learned about the nearby Black community of Ezekiel's Mill and the controversy over sending kids from there to schools in Avalon.

"That must have gotten some people riled up," David said.

Mick shrugged. "It did at first, but things died down after a few weeks."

David glanced around the diner. He lowered his voice. "What about the Klan? Surely they had something to say."

"Oh, they had things to say all right, but they're all bark and no bite. They like to hide behind the hoods and make all kinds of threats, but in the end they're too scared to actually do anything. Most of them own businesses. Family men. Good Christians. Upstanding members of the community. All that shit. You want a list of members? I can give it to you."

David sat up. "That ... would actually come in quite handy."

They made plans to meet again. David let Mick pick the time and the place. He hadn't expected Mick to pick a cemetery, but he wasn't going to judge.

David took a seat on the bench next to him and handed him the chocolate shake he'd order to go with his burger and fries. "Two days in a row skipping school. Aren't you worried about getting into trouble?"

Mick dug into the sack of food. "Nobody's going to miss me."

"Surely somebody will," David protested.

"Trust me. No one's going to." Mick stuffed a handful of fries in his mouth. "So, are you CIA?"

David shook his head. "Nope."

"FBI?"

David grinned. "Not even close. And even if I were, do you think I could tell you?"

"Well, then what are you?"

"I told you. I'm a journalist."

Mick smirked. "So, what the hell are you doing here?"

David held up his hands. "I'm doing what journalists do, writing a story."

"No, you're not. Why would anybody want to write a story about here?" He shoved his hand into the bag and pulled out a cheese-burger. "Extra pickles?"

"Extra everything," David replied. "Did it ever occur to you someone might be interested in what people in places like this think about what's going on in the world?"

Mick laughed. "Now I know you're full of it. Nobody here knows anything about anything. All anyone ever does is go to church and talk about their neighbors."

"What about you? What do you do?"

He took a hunk out of the cheeseburger. "Don't know. Sit around. Maybe graduate. Maybe not. Wait for a factory job to come up. One where I don't have to do all that much."

"But don't you ever think about anything more than that?"

"Like what?"

"Buy a bus ticket. Go to New York. Or Los Angeles. Find a job. See a different part of the country."

Mick rolled his eyes. "Yeah, that only happens in books and movies."

"So, you want to spend the rest of your life going to church and talking about your neighbors?" David waved a hand at the tombstones all around them. "And when it's all over, you'll wind up here."

"I can't go anywhere."

"Why not?"

"I just can't. That's all."

They were silent for a moment. Everything was still and quiet in the way only a Southern summer afternoon could be. Even the birds seemed to be in a stupor from the heat.

"What's it like in New York anyway?" Mick asked finally.

"Busy all the time," David answered. "People everywhere, crammed together. Not like this, not all this open space. But there's always something to do, someone new to talk to from somewhere you've never been or sometimes never even heard of."

Mick looked out over the cemetery toward the spire of the Episcopal church across the street. "That does sound a whole hell of a lot more interesting than here."

"I'm sure interesting things happen here, too."

Mick gulped his shake between mouthfuls of fries and burger. "When the kids from Ezekiel's Mill came to school, it was kind of a big deal. Reporters came to town to cover the story, but they only stayed a few days. I guess they lost interest when they figured out the

National Guard wasn't going to get called in and no one was going to get shot."

"Ezekiel's Mill. Weird name. Where did it come from?"

Mick shrugged. "Don't know. A guy named Ezekiel had a mill?"

David winced. He'd walked into that one. "What about Avalon? That's a pretty ... ah ... lofty name for a town like this. Do you know where it came from?"

"Oh, yeah, we get the story every year in school." The irritation dripped from Mick's words. "The town wasn't always called that. They changed it sometime last century, before the Civil War. They chose Avalon to let everyone know the town is a 'tranquil haven from the evils of the world,' or something like that. Before, it was called Bent Oak."

David let out a chuckle. "Let me guess, because there was a bent oak tree."

"Maybe? That's just what the Native Americans called it."

"And then the white people took their land," David added.

"Not exactly." Mick shot him a sly look. "There weren't any Native Americans living here. They avoided this area."

That perked up David's ears. "Don't you think that's something the settlers should have been curious about?"

Mick slurped the last of his shake. "Probably."

David found himself wishing he'd ordered a shake for himself. The couple of shots of whisky he'd had earlier weren't doing much to ward off the sun. "So, nothing else interesting has ever happened? No scandals? No murders?"

"No. Maybe before I was born." Mick licked the grease off his fingers.

"I saw something in the paper about a missing woman," David offered.

"I haven't heard anything about that."

David frowned. He was beginning to rethink his choice of informant, but he made one last try. "So, who runs this town?"

"Well, the mayor's been reelected four times. The sheriff's had the job as long as I can remember. There's Mr. Porter, who owns the bank." Mick pointed to the church. "And then there's the minister at the Episcopal church. That's where all the older families go."

"That's not exactly what I meant. I mean who really runs things? Who's everyone afraid of?"

"Looking for trouble, then? My dad always talks about the Hawkins brothers. They run moonshine. Closest thing to a criminal enterprise around here. Most people won't cross them." Mick grinned. "But if you really want to poke the hornets' nest, you should go asking about the MacNeils. There's three brothers. Rhett is the oldest, Danny is in the middle, and Billy is the youngest. They own the hardware store and have their hands in a few more businesses besides that. Everyone knows they bought and paid for the mayor and the sheriff and the minister at the Episcopal church."

"Good to know."

It sounded like David needed to get acquainted with the MacNeils.

Mick dug the last couple of fries out of the bottom of the greasy bag. "Now you're not going to go around telling everyone I said that, are you?"

David placed a hand over his heart. "Absolutely not. You have my word."

"By the way—" Mick shoved his hand in his pocket and handed David a folded piece of paper. "Here's that list I was telling you I could get for you."

David took the list of local Klansmen from him. "Thanks." He reached into his own pocket and held out a slip of paper for Mick. "I'll trade you. If you think of anything else you want to tell me, here's my phone number and the address where I'm staying while I'm here."

Mick grabbed the paper and stood up. "I should be going. Thanks for lunch. Any time you want to buy me a meal, it's cool with me."

"Hey, wait," David called as Mick walked away, "why'd you pick here to meet?"

Mick pointed to a gravestone nearby. "That's my grandfather over there. He's the only one who was ever nice to me. I like to stop by from time to time to say hello. Besides, it's quiet here. No one ever bothers you when you're visiting a graveyard."

David wished that were true.

———

IT WAS DARK. Everyone had gone to sleep long ago. Everyone except for Jamie. He sat in the bed of the pickup truck in his back yard. Another sleepless night. Another damned nightmare. Always the same.

He's back in the army. Back in Korea, and those goddamned Commies were shelling their camp. Missiles whistle through the air before they hit the ground and explode. Dust and smoke everywhere. He's choking. His eyes are tearing up. Someone calls out to him. He shouts back, but another explosion cuts off the reply.

He goes in the direction of the voice only to have the ground disappear from underneath him. When he stops falling, he's on his back, looking up at the yellow sky above him. He tries to stand, but a searing pain shoots up his leg. Is it broken? He can't tell. All he knows is he can't move. And then, he hears that awful whistling sound.

The last thing he knows he'll ever hear.

Off to the west, a flash of lightning lit up the clouds, followed a few seconds later by a crack of thunder that rumbled across the sky and shook Jamie's very bones.

"I remember nights when I was little sitting on our front porch while we watched the summer storms roll in," he said to the picture of his parents he clutched between his fingers. "I can smell the rain on the wind and feel a tingle in the air. I still get excited over thunderstorms. This is the time I can almost believe magic is real and that anything's possible. But tonight, tonight I'm scared of what the storm is going to bring, and I don't know why."

The silent figures in the picture stared back at Jamie.

"Storms are dangerous. You should be scared of them."

Jamie leapt nearly three feet out of the truck bed. His shotgun, unfortunately, was in his other truck. "Who's out there?"

A man stepped forward out of the shadows. "Sorry. I didn't mean to scare you."

He looked like he'd come straight from a bar fight. His clothes were wrinkled, and his untucked shirt was mis-buttoned. Dark, messy curls fell in front of his face.

"Could have fooled me," Jamie spat. "Who the hell are you? Do you have any idea what time it is?"

"My name is David Ben-Ari, and it's three thirty-seven in the morning. Believe me, if there were any other way I could have arranged this meeting I would have, but I don't have a lot of options these days." He spoke with a slight accent.

Jamie hopped out of the truck and came toward the stranger, his chest puffed out. He stopped when he was close enough to smell the alcohol on the man's breath. "Well, Mr. Ben-Ari, I'd like to remind you that what you're doing right now is trespassing, so you should get moving before I decide to kick your ass off my property."

The corners of the man's mouth turned up slightly, as if the idea were funny somehow. "I'll go, I promise, but first I want to talk with you about the car you've been keeping at your garage, the one the sheriff asked you to look at."

"Why?" Jamie asked. "Is it yours?"

"No, I just have some questions about it. It has some ... unusual damage, or so I've heard."

Jamie eyeballed the stranger. "How do you know that?"

The man shrugged. "In a town like this it's hard to keep anything a secret. I overheard a conversation or two while I was having break-fast at the Tick-Tock Diner. Lovely establishment, by the way. Good people there. Especially Peggy. She's a peach."

"If it's not your car, I don't see how it's any of your damn busi-ness." Jamie got in his face. "Now I'm going to ask you again to leave. I won't be nice about it the next time."

The man put a finger on Jamie's chest and pushed him back-wards. He was shorter than Jamie, but he had a compact build. "It's my business because I was supposed to meet with the man driving that car on the night it went into the ditch. He had something to give me. You didn't happen to find anything in the car, did you?"

"An envelope." The words slipped out of Jamie's mouth before he realized.

The man raised an eyebrow. "Now we're getting somewhere."

Jamie cursed himself. "I'm going to turn it over to the sheriff."

"Can you trust him?"

"I can trust him more than a stranger trespassing in my back yard in the middle of the night," Jamie snapped.

"But do you know everything about him? What's his favorite cereal? Or his favorite TV show?" The man snickered. "Who's the actress he thinks about when he's with his wife?"

Jamie scoffed. "Of course, I don't know things like that."

The man persisted. "So, it's possible there could be something you don't know, something that would change your opinion of him."

Jamie frowned. "What exactly are you getting at?"

"I need that envelope."

"And I haven't heard a reason yet why I should give it to you."

"Because if you don't, your life and the lives of your wife and daughter will be in danger." Each of the man's words came out sharp as a knife blade.

Jamie's hackles rose at the mention of Ginny and Amy Lynn. "Is that a threat?"

"A warning," the man replied. "This isn't about illegal liquor, Mr. Fletcher. There are some evil people in this world. If you give me the envelope now, before anyone figures out you have it, you might be okay. You looked through the papers inside, I'm sure. Think about what you've seen."

Yellowed pages all in German.

Jamie shook his head. "I never said anything to you about bootleg liquor."

"But that's what you thought, after you looked at the car and saw the modifications made to it, right?" He took a step toward Jamie. "You thought about the Hawkins brothers, but it's too nice of a car for them to ever own. And you asked yourself why someone would go to the trouble to soup up a car like that to begin with. What exactly made the gouges in the side, and why did the car go into the ditch that night? Those are all very good questions, but they're ones you need to forget about."

Giant swastikas.

Jamie backed away. "Who are you exactly, Mr. Ben-Ari?"

"You're still not asking the right question."

Werwolf.

"What question should I be asking?"

He had Jamie pinned against the truck. "You should be asking how you can protect yourself and your family. Your sheriff, your congressman, your FBI, they're all pretty much useless to you in this situation."

Jamie studied him a little more closely. *"Your FBI?* And the funny accent. You're not American, are you?"

The man narrowed his eyes. "You're one to be talking about funny accents. I'm Israeli."

"A Jew," Jamie said.

He nodded. "Is that a problem for you?"

"Not at all. There's just not many of you around here." But some things suddenly made a little more sense to Jamie. "I know what you're doing. You're one of those people who hunt Nazis who escaped after the end of World War II. Is that what this is all about? Are you saying there are bona fide Nazis here, in Avalon?"

"If you give the sheriff those documents, you may as well set them on fire. He won't know what to do with them." He flashed a feral grin. "But I do."

Jamie chewed his lip. "Nothing about this makes any sense."

"It doesn't have to," the man insisted. "All you have to do is give me the envelope and I'll go away. You can tell the sheriff you're really sorry, but you don't have a clue what happened to the car. He can take it and sell it for scrap metal or whatever he wants to do with it, and you can go on with your life, forgetting I was ever here."

Jamie thought for a moment. That's really want he wanted, to forget he'd ever laid eyes on the silver Chrysler. "I don't have the envelope with me. It's in my office in my desk at work."

"Have you told anyone about it?"

"Not a soul."

Lightning streaked across the sky, and almost immediately a peal of thunder rattled the windows in the old truck.

"You should get inside before the storm hits," said David Ben-Ari. "I'll see you tomorrow."

7

TUESDAY, AUGUST 21, 1962

Jamie cursed the alarm clock when it went off the next morning. Still, he dragged himself out of bed and staggered down the stairs. Amy Lynn was already finished with her breakfast and headed out the door for school. Most days, if the weather was nice, she rode her bike there. Jamie called her back for a quick hug and a peck on the forehead.

"You're up early," Ginny said, handing him a plate of scrambled eggs and sausage.

Jamie sat down at the kitchen table. "I need to get to the garage before everyone else."

"What for?" Ginny asked.

"Paperwork. Things have been so crazy, I'm behind on the invoices."

Not entirely a lie.

She set a cup of coffee on the table next of him. "You know you could hire someone to do that for you."

"But why when I can do it myself?" He stabbed a sausage with his fork and popped it in his mouth.

Ginny sat down across from him and looked him in the eye. "You don't have to do everything yourself."

Jamie grunted. "I do if I want it done right."

Ginny didn't answer. She rolled her eyes and left him to finish his breakfast alone.

After the previous night's thunderstorm, the air smelled like fresh, damp earth. The sun beat down from a nearly cloudless sky, and steam rose up from the wet ground, hanging like a silent army of ghosts. Jamie broke a sweat just walking from his truck to his office.

He unlocked the door and slipped inside. The office was dark and cool. He pushed the door shut behind him and stood for a moment with his hand resting on the doorknob while he let his eyes adjust to the dimness. He hadn't changed much since taking over from Old Carl, other than the dead fern on top of the filing cabinet—the one Ginny had given him and he'd promised to take care of—and the Chevy truck calendar on the wall. It was at least for the current year, even if Jamie hadn't flipped the pages since May. He headed for the desk drawer where he'd stuck the envelope. He didn't know when or where this David Ben-Ari was going to show up again, and he wanted to be ready.

But when he looked in the drawer, his heart leapt up into his throat.

The envelope was gone.

"No," he whispered.

He reached deep into the drawer but failed to place a hand on it.

"No, no, no," he repeated.

He tore through all the rest of the drawers in his desk. The envelope wasn't anywhere to be found. Jamie glanced around his office. The papers on top of his desk were all where he left them. His filing cabinet was still locked, and so was the safe. It didn't look like anything in either place had been touched. His stomach lurched as he realized someone must have broken into his office with the purpose of stealing the envelope and the papers inside.

Jamie stared at the door. He knelt down so he was eye-level with the doorknob. He opened the door and shut it, watching it catch. Then he took out his key and locked and unlocked the door, over and over. It didn't seem tampered with. There wasn't any sign of a break-in at all, but no one else had a key to his office. And no one else knew about the envelope, let alone where he put it.

A noise outside brought Jamie back to the present. He came out of his office to find Bobby and Eddie both arriving for work.

"That's two days in a row you've beaten us all here," Bobby said. "You want to start opening the garage earlier? Not sure who you're going to find to come in, because it ain't going to be me."

Jamie laughed. "No just trying to keep from getting buried in invoices."

Bobby's gaze went past Jamie, to the open door of his office. "You could hire someone to help with that, you know."

Jamie glared. "Now you're starting to sound like Ginny."

Bobby grinned. "Well, there's a reason everyone calls her the smart one."

Jamie held up a chiding finger. "Hey, watch it now, or I *will* start making you come in at six every morning." He was grinning, too, though. "Now get going on Mrs. Adams' Ford before she calls me again screaming about when she's going to get her relic of a car back."

"Yes, sir," Bobby said.

Jamie spent the rest of the morning eyeing his own employees, wondering if any of them had taken the envelope, but he didn't know when or how they could have gotten into the office. As he was eating his lunch another idea occurred to him. What if David Ben-Ari had taken it? If he was really some kind of Nazi-hunting secret agent, then maybe he had the skill to break into the office without actually breaking anything. What if he had left Jamie's back yard and come straight to the garage? If that was the case, Jamie didn't have anything to worry about. The problem was solved and he'd never see David Ben-Ari again. Or maybe Ginny was right and he'd been watching too much TV.

At about four, a sheriff's car pulled up.

Jamie went out to meet the deputy as he was getting out of the car. "Hey, Rick, tell me you've figured out who that car belongs to and you're sending a tow truck to get it out of here."

"I wish I could," Rick said, taking Jamie's outstretched hand.

Jamie frowned. "Why? What's wrong?"

Rick put his hands on his hips. "Well, it's the darnedest thing. They ran the VIN on the car, and they couldn't find it."

Jamie's stomach twisted in knots again. "Couldn't find what? The car? What do you mean?"

"They couldn't find any record of it." Rick gestured toward the garage bay. "Technically, that silver car in there does not exist."

Jamie felt like he might throw up, but he did his best to hide it. "How do they lose track of a car?"

Rick shook his head. "They don't, not usually."

"Do you think it's possible someone erased the record on purpose?"

Rick looked at him like he also thought Jamie watched too much TV. "I don't know if I'd go that far, but it's possible."

"Any reason why someone might want to do that?" Jamie asked the question to himself as much as Rick.

The sheriff's deputy threw up his hands. "Your guess is as good as mine on that one."

Jamie let his gaze wander over to the Chrysler. "So, the car's staying here."

"Only for a few more days. I promise," Rick said, "while they're re-reviewing their records."

Jamie opened his mouth to tell Rick about the missing envelope and the secret compartment in the car, but David's question from the night before echoed in his head. *Can you trust him?* Jamie had known Rick basically his entire life. He didn't have a reason not to trust the sheriff's deputy, but the way David acted, it made Jamie think he knew something about Rick.

"As long as you promise," he muttered.

"Any progress on finding out what sent the car off the road?" Rick asked.

Jamie shook his head. "None at all. Other than the strange gouge marks on the side, pretty much all the rest of the damage is consistent with the car's trip into the ditch."

"Do you have any idea what made those marks?" Rick looked at him expectantly.

Jamie shrugged. "Not a clue. At least not anything that would send a car off the road."

Rick made a face, obviously disappointed. "Well, you let me know if you figure anything out."

Jamie nodded. "Yeah, you do the same."

When closing time came, there still wasn't any sign of David Ben-Ari. By then, Jamie had all but convinced himself David must have come in the middle of the night and taken the envelope. He was still mulling over the idea when he found David leaning against his truck after he finished locking up.

"Busy day?" David asked before taking a drag from his cigarette.

He hadn't changed clothes from the night before. His shirt was still mis-buttoned. His eyes were bloodshot, and he smelled like bourbon again. The only difference was the thicker stubble on his face.

Jamie scowled. "Do you know how to make a regular entrance?"

"I do," David replied, "but it's not really something that's recommended in my line of work."

Jamie stopped and wiped the sweat off his forehead with his sleeve. The heat hadn't let up all day, and this was the last conversation he wanted to be having. All he wanted to do was go home. "And what exactly is your line of work?"

David chuckled. "You asked me that last night, and I didn't answer you. What makes you think I'm going to answer now? I'll take that envelope, if you don't mind, and then you can forget all about me."

So, David didn't steal it from his office. Wishful thinking. Jamie took in a deep breath and let it out slowly. "As much as I want to do that very thing, I can't."

David groaned. "Do we have to go through this again? You didn't give it to the sheriff, did you? I thought we—"

"I can't because it's gone."

David's face fell. "What do you mean by that?"

"I mean it's gone," Jamie spat. "Someone took it from my desk."

David swore. "This is bad. This is really bad."

He stood so he blocked Jamie from the door to his truck, and he didn't show any sign of moving.

"Yeah, I guess you've got a real head-scratcher on your hands, then."

Jamie went to go around him, but David held up an arm to stop him.

"I mean it's bad for you. They know you found it." David's gaze darted around the area, as if he were looking for anyone who might be spying on them. "We should have some time, though. They'll try to figure out how much you really know before they decide what to do with you."

"What to do with me? And who are 'they'? This is insane. I've had about enough of you." He tried to push David's arm away. "Let me—"

David didn't give him a chance to finish. He seized Jamie's arm, spun him around, slammed him against the side of his truck, and held him there, his arm pinned behind his back.

"You looked in the envelope," he growled, his cigarette still clenched between his teeth. "You know who 'they' are."

Jamie smirked, despite his face being pressed against the driver's-side window of his truck. "So, you're admitting to me you really are a Nazi hunter."

With one more hard shove, David let him go. "It's unfortunate you know that."

"For me or for you?" Jamie asked, rubbing his wrenched shoulder.

David dropped the butt of his cigarette on the ground and stamped it out with his heel. "Both."

"So, these Nazis of yours. What are they doing here of all places?"

"That's what I aim to find out," David said as he retrieved a pack of cigarettes and a lighter from his back pocket.

Jamie watched as he lit up another one. "Well, maybe you could answer a question for me in the meantime."

David took a long drag and blew out a puff of smoke. "Sure. What's the harm in spilling a few more state secrets at this point?"

Jamie chose to ignore the remark. "I couldn't read any of the documents in the envelope seeing as how they were all in German, but I figured I didn't need to. The big swastikas everywhere gave me a pretty good idea of what they were all about, but one word kept coming up again and again. *Werwolf.* Does that mean what I think it means?"

David stood silent for a moment. The corner of his mouth twitched. "It would be easier to show you, if you've got a little time."

Jamie shook his head. "I really shouldn't be late getting home again."

"It won't take long, I promise. The place where I'm staying isn't very far from here. And you should know what we're up against. You deserve at least that. You can follow me." He turned and walked toward his car, a navy-blue Ford Fairlane that had seen better days.

Jamie hesitated. He should go home. He should forget David and his Nazi conspiracies. Those papers could have gotten in that car any number of ways. A World War II vet. There were a lot of those around. Ginny's father was one. He could have found them marching through one German village or another and brought them back as a weird souvenir. But there was the car. And the blood. And the missing driver.

Cursing himself, he climbed into his truck.

They took Old Avalon Road south of town. David turned left onto Hidden Lake Road and then left again onto a side road Jamie didn't even see until they were right on top of it. He failed to catch the name. The road skirted the lake for a mile or two and then the pavement ran out. They kept going for about another mile on gravel. Finally, the road ended in front of a wooden shack that looked like it would fall over in a stiff breeze.

"You live here?" Jamie asked as he climbed out of his truck.

"For the time being," David said. "Rent's cheap at least."

Jamie followed him inside. The house was one giant room. The kitchen occupied one corner. It had a two-burner stove and a small refrigerator, and room enough for a dinette set. A few empty liquor bottles stood on the table. An unmade bed occupied the opposite corner. An open suitcase lay on the floor next to it. There was also a small desk covered in loose papers, but the most curious thing about the room was the display on the wall above the desk. Photographs, news clippings, maps, and drawings covered the wall in a haphazard jumble.

"Welcome," David said as he led Jamie in. "Hope you don't mind the mess. I wasn't expecting to entertain visitors."

"That much is pretty clear," Jamie muttered under his breath.

David nodded toward the display on the wall. "Here's what I wanted to show you. To answer your question, yes, *Werwolf* is the German word for werewolf." He pronounced it *vehr-vohlf*. "It was also the codename given to the Nazis who tried to fight a guerrilla war against the Allies after Germany surrendered," he continued. He pointed to a symbol drawn on a scrap of paper, a straight line with hooks at each end and a diagonal slash through the middle. "See that. It was their symbol. It's called a *Wolfsangel*."

It looked familiar to Jamie, but he couldn't place where he'd seen it before.

"Some of them are still fighting, almost twenty years later," David went on. He pointed to a set of pictures, all of the same person. The first one was labeled April 28, 1943, and showed a man with light hair and piercing light-colored eyes in a Nazi SS uniform. "His name is Heinrich Albrecht. He was a fairly high-ranking official in the Nazi Party, right under Heinrich Himmler. After Germany's surrender, he vanished despite efforts to capture him, but he has turned up a few times since then. The last time he was seen was about ten years ago. No one knows what happened to him, until I got a call he was living here under a different name."

"Living here? In Avalon?" Jamie studied the pictures. "I don't recognize him."

"I'd be shocked if you did," David said. "I'd venture to guess he's pretty good at disguising himself."

Jamie's gaze wandered over the photos on the wall of the Nazi officer. Even though they were taken years apart, the man didn't seem to age. "Don't you know the name he's been living under?"

"That's just it. I don't. My informant wouldn't tell me over the phone. He said we needed to meet in person before he would share all the details with me."

"So, this Heinrich Albrecht could be almost anyone."

David went to rummage around in the kitchen. He dug a half-empty bottle of whisky from underneath a chair and swiped a glass from the counter next to the sink. "Anyone at all. And we have to find him before the next full moon."

Jamie frowned. "Why? What happens at the next full moon?"

David pointed to some newspaper clippings. "Someone else dies."

Jamie read the headlines.

Camden woman missing for four days. Police at a loss.
Family pleads for help finding missing grandmother.
"Please help find our baby girl," says distraught father.

"That doesn't make any sense. What does the full moon have to do with any of these people?" But right then Jamie put two and two together in his head. The idea was so absurd he laughed out loud. "Next you'll be telling me we're going up against real werewolves."

David didn't laugh with him. "You keep saying you don't know what made the giant gouges on the side of the car. You know, the ones that look like giant claw marks? Now you do."

Jamie's blood rose. He felt stupid for falling for the ramblings of someone who obviously wasn't right in the head. "You've got to be kidding me. You're nuts. There's no such thing as werewolves or vampires or ghosts or any of that shit."

David took a giant swig of his whisky. "Are you sure? Nothing's ever happened to you that you can't explain?"

"Lots of stuff," Jamie admitted, "but just because I can't explain it doesn't mean a ghost did it. Look, Ginny's going to be mad at me for being late again. Sorry your envelope went missing. You get in touch with me when you have a plan that doesn't involve fighting imaginary monsters, okay?"

He stormed out of the shack and left David to his wall of crazy. David didn't try to stop him. He stood at the door and watched Jamie get into his truck. All the way home Jamie seethed, thinking he had to be the butt of some stupid practical joke, like David left him in the middle of the woods holding the bag at the end of a snipe hunt.

When he got home finally, Ginny asked him why he was so late, and he lied again, saying he had a lot of paperwork to do. She looked at him a little sideways, but she didn't say anything. Jamie got the impression that particular lie was wearing thin. He'd have to come up with something else next time.

Except there wasn't going to be a next time.

No more Nazis. No more David Ben-Ari. No more thinking about mysterious car crashes. Ginny was right. None of it was any of his business, and he promised himself then and there he was going to stay out of it. He didn't go a day without breaking that promise.

8

WEDNESDAY, AUGUST 22, 1962

Jamie nodded off again. The tip of his pencil snapped and made a giant smudge across the spreadsheet splayed out on the desk. He swore as he frantically tried to erase the mark without obliterating that month's expense figures. After spending the better part of the day trudging through row after row of numbers, Jamie began to think maybe Ginny was right about hiring someone to take care of the garage's finances. Maybe. As he tried for the third time to add up the same column, a knock on the door of his office nearly made him fall backwards in his chair.

"What is it?" he barked.

Bobby opened the door and poked his head inside, a strange look on his face. "Jamie, there's a guy here to see you."

Jamie squinted hard at him. "Does this guy have a name?"

Before Bobby could answer, someone else popped up behind him. Calvin Jordan, Sarah Jordan's oldest brother. Tall and lanky, he had always reminded Jamie of a marionette jerking around as someone tugged on the strings.

"It's just me, Jamie."

Jamie and Calvin were the same age. They had gone to school together, whenever Calvin bothered to go to school. They were never exactly friends, but they were always at least cordial to one another.

Jamie waved him inside. "Come on in, Calvin. What can I do for you today? Got a car for me to look at?"

Calvin's eyes darted nervously around the room as he entered. "Not exactly."

Jamie noticed he had put on his Sunday clothes. "Then what brings you by today?"

His hands shook. He glanced over his shoulder at Bobby and the other mechanics right outside Jamie's office, all looking busy while trying to overhear. "Can I shut the door first?"

Jamie let his smile slip, just a little. "Sure."

The Jordans had always been odd. They mostly kept to themselves, but when one of them did venture into town, they managed to have the most awkward encounters. Jamie was all but sure he was about to have one of those encounters.

Calvin closed the door carefully before he folded himself into the chair across from Jamie's desk. "Sarah wants to meet with you."

Jamie stared at him. "She wants to meet with me? I don't understand, exactly."

"She wants you to come over to the house and have a talk with her," Calvin explained as if it were the most obvious thing in the world and Jamie was being dense.

"About what?"

Calvin shook his head. "She wouldn't say. She never does."

Jamie thought back to the incident at the church service the past Sunday, how Sarah had seemed to look at him while she danced in front of the congregation, and then how they had all stared at him in the parking lot afterwards.

"Is this about what happened at church?"

Calvin shrugged. "It could be."

Jamie eyed the stack of papers on his desk. He didn't have time for games like this. "I don't know, Calvin. I'm kind of busy right now."

Calvin grasped the top of Jamie's desk with both hands. "Please. Look, I know my sister can make people sort of uncomfortable sometimes, but she *knows* things, like things she shouldn't be able to know." He lowered his voice even more. "She says the angels and the demons talk to her."

More magical bullshit.

"Do you believe her?"

"I do." Calvin swallowed hard. "I'm going to tell you a story. This is something that happened when we were kids, right after our grandmother died. All five of us were sleeping in a room together because we had family staying with us. I was on some blankets on the floor. I woke up all of a sudden in the middle of the night. I'm not sure if I heard a noise or I felt something touch me, but I knew right away something wasn't right. There were no night noises. It was summertime and all the windows were open. I should have heard crickets and frogs and all sorts of things, but everything was completely silent.

"I sat up, and I wished right away I hadn't. Like I said, it was summertime, but I was so cold I was shivering. There was a shadow in the corner of the room that shouldn't have been there. I thought at first it might be our daddy come to check in on us, but it didn't move at all, and even though it didn't really have a head, I knew it was looking at me. I couldn't move or scream. It put out all kinds of bad feelings. It was evil, and it wanted to hurt us."

Jamie couldn't say he wasn't familiar with what Calvin was saying. There were times when he woke up in the middle of the night, convinced if he looked, there would be something looking back at him, but of course he always blamed his overactive imagination.

Calvin went on. "Then I saw Sarah get up. I wanted to warn her, to call out to her and tell her to stop, but I still couldn't speak. She went directly up to the creature, and she said, 'Don't worry, Calvin, Grandma told me she won't let the monsters get us.' Then she reached up and touched the shadow, and the thing vanished like smoke."

He looked expectantly at Jamie, who didn't know exactly how to reply. It was just a misremembered childhood dream. It had to be. Right?

"That's ... quite a story, Calvin. How long ago did that happen?"

Calvin's expression soured. "It was real. Sarah remembers it, too. And that's only one of the stories I could tell. I don't know if Sarah really talks to angels and demons, but it's as good an explanation as any. She wants to talk to you because she needs to tell you something important. It's probably in your best interest to listen."

Jamie sat back, surprised at the sudden forcefulness of Calvin's words. "Okay, I'll see what I can do. Maybe tomorrow afternoon?"

Calvin broke out in a smile. "That'll be fine. I'll let her know to expect you. Thank you. You have a nice rest of your day, okay?"

After he left, Jamie wondered what he'd gotten himself into.

———

WHEN THE BELL RANG, twenty-five eight- and nine-year-olds ran yelling out the door. Addie sank down in her chair. The first week of school was more than halfway over, and nothing bad had happened. Well, nothing too bad. She'd had to break up one fight, not to mention the barbed comments from Rose she'd been forced to endure at the first faculty meeting.

She straightened up the desks, put all the books back on their shelves, and cleaned the chalkboard. Then she packed up her things, turned off the lights, and hoped she wouldn't run into Rose on her way out.

As Addie passed by Cassandra Miller's classroom, though, she overheard Cassandra and another teacher talking. Addie wasn't trying to be nosey, but she slowed her pace a little.

"It's a shame. Edda's been such a good neighbor since we moved here, almost like a second mother. She's taking this so hard."

Addie recognized the voice of Carol Robertson. She and Cassandra both taught combined first- and second-grade classes. It was the first year teaching for both of them.

"Well, what would you do if your daughter was missing?" Cassandra asked.

"I don't think I'd handle it well either," Carol conceded. "You know they put out an ad in the paper asking anyone who might know anything to come forward. I don't think anyone has yet. I just can't believe the sheriff hasn't found any clues."

Cassandra let out a bitter chuckle. "He'd have to be looking for them to find them."

"What's that supposed to mean?"

"You know how the authorities are around here. How hard do you think they're going to try to find a girl from Ezekiel's Mill?"

"But that's what they're supposed to do. It's their job."

"It's their job to protect the good people of Avalon," Cassandra corrected, "and not all of them agree on who those good people are."

Addie didn't stick around for Carol's response. The conversation brought back memories of when Addie's sister went missing. They'd gone to the police, but the police didn't seem too interested in helping. They had the audacity to suggest maybe Cora ran off on her own.

It took more than a week and constant badgering from her parents before the police finally opened an investigation, but they never really took it seriously. A couple of deputies looked through the woods near their home and asked the neighbors if they'd seen anything, but that was it. When a month passed without any sign of her sister, they basically gave up.

And now the same thing had happened to someone else's daughter, maybe someone else's sister. Addie didn't want to think about it. As she walked home on another sweltering afternoon, she began humming her grandmother's tune again. Almost immediately, she felt something warm in her bag. She stopped to dig through it and fished out her grandmother's red cookbook. She didn't remember putting it there.

The warmth spread into her as she held the book, filling Addie with the sensation of being protected, being loved, like her grandmother made her feel. She hurried home and went straight to her bedroom, shutting the door behind her.

Fortunately, her mother was out, and her father wasn't home from work yet, so she didn't have to deal with questions from either of them. She sat down on her bed and pulled the red cookbook out of her bag again. The warmth still radiated from it, pulsing almost like a heartbeat.

Again, she wondered how she was supposed to read it, given that her grandmother hadn't used any sort of standard English, but as she watched, the flowing, loopy lines of her grandmother's handwriting rearranged themselves. She blinked and looked again. The words were the same as before, yet also different. Both foreign and familiar, cryptic and clear. The effect was jarring, but she found if she concentrated, she could actually understand.

Addie read with her mouth hanging open. The book wasn't a cookbook at all. It was full of magical rituals, everything from attracting your soulmate to generating luck to making someone you disliked sick. Her grandmother described each ritual down to the smallest detail—the exact words that needed to be said, the time of day the ritual had to be performed, the ingredients required, even the clothes the person performing the ritual should wear and what they should eat and drink beforehand.

Grandma Zee had told Addie stories from growing up near Charleston, of ghosts and witches and magical creatures that lurked in the marshes and woods, and what you were supposed to do to fight those things if they ever came after you.

But they were only stories.

Surely her grandmother had just meant to scare her and her sister. Surely no one was supposed to take those stories seriously.

And yet.

Addie stopped when she came to a page with the words "For Finding Lost Things or People" written across the top. The rest of the page was taken up with instructions on how to perform a magic ritual to do exactly that, complete with a diagram on how to set everything up. Addie scanned the list of ingredients. Most of them were either things they already had in the house or things she could get easily, but a few ingredients she'd never heard of before. She had no clue what "High John the Conqueror root" was.

Addie kept going, reading through all the spells until she came to the very last page, where she found another note from her grandmother.

I left a box for you, Addie. There are some things in it you'll need. I'm sure your mother won't give it to you. She means well, but she doesn't understand. You look for it. The box wants you to find it.

She flipped back to the spell for finding lost things and people. Reading over the ingredients again, she wondered if the more ... uncommon ones were in the box her grandmother's note mentioned. She needed to go back up in the attic and poke around some more when she got the chance.

And in that moment, it dawned on her she'd gone from merely reading about magic spells to actually intending to try one. If the spell could find lost people, maybe it would help find her sister. The idea was ridiculous, but her grandmother was not a ridiculous woman. Far from it. And if her grandmother believed in magic, could there be a tiny bit of truth to all those stories she told?

Addie glanced at the photo of her sister she kept by her bed. What did she have to lose?

9

THURSDAY, AUGUST 23, 1962

Jamie showed up at the Jordan farm a little bit after noon. He'd told the guys at the garage he had to go track down a part he needed to rebuild the drivetrain of Bennett Blake's '59 Chevy El Camino. Not entirely a lie. He planned to swing by Sam Murphy's after his visit to the Jordan farm. Sam said he might have the part in question, but Jamie wouldn't know until he got there, and that was only if Sam wasn't already fall-down drunk.

As Jamie approached the front of the old farmhouse, he glanced up at the gables and the gingerbread trim around the roofline. From the road it looked like a tidy little white house set up on a hill, nestled in among some trees, but up close Jamie could see clearly the signs of neglect and decay. The white paint was peeling. The bushes around the house were overgrown, and he nearly turned his ankle on a loose board on the porch.

More importantly, though, all the windows on that side of the house provided a clear view of Dry Creek Road. Anyone looking out on the night of the accident would have seen it. And given the godawful sound he heard from almost a mile away, Jamie couldn't help but wonder why no one had come running, out of curiosity at the very least.

He knocked on the door and waited.

And waited.

And waited.

He absentmindedly shoved his hands into his pockets. In his left pocket, his fingers hit something hard. Confused, he fished out a flat stone, shiny and black, worn smooth in a stream somewhere. The most curious thing about it, though, was the perfectly round hole in the middle. Jamie knew it hadn't been in his pocket when he put his pants on that morning. At least he was pretty sure. Why hadn't he felt it before now?

He was still examining the rock when the door creaked open. Jamie glanced up to find Calvin and all his brothers confronting him. The expressions on their faces ranged from Calvin's vague welcome to open hostility. Apparently not everyone agreed on his visit. Sarah, Jamie noticed, wasn't among them.

Jamie slipped the rock back into his pocket and smiled as wide as he could, trying to appear cordial. "Uh, good afternoon."

Calvin returned his smile, but the gesture seemed forced, as if he did it only because he knew he was supposed to. "I'm glad you could make it, Jamie. Come on in."

He and his brothers stepped aside for Jamie to enter. Though he had known the Jordan family most of his life, this was the first time Jamie had ever set foot inside their house. A table stood in the small entryway. On top was a vase full of daisies, the petals browning at the edges. A giant Bible rested next to it, no doubt full of generations of Jordans who had been born and died in that house. A staircase led up to the second floor. Next to it, a hallway led to the back of the house. To Jamie's right was a small, sparely furnished sitting room.

Calvin pointed up to the second floor. "Sarah's waiting for you upstairs. First door on your right."

His brothers all continued to glare silently.

Jamie hesitated. "You ... want me to just go on up? You sure that's okay?"

Calvin looked at him like he had grown three heads. "Well, of course. Why wouldn't it be?"

Jamie drew in a breath, ready to explain the etiquette for visiting another's home, about how it wasn't proper for a visitor to go alone into the more private parts of the house, and about how it certainly wasn't proper for a married man to visit with an unmarried woman in her bedroom. At the perplexed look on Calvin's face, though, he decided not to waste his time.

Slowly, he climbed the stairs. With each step, the old boards creaked and groaned, announcing his approach. Definitely no sneaking around in a house like that. At the top, Jamie came to a long hallway lined with closed doors. The end was lost in darkness. It occurred to him again that no one had seen Calvin and Sarah's parents in a while. Why didn't they come out to meet him? Were they in one of those other rooms? Were they ailing in some way?

He knocked on the first door to the right, like Calvin said. There was no answer. He glanced over his shoulder, back down the stairs. Calvin and his brothers had all gone ... somewhere. He could go back down and leave through the front door. No one would seriously blame him. Maybe Sarah fell asleep, in which case it would probably be best not to disturb her.

But she was the one who wanted to meet with him, he reminded himself, so he knocked again. Still no one answered, although he could hear someone moving inside, a light shuffle of feet, a slight scrape of wood on wood. Tentative fingers curled around the doorknob, and he turned it carefully. The latch was rusty and gave with a screech that made him cringe. He pushed the door open a crack.

"Sarah?" he called. "Is that you in there? Are you okay?"

A high, girlish voice floated from inside the room. "I'm fine, Jamie Fletcher. Why don't you come in and shut the door behind you?"

Jamie did as he was told, and that was how he found himself in Sarah Jordan's bedroom. She sat in a rocking chair at the foot of her bed. Besides the small table next to the chair, the only other furniture in the room was the bed itself. It was covered in a blue and white checked quilt. The bare walls were painted the same shade of light blue. No pictures or mirrors hung anywhere. The faintest scent of lilac perfume hung in the air.

Sheer curtains filtered the sunlight coming in through the window, which, as Jamie suspected, looked directly out the front of the house toward Dry Creek Road. If Sarah had her window open that night, she would have heard the crash.

"Have a seat," Sarah told him.

The only place for Jamie to sit was on the bed. He eyed it nervously. "I'm not sure—"

Sara sighed and rolled her eyes. "Please, Jamie, for the love of God, sit down on the bed. Ain't nothing going to happen."

Jamie perched himself on the very edge of the bed, both feet firmly on the floor and hands resting on his knees.

Sarah tilted her head to the side and looked him up and down with her pale blue eyes. "Aren't you going to ask me about what happened in church last Sunday?"

Jamie shook his head. "No, ma'am. I don't believe that's any of my business."

She let out a bitter chuckle. "You don't, now? Seems like the rest of this town has a different opinion. Most people think pretty much everything I do is their business."

"Not me," Jamie insisted. "I don't believe in gossip."

"Well, that's mighty admirable of you, Jamie Fletcher, but whether you like to gossip or not isn't why I wanted to talk to you."

"Why do you?"

She rocked back and forth for a minute before she said anything further. "What do you think you saw me doing in church?"

"Speaking in tongues?" Jamie ventured. "That's what Ginny said it looked like anyway."

She laughed, this time for real. "If God ever uses me to speak through like that, we're all well and truly done. No, I was seeing through someone else's eyes."

"Whose?" Jamie asked.

She shrugged. "I don't know, but they know you. They recognized you when they saw you sitting there next to your wife and daughter and your father-in-law."

The mention of his family made Jamie doubly uncomfortable. "Do you know what you were saying, what the words meant?"

"Not exactly, but it ain't good." Sarah gestured toward the window. "I saw you outside the other day, looking at where that wreck was."

"I think I heard it when it happened." Jamie kept an eye on her for any sort of reaction. "There was a loud noise."

She merely nodded. "I heard it, too. We all did."

Jamie bolted to the window. "You did? Then why didn't anyone from the house go try to help? The driver was hurt pretty badly."

She held up a hand. "He wasn't hurt in the crash, Jamie. As soon as the car stopped moving, he threw his door open and ran into the woods."

"But still—"

Sarah silenced him with a look. "Something else was out there, too. It followed him into the trees. And that was that. There wasn't anything anyone here could do to help him at that point."

Jamie's gaze went to the woods on the other side of Dry Creek Road. "Something else? What do you mean by that?"

"I mean, something else. Something dark. Something evil. There's a reason people shut their blinds at night and don't look outside when they hear strange noises. They're afraid of what they'll see if they look. Maybe it's only a fox or a raccoon. Maybe it's not."

Jamie turned back toward her. "But you looked."

"I'm not afraid." She jutted out her chin. "I've known all my life what the devil looks like. He can't scare me."

"Why are you telling me all this?" he asked, sitting down on the bed again.

"Because you want to know all the answers. You want to know what made that car crash and what happened to the driver. Because you're not going to be able to let it go after you leave here today." She leaned in closer. "Because you already know who the driver was."

Jamie backed away. "What? How is that even possible?"

"His name was Jeffrey DiCarlo," Sarah continued.

Jamie stared at her. His old army buddy. A fellow mechanic. Jeff could fix anything, not only Jeeps—radios, lights, generators—and usually make them better than they were before. He hadn't spoken to Jeff in almost ten years.

"Where did you get that name?" he whispered.

"The spirits told me."

This was a trick. Some kind of cruel joke. Jamie didn't believe it. "No, I must have talked about Jeff to you or to someone else at one point. That's where you got it from. Why would he be here? Why wouldn't he look me up? And why would he have been driving that car at three in the morning?"

Her mouth twisted into a smirk. "I told you you wouldn't be able to let it go."

He ran a hand through his hair. "Nothing about this makes any sense."

"I can't help you with that if you don't see it yourself." She leaned back in her rocking chair. "Now, I've got one more thing to tell you before you go. Be careful tomorrow. Think before you make any big decisions."

His big meeting his father-in-law had set up with some "important people" was the next day, but no one knew about that except for his father-in-law and these "important people." He hadn't even told Ginny.

"How do you know about tomorrow?"

"Just a feeling I had."

After taking his leave, Jamie hurried back downstairs. Thankfully, he didn't see any sign of Calvin or his brothers anywhere. On his way out, he passed the table in the entryway with the family Bible. It lay open. He was pretty sure it had been closed before. One verse on the page was underlined in red pen: Romans 1:18. *For the wrath of God is revealed from heaven against all ungodliness and unrighteousness of men, who hold the truth in unrighteousness.*

Something told him not to look back.

THE BOX WANTED Addie to find it. Grandma Zee was right. It sang to her in her dreams, the same melody she had come to associate so closely with her grandmother. As soon as she got home from school that afternoon, she clambered up into the attic. She found the box packed up with a bunch of her grandmother's clothes, only a few feet away from where she'd discovered the red cookbook. She still hadn't gotten used to calling it a spell book.

She lifted the old cigar box, beaten up to the point the lid barely hung on. A rich, earthy scent hit her nose, bringing up vague memories of her grandfather, who died when she was little. Inside she found vials and jars and bags full of powders and dried herbs. She didn't understand half the labels, but they all apparently meant something to her grandmother. There were also a number of candles in different colors.

The rest of the day passed by at a snail's pace. Addie could hardly contain herself through dinner with her parents. Her mother kept shooting her looks over the pork chops and green beans, no doubt wondering why Addie was so antsy, but thankfully she didn't ask any questions.

Later, once her parents were asleep, Addie went to work. On the desk next to her bed, she set out a sheet of paper and a pencil, a blue candle, a jar of cooking oil she stole from the kitchen, and a jar of the reddish powder her grandmother had labeled "High John the Conqueror root." Open by her side was her grandmother's red cookbook.

When everything was ready, she closed her eyes and took a deep breath and tried to clear her head. She thought of her sister Cora the way she wanted to remember her, laughing, singing, seeking out joy wherever she could, even if some of the things she did earned a disapproving frown from their mother. With a bittersweet smile, Addie picked up the pencil and wrote, "Return to me," on the sheet of paper. Then she folded it in half and wrote, "Return to me," again. Over and over, she repeated the steps, folding the paper and writing the phrase.

Return to me.

Return to me.

Return to me.

When she was done, she had folded the piece of paper in half nine times. Then she used a nail to etch her sister's name in the candle. She mixed about a teaspoon of the High John the Conqueror root with the cooking oil and dipped the candle in it.

She recited the Bible verses the spell said to recite and ended with a short prayer before she placed the candle in its holder with the folded piece of paper underneath.

She lit the candle and stared at the dancing, sputtering flame. The residue of the High John the Conqueror root gave it a peculiar smell. She hoped the scent didn't make its way down the hall and wake up her parents.

She wasn't sure what to do next. Her grandmother's instructions didn't say anything about how long to let the candle burn or what would happen after it burned out.

So, she kept watching.

Outside, the crickets and the frogs and the owls fell mute. Silence reigned through the house. Her father even paused in his relentless snoring. As Addie stared, shapes emerged from the flame, abstract at first, but gradually forming faces of people she'd never seen before, screaming in terror and pain. She didn't want to see them, but she couldn't look away. At the same time the shadows moved at the edges of her vision, more than merely responding to the flickering of the candle flame. They swirled and churned, brushing against her bare arms and legs, tugging at her hair. And then she saw a face in the fire that chilled her blood.

Cora.

All at once, the orange flame flared up, and a scream shattered the silence. The black shadows danced in a frenzy around the room. They looked like people now, arms waving and heads bobbing in rhythm to some unheard drumbeat. Addie squeezed her eyes shut and covered her ears. But as quickly as everything happened, it was over. The candle flame died, the candle having melted completely. The dancing shadow figures were gone.

She wondered why her parents didn't come running into the room. The scream had to have woken them up. She sat in the renewed silence, waiting, but her parents never did come. Soon her father's resonant snoring started up again, and Addie decided to go to bed. Surely that hadn't been Cora's face in the candle's flame. She must have dozed off for a moment and dreamed the whole thing. What else could explain why her parents hadn't heard the scream? She shook her head, feeling slightly foolish. Dried herbs, candles, and some words. How was that going to bring Cora back?

She didn't see the shadows rising up behind her.

10

FRIDAY, AUGUST 24, 1962

A maze of tall shelves confronted David when he entered the hardware store, hiding most of it from view, but a few conversations floated about, conversations that all paused when he opened the door and started up again a lot quieter.

David pretended to browse as he eavesdropped. Two men in the second aisle he came to—farmers from the sound of it—were having a serious discussion about corn. He passed them by and made his way deeper into the store. A few aisles over, he came across another group of men whose conversation was far more interesting. David stayed out of sight while he listened.

"Just you watch," one of them said. "Next they'll be sending in the National Guard."

"Let them try," a second one replied. "Me and my boys are all pretty good shots."

"Nah, they won't do that, not here," a third one, a man with a nasally voice, offered. "We're a peaceful little town. Things like happened in those other places, they don't happen here."

"Maybe that's the problem," the first one returned. "They never should have let these kids into our schools to begin with. If people would have put up more of a fight last year, we wouldn't be talking about this now."

"I don't know. Did you see the arm on that boy in the football game last Friday?" The nasally one chuckled. "I don't think I'd mind getting more like that."

"Well, I guarantee you the rest of them ain't like that," the first one said. "They won't bring anything but trouble, and I for one am not going to stand by and let it happen. I'm a pretty good shot, too."

David clenched his fists and bit his tongue. He would have liked to introduce these men to his parents. Certain people once said they were nothing but trouble, too, that they shouldn't be allowed to mingle with the rest of society. But these men could never meet his parents because they went to Dachau in 1941 and never came back.

He grabbed a couple of boxes of nails and continued on.

Three men were gathered near the register as he approached. Two of them were obviously brothers—Rhett and Danny MacNeil— the oldest and middle of the three MacNeil brothers. The other man, a little older, was Boyd Parker, the owner of the feed and seed store. David recognized them because Mick had been helping him with his "Who's Who" of Avalon. Thanks to Mick's handy list, David also knew all three happened to be active members of the Klan. Their conversation died when David came near. He wasn't able to pick up on anything important except for the word *tonight*.

David grinned and nodded at them as he placed his intended purchase on the counter. "Good afternoon!"

None of them smiled back at him.

"That'll be all?" asked the clerk, a scrawny teenaged boy with a wisp of a mustache. He glanced back and forth between David and the group of men.

"That's it for today," David answered cheerily.

"Really? That's it?" Danny MacNeil glanced down at the boxes of nails. Despite being younger, he was the larger of the two brothers. He also had a scruffy beard while Rhett was clean-shaven. "What do you think you're going to do with a couple of boxes of roofing nails?"

So that's what they were. David shrugged. "Working on a house. Ran out of nails."

Rhett's eyes narrowed. "I'm not sure I've seen you before. What's your name?"

"David. David Ben-Ari. And you're right. I'm renting a little house south of town from Otis MacAndrew. Needs a lot of work, though. I'm helping him fix it up."

The two brothers eyed each other. Some secret communication passed between them.

"Ben-Ari? What kind of name is that?" the older MacNeil asked as the clerk, now visibly nervous, rang up David's purchase.

"Israeli."

Rhett grunted. "Hmm. Don't get a lot of your kind around here."

David handed over a couple of bills to the clerk. "So I've heard."

The clerk, hands shaking, struggled to maintain his smile as he bagged up the boxes of nails and gave them to David along with his change.

With a quick salute to the three men, David turned to leave. He could feel them watching him as he walked away. Exactly what he wanted. He had spent most of his adult life working to deflect attention away from himself, to become invisible, but sometimes the only way to get the job done was to let them know your name. Now they knew it.

Let's see what they do with it.

———

JAMIE TOLD Ginny he was going to a special meeting of the Chamber of Commerce. Arriving at the address he'd been given, he realized it wasn't entirely a lie.

He'd passed by this house a thousand times, one of the big, old white houses on Independence Street with columns and double front porches and porte-cochères meant for fancy carriages. These houses were where Avalon's "old money" lived. Jamie never expected to be invited inside any of them, let alone the one he pulled up in front of, the house of Rhett MacNeil.

Several other cars were already parked there in the big circular driveway—Rhett MacNeil's navy-blue Caddy, Boyd Parker's white Ford pickup truck, a gold Chevy Bel Air belonging to the Reverend Fenton Graham, pastor of Avalon First Baptist Church, and a green Buick Electra Jamie recognized as belonging to Archie Brown, the owner of the drug store. His father-in-law's car was nowhere to be seen.

He knocked on the front door. While he waited, he fiddled with the collar of his shirt. He'd opted for the button-down shirt Ginny gave him for his birthday, along with one of his three neckties and a pair of his Sunday trousers. Jamie wanted to make a good impression for Ginny's father, even though he still didn't have a clue what this meeting was supposed to be about. Strange his father-in-law wasn't there. Jamie wondered where he was.

He put a hand in the pocket of his trousers only to discover something small and round, like the day before when he'd visited Sarah Jordan. This time he fished out a Mercury dime. The year stamped on it was 1929, the year he was born. He was absolutely certain the coin hadn't been in his pocket when he left his house.

At that moment, Rhett MacNeil himself answered the door. Jamie stuffed the dime back in his pocket. In one hand Rhett held a glass filled with some brown liquid while in the other he held a smoldering cigar. He was a large, imposing man. All the MacNeil brothers were, but Rhett, as the oldest, was the one everyone was afraid of. Jamie knew the stories. You didn't want to cross the MacNeils. Their money typically got them what they wanted, but when that wasn't enough, Rhett's yelling and cussing did the trick. He'd once stormed into the sheriff's office and called the sheriff himself a fucking moron to his face because he'd gotten a parking ticket. Not only did he not get thrown in jail, but after that he could park his blue Caddy anywhere he wanted.

He eyed Jamie up and down and grinned, baring his teeth. "You're a little early, ain't you?"

Jamie checked his watch. His father-in-law has said to be there at seven o'clock. It was five till. That didn't seem too early to him.

"Better than late, right? My momma would skin me alive if I was ever not on time." He chuckled nervously.

Rhett didn't laugh or say anything. He just motioned for Jamie to follow.

Stepping inside, Jamie couldn't help but gawk. Rhett MacNeil never married, and it was evident. There wasn't a feminine touch to be seen anywhere—no flowers, no flowy, lace-trimmed curtains, no delicate furniture. Dark wood paneling covered the walls of the entryway. The thick, heavy drapes blocked out the light. What little artwork there was tended toward hunting scenes.

Even so, Jamie couldn't help but be taken in by everything he saw. The entryway was two stories high. A winding staircase led up to a landing on the second floor. A great crystal chandelier hung from the towering ceiling over a large round table. The one piece of art that wasn't dogs and horses and men with rifles was a giant portrait of a well-dressed couple, the woman seated in a high-backed chair and the man standing behind her with his hands on her shoulders— Rhett, Danny, and Billy's parents.

Rhett led him into a room off the entryway. "I need to take care of something real quick. You can wait in here."

He shut the door and left before Jamie could even reply. The room turned out to be a small study. Like the entryway, it betrayed nothing of a woman's influence. Big, bulky leather chairs were arranged in front of a heavy wooden desk. A deer head held the place of honor over a brick fireplace. A grandfather clock loomed in one corner while an antique globe on a pedestal took up another. Bookshelves lined two of the walls, full of dark, leather-bound volumes with gold lettering on the spines. Jamie scanned some of them—the complete works of William Shakespeare, plus Charles Dickens, Nathaniel Hawthorne, Henry David Thoreau, and a dozen or so other authors he should have read in high school English but never bothered to. They were all covered in a thick layer of dust, like no one had touched them in years.

Muffled voices came through the wall, boisterous laughter and animated talking, but Jamie couldn't make out what they were saying. He wondered why Rhett had shoved him into a side room but couldn't come up with a good reason other than maybe he was waiting for some others to show up, like his father-in-law. Jamie figured Rhett would come to get him soon enough.

He made himself comfortable in one of the leather chairs, but the clock ticked off the minutes without any sign of Rhett returning. Eventually the voices died away. Jamie had almost dozed off when the click of the door latch startled him. Rhett stood in the doorway.

"Hey, Jamie," he said, "let's you and me go have a little chat, all right?"

Rhett led him to a large sitting room, and for a moment Jamie thought he'd entered a different house. Everywhere there were over-stuffed Victorian chairs, pie crust tables with carved legs, lamps with hand-painted glass globes, lace doilies, and porcelain figurines. Another portrait hung over the fireplace. Rhett's mother, by herself this time and several years older, sat with her hands crossed in her lap and an odd half-smile on her face.

"Where is everyone else?" Jamie asked. "Reverend Graham and Boyd Parker and Archie Brown? Aren't they joining us?"

Rhett shot him a look. "How did you know they were here?"

Jamie smirked. "I recognized their cars. I *am* a mechanic, after all."

Rhett chuckled. "That's mighty clever. No, they were here for ... a different meeting." He took a crystal decanter and poured himself another glass of the same brown liquid—bourbon if Jamie had to guess. He didn't offer any to Jamie. Not that Jamie would have accepted. "Have a seat, why don't you?"

Jamie chose a faded green high-backed chair, the same one Mrs. MacNeil posed in for both portraits he realized after he sat down, but it would have been awkward to change.

Rhett sat in a chair opposite him. "Your father-in-law tells me you've got a pretty busy business."

"It's hectic, but we manage. Some days better than others."

"A lot of people trust you—" Rhett took a sip from his glass. "—with their cars, I mean."

Jamie studied the other man. Something about what he said wasn't right. Jamie felt he should choose his words carefully. "I don't do or tolerate shoddy work. I think people appreciate that. They know they can count on me to get their cars fixed."

"You and I are alike that way. I don't tolerate bullshit either. In fact, I think we have a lot in common. We both were born in Avalon. We both grew up here, and we both stayed."

Jamie shrugged. "I never saw a reason to leave. It's a nice place to live."

Rhett nodded. "That it is, but you know what, Jamie?"

"What?"

Like a restless spirit, the smoke from Rhett's cigar curled in the air above his head. "It takes work to keep this a nice place. Work I and many others do."

The unsettling feeling grew, but Jamie couldn't put his finger on exactly what bothered him. The cigar smoke continued to take on bizarre shapes. Something moved in it, something he couldn't see when he looked straight on. He was only able to catch glimpses out of the corer of his eye. Some kind of taint in the air. He didn't know why he picked that word, but it fit better than anything else.

Jamie smiled nervously. "We all do what we can, I'm sure."

Rhett didn't smile back. "I'm not sure you get my meaning. I'm talking about work that happens behind the scenes, work that most people can't know about."

He tossed something shiny toward Jamie, who reached out and caught it. When Jamie opened his hand, he discovered a small pin, a square white cross situated on a red background. In the center of the cross was a white diamond outlined in black, and in the center of the diamond there was a teardrop shape—red, like blood.

Jamie glanced back up at Rhett. It must have been a trick of the light, something to do with the cigar smoke or the hazy whatever-it-was in the air, or the fact he hadn't been getting much sleep, but the shadow behind Rhett grew. Up the wall it went, stretching out until it tapered off to a point at the ceiling.

Jamie blinked, and the illusion dissolved. "I'm not sure what you mean by 'behind the scenes.'"

Rhett scowled. "You love your family, don't you?"

The way he asked the question made every hair on the back of Jamie's neck stand on end. He didn't know how, but he knew he was in danger. "Of course I love them."

Rhett pointed to the portrait of his mother. "Nothing's more important than your family. You'd do anything to protect them, I'm sure. Now your father-in-law said you were a sharp man, that you were ready to be shown how things really work in the world. Think about your customers, Jamie. Would you trust any of them to make decisions about your life or you family?"

Jamie's heart pounded. He didn't want to be there anymore. It was all he could do to stay in his chair. "No."

"That's right, you wouldn't. All we're saying is that this is our town and we don't trust all those people out there to know what's best for us. Take this whole school integration bullshit. We've come this far without doing it, and I for one don't see the need, but there are a lot of people for it because they're afraid of what the boys up in Washington will do if we don't integrate. Can you imagine, making our children go to school with those colored children from over there in Ezekiel's Mill?" Rhett's lip curled up in disgust. He wagged a finger at Jamie. "The next few months are important, Jamie. We need all the support we can get. Do you understand?"

Jamie glanced down at the pin in his hand. "I do."

Rhett stood, a signal their meeting was hopefully over. Jamie shot out of his seat, never so relieved in his entire life.

"I'm glad we see eye-to-eye." Rhett put a hand on Jamie's shoulder. "You think on what we said tonight. If you're interested in joining us and helping keep Avalon a nice place to live, you let your father-in-law know. And I assure you, we can make it worth your while."

Outside, Jamie paused next to his truck and looked back at the darkened windows of Rhett MacNeil's house. He turned the pin over in his fingers before he shoved it in his pocket. He knew the symbol. He had seen it before, even though he wasn't supposed to. He couldn't let Ginny know. How would he ever explain to her that her own father was a member of the Klan?

———

ADDIE WOKE up to a cold and clammy hand covering her mouth. Panicking, she kicked her legs and flailed her arms, but no matter how much she thrashed around, she couldn't get up or break free. Whoever held her down was too strong.

"Stop fighting," a voice said, one she recognized, one she hadn't heard in five years.

Addie did as she was told. Then a face appeared above her. She should have been overjoyed, but instead she was terrified. The face belonged to Cora, her sister.

"You have to promise not to scream," she said.

Addie nodded, and Cora removed her hand.

Addie immediately scrambled up out of the bed. "Cora, are you … are you real? You're really here? This isn't some dream."

Cora shook her head. Her stony expression never changed. "Oh, Addie, I wish it was a dream, but no, this is real. I'm here."

Addie reached for her, wanting to hug her, to hold her close, not understanding why Cora stayed away. "Why? After all this time."

"You called me," Cora replied. "With the spell from Grandma Zee's spell book."

Addie stared at her, puzzled. "But how would you know about Grandma Zee's book?"

Cora met her gaze dead on. "You know how, Addie."

Addie started to protest, but as she studied her sister illuminated in the moonlight shining through the window—her ashen skin, her dull, sunken eyes, her stringy hair—a knot formed in the pit of her stomach. Cora was wearing the same clothes she disappeared in five years earlier.

Addie covered her mouth. Her legs gave out from under her, and she collapsed back on the bed. "You're dead, aren't you? I'm talking to a ghost."

Cora sat down on the very edge of the bed. "Did you expect anything else? It's been five years."

"I hoped," Addie croaked. "We all hoped."

Cora drew her mouth into a thin line. "You shouldn't have."

She was as contrary as she always had been, saying things that shouldn't be said out loud. Addie forced down the retort that nearly escaped her lips. "What happened to you, Cora?"

Cora didn't answer right away. It seemed to Addie she was trying to choose the right words. "A monster killed me."

She was murdered. That's what Cora was trying to say. Addie had always secretly feared as much, but now that she knew for sure, anger mixed with her grief. "Who did it, Cora? Who murdered you?"

Cora frowned. "No, you're misunderstanding me. I mean a real monster. It had giant teeth and claws and everything. It attacked me on that road that night. It pounced on me out of the shadows, and it killed me."

Addie found what her sister said easier to believe than she expected. If there were ghosts then why not monsters? But something still bothered her. "Why didn't we find a body?"

Cora brought her knees up and hugged her legs. "There wasn't any body to find."

Addie shivered. "You mean ..."

The curtains fluttered in the breeze and the shadows played across Cora's face in a way Addie didn't like. "I didn't feel any pain if that makes it better. The thing snapped my neck right away. I was dead before I hit the ground."

That was too much for Addie. She wanted to cover her ears with her hands and yell so she couldn't hear any more. "Oh, Cora, please don't talk that way."

"What's the good putting on a pretty gloss now?" Cora asked, her jaw clenched. "It happened."

Addie couldn't hold the tears welling up in her eyes back any longer. "I'm so sorry. If I could have done something different, if any of us could have done something so that you weren't out on that road by yourself, we would have."

For the first time, the corners of Cora's mouth turned up in a faint smile. "Don't blame yourself like that. You couldn't have known."

Addie had never felt more helpless. "But still."

Cora held up a hand. "Addie, there's something else I need to tell you. You didn't only call me. There are dozens of us. Whether you want to or not, you're about to have a lot more late-night visitors."

"Dozens? You mean more ghosts?"

Cora nodded. "You're also going to have some choices to make in the coming days."

It didn't seem like Addie and Cora were the only ones in the room anymore. Addie felt other eyes on her, watching, waiting for ... something. "What do you mean?"

"You can kill this monster, or you can walk away and let someone else take up that burden. The choice is yours. It's a lot to ask, I know. If you choose to walk away, no one will judge you for it."

Addie looked at her sister, completely taken aback. "Me? How do I kill a monster?"

"You got Grandma Zee's spell book. That's nothing to shake a stick at. And Fate might throw a couple of other things your way. Just keep your eyes open." Cora stood up from the bed. "I have to go now, Addie. But you remember you are never alone. Do you promise me you'll remember that?"

"Yes, I promise. Do you really have to go?" She reached out for her sister again.

Cora took a step back. "Best not. Good-bye, Addie."

She withdrew into the shadows in the corner of the room and vanished.

Addie cried herself back to sleep.

11

MONDAY, AUGUST 27, 1962

I t started raining in the morning as Addie walked to school, and it didn't let up all day. Addie put a trash can in the corner of the room by her desk to catch the water leaking from the ceiling, but the constant *drip-drip-plop* all day long threatened to drive her crazy. It didn't do too much for the kids' conduct either. The rain was still coming down hard at the end of the school day, and Addie didn't look forward to the walk home.

As she left her classroom, Carol Robertson flagged her down. Addie sighed inwardly. The last thing she wanted to do was socialize.

"Hi, Carol. What's going on?"

"Addie, did you hear the news?"

Carol was a notorious gossip. Addie didn't particularly care who was having trouble in their marriage, but she answered anyway. "No. What news?"

"About the school. About them coming in to make us integrate with the white schools."

Addie could hardly keep from rolling her eyes. "And how are they going to make us do that? They sent how many of our kids over there? Twelve? And not a peep since. They were just making show. They're not planning on doing anything more."

Carol shook her head. "But this time it's different. They're talking about bringing in the National Guard like they did in Arkansas."

"Carol, think about it. Why here? Why not someplace like Columbia or Charleston first?"

But Addie knew the reason why. Ezekiel's Mill and Avalon would be practice. If everything went right, they'd move onto the bigger cities. Avalon was so small, if something went wrong, they could sweep everything under the rug and pretend like nothing happened.

"Maybe because we all get along here already," Carol offered.

Addie shot her a look. "Maybe what?"

Carol seemed genuine in her response, though. "There really isn't any violence here, and there hasn't been for a long time. We all get along pretty well."

On any other day, Addie would have given her a lecture. Everyone got along because no one dared to rock the boat. It wasn't worth it, and even if there wasn't any violence, the threat of it was always there. She'd heard her grandmother's stories, not the ones about the supernatural creatures in the woods, but the ones about the real flesh and blood monsters.

And she'd never forget that one time when she was little and she'd watched her parents pacing and glancing out the window, worried looks in their faces as the drums from a Klan rally in the woods echoed through the night. She didn't know it then, but she realized later they'd been afraid they were going to see a burning cross in their yard.

But Addie was tired and didn't have it in her. "Well, we'll have to wait and see what happens, I guess. Looks like the rain's let up a little. I probably ought to be going on home. I'll talk to you tomorrow."

She turned to leave, shaking her head. People never ceased to amaze her, though she supposed you really didn't understand a place unless you'd been there a long time. The thought triggered something in the back of her mind about her sister, but she couldn't think of what. Her head was so muddled, and she was so tired. Maybe she'd be able to sneak a nap before dinner, but there were tests to grade.

Before she could make it too far, though, she ran into the absolute last person she wanted to see. Rounding a corner, she found Rose Ellison standing in her path with Mr. Deakins by her side. Rose practically beamed when she saw Addie. Addie wondered what scheme she had cooked up.

"Why, Addie, I'm glad we could catch you before you left for the day," Rose said. "Martin and I were just talking about you."

No one ever called Mr. Deakins by his first name like that. To Addie's shock, he didn't correct her, though he did look a little uncomfortable at how close she was standing to him.

"Why would you be talking about me?" Addie asked.

"Well, Rose came to me with an idea this morning," Mr. Deakins began, still looking uncomfortable, "and I thought it was a good one. We ought to be doing more to encourage our kids to read, and Rose said we should put on a storybook pageant."

Addie felt a little like a cornered animal as her gaze went back and forth between Mr. Deakins and Rose. "That does sound like a good idea, Rose, and obviously I'd be glad to help out."

Mr. Deakins and Rose eyed each other.

"I was actually going to ask you to be in charge of it if you didn't mind," he said.

And the trap was sprung.

"Me?" Addie balked. "But it was Rose's idea. I thought she was volunteering to do it."

Rose plastered on her best smile. "Oh, I would, but I simply don't have the time. I'm so busy with my class. I immediately thought of you when I had the idea and told it to Martin."

"What do you say, Addie?" Mr. Deakins asked. "I think it would help out the kids a lot."

Before Addie could protest any more, a loud crash came from the direction of her room. The three of them ran in to find a chunk of the ceiling on her desk and water pouring from the hole. Addie bit her lip to keep from crying.

Mr. Deakins sighed. "I'll go get someone to come clean up the mess. Maybe we can get someone out here to fix the hole by next week. Hopefully it won't rain again."

Rose placed a hand in Addie's shoulder. "Don't worry, Addie, if anyone knows how to make do with a bad situation, I'm sure it's you."

———

JAMIE WALKED into the house that evening to find Ginny getting ready to put dinner on the table. Amy Lynn sat in her spot, reading a book, as usual. He greeted each of them with a quick kiss, then went to change out of his work clothes and wash up.

"Hi, sweetheart, how was school today?" he asked Amy Lynn as he took a seat at the table after he came back downstairs.

Amy Lynn hadn't had much to say about skipping a whole grade. She didn't even seem to notice, so her answer surprised Jamie a little.

"I made a new friend. She's really nice."

Jamie looked at her askance. "You made a friend? Really?"

Ginny slapped his arm as she put his plate down in front of him. "Don't sound so shocked."

"What's her name?" Jamie asked.

"Ellie," Amy Lynn replied, putting her book aside as Ginny set her dinner down.

Jamie pressed her. "Ellie who?"

"Ellie Morris."

The name seemed familiar to Jamie.

"Who are her parents?"

Amy Lynn shrugged. "I don't know. I didn't ask. Anyway, she says she got a new Barbie doll for her birthday, and she has a swing set in her back yard, and maybe one day after school I could go over to her house and play. Do you think I could, Daddy? Please?"

Jamie glanced over at Ginny, pleading silently for help, but she just grinned. He tried to be stern. "Well, first we'll have to wait for an actual invitation, and then we'll see."

Amy Lynn didn't seem too happy with that answer, but she didn't say anything else. When Ginny brought her own plate over and sat down at the table, the conversation shifted to other things.

Jamie told Ginny about his day. Thankfully the garage had been a little less busy. He *didn't* tell Ginny about the dark cloud hovering at the edge of his thoughts. About his odd encounters with David Ben-Ari and Rhett MacNeil. About the nagging feeling that things were going to get stranger.

"You haven't spent any more of your time playing detective, have you?" asked Ginny.

He didn't answer.

Ginny narrowed her eyes and cocked her head the way she did whenever she caught their daughter in a lie. "Jamie, you can't tell me you're still trying to figure out what happened to that car."

He shook his head. "No, I've got something else on my mind. Something I forgot to do today. It's no big deal, I can do it in the morning when I get to the garage."

Ginny raised an eyebrow slightly but didn't pursue the issue any more. After dinner, she sent Amy Lynn upstairs to get ready for bed. Jamie lingered in the kitchen.

"What do you think about Amy Lynn's news?" he asked.

"What, that she made a friend? What do you think?"

He leaned against the counter while Ginny filled the sink to do the dishes. "I don't know. Her name sounded familiar, and I remember now why. That's one of the kids they sent over from Ezekiel's Mill."

Ginny glanced sideways at him while she scrubbed the pan from that night's chicken. "What about it? You're the one who's been wanting her to make friends."

"I know, but this makes it more complicated, doesn't it? I heard how they treated those kids when they first came. It wasn't pretty. What if they're mean to Amy Lynn, too? What if something worse happens?"

Ginny stopped scrubbing. "Look, I can't say that doesn't have me worried a little, too. I know how people can get, but we've made it this far without any real problems. I don't see why there should be any now." She handed him the pan. "Here, as long as you're standing there, you could make yourself useful. Dry."

Jamie took the pan and absentmindedly ran a dishrag over it.

"And since when is she into Barbie dolls? She's barely ever touched the one she has."

Ginny chuckled. "Little girls are complicated creatures. Trust me. I was one at one time. You should be happy for her."

Jamie sighed. "I am. I guess I'm afraid she's going to get hurt. She's never really had friends before. I don't want her to put too much into this."

Ginny put the plate in her hand down and hugged him around the waist. "And that's why you're a good dad, but you know you can't protect her from everything. She's going to have to find her own way eventually."

Jamie put his arms around her. "I know. I know. But if I could keep her from getting any older, I would." He spotted her book on the table. "At least some things haven't changed."

Ginny followed his gaze. "She's been glued to that book."

Jamie walked over to the table and picked it up. "I'll carry it up to her. She'll want it to read before she goes to bed. You know she thinks she's tricking us by staying up past her bedtime and reading."

As Jamie climbed the stairs, he leafed through the book. Like Amy Lynn said, it had anything anyone would ever want to know about the moon. There was a section on the phases of the moon and one on theories on where the moon came from and another on moon folklore. There was even a section on what a mission to the moon by real astronauts might be like.

He stopped outside the door to Amy Lynn's room. The door was opened a crack. Jamie peered in. Amy Lynn sat on her bed, brushing her hair and singing to herself. He'd never known her to voluntarily run a brush through her hair, and he'd certainly never heard her sing to herself. He had to admit, he hadn't seen her this happy in a long time. Still, he worried.

He knocked before he went in. Amy Lynn immediately stopped singing and hid the brush behind her back.

He handed her the book. "You left this downstairs."

"Oh, okay, thanks." She snatched it from his hands.

"What is it about that book that's got you so fascinated, anyway?" Jamie asked.

Amy Lynn opened the book up to somewhere in the middle. "I don't know. It's just got a lot of interesting facts. Like did you know it's good luck to have a full moon on a Monday, but it's bad luck to have a full moon on a Sunday?"

Jamie gave her a quizzical look. "And why is that?"

"It just is." She held the book up and pointed to the page. "That's what it says anyway."

Jamie laughed. "Well, don't believe everything you read. You finish getting ready for bed, okay? I don't want you staying up too late."

She nodded. "Okay, Daddy."

He went to leave, but paused at the doorway. "Hey, Amy Lynn, I'm happy you're making friends, but I want you to remember one thing for me. You promise to always be yourself, okay?"

She frowned. "But who else would I be?"

Jamie smiled and shook his head as he shut the door.

———

A DARK MOOD settled over Addie as she sat at the kitchen table after dinner, grading the spelling test she had given her students the day before. She didn't know which was worse, the liberal use her red pen was getting—the words *friend*, *fiend*, and *weird* seemed to have stumped a lot of her students—or Rose's barbed comments after volunteering her for a project she didn't have the time to do.

The more she thought about what Rose had done, the more she seethed, and the less she could concentrate on grading. She dropped her pen on the table and closed her eyes while she massaged her temples. When she opened her eyes again, her mother was sitting at the table next to her, a concerned look on her face.

"Sweetie, go to bed," her mother said. "You look exhausted."

Addie shook her head. "I can't. I have to finish grading these tests—"

Her mother held up a hand. "The tests will wait another day. Go to bed."

"But—"

She silenced Addie with a glance. "Not another word. You need your rest."

Addie sighed and gathered up her papers. No use arguing when her mother used that tone.

"Is everything all right?" her mother asked. "You seem a little on edge today."

Addie smiled faintly. "Just got a lot going on right now at school. That's all."

"Well, you don't let those kids get to you, you got me? You're the one in charge, remember."

It's not the kids, she wanted to say, but she didn't really have it in her to explain everything that was going on. She told her mother good night and retreated to her room.

She tossed her folder with all the test papers down on her nightstand. In doing so she accidentally knocked her grandmother's red cookbook to the floor. When she picked it up, she saw it had fallen open to a page she hadn't read yet. Three words stretched across the top in her grandmother's perfect handwriting. "Spells for hexing." Addie frowned. Her grandmother was certainly one to speak her mind, and anyone who got on her bad side was likely to get a tongue lashing, but Addie couldn't imagine her grandmother actually doing anything to hurt anyone.

Curious, though, she sat down on her bed and read through the spells listed, everything from giving a person bad luck to making them sick or making them leave the area. There were explanations written out for every outcome someone might want, as clear as if her grandmother were writing out the recipe for her famous honey biscuits, and judging by the stain or two on the pages, it looked like her grandmother had actually used a couple of the spells.

A thought occurred to Addie. An awful one, but one that wouldn't let go of her. She literally held the power in her hands to take Rose Ellison down a peg or two, maybe for good. Before she could talk herself out of it, she went rummaging through her grandmother's box of supplies for the things she needed. When she was done, she laid everything out on her desk, the spell book propped open at her elbow.

She took a black candle and etched Rose's name in the side backwards, starting at the bottom. She set the candle in its holder and stuck a pin in the side, by the first letter. The spell said the good fortune of the person being targeted would drain out as the candle burned down. The more letters, the worse their luck. Addie didn't want anything really bad to happen to Rose. She only wanted to teach her a lesson, so she decided she would only let the candle burn through the first letter.

The spell said it would work better if you had some personal effect of the person you were trying to hex. All she had was a picture of Rose from the school yearbook from the year before. She cut it out and put it under the candle base. She hoped that would be enough.

Addie struck a match and lit the wick. Like before, she recited a few Bible verses and said a prayer, this one asking God to humble Rose.

The candle flame swirled and danced. Again, she saw shapes in the fire, twirling around, threatening to lull her to sleep. She jumped when the pin she stuck into the wax clattered to the desktop after the candle had burned all the way through the first letter. Addie blew out the candle. Then she picked up the pin and stuck it through the picture of Rose.

Nothing happened. No screams. No dancing shadows.

The spell book said to dispose of the elements used in the ritual by tossing them into running water. There was a little creek in the woods not too far of a walk from the house. She could go there the next day after school. In the meantime, she hid everything back in her grandmother's cigar box.

She got herself ready for bed, and pulling the covers over her head, she wondered if the ritual had worked at all. Was it ridiculous to believe in magic spells? Had her sister's visit been a dream? She closed her eyes and tried to push the thoughts out of her head.

The shadow things came out from their hiding places.

———

ADDIE WOKE up to someone quietly sobbing. She lay in bed and listened for a moment. Her sleep-fogged brain told her the noise was coming from outside, through her open window. Sound traveled funny sometimes, and the humid August air had a way of warping and bending things. It was probably one of her neighbors. She slipped out of bed and peered outside into the darkness, but no lights were on at any of the neighbor's houses.

Then she heard the sobbing again, coming from behind her.

Addie turned around to see the figure of a woman in the dim moonlight, sitting in the chair at her desk. She looked at Addie with the same hollow eyes as her sister, the same ashen skin, the same stony expression. She was wearing a long skirt with a blouse and a cardigan sweater, and she had a scarf around her neck—clothes that would have been popular maybe ten years earlier.

Addie's heart threatened to beat out of her chest. "You're another ghost, aren't you? Cora said there would be others. The same monster killed you, whatever it is."

The woman nodded, struggling to dry her eyes.

"What's your name?" Addie asked.

"Minerva. Minerva Oliver."

"How long has it been? Do you know?"

Minerva shook her head. "Time is ... it doesn't work the same as it used to."

"When did you ... When did it happen?"

"October 22, 1953."

"Almost nine years ago," Addie said.

Minerva seemed surprised. "Has it been that many years? Really? I suppose everyone's moved on by now."

Addie reached out to her, but stopped short of touching her. "You never know. I'm sure you're not forgotten."

"Maybe not, but life still goes on for the living." Minerva

grimaced. "Life I'm not a part of anymore."

"Tell me what happened," Addie prodded.

"I was walking home from my best friend's house. I know I shouldn't have been out that late, but we were having such a good time talking and playing records, I forgot to look at the clock. I thought I'd be okay walking. The full moon made it easy to see." She was so much like Addie's sister. So young. So much of her life still ahead of her. "The thing came up behind me and knocked me to the ground. I never heard it. I just felt it on top of me and smelled its awful stink. Something warm and wet ran down my back. I didn't realize at the time it was my own blood. After that I don't remember much."

It wasn't fair. The more Addie listened, the angrier she got. This monster, this thing, denied her sister the rest of her life, and Minerva too, and many, many others if what Cora said was true.

"I didn't mean to call you," she said. "I didn't mean to disturb your peace."

Minerva laughed, but there wasn't any humor in her voice. "Peace? There isn't any peace."

Addie frowned, thinking of Cora's face in the flame of the candle. "I want to stop this monster, but I need to know more about it. I just don't know where to look."

Minerva cocked her head to the side. "Other ghosts might have the answers you're looking for."

"You mean other ghosts like you?"

"We aren't the only restless ones. There are ghosts in this town that have been here for a very, very long time. They've seen a lot, and they know a lot. Find them. Ask them."

"How do I—"

But Minerva was already fading away. In an instant, she was gone, dissipated like smoke.

Find them. Ask them. The moonlight glanced off the red cover of her grandmother's cookbook. Addie had already called ghosts by accident. There had to be a way to call them on purpose.

The shadow things watched in silence.

12

TUESDAY, AUGUST 28, 1962

W hen Addie arrived at the school the following day, she walked into utter chaos. All the teachers were gathered around the door to Rose's classroom, pushing on each other, craning their necks and hopping up to try to see in, like a bunch of unruly kids wanting to see the elephants at the circus. Above all their chatter, Rose screamed, her cries punctuated by yelps from Mr. Deakins.

Addie attached herself to Cassandra Miller and Carol Robertson, who were standing at the edge of the crowd, both of them trying to get a good look at whatever was going on.

"What's happening?" Addie asked.

"We're not sure," Carol answered.

"I was in my room getting things ready for the day," Cassandra said. "Everything was quiet and then all of a sudden Rose started screaming. I saw Mr. Deakins run by, and then he shouted for someone to get Harold. I don't have the faintest idea what could be causing such a ruckus."

A raspy, unpleasant voice whispered in the back of Addie's head. *You did this. It was you.* Addie tried to shoo it away as one would a bothersome fly. She stood on her tiptoes in an effort to see over everyone, but there were too many people in her way. She finally gave up with a huff and pushed her way through, stepping on a few toes, until she came to the threshold of Rose's classroom.

Addie's mouth fell open. Rose, Mr. Deakins, and Harold, the janitor, fought against what appeared to be a flock of tiny brown sparrows. Harold chased them around with a broom, trying to get them to fly out the open window, but he wasn't having any luck. The little birds dodged the broom and dove down at their heads. Rose waved her arms and yelled for them to get out, while Mr. Deakins stood helplessly, swatting at the air. The birds had made a mess of Rose's perfect room.

Seeing Rose's face as she surveyed the damage to her room while she ducked the birds almost made Addie feel sorry for her, but then she remembered all the tiny slights Rose had made toward her and thought maybe this was the comeuppance she needed. Addie *had* asked for it, after all. She covered her mouth to hide the unbidden smile that came to her face. The raspy voice in her head gave a satisfied chortle.

———

TWO YELLOW LIGHTS appeared in the distance. David frowned. He was driving back to his cabin, back from another meeting with Mick, who had more than earned his pay in cheeseburgers and milkshakes. The boys in the home office weren't going to be very happy with all the things they'd gotten wrong about small Southern towns in the briefing they'd given him before he came to Avalon, but that couldn't be helped. Who could ever know "bless your heart" was a deadly insult?

The lights grew bigger by the second, and soon a pickup truck came into view. The truck sped by, spraying gravel as it passed and nearly running David into the ditch. His cabin was the only thing on that road. David didn't have to guess too hard where the truck was coming from.

Sure enough, when he got to the cabin, he found tire marks in the muddy ground. A quick inspection revealed a window that had been jimmied open. Whoever was there had tried to cover their tracks, but they were pretty sloppy about it.

Once inside, David took an inventory. One of the empty bourbon bottles on the kitchen table had been knocked over, and even if he didn't make his bed, he didn't leave the sheets in as much of a jumble. Near his desk, a few of his papers were scattered on the floor.

He'd expected someone to come calling sooner or later. Of course, the MacNeils were going to try to find out whatever they could about him. The only question in his mind had been whether they would leave his place ransacked, or try to cover up their snooping.

That they'd chosen to try to cover up their little visit to his humble shack told David a few things. Their attention wasn't only because he was an "outsider." Otherwise they wouldn't have been so subtle. They would have wanted to send a message. No, they were looking for something else. They wanted to know *why* he was there before they ran him out of town on a rail.

Glancing at his wall with all its pictures and newspaper clippings, he figured he'd certainly given them something to wonder about. None of what he'd tacked up there would make sense to someone who didn't know the truth about *Unternehmen Werwolf.* He'd probably come across as some lunatic, which wasn't completely false, all things considered. If they did know anything about the real Nazi contingency in place at the end of World War II—the one with the real werewolves—that was a different story.

Luckily, they hadn't found anything important. His extra passports, his fake IDs, and all the papers that were supposed to keep him from causing an international incident were still in their top-secret hiding place, a folder in the back of the refrigerator.

Let them all wonder. Let them talk about his wall full of crazy conspiracies. It would only serve to draw out his quarry. David opened a new bottle of bourbon and poured himself a generous glass. He slumped into a chair, propped his feet up on the table, and saluted the pictures of Heinrich Albrecht. He was there, somewhere,

David was certain of it, and when he showed his true face, David would be ready.

———

ADDIE FELT a little like Ebenezer Scrooge, waiting for the next ghost to make its appearance. Her parents had long since gone to bed. Her father's snoring reverberated through the wall. She sat in her bed, reading through her grandmother's spell book. There were stories in it, too, interspersed throughout, some about her grandmother, some even about her grandmother's grandmother, and they were all too fantastical to believe, full of spirits and creatures and magic, of course. Yet, Addie could hear her grandmother's reassuring voice in her head, and she didn't find it hard at all to take every word as true.

The ghost didn't appear with quiet sobbing or even her sister's silent assault. A giant thud caused Addie to jump, and she glanced up to meet the eyes of an equally startled ghost standing in the middle of her bedroom.

The sudden appearance wasn't the only thing that surprised her. Cora and Minerva were both black and both women. The missing neighbor Addie had overheard Carol and Cassandra talking about at the school was a black woman, too, and Addie grimly suspected she was also one of this monster's victims. None of them the kind of people the police would try too hard to find. But the ghost standing in front of her was a white man, maybe in his thirties, with dirty blond hair and pale blue, almost gray eyes.

He eyed her up and down. "Who the fuck are you?"

"I could ask you the same question," Addie snapped. "You know you're dead, right? You know you're a ghost."

His expression softened a little. "Yeah, I know I'm dead."

"Then maybe you could show a little more respect to your one connection to the real world." Addie used the same tone as when she caught one of her students doing something they weren't supposed to. "Now, as near as I can tell, you're here to tell me about how you died, but I think I already have a good idea. The same as the others. A monster."

The man sneered. "A monster nothing. It was a wolf. A giant fucking wolf. I saw it, and when it howled, the sound froze my blood. It chased down my car and caused me to wreck. I tried to get away from it in the woods, but I might as well have been trying to outrun a bullet. The thing tore me in half before I even knew it." He patted his legs. "At least I'm all in one piece here."

Addie grabbed her grandmother's spell book and leafed through it. She hadn't come across any stories about wolves, so far. "A monster wolf. You mean like a werewolf from the movies?"

He shook his head. "I don't know anything about that. All I know is what I saw."

Addie wasn't sure she liked this ghost very much, but he still didn't deserve to die the way he did. "I'm sorry that happened to you. What's your name?"

"Jeffrey. Jeffrey DiCarlo." The man knit his brows together. "You said there were others?"

"Dozens of others," Addie replied.

Jeffrey swore. "This thing needs to be stopped."

"That's what I intend to do."

The ghost let out a humorless chuckle. "You? You're crazy if you think you can do anything by yourself. There's a lot more going on here than you realize. I don't think I have time to explain it, but you should remember, sometimes the monsters are monsters, and sometimes ... well, they're just people. Good luck. You're going to need it."

Addie nodded. "I think I understand, but this is something I have to do."

Jeffrey, even as a ghost, looked stricken. "I didn't mean for things to get so out of hand. Do ... do you know a man named Jamie Fletcher?"

The name seemed familiar to Addie, but she couldn't place a face to it. "No, I can't say that I do."

"I want to tell him I'm sorry. He's going to get mixed up in all this because of me. I need to warn him—"

"Warn him about what?"

But Addie was talking to an empty room.

———

SWEAT TRICKLED down the boy's naked chest. His heart pounded. The fear radiated off him. It was intoxicating.

"Why did we have to come all the way out here in the middle of the woods?" the boy asked.

He looked over Cole Carter's athletic form in the moonlight. "Because no one can find out about what we're doing tonight."

He had driven them almost an hour away from Avalon, out into the pine barrens. They left the car by the side of the road and hiked into the woods for about a mile, to a small clearing—a desolate place, one people instinctively stayed away from. The tall, vertical trunks of the pine trees surrounded them, never-ending rows of columns, stretching out in all directions. It was easy to imagine things sliding through the darkness other than a fox or a bobcat looking for its next meal. Ancient things. Alien things. Unwelcoming things. Maybe something hid behind the trunk of the tree up ahead, poised, waiting, ready to spring out at you and drag you back into the shadows.

Cole shied away from his gaze. "Why did you tell me I had to take off my clothes?"

"Trust me, it's easier this way." He leaned in close to Cole's ear. "Don't you trust me? Don't you want this?"

Cole nodded. "Yes, sir."

He placed a hand on Cole's shoulder. "You'll be fine if you listen to me and do exactly as I say. Do you understand?"

If the boy didn't go crazy first. That was always a danger. He didn't remember much after it happened to him, except pain ... and hunger. He didn't think he could handle the changes, but he forced himself to maintain control. Cole would have to do the same.

"Yes, sir." To his credit, the boy didn't flinch at his touch.

"Tell me what happened at the football game last Friday, Cole."

Cole frowned. "You were there. You saw."

"I want to hear about it from you."

"Coach was supposed to put me in at the beginning of the second half," Cole said, clenching his jaw. "He promised he would, but he didn't."

He chuckled softly. "Marcus threw three touchdowns and nearly ran one in himself. Seems to me your coach was doing what was good for the team."

Marcus Jones, the colored boy from Ezekiel's Mill, had started that game as the quarterback. Now, some people were saying he should start more games. Cole had, of course, heard everything those people said.

"I could have done better," Cole spat. "Coach should have sent me in sooner."

Fear and anger. The fire was set. He only had to stoke the blaze. He raised an eyebrow. "Is that right? You upset about that?"

The dam burst.

"Yeah, I'm upset. I'm supposed to be starting quarterback. This was my year. I was going to lead us to the state championships. Marcus can't do that. No one's going to follow ... someone like him. Coach won't budge, though. He can't see it. My dad even went to talk to him, but he couldn't get Coach to change his mind, either."

"It's not right, is it?"

"No, it isn't," Cole replied.

He circled the boy, like a predator circling prey. "It goes against the natural order of things. You're better than he is, Cole. You deserve to be the star of the team, but you know what? No one is going to just give you what you want. Not your parents, not your teachers, not your friends, and not your coach. You have to take it. Are you willing to do that?"

"Yes, sir."

"Did you know your father's a member of the Klan?"

Cole nodded. "Yeah, I found his stuff in a closet when I was maybe eleven or twelve. I just shoved it all back in. I never told him about it. I know he still goes to the meetings and stuff."

"And what do you think about that?" he asked.

Cole shrugged. "I don't know."

"What if I told you the Klan's time is past? They had their opportunity to do something with this country, and they wasted it, but you represent the next generation. You'll do things they only dreamed of. You'll be more powerful than your father ever could be."

Cole smiled nervously. "Sound like a lot. All I want to do is play football."

"There's more to life than football," he admonished.

Cole shook his head. "Not for me."

He moved close enough to feel the heat coming off the boy's body. "There'll always be another Marcus, Cole, ready to take away things that are supposed to be yours, but if tonight goes the way it's supposed to, you'll never have to worry about that again."

Cole, clearly uncomfortable, tried not to look at him. "What am I supposed to do now?"

"Just stand still. It might help if you close your eyes."

"Why is that?"

He brushed a clawed finger across Cole's cheek, making a thin, red line. "Because this is going to hurt. A lot."

13

WEDNESDAY, AUGUST 29, 1962

Sarah Jordan hummed softly to herself as she laid out the cards one by one on the table in front of her. The flickering light of a candle threw dancing shadows across the walls of her room. The song was an old tune her grandmother used to sing. She remembered asking once what the words meant. Her grandmother told her they were just nonsense. She didn't learn the truth until she was older.

Sarah's frown deepened with each card she turned over. Again and again the same cards confronted her. The Ten of Swords, the Devil, the Moon, the Knight of Swords, the High Priestess, the Hanged Man. They were in for some trouble, it seemed. She scooped up the cards and returned them to the deck, then gave the cards a good shuffle.

But as she sat poised to turn over the top card, the wind caused the curtains to billow, and the air turned electric all around her. Someone nearby was working some powerful magic. A wolf howled in the woods. It seemed she wasn't the only one to notice, either. Jamie Fletcher needed to figure himself out before it was too late for all of them.

THE WOLF STOPPED and sniffed the air before throwing his head back and letting out a long howl. There was magic about that night, but this magic was different, not like any he'd ever felt before. Powerful, but raw, unfinished, ragged around the edges.

He sniffed the air again. He couldn't tell where the magic came from, but it was close by. He needed to find it. He needed to know what its purpose was. Too much was at stake to leave anything to chance.

He sprinted through the woods, enjoying the feeling of his lean, muscled body, reveling in the grace of his movements as he leapt over gnarled roots and dodged crooked tree trunks. So few would ever understand what it was like to run free on a warm summer night, the smells of the earth and the trees and the blood of all the creatures cowering as he passed mingling in his nostrils, the night's chorus singing in his ears. He wanted to let go completely, to give in fully to the urges inside him, but not yet. It wasn't time. He stopped at the edge of the woods and let out another howl before dashing across the open field, following the magic.

———

JAMIE NUDGED Ginny gently to make sure she was asleep. She muttered something he couldn't understand and rolled over, wrapping herself up in the covers. He slipped out of bed, pulled on a pair of jeans, and left her to her dreams.

The warm, sticky air practically smacked him in the face the moment he stepped through the back door, headed for his pickup truck in the backyard. He hopped into the bed, laid down on his back, and stared up at the clear night sky. There was no moon. The stars sparkled against the uninterrupted blackness. Jamie traced the meandering flow of the Milky Way like he did on those rare nights in Korea when everything was still and quiet. It helped then to think Ginny and everyone else he'd left behind were looking up at the same stars.

He hadn't gotten much sleep since his visit to Rhett MacNeil's house. He'd gone through every interaction he'd ever had with Ginny's father, starting from the time he and Ginny met as teenagers, right after her family moved to Avalon. He sifted through his memories for any sort of give-away that his father-in-law was a Klansman, but he couldn't find one. And that bothered him even more.

Not that he was naïve. He knew a lot of fine, upstanding, church-going people were involved with the Klan, but as long as they kept it to themselves, he could pretend otherwise. Now that he knew some of their names, he couldn't lie to himself anymore.

"What do you do if you find out something about someone that changes the whole way you think about them?" he asked no one in particular. "And what if you know that something will hurt someone else? Do you tell the truth and hurt them, or do you lie to them forever?"

As if to respond, a wolf's howl shattered the night's peace. Jamie's blood ran cold. He sat up in the truck bed. He didn't think he'd ever heard a wolf so close before. A few moments later, the howl came again. Jamie scanned the tree line, but failed to spot any dark shadows lurking in the woods.

He was still trying to see through the murky darkness when the ghostly hand clamped down on his shoulder.

———

MOST PEOPLE DROVE by on Highway 231 never even realizing an old plantation house lurked merely a few hundred feet off the road. The house was built in 1823 by Daniel Bray, a wealthy farmer who moved down from Greenville. By 1833, the surrounding plantation boasted forty acres of cotton worked by twenty African slaves. By 1843, the plantation had expanded to sixty acres and thirty slaves. In 1845, though, a horse-riding accident left Daniel Bray paralyzed and unable to walk, and his oldest son Bernard took over the day-to-day management of the plantation.

While it couldn't exactly be said that Daniel was kind to his slaves, he didn't go out of his way to be cruel. Bernard, on the other hand, had a mean streak a mile wide by all accounts, and took a certain amount of pleasure in tormenting the slaves who worked the fields.

No one knows exactly what happened on that sweltering July day in 1848. The last anyone saw Bernard alone, he was headed out to one of the far fields. As always, he carried the horsewhip with him he used to beat any slave he didn't think was working hard enough. When he didn't come back by dinner time, they went out looking for him and found him among the rows of cotton, beaten to death. Ultimately it was decided a slave named Ishmael had murdered him, but Ishmael vehemently denied he was anywhere near where the body was found on that day. Of course, his word carried no weight, and he was put to death for the crime.

After that, the family fortunes fell. None of Daniel's other sons were interested in working the family plantation, and the land was sold off piece by piece until only the small bit around the house itself remained. Daniel died in 1861 as the Civil War was getting underway. One son lived in the house for a few more years, but by the end of the war, he was gone. No one came back. The house sat empty.

After a while, people reported seeing things at night—strange shadows, weird lights. Anyone brave enough to venture closer might hear singing—spirituals and work songs where the old slave quarters used to be. And the truly unfortunate might encounter a lone figure wandering through the abandoned fields carrying a horsewhip.

Addie pulled her father's car up to the gates of the Bray plantation. Her heart pounded. Taking the car without permission was the most brazen thing she'd ever done. She'd waited until her parents went to sleep before she slipped out of the house.

Of the wall that once surrounded the abandoned mansion, the gates were all that was left, and even they had mostly crumbled. Addie, toting a bag full of the things she needed that night as well as a flashlight, stepped over the rusted remains. Nature reclaimed the grounds long ago. Addie's skirt snagged on branches as she passed, and she winced as her shoes sunk into the damp soil. She wished she had other clothes to wear. Maybe she should have borrowed a pair of her father's work boots, but it was too late to turn back. The only thing she could do was keep walking.

In front of her the house loomed. The Georgian-style mansion had obviously once been grand. Its three-story brick façade was full of large, ornamented windows, and columns lined a massive porch, but time had done what time does. The porch sagged. Much of the roof was missing. One of the two enormous chimneys had collapsed. Vines of Virginia creeper snaked their way up the sides and into the broken windows. The house looked like it might fall down at any moment, but fortunately for Addie, it was not her ultimate destination.

She slogged across the grounds until she came to a small clearing. Stacks of stone outlined the foundations of several small, square buildings—the former slaves' quarters—and behind she found the place she was looking for: the burial plot for the slaves. She put down her bag and pulled out the things she had brought, including her grandmother's spell book.

Addie lit six black candles in turn, spilling a little wax from each onto a plate to fix it in place. In the middle of the plate, she put a handful of dirt she scooped up from the burial plot. To the dirt, she added mullein leaves and more ingredients from the jars she found in her grandmother's cigar box—sulfur powder and something called vandal root. She took a deep breath and calmed herself before reciting the Lord's Prayer.

Then she opened her eyes and called out, "Any spirits present here tonight, I ask that you make your presence known and answer my questions, in the name of the Father, the Son, and the Holy Ghost."

She lit another match and set fire to the mixture of ingredients in the middle of the plate. The smell rising up almost caused her to retch, but she managed to keep her dinner down. As the smoke ascended, she watched and listened, but nothing happened. After a few minutes of sitting in the eerie stillness of the plantation grounds, she wondered if she had performed the spell right, but she told herself to be patient. She closed her eyes and focused on slowing her heartbeat.

As Addie was about to drift off to sleep, she heard a noise. When she opened her eyes, several figures stood in the burial plot, staring back at her. Their edges were unclear, and many of them faded in and out. She had to struggle to keep them in focus. They were all dressed in rags and seemed on the point of starvation. The expression on their faces ranged from mild curiosity to indifference to irritation.

"Thank you for answering my call," Addie said to the assembled spirits.

"What is it you want, child?" one of the closer, more distinct spirits asked. She was an older woman who seemed annoyed at being called. "One so young as you should not be dabbling in the magic you do. You can't contain it. It's spilling over."

Addie withered under her glare. "What do you mean by that?"

"You have power, a lot of it, but you don't know how to use it," the woman answered. "You were able to call us here, but the spell you cast reached beyond this place. Who knows what spirits you've riled up?"

Addie glanced down at the smoldering remains of her ritual. "I'm sorry. I didn't know."

"That's not an excuse," the woman snapped.

Another spirit stepped forward, a tall, lanky man. "Never mind. What's done is done. She can deal with the consequences later." He turned to Addie. "You called us here to answer your questions. Now ask. Time is short."

"I need to know about a monster," Addie said. "It's been killing for years. People like us, mostly."

The older woman barked a laugh. "People like us? You may look like us, but you're nothing like us. You have no idea what it was like to live our lives."

"Tell us more about this monster," the man said to Addie, ignoring the woman's rebuke.

"It takes the form of a giant wolf," Addie explained, "and it's powerful enough to rip a man in half. It hunts at night and stalks its victims, taking them by surprise."

Another ghost spoke up, this one of a young woman. "That sounds like a rougarou. We had stories of such creatures where I grew up in Louisiana. A man who can become a wolf."

The man nodded. "I know stories of monsters like that, too. A man who transforms under the light of a full moon into a blood-thirsty creature that can only be satisfied by killing."

"I need to know how to stop one of them," Addie said.

The older woman laughed again, this time a hearty chuckle. "You are going to stop a rougarou? By yourself? There are easier ways to die if that is what you want."

The man looked at Addie so intensely she was afraid he could peer into her soul. "But she has power. It's true that it's unfocused, but the power is there." He addressed Addie again. "There are a number of weaknesses they have. A potion made with monkshood will trans-form the wolf back into a man, even under the full moon."

"If you can get the rougarou to drink it," the older woman added with a smirk.

The man gave her a sideways glance. "Some say placing iron nails through its hands will also cause it to turn back into a man."

"And, anything silver will harm it," the younger woman offered. "A rougarou is normally very hard to injure, but wounds made by silver weapons don't heal easily. Fire will work as well. Or beheading."

"Fire and beheading will kill a normal person," Addie muttered.

The man held up a chiding finger. "You asked the question. It's not our fault you don't like the answers."

Addie choked down a retort of her own. "Is there any way to tell if a person is a rougarou?"

"Not unless you see them change," the older woman replied, "and then you're unlikely to survive the encounter."

The man shook his head. "Now you know that's not entirely true. A rougarou keeps his weakness to silver even as a man. If you get close to someone with a silver trinket and they get nervous about it, that's a pretty good hint."

Addie looked dubiously at the ghosts. She didn't want to appear ungrateful, but she still didn't know exactly how she was supposed to fight against the creature. "What else can you tell me?"

The man turned up his hands. "That's all we can offer you now. Be careful. A powerful rougarou can change any time he wants, though he must change by the light of the full moon, and that is when he is at his wildest, more beast than man."

They all stepped back and faded from view, first the older woman, and then the man, and finally the younger woman, who lingered for a few seconds before she too disappeared.

"Wait," Addie called, "I can't fight this thing by myself."

"You will not have to fight by yourself," a new voice said.

Addie turned to see another ghost. She wasn't like the others. She stood up straight and tall, and she wore a woven dress of purple and green and gold with a matching shawl draped over her shoulders. Her hair was tucked under an elaborate head wrap. Her age was impossible to say.

She held a man's hand. A white man. Addie didn't know who he was, but she recognized him.

————

JAMIE STARTED at the ghostly fingers wrapped around his shoulder. He wrenched himself free and scrambled out of the truck bed to come face to face with a dark-skinned woman. She didn't look like any black person he'd ever seen. She wore a fancy dress and some kind of complicated covering on her head.

It was hard for Jamie to look at her for too long, though. The outline of her body was indistinct, and Jamie had trouble keeping her in focus. Plus, if he didn't know better, he would have sworn she gave off a faint light of her own.

"Who the hell are you?" he asked.

"There is no time." The woman's voice was like a rushing river. She reached toward him. "Take my hand."

Jamie took a step back. "Why should I do that?"

The woman thrust her hand at him again. "Because otherwise you'll die."

Jamie crossed his arms. "You know, I've just about had it with threats like that."

She drew herself up and peered down her nose at him. "I don't have need for threats."

Jamie let out a dry laugh. "Well, the last person who showed up unannounced in my back yard in the middle of the night said the same thing, and then he tried to sell me on some half-cocked idea about Nazi werewolves running around howling at the moon."

The woman did not seem moved.

"And while we're at it," Jamie continued, "we might as well talk about the nice and not at all awkward visit I had with the girl who talks to demons and might possibly have something to do with the disappearance of her parents. She made some scary doomsday predictions, too, so pardon me if I've had enough crazy for a while."

The woman's expression changed, and for the first time, Jamie was genuinely afraid. In her eyes he could see gravestones and funerals and coffins and hearses and death. She seized his hand, and then he was no longer in his back yard. He stood, instead, in the middle of what looked like an overgrown garden. The ruins of a large house stood nearby.

He faced a very startled Black woman. "Where am I?"

"You are not truly here," his escort said. "Only your spirit has traveled here. Your body is where you left it. I will return you to it when you are done here."

Puzzled, Jamie glanced at the spirit. "When I'm done? What am I supposed to do?"

She let go of his hand and faded away, a faint smile on her face. Jamie turned back to the woman staring at him. She appeared to be about his age, maybe a little younger, and was completely out of place in her skirt and blouse. She'd be more at home in a classroom, Jamie thought.

"You're at the old Bray plantation," the woman answered. Then she narrowed her eyes. "I know you."

"You do?" Jamie tried to place her face but couldn't.

"I mean I don't know you, but I've seen you before." She shook her head. "It's hard to explain."

Jamie looked around. "Like any of this is easy to explain? Why don't you try?"

"Last Sunday when I was in church. I saw a ... vision, I guess. A different church. A woman was dancing and singing. You were there, sitting among the pews with your family."

A feeling inched up Jamie's spine like a thousand tiny spiders. "Sarah Jordan. She was dancing and speaking in ... a weird language."

"That wasn't a weird language. That was Gullah. They speak it around Charleston. It comes from the languages the African slaves spoke."

Jamie nodded. "I thought it sounded familiar."

"What's your name?" she asked.

"Jamie Fletcher."

She let out a short gasp. "Did you say Jamie Fletcher?"

"Yes." He studied her face again. "Are you sure we haven't met before?"

The woman regained a bit of her composure. "No, I'm sure we haven't. I'm ... my name is Addie Prichard."

Jamie gave a quick salute. "Pleased to make your acquaintance, Miss Prichard. So, what exactly am I doing here? Do you know?"

She chewed her lip, putting some thought into her answer. "I think you're here to help me stop a werewolf."

The feeling of crawling spiders returned. "Werewolf?"

Addie threw up her hands. "I know. It sounds crazy."

"Not as crazy as you might think. We should talk, but not like this. Maybe we could meet face to face for real."

Before she could respond, a shriek tore through the night. A dark shape swooped down from the sky, and a clawed hand swiped at Addie. She ducked at the last second, escaping the claws, but the thing banked and turned, readying for another pass. And it wasn't alone. Two other dark shapes joined it.

Jamie ran toward Addie. "Get down," he yelled, "all the way to the ground."

As the things dove at Addie again, she threw herself into the dirt. Its claws barely missed her, and it let out a frustrated scream. Jamie desperately scanned the grounds, looking for some way to get away from the black shapes, until he spotted a small building close by. He ran to where Addie was huddled. He tried to put a hand on her shoulder, but his whole arm went straight through her. *Because only his spirit was there.*

"There's a shed about twenty yards from here. I think if you hurry you can make it. Maybe you can hide from those things there."

She looked toward where Jamie was pointing, and then she glanced over at some kind of shrine on the ground nearby—six black candles set up on a plate with something piled in the middle. The three things in the sky dove at them again. Jamie put up his hands to block the attack, but of course, they went straight through him.

He did, however, get a good look at them, and he would never forget what he saw. The things were women, completely naked, without any skin. They looked at him with bulging lidless eyes and screeched through lipless mouths full of yellow teeth. The razor-sharp claws flashed from their fingertips. Addie tried to dodge, but one of them managed to catch her arm. She cried out and grasped the wound.

"Are you hurt bad?" Jamie called

She shook her head even as she clutched her arm, a red stain spreading across the white sleeve of her blouse "No, it isn't that deep."

The three monstrous women flew up on the air in preparation for another attack.

"Now! Go now and you can make it."

"No," Addie said. "There's another way."

Still clutching her arm, she jumped up and ran over to the

shrine. Jamie followed her. She pulled a small book out of a bag resting on the ground and flipped through it until she came to the page she wanted. Then she put the book on the ground in front of Jamie.

"Start reading out loud," she told him.

Jamie crouched down. The book was a Bible, turned to Psalm 121.

"I will lift up mine eyes unto the hills, from whence cometh my help," he read. "My help cometh from the Lord, which made heaven and earth. He will not suffer thy foot to be moved: he that keepeth thee will not slumber."

The things screamed and halted their descent, clutching their heads as if in pain.

Addie scooped the mound of dirt in the middle of the plate into her hands. "Keep going."

"Behold, he that keepeth Israel shall neither slumber nor sleep." Jamie was shouting now over the screams of the things in the air. "The Lord is thy keeper: the Lord is thy shade upon thy right hand. The sun shall not smite thee by day, nor the moon by night. The Lord shall preserve thee from all evil: he shall preserve thy soul. The Lord shall preserve thy going out and thy coming in from this time forth, and even for evermore."

With the last word, Addie tossed the ashes at the monsters. They screeched as they flew off into the night.

"What were those things?" Jamie asked, watching them fly away.

"Boo hags," Addie answered. "Horrible things that feed off people."

"What were they doing attacking you?"

She looked down at her dirty hands and wiped them off on her skirt. "I don't know. The ghosts I came here to speak with said I didn't do a good job of containing the spell I cast to call them up. I let the magic spill over. I guess maybe I attracted their attention."

Jamie glanced over at the tiny shrine. A few of the black candles had toppled over. "What did you throw at them?"

"A mixture of grave dirt and sulfur." *As if that was something everyone used, like headache powder.* "They hate sulfur. Of course, I just used up the rest of my grandmother's supply of sulfur powder, and I don't even know where to get more."

"How did you know what to do?"

"It's all in a book my grandmother left for me." She grabbed up a red book from the ground where it had come to rest in the chaos. "But that might be one of those things easier to explain ... at a different time. Friday maybe? I'm a teacher at Ezekiel's Mill Elementary School. We could meet in the parking lot after school. Seems like we both have some things to share."

"I think I can do that," Jamie said, "but as for right now, you wouldn't know anything about getting me back to my body, would you? I don't suppose you know a way to call the ghost lady."

Addie shook her head. "I don't think she's a ghost."

Jamie remembered the tombstones in the woman's eyes. "Then what is she?"

Addie didn't answer. Her gaze went to something behind him, and her eyes grew wide.

Jamie turned to see the spirit waiting in silence. "Well, perfect timing. Until Friday, Miss Prichard."

When the woman held out her hand, Jamie didn't hesitate to take it, and in a blink, he was in his own back yard again, lying in the back of his truck, alone. Everything was quiet, but the shrieks still echoed in his head, and he couldn't help but scan the moonless sky for those dark shapes.

14

THURSDAY, AUGUST 30, 1962

J amie hesitated outside the hardware store, wishing he'd sent Eddie to get the stuff they needed for the garage. Doing it himself seemed like a good idea at the time. Get out. Clear his head. Try to forget those skinless things with their sharp claws and terrifying grins flying through the night.

But as he stared at his reflection in the store window, he realized he'd just as soon smack a bear on the nose while naked and covered in honey than talk to Rhett MacNeil again. Hell, he'd even fight the boo hags. He hadn't given an answer yet to Rhett's proposal, and he didn't know how much longer he could put it off, but seeing as how he was already there, he took a deep breath and pushed open the door.

Jamie navigated the maze of shelves without managing to run into anyone, a small feat in and of itself. He just wanted to get in and out of the store as fast as he could, so when he rounded a corner and found a group of four or five men gathered, he grimaced. One voice was louder than the rest. Caleb Murray. He had been in the army in Korea at about the same time as Jamie, but while they taught Jamie to fix jeeps, they taught Caleb how to blow things up, a skill not as easily transferrable to civilian life.

That didn't seem to matter to Caleb. The thing he was proudest of in life was the time he blew up a bridge near the city of Wonju as a convoy of North Korean soldiers was crossing. He probably saved a lot of American lives that day, and maybe even helped win a battle. To hear Caleb tell it, though—and Jamie had heard the story quite a few times—he'd won the whole damn war.

But to Jamie's surprise, that wasn't the story Caleb was telling.

"So, I got an interesting phone call the other day," Caleb said to the group gathered. "The man on the other end of the line told me his name was 'Agent Johnson.' Said he was with the federal government. A revenuer. He said they'd found a still down past the old Barton's General Store off Highway 94. Now, of course I assured him I had nothing to do with that."

One of the other men—Herbert Paige—interrupted him. "You know it's a crime to lie to a federal agent."

The others chuckled.

Caleb didn't seem to notice. "Seems they had a problem. The still was buried underground. They couldn't figure out how to get it out without it going sky high."

"So, what's this got to do with you?" Herbert's smirk twisted up even more.

Caleb held up a hand. "I'm getting there. They decided the best way to take care of it was to blow it up on purpose. Seeing as how I'm a demolitions expert, they got in touch with me about the best way to go about that."

Herbert all but laughed in his face. "Well, if you're the expert they're calling, then we're all in trouble. How did this 'Agent Johnson' get your name anyway?"

"Beats me, but apparently I have a reputation." Caleb grinned. If the story was true, he was only going to get worse. "I told them how much dynamite to use and where to put the charges. When everything was said and done, the explosion left a crater ten feet deep. I'm sure the Hawkins Brothers were hopping mad when they found out."

Of course, everyone assumed the still belonged to Roy and Vance Hawkins. Their favorite hobby wasn't exactly a secret. The real mystery was why they never went to jail for it. They weren't exactly criminal masterminds. Jamie figured locking them up was probably more trouble than it was worth, and the revenuers contented themselves with busting up their stills whenever they found them.

Jamie finished up his purchases and came up to the register with a knot the size of Texas between his shoulders, but at the sight of Billy MacNeil sitting behind the counter, the tension drained away. If Billy was there, then Rhett wasn't.

Jamie gave him a curt nod while the cashier rang him up. Billy nodded back. Jamie didn't mind Billy as much as Rhett or Danny. In fact, he felt a little sorry for the youngest MacNeil. Rhett and Danny always treated Billy like an idiot who couldn't do anything right. Of course, there wasn't a lot Billy did do right, but surely he was good for something. A stopped clock, after all ...

When Jamie came out of the store, he nearly ran into Hank Porter exiting the feed and seed with two giant bags of fertilizer, one perched on each shoulder.

"Hi, Hank," he said. "How are you doing today?"

Hank fought to keep from dropping the fertilizer bags. "Oh, I can't complain."

Jamie cocked an eyebrow. "Need help with those?"

Hank shook his head. "Nah, Jamie, I'm good."

"You sure? You look a little top-heavy there."

Hank grunted as he heaved one of the bags back up onto his shoulder. "No. I can make it."

"Well, okay if you think so." Jamie gave him a salute. "You have a good day."

"Thanks, Jamie. You, too."

Jamie watched, shaking his head as Hank staggered down the sidewalk, the bags of fertilizer threatening to topple him at any moment. As he headed toward his pickup, though, he felt something in his shoe. He tried to ignore it, but it dug into the sole of his foot. Every step threatened to drive him around the bend, until finally, he had to stop to take off his shoe and fish out whatever was in there. He knelt on the sidewalk with his shoe in his hand and pulled out an

Indian Head penny. It was warm, and the coppery smell filled Jamie's nostrils when he held it close. The year stamped on it was 1899. It couldn't have been in his shoe all day. Where the hell did it come from?

Jamie didn't have time to dwell on the thousands of questions that ran through his head, though. He needed to get back to the garage. He slipped the penny in his pocket and put his shoe back on. When he looked up, he spotted a flyer posted on a nearby telephone pole. It had a picture of a giant American flag surrounded by a group of smiling kids. Underneath, it talked about how the federal government wanted to violate the sovereignty of the state of South Carolina by forcing the integration of the public schools. Everyone chose to live where they lived, after all. If they had separate communities then they should be okay with separate schools.

Except for that boy who keeps winning all the football games for the high school. Jamie didn't hear anyone arguing to send him back.

Remembering what Rhett said to him when they met, Jamie was pretty sure he was behind the flyer. Jamie didn't know what he was going to do, how he was going to say no to Rhett MacNeil. What would that mean for his father-in-law? Jamie had barely been able to look him in the eye on Sunday, either in church or afterwards when they went for dinner at Ginny's parents' house. He laughed at all his father-in-law's old jokes, like he always did, but it seemed like a role he was playing, now that he knew the truth.

Another flyer was stapled to the telephone pole right above.

Do you know where you'll go when you die?
Will you spend Eternity with your Heavenly Father?
Or will you suffer endless torment in Hell?
Listen to the Words of Jesus as spoken by the renowned orator the Reverend Ewell Holt.
Experience the Miracles of God.
Daily Services 7:30 p.m. sharp.
Saturday, August 18 to Saturday, September 15, 1962.
The big tent in the field near Mile 23 on Camden Highway.

It seemed every summer there was a tent revival somewhere, and always led by some renowned orator Jamie had never heard of. Ewell Holt was no exception.

As he passed the sheriff's office, the door suddenly opened, and two Black women stepped out. One of them was yelling and flailing her arms while the other woman, probably her daughter, tried to calmly usher her away.

"Y'all ain't doing nothing to find my baby," screamed the older woman. "She's been missing for four months and y'all don't know anything about where my Agnes is. Y'all promised. You said you'd do everything you could, but you haven't done nothing. Y'all promised."

Jamie stared. His mind went back to the newspaper clippings David had pinned to his wall, people pleading for help finding their missing daughters and sisters and mothers. *All women.* That seemed important.

The younger woman quietly pleaded with her mother to calm down, but that only seemed to make her shout louder. In the midst of her yelling, she wasn't paying attention and tripped on the curb. Down she went. Jamie ran over to help her.

"Ma'am, are you hurt?" he asked, reaching out a hand.

Her daughter grabbed her by the shoulders, trying to lift her to her feet. "She already has help."

Jamie stooped to help pick the woman up. "Here, let me—"

"I said she already has help," the younger woman snapped, glaring at him.

People stopped to look, including a couple of sheriff's deputies who had followed the commotion outside.

Jamie, a little flummoxed, backed away. "I just wanted to make sure she was okay. Sorry for intruding."

He left the two women behind, but he didn't make it far before nearly colliding with someone walking in the other direction. He muttered an apology. The other person kept walking without saying anything, but he dropped a crumpled piece of paper at Jamie's feet. Jamie snatched it up, mentally cursing the litterbug. He flattened the piece of paper out to find it was one of the anti-integration flyers.

Someone had written a date and a time with a black marker. August 31, 4:30. Glancing at the receding figure, Jamie made out the disheveled profile of David Ben-Ari.

————

WHEN JAMIE CAME HOME from work, he found Amy Lynn standing at the door waiting for him. For once, she didn't have a book in her hand.

She stared at her feet. "Daddy, I have a question for you."

Jamie looked at her quizzically. "What is it?"

Her words came out all at once, tumbling over one another. "Ellie invited me to a sleepover at her house this Friday. Can I go? Please?"

A sleepover, with the girl from Ezekiel's Mill. Amy Lynn had never been to a sleepover before.

"What did your mom say?"

"She said to ask you."

Jamie shot daggers at Ginny, who appeared at the door to the kitchen. He hated when she did that. "What time does it start?"

"Ellie said you could drop me off at her house around six-thirty."

"And what time does it end?"

"Saturday morning around ten. We're going to have waffles for breakfast."

"How many other girls are going to be there?"

"Just me and Ellie." She hopped up and down. "Can I go, Daddy? Please? I'll do extra chores for a month."

Jamie had never seen her so excited. But what would his father-in-law think letting her sleep over at the home of a Black family? What would Rhett MacNeil think? Jamie wasn't naïve enough to believe word wouldn't get back, just like he was sure everyone already knew about what happened with the two women in front of the sheriff's office.

On the other hand, if he was already planning on declining Rhett's offer, what exactly did he care what they thought? Amy Lynn had never had a friend before, and looking into her eyes, he didn't have the heart to crush her spirit.

He sighed. "Well, okay."

She squealed and hugged him around the waist, despite his dirty coveralls. "Thank you! Thank you! Thank you!"

"You're welcome." He pointed toward the bathroom. "Now go wash up. It's time for dinner."

After dinner, Amy Lynn went upstairs to get ready for bed. Ginny cleared the table and carried the dishes to the kitchen, and Jamie went outside on the front porch for a cigarette. The days were definitely getting shorter, but there was still time enough to watch the sunset.

Ginny joined him after a while. "What's bothering you?"

Jamie tensed. "What makes you think something is bothering me?"

"I know you, Jamie. Something's eating at you. What is it?"

There was so much he wanted to tell her, but he didn't know where to begin, how to make sense of any of it. How was he supposed to explain the Jew who'd come into their back yard in the middle of the night and his crazy stories about Nazi werewolves? Or the little trip his spirit had taken the night before and the attack of the boo hags? And that was before the issue of her father's membership in the Klan and Rhett MacNeil's invitation for Jamie to join. "Just busy at the garage, that's all."

She clicked her tongue, a noise she made sometimes when he said something she really didn't believe. "Whatever it is, I don't understand why you won't talk to me about it."

"Because I don't think I can."

She jabbed his side with her elbow. "So, there is something."

Maybe telling her part of the truth might be enough for the moment. "Someone stole something from my office the other day, and I don't know who did it."

"You think it was one of the boys?" Ginny asked.

"It would have to be. No one else has access to my office."

Ginny frowned. "I can't imagine any of them doing something like that."

"Neither can I. That's what's got me so preoccupied."

She leaned into him. "There, was that so hard?"

He put his arm around her. "No, I suppose it wasn't. Now what do you really think about this sleepover?"

"I think it'll be good for her."

"So why did you punt to me?"

"So, I wouldn't be the bad guy if you said no."

Jamie grunted. "I thought so."

"You made her year."

Jamie pulled Ginny in tighter and kissed her on the forehead. "Yeah, well, we'll see if she actually does those extra chores."

———

GRANDMA ZEE TOLD Addie stories about boo hags. She'd believed them when she was little, listening wide-eyed at her grandmother's kitchen table as she recounted tales of all sorts of fantastical things while she cooked. As Addie got older, she realized boo hags were only made-up monsters meant to scare little children into doing what their parents said.

But her grandmother had been telling the truth.

It was well after midnight. Addie sat in her bed, pawing through her grandmother's spell book, looking for anything she could find that had to do with her magic "spilling over" as the ghosts said. She didn't know how she was supposed to contain it, if that was even how the magic worked, and her grandmother's scribbled words weren't offering much in the way of aid, despite how peculiarly helpful Grandma Zee had been so far. Maybe what the ghosts were talking about was one of those things that just got passed down. Only, her grandmother wasn't there to pass anything down to her.

Frustrated, Addie tossed the book across the bed, leaned back, and closed her eyes. She was tired. She needed to sleep, but that didn't seem very likely. Another ghost was only going to come along and wake her up. The night before, she'd come home, exhausted from her experience at the Bray plantation. She'd collapsed into her bed, but the ghost arrived before sleep did. Her name was Mae. She came from Lake City, almost an hour away. The story she told was exactly the same. A walk alone at night. A full moon. No warning.

Like Ezekiel's Mill, mostly Black people lived in Lake City, so no one was going to look too hard if someone went missing. The same as Addie's sister. They were easy prey.

The ghost, when she appeared, did so with little more than a subtle flutter of the curtains and a slight shift in the shadows.

"Oh, mercy me," she muttered quietly, gazing back at a startled Addie from a dark corner of the bedroom.

Her name was Cynthia Jefferson, and she was Addie's teacher in the fifth grade at Ezekiel's Mill Elementary School. She had retired a few years later, and since then they hadn't really kept in touch.

"I'm so sorry," was all Addie could say.

The ghost spoke with a gentle, soft voice. "What's done is done. It's not your fault."

"But the next one will be my fault," Addie insisted. "The next full moon is only two weeks away, and if I can't stop this thing by then—"

"Is that what you think? Honey, you didn't bring this evil into the world. The only way it could ever be your fault is if you walked away from your calling, and I know your family raised you better than that, Addie Prichard, Besides, you have the power." She pointed to the spell book. "And you have the knowledge."

"What good is having power and knowledge if I don't know how to use either one?" Addie asked. "I don't have anyone to show me."

Cynthia shook her head. "You're wrong, Addie. You do. I knew your grandmother. She may be gone from this earth, but she is still helping you. I can even sense something of her here right now."

Addie's heart fluttered. "You can? Can I talk to her?"

"You mean have a conversation? I don't think so."

Addie fought back tears. "I just want to hear her voice one more time."

Cynthia picked up the spell book and handed it to Addie. "There are other ways you can talk to her."

Addie stared down at the book. "But I've already read through the whole thing."

Cynthia looked at Addie over the edge of her glasses the way she used to whenever Addie misbehaved in class. It made Addie feel like she was eleven years old again. "Now Addie, I taught you for a whole year. You can be obstinate, but you're no dummy. Remember what I said about how you can tell a good book?"

"You can read it more than once and find something new every time," Addie recited.

She pushed the spell book toward Addie again. "This is a good book. Read it one more time."

Addie took the book from Cynthia as she began to fade out. "I looked up to you. You made me want to be a teacher. I just want you to know that."

Cynthia disappeared with a faint smile on her face, leaving Addie alone holding her grandmother's book. She opened it, not exactly expecting much, but almost immediately, she happened upon a page she'd never seen before. "Prayer," it said at the top. Having a strong faith was vital, her grandmother wrote. Without it, the magic wouldn't work. That was why so many spells required reciting verses from the Bible, but God wasn't the only one who heard prayers.

Lesser spirits existed. Angels. Demons. Half breeds. Others. The Bible was full of stories about them as well, if you knew how to read it. The woman who appeared with Jamie Fletcher at the Bray plantation had to be one of those spirits. An angel maybe, but without knowing her name, Addie couldn't summon her. She flipped through the pages of the book, searching for a certain spell she'd seen before. She could summon someone else, someone who certainly wasn't an angel.

15

FRIDAY, AUGUST 31, 1962

D avid threw some money down on the counter as he stood to
leave. Since coming to town he'd become something of a
regular at the Tick-Tock Diner. He'd even developed a little bit of a
rapport with Peggy the waitress. They had a little game they played.
Every time he came in, she greeted him with her unwavering plastic
smile, called him "Sweetie," and asked whether he'd changed his
mind about the bacon. He called her "Darling" and told her he
hadn't. Then she gave him a "suit yourself" shrug and took his order.
Of course, she called everyone "Sweetie," but deep down inside
David liked to think they had a connection.

After the first few days no one paid much attention to him. Eyes
still occasionally followed him from the door to the counter, but once
he sat down, everyone went back to eating their breakfast, drinking
their coffee, reading their paper, talking about cows and shotguns
and pickup trucks. Today, though, someone's gaze bored a hole in the
back of his head. On his way out, he spotted Billy MacNeil sitting in a
booth by himself, hunched behind the sports section of the paper
with a hunting cap pulled low over his eyes. Curious. From what
David had heard, if Rhett was the boss and Danny his trusted lieutenant, then Billy was the screw-up.

Outside the diner, he caught a glimpse through the window of Billy rising from his seat. David walked, slow enough to make it easy for someone to follow, but fast enough to seem like he had somewhere to be. It didn't even take a block before he spotted Billy's reflection in the window of the antique store across the street.

Sometimes David met up with Mick after breakfast. The kid continued to be helpful, feeding him little bits of information regarding the comings and goings of various townsfolk. Nothing he could really sink his teeth into so far, but David had hope.

Fortunately, he didn't have an appointment with Mick today. He had planned to go straight back to his shack, but screwing with Billy seemed more fun. He walked down Assembly Street, slowing as he passed the drug store, pretending to look at something in the window display. In the glass reflection, he watched Billy cross the street and loiter in the shadow of the movie theatre's marquee. Giant black letters spelled out the titles of *Ben Hur* and *G.I. Blues* though the *H* in *Hur* was slipping. After a minute, David moved along, past MacNeil's Hardware and the office of Bennett Blake, attorney at law, until he came to the intersection of Assembly and Independence Street. A quick glance over his shoulder confirmed Billy still behind him.

David turned left and walked down Independence for a couple of blocks before making another left turn and doubling back. This street skirted the cemetery where he met with Mick. The morning mist still clung to the gravestones, like spirits late in returning to their resting places. With a wicked grin, he considered leading Billy into the cemetery and trying to lose him among the quiet graves, but then he struck upon a better idea.

Once David passed the sheriff's office, he turned left again, this time onto Tyler Street, back toward Assembly. That would get Billy wondering. David picked up his pace. When he rounded the corner onto Assembly once again, he stopped, pressing himself against the side of the building, and waited. Not more than a minute later, Billy turned the corner.

"Morning, Mr. MacNeil," David said casually. "Hot weather we've been having, isn't it?"

Billy was so startled he stumbled backwards and fell on his ass. Once he scrambled to his feet again, he spun around and ran away. David watched him go. He would have liked to be a fly on the wall when Billy told his brothers about what happened.

———

JAMIE PULLED his pickup into the parking lot of Ezekiel's Mill Elementary School as the kids were letting out. He chose a spot as far away from the entrance as he could get, hoping to avoid being noticed, and watched as scores of kids spilled out of the school. They were running and playing with each other and screaming and laughing. No different really than Amy Lynn's school on those occasions he'd gone to pick her up. Kids just being kids.

The teachers followed about ten minutes after the last of the stragglers. Jamie looked in vain for Addie among the clumps of two or three that came out at a time, chit-chatting before going their separate ways. After a while he got worried she wasn't going to show up. Maybe she was sick and didn't come in.

Jamie wiped his forehead with his forearm. There was no breeze that day, and the afternoon heat made the cab of his pickup into an oven, even with the windows down. He considered giving up and calling it a day, when Addie exited the school building by herself, wrestling with a heavy looking bag. She scanned the parking lot until her gaze landed on Jamie's truck. Jamie opened his door, but a curt shake of Addie's head stopped him before he could get a foot out, and he eased the door shut. She peered over her shoulder before striding toward the pickup.

"I live down the road about a mile from here if you go right out of the parking lot," she said, pausing when she got near. She didn't look at him. "I'm going to start walking. Wait a little while and then come pick me up. I'll take us to a place where we can talk in private, okay?"

Jamie nodded.

Addie glanced back toward the school as she walked away. Jamie counted off a few minutes and then started his truck. It didn't take long for him to catch up with her as she walked along the edge of the dusty road. He pulled up beside her and stopped. She threw her bag into the seat and climbed in after.

"Do you walk to and from school every day?" he asked.

"I do. It only gets bad when it rains hard, but fortunately that doesn't happen too much." Addie pointed to the side of the road. "Pull off to the right here."

Jamie would have missed the turn if she hadn't said anything. His pickup bounced over a dirt driveway overgrown with weeds. Soon a small house came into view.

Jamie brought the pickup to a stop. "What is this place?"

Addie shrugged. "Just a house. My parents told me an old lady used to live here by herself. Her husband had long passed away and all her children were grown. My parents would give her rides to church. But when she died, no one else ever moved in. Supposedly all her things are still in there. It's been abandoned as long as I can remember. My sister and I used to think it was haunted. We wouldn't go near it. We convinced ourselves we heard noises coming from inside and saw shapes in the windows."

Pain flashed in her eyes at the mention of her sister.

Jamie studied the little house. At one point it had been painted a cheerful yellow, but now the paint was chipped and faded to almost white. Rows of bricks outlined places where flower beds used to be, and he was sure at one point they were full of color. Sunlight streamed in through the broken windows. Jamie easily imagined the ghost of the old woman hanging around, but the idea was more sad than scary.

"I don't know. After what I saw, maybe you did see and hear things. Maybe this house really is haunted."

Addie scowled. "Yeah, well, I think I've had my fill of ghosts."

"How did you come to be at that plantation in the middle of the night anyway?"

"I guess that's the reason we're here talking, isn't it?" Addie told Jamie about her grandmother's melody and how she found the cookbook in the attic, about her sister and all the ghosts that visited her of the people the werewolf murdered, and the reason she was at the Bray Plantation. "One of the ghosts that came to visit me, he said his name was Jeffrey DiCarlo. He wanted me to tell you he's sorry. He didn't mean for you to get dragged into all of this."

Jamie swallowed hard. So, Sarah was right. "Jeff was an army buddy of mine. We were in Korea together. He ... he saved my life once, when our camp got shelled. I fell and twisted my ankle pretty bad. I thought I'd broken it at the time. I couldn't run. He picked me up and carried me into the bunker. I don't understand what he was doing here in Avalon. Why didn't he try to get it touch with me?"

"I'm not sure he could," Addie said quietly.

According to David, Jeff was there to meet him. To give him the Nazi papers Jamie found in Jeff's car. The more Jamie thought about it, the less sense it made. Jamie shook his head, trying to sort out all his jumbled thoughts. "Did you at least find out anything useful from your ... uh ... ritual at the plantation?"

Addie made a face again. "I wouldn't say useful. The ghosts said a werewolf can turn any time it wants, but every full moon the blood-lust is overwhelming, and it has to kill. The next full moon is only two weeks away."

Someone else dies. That's what David had said.

"But that's twelve people a year at least." Jamie did some quick math in his head. "You're talking about more than a hundred murders in only nine years. Surely someone would have noticed that many people missing by now."

"What if he's being deliberate, though?" Addie argued. "What if he's choosing victims over a wide area, maybe even as far away as Columbia or Florence? He could go more than a year without visiting the same place twice."

"But even so," Jamie persisted, "no one's noticed a pattern?"

Addie shook her head. "Different counties. Different cities. Different cops. They don't talk to one another. And anyway, no one's likely to take much notice when all the victims are black, and especially when they're women."

The woman at the sheriff's station. She said no one was looking for her missing daughter.

"I guess I never really thought about it that way," Jamie said.

"You've never had a reason to think about it that way."

He winced. She was right, but he wasn't ready to explore that topic any deeper. He decided to steer the conversation in a different direction. "So, how do we stop this thing?"

Addie sighed. "The ghosts told me what a werewolf's weaknesses are, but as for actually finding one and killing it, they were a little vague."

"Could you ask them again?" Jamie offered tentatively.

"They probably wouldn't answer." Addie grimaced. "Besides, I don't want another run in with those boo hags. The ghosts said I needed to learn how to contain the magic, but they weren't very clear about that, either."

"You don't have anyone to show you?"

She reached into her bag and pulled out an old, tattered book with a red cover, the same book she'd had at the plantation. "No, all I have is this, my grandmother's spell book, but she's been gone for a while."

In that moment Jamie made a decision. He wasn't sure everyone would agree. In fact, he was pretty sure there would be some words exchanged, but if what Addie said was true, they didn't have a lot of other options. "Look I don't know why whatever Powers that Be picked me to help you. I don't know the first thing about any of this hoodoo business or occult hocus-pocus, but I do know someone who is knowledgeable, if he's sober today. In fact, he's sort of the one who got me mixed up in all this to begin with. I think you should meet him, and I think we should go now."

She worked her jaw as she deliberated for a moment or two. "I can't be gone too long. My parents will wonder where I'm at."

He shot her a sidelong glance. "You still live with your parents?"

The look she gave him made him immediately regret asking the question. "Not exactly a lot of options around here for an unmarried teacher."

"No, I guess you're right," he said sheepishly.

"So how *did* you get mixed up in all this?" she asked.

Jamie started the truck and put it in reverse. "I can explain on the way."

————

JAMIE AND ADDIE got to David's shack at four-thirty on the nose, but David's blue Ford Fairlane wasn't anywhere to be seen. That didn't stop Jamie from pounding on the door. When he didn't get an answer, he peered through a window, half expecting to see David passed out on the floor, but the darkened interior of the shack was empty save for the piles of clutter. Jamie threw up his hands and sat down on the front steps.

Addie stood, surveying the falling-down structure. "Someone actually lives here?"

Jamie let out a chuckle. "Surprised me, too."

She pursed her lips. "Who is this person we're here to meet, exactly?"

"His name's David Ben-Ari. He's Jewish. Near as I can tell, some kind of Israeli secret agent. A Nazi hunter."

Addie's eyes got big. "Nazis? What do Nazis have to do with any of this?"

Before Jamie could reply, the sound of crunching gravel alerted them both to an approaching car. Seconds later, David's Ford rumbled into view.

Jamie gestured toward the vehicle. "I'll let him explain it. He can do a better job than I can."

David parked his car next to Jamie's truck. He climbed out, a cigarette hanging from his lips. He'd changed his shirt, but otherwise he was still as mangy as ever. He ran his fingers through the tangled mess of his hair, threw the cigarette to the ground, and stalked toward them, looking daggers.

Jamie stood, dusting the back of his pants off. "Nice of you to make it."

David kept his eyes on Addie. "Who's this?"

Jamie rubbed his shoulder, remembering how David had pinned him to his pickup truck. Still, he wasn't going to let the other man forget his manners. "Is that any way to make an introduction? David Ben-Ari, I'd like you to meet Addie Prichard. I think—"

"I don't care what you think," David shouted, crowding Jamie against the door of the shack. "Did I say you could bring a friend? What the hell are you thinking? This isn't some sort of schoolyard game. You can't just invite others to play."

Jamie held up a hand. "Look, David, I'm sorry for the way I spoke with you the other day. Some ... things happened to convince me you were telling the truth about Nazi werewolves." He glanced toward Addie. "And I think Addie here can help us."

David rolled his eyes. "You do, do you? Is she going to help us learn to talk nice to the werewolf? What made you think you could involve whoever you wanted?"

"She's already involved," Jamie said through clinched teeth. "That thing killed her sister."

"Well, I'm sorry to hear that, but it doesn't change anything." David turned to Addie, addressing her for the first time. "You have my condolences, but this still isn't any of your business."

Addie stuck out her chin. "I think it is, Mr. Ben-Ari."

David smirked. "And what makes you think that?"

"My sister's ghost told me," replied Addie.

David frowned. "Your sister's ghost?"

"I called her. By accident," Addie explained. "And I've called other spirits too. All victims of the werewolf."

And just like that, all of David's bravado left him. "You know magic."

Addie nodded. "A little."

"I used to know a little magic myself," David said, a slight, wistful smile on his face.

Jamie cleared his throat. "So, are you inviting us in or what? I'm sweating like a horse standing out here."

David took in a deep breath and let it out slowly. "Fine, but I'll warn you the place is a mess. If I had known I'd be entertaining female company, I'd have made an effort to tidy things up."

It wasn't much cooler inside the shack. Things looked pretty much the same as the last time Jamie was there, except the bourbon bottles on the kitchen table had gained some friends. Addie wrinkled her nose as she stepped carefully over a pile of trash. She shot Jamie another look, no doubt questioning his judgment for bringing her there and her own for agreeing to come.

Jamie turned to face David. "Before we get to why you wanted to meet with me, why didn't you tell me the name of the guy you were here to meet? Jeffrey DiCarlo? That would have saved us all a lot of grief."

"I didn't know his name," David shot back. "All I knew was that I was meeting with an FBI contact. Besides, even if he had given it to me, he probably wouldn't have told me his real name."

Jamie grunted. "Spy stuff."

"Yeah, I guess you could call it that," David locked the door and drew the blinds on all the windows. "Does the name mean something to you?"

"He was my army buddy," Jamie said. "We saw a little fighting together over in Korea. He saved my life once. We spent a lot of long nights talking to each other about everything we missed back home, what we wanted to do once we got out. We told each other about our families. I learned all about his parents and his three sisters and the neighborhood he grew up in Philadelphia. I felt like I knew them all. He and I lost touch after we came back, but you never abandon your battle buddy."

"So, did you know your battle buddy was an FBI agent?" David asked.

"Not until right this moment, but after all we went through, I owe it to him to make sure he didn't die in vain." Jamie pulled the crumpled flyer out of his pocket. "Now, you're the one who wanted to meet with me. What for?"

David flashed a lopsided smile. "I made some additions to the wall I thought you might be interested in seeing."

Addie frowned. "The wall?"

Jamie was coming to dislike David's crooked grin greatly. He pointed to the array of pictures, maps, drawings, news articles, and other scraps of paper David had tacked to the wall of the shack near his bed. "He means that."

Seeing David's handiwork, her eyebrows immediately shot up. She crossed the room and spent several minutes taking it all in. As she read the newspaper clippings of people begging for help finding their missing family members, she teared up.

"We have to stop him," she whispered, "no matter what it takes, we have to stop him."

By then, David and Jamie had both joined her.

David pointed to the picture of the man with the piercing light-colored eyes. "The guy dressed in the Nazi SS uniform is Heinrich Albrecht. He's wanted for war crimes. He's been on the run ever since the end of World War II. You wouldn't happen to recognize him, would you?"

Addie squinted as she scrutinized the face in the picture. "No, but of course he'd be almost twenty years older now, wouldn't he?"

David shook his head. "Not exactly. Werewolves don't age as fast as the rest of us."

"That would be pretty inconvenient," said Addie.

David regarded her with an arched eyebrow. "What do you mean?"

Addie looked over the pictures of Heinrich Albrecht taken over a ten-year span. "I mean he wouldn't be able to stay in any one place for very long. People would start asking questions. Even if he's disguised, he can't be someone who's lived here for any considerable period of time."

"That's a good thing, right?" David said. "A small town like this? That narrows the list quite a bit."

Normally, Jamie would have enjoyed bursting David's bubble, but not that day. "Avalon isn't the backwater hick town you think it is. You're in the New South. When the chemical plant came in after the war, it brought a lot of people in with it. Since then, a couple of other plants have opened. Not to mention the Air Force base not too far from here. This Albrecht character's got a lot of company."

David didn't seem too discouraged, though. "Well, maybe we can narrow the list anyway."

Jamie scanned the wall. "You said you added some things."

David chuckled. "It's right in front of your nose."

Jamie focused on the piece of paper tacked on the wall in front of him. *These are people I can confirm are members of the KKK*, it said at the top in shaky cursive handwriting. Some of the names surprised Jamie. Some of them, like the MacNeil brothers, didn't. He found his father-in-law's name. Jamie knew it would be there, of course, but seeing it in writing was still like a punch in the gut. One other name that stood out was Richard Burke, the sheriff's deputy who had brought him the silver Chrysler still sitting in his garage. What did David say? *Can you trust him?* Had he known about Rick?

Next to the list, David had tacked up another sheet of paper covered in the same handwriting. This one had times and dates on it. *August 22, 6:30 p.m. Bartholomew Avery, Bennett Blake, and Danny MacNeil arrive at Rhett MacNeil's house. 7:45 p.m. Bartholomew Avery, Bennett Blake, and Danny MacNeil leave Rhett MacNeil's house. August 23, 6:00 p.m. Fenton Graham, Danny MacNeil, and George Owens arrive at Rhett MacNeil's house. 7:10 p.m. Fenton Graham, Danny MacNeil, and George Owens leave Rhett MacNeil's house.*

A knot formed in Jamie's stomach, knowing what he'd see when he read the entry for the next day. *August 24, 6:00 p.m. Boyd Parker, Fenton Graham, and Archie Brown arrive at Rhett MacNeil's house. 6:55 p.m. Jamie Fletcher arrives at Rhett MacNeil's house. 7:15 p.m. Boyd Parker, Fenton Graham, and Archie Brown leave. 7:50 p.m. Jamie Fletcher leaves.*

"Where did you get all this?" Jamie asked.

"I have my sources," David said, still grinning.

Jamie resisted the urge to slap the smile off his face. "Everyone meeting with Rhett is a member of the Klan, according to your list."

"Except you," David added.

Jamie nodded. "Except me, yes."

David cocked his head to the side. "So, what were you doing there?"

Jamie sighed. "I was invited."

He told David and Addie about his father-in-law's invitation and what Rhett MacNeil had said to him. Addie tried to keep her face as unemotional as possible, but Jamie could tell by the way her lower lip trembled the things Rhett said upset her.

"I haven't given them an answer yet," Jamie finished, "but they're expecting one soon."

"What are you going to say?" David asked.

Jamie looked sideways at him. "I'm going to tell them no. I can't. After my parents died, I was raised by an aunt. She was ... a character, and she had opinions on things like the Klan. She taught me everyone is equal in the eyes of God. It doesn't matter the color of your skin, if your car breaks down, I'll still fix it for you."

David spent a moment scratching his chin. "I think you should do it."

He might as well have said he wanted Jamie to jump in front of a bus. "What? Why? You of all people should understand why I don't want to."

David held up a finger. "I don't mean seriously. I mean so we can find out more about what's going on."

"More spy stuff."

"Sort of, yes. My source tells me the Klan's been pretty quiet here for a while, but from what I'm seeing, that's not going to last. They're planning something." David rapped the wall with his knuckles. "I'd be willing to bet Herr Albrecht is tangled up in it somehow."

Jamie's attention went back to the list of KKK members. "That's asking a lot. This isn't the church bridge league. This is not an organization you get involved with lightly."

"I understand that." Steely resolve shone in David's eyes. Gone was the smile.

Jamie had the sense once again he was far more dangerous than he let on. He cupped his face in his hands as he struggled to think through the idea. "If I did this, I would need your word that no matter what, my wife and daughter are protected. Can you do that for me?"

David placed his hand over his heart. "You have my word."

Jamie looked to Addie. "What do you think?"

"Anything you can do to stop this monster." Her expression mirrored David's.

Jamie made his second big decision of the day, one he was sure he was going to regret. "Okay then, I guess I should talk to my father-in-law."

On the ride back from David's shack, Jamie kept glancing over toward Addie, who spent her time staring out the window. Neither of them said very much.

As they neared Ezekiel's Mill, Jamie finally worked up the courage to say what was on his mind. "You're sure you're okay, I mean with me joining the Klan?"

Addie answered without turning away from the window. "If that's what it takes, then that's what you need to do."

Jamie shifted in his seat. That wasn't exactly the answer he wanted to hear. "You know I don't believe in what they stand for. You understand that, right?"

Addie almost, but not quite, placed a hand on Jamie's arm. "Jamie, it's okay. Really. I understand. You don't have to justify it to me."

"All right. Just making sure."

Addie returned her gaze to the passing scenery. "But there is something you could help me with."

"Okay, name it."

"I think it would be easier to show you, though I have to warn you it might be a little dangerous."

"Is this another magic trick?" Jamie asked.

She glared at him again. "They aren't magic tricks, but yes, I need to do another ritual, and it has to happen tomorrow at midnight. Is there any way you could meet me back at the abandoned house a little bit before then?"

Jamie sucked in air through his teeth. That was going to be hard to pull off. Still, he did promise. "I'll do my best."

He already regretted all his decisions.

———

FOR THE SECOND time that day, Jamie drove to Ezekiel's Mill. Amy Lynn sat in the pickup next to him, the biggest grin on her face he had ever seen. Her duffel bag was on the seat in between them, packed for her very first sleepover. She'd probably packed it and unpacked it a dozen times, making sure she had everything she needed—pajamas, her toothbrush, her comb, clothes for the next day, and of course Jamie had caught her sneaking a book in as well.

"What do you think you're going to do tonight?" he asked.

Amy Lynn shrugged. "I don't know. Ellie said she'd show me her dolls. Maybe we could build a pillow fort, or tell ghost stories, or read books."

Jamie laughed. "Does she like books as much as you do?"

Amy Lynn considered for a moment, a serious look on her face. "Almost. But she doesn't have all that many. I thought maybe she could borrow some of mine."

"Well, that's awfully nice of you, Amy Lynn, but can't she check out books from the library at school?"

"She can, but we're not allowed to check out more than one book at a time," Amy Lynn explained. "That's not enough to get through a whole week. She said she really likes our library, though. It's twice as big as the one at her old school, and the books aren't all beat up. I asked her why they had beat-up books. Why couldn't they buy new ones? She didn't know. Do you, Daddy?"

Jamie shifted uncomfortably in his seat. "Well, sometimes there isn't enough money for new books."

Amy Lynn frowned. "But why does our school have money for new books and her old school doesn't?"

Thankfully, they arrived at the Morris' house before Jamie had to answer any more questions. It wasn't very big, but it was kept up, painted white with green awnings over the windows and the front door, and a hedge of azaleas all around. A brick walk led from the driveway.

Amy Lynn leapt out of the truck before Jamie even had a chance to turn it off. At the same time, a girl about Amy Lynn's age, with deep brown skin and hair in pigtails, came bounding out of the house. She grabbed Amy Lynn by the hand and pulled her toward the door, nearly colliding with a man coming down the walkway. Of course, Amy Lynn completely forgot about her duffel. Sighing and rolling his eyes, Jamie grabbed it and climbed out of the truck.

The man met Jamie by the side of his pickup. He held out a hand. "Pleased to meet you, Mr. Fletcher. I'm Isaac Morris."

His skin was the same deep brown color as the girl's but weathered around the eyes and mouth. A little gray crept into his hair around his temples. He was a carpenter by trade, Jamie had learned. Jamie could respect that.

He took Isaac's offered hand. "There isn't any Mr. Fletcher here. It's just Jamie."

Isaac reached for the duffel. "Here, let me take that. I'll make sure Amy Lynn gets it. You know, this sleepover is all Ellie's been talking about."

"Amy Lynn, too," Jamie said as he handed over the bag.

"She talks a lot about Amy Lynn. I'm glad she finally found a friend."

"It's been hard for her, I imagine."

"It has, for all of us, but Ellie was never good at making friends, even at her old school."

Jamie hesitated, not sure if he should ask the question, but his curiosity got the better of him. "Why did you do it? I mean move her to the—to Avalon Elementary."

"We couldn't let an opportunity like that pass by. Ellie gets to go to a better school where she can get a good education and have a chance to do something with her life. Not that we don't have good teachers here, but they can only work with what they have, and that's not much." Isaac paused, his jaw set, his shoulders tensed. He seemed like he was trying to hold back some stronger feelings. "At the end of the day, we left the decision up to Ellie, and she said she wanted to do it. I'd be lying, though, if I said there aren't some days I ask myself if we made the right decision."

Jamie suddenly felt as if he'd tread on a place he shouldn't have. Of course, it couldn't have been an easy decision to make. Of course, they'd had to put up with a lot. He didn't need Jamie reminding him. "Well, Amy Lynn hasn't had the easiest time making friends either. For what it's worth, I think it's good they found each other."

Isaac nodded. "I appreciate that."

"Listen, you give us a call if you have any problems. I'll be back at ten tomorrow morning to pick her up."

A burst of squeals and giggles came from inside the house.

Isaac grinned. "Sounds like they're going to be just fine."

On the way home, Jamie thought back to the smile on Amy Lynn's face and how it could have powered the whole town, but he couldn't share her joy, not completely, not knowing what was going to happen once he made a certain phone call.

16

SATURDAY, SEPTEMBER 1, 1962

A t ten-thirty that morning, someone knocked on the front door. Three quick, crisp raps. Addie was home alone. Her parents had gone to visit a cousin in Lynchburg. She seriously considered not answering, staying really still, and hoping whoever was there would go away, but three more quick raps made her give up on that idea. When Addie opened the door, she stifled a yelp.

"Good morning, Addie," Rose said, dressed like she was going to church. "I hope I'm not intruding. I was just out running some errands, and I thought I'd stop by for a moment."

Addie swallowed the reply she wanted to make and forced a smile. "Of course, you're not intruding, Rose. Please, come in."

Rose stepped inside. Her sharp gaze swept the living room, like an accountant making an appraisal. "You have a ... charming home, Addie."

"Thank you. It's actually my parents' house."

"Is that so?" She fingered the lace doily on the table by the door. "Well, your parents certainly know how to make the most of what they have."

Addie did her best to ignore the backhanded compliment. "Please, Rose, have a seat."

Rose sat down in one of the high-backed chairs by the window, her purse tucked in her lap. Addie took a seat on the sofa, on the opposite end of the room. Rose smiled. Addie smiled back. A moment or two of awkward silence passed.

"Hot weather we've been having," Rose said finally.

"Well, it's summer. It *is* generally hot this time of year." Addie tried desperately to suss out why Rose, who had never before made any sort of social call, was in her house.

"How is your class this year?" Rose asked. "Not too unruly I hope."

"They're fine. You know kids that age. Full of energy. The trick is to channel it before they tear up the classroom."

Rose laughed, a high-pitched titter that grated on Addie's ears. "That is the trick, isn't it?"

Addie knew what she was about to say wasn't terribly polite, but she didn't really feel like playing this game anymore. "Rose, did you really just stop by to chat, or is there a particular reason for your visit?"

Rose twisted up her mouth and wrinkled her nose like she'd smelled something rotten. "Well, since you brought it up, I saw you yesterday, when you got into the pickup truck with that white man. Of course, someone else might think something untoward about what I saw, but I know you would never do anything inappropriate."

Addie froze. "You would have had to follow me to see that, Rose."

"Who was he?" she asked.

Addie couldn't think of a good lie. "He's a friend of the family, and it's none of your business."

"Well, that may very well be the case, but my business or not, it won't keep other people from saying things."

Addie regarded Rose, whose pleasant, friendly, innocent smile had returned. "Why would they say things, Rose? If you're the only one who saw me, then you're the only one who knows. You'd have to be the one to tell them."

Rose drew herself up and peered down her nose at Addie. "All I'm trying to say is that as teachers we have certain appearances we have to keep. We have to be examples. You should be more careful, Addie."

"I don't need your advice, Rose." Addie did her best to keep her voice even.

Rose leaned forward. "Just promise me you'll think about what I've said."

Addie stared out the window at the oak tree in the front yard to keep from having to look her in the eye. "I really shouldn't keep you from your errands any longer, but thank you for stopping by."

Once Rose left, Addie stormed to her room and pulled her grandmother's spell book from underneath the pillow on her bed. There had to be a way to keep Rose from telling anyone about Jamie. Addie angrily flipped through the pages, unaware of the shadows boiling around the edges of the room. Finally, she found a spell she thought might work. The low, raspy voice in her head returned, telling her this was all for the good. There was a werewolf on the loose, killing people, their people, and all Addie was trying to do was stop it. She couldn't let Rose jeopardize that.

The spell called for another black candle and something called crossing oil. She found those things among her grandmother's supplies. The rest of the ingredients—a lemon, vinegar, and a glass jar—she found in the kitchen.

Like before, she etched Rose's name in the candle. Then she rubbed it with the crossing oil and put it on the holder before lighting it. She dug out the picture of Rose she had used for the last spell. With a pen, she crossed through the picture and then folded it in half twice. She cut a slice in the lemon and shoved the picture inside.

Then she closed the cut in the lemon with a straight pin, put the lemon in the jar and filled it with vinegar. She sealed the jar shut and shook it while she said a prayer asking the Lord to remove Rose from her life.

The book said she was supposed to leave the jar by the candle until it burned down, and then she was supposed to bury the jar in the ground. The voice whispered in her ear, telling her Rose deserved whatever happened to her. If she didn't get out of Addie's life, it was her own fault for anything bad that happened. The shadow things danced and reveled in the light of the candle as Addie gazed into the flame. The voice let out a satisfying laugh.

———

JAMIE PICKED up the phone to make a call he didn't want to make, one that every fiber of his being screamed at him not to. Maybe the line would be busy, he thought, but the first ring came, and he deflated. After three rings, maybe he thought no one would pick up. Maybe they were out somewhere. But those hopes were crushed, too, when his mother-in-law answered the phone.

"Hello?" she said.

"Hi, Evelyn, this is Jamie. Is George there?"

Maybe he wasn't home.

"Oh sure, he's right here." She hesitated. "Is everything okay? You don't usually call us at this time of day."

Damn.

"Everything's fine. He asked me a question about a car, and I told him I'd have to get back to him. I was calling to tell him what I found out."

"Oh, okay, dear. Here he is."

There was a pause while she handed over the phone, and then his father-in-law's voice came over the line. "Hi, Jamie, what is it?"

"Hi, George. I told Evelyn you had a question about a car. I wanted to let you know I've made a decision."

"All right then." George's voice changed, taking on a stiff, impersonal tone Jamie had never heard before. "What's it going to be?"

Jamie closed his eyes and took a deep breath. "I'm in."

"That's good news. I'm glad to hear it." But his words didn't have any joy in them. "I'll let the others know."

"What am I supposed to do now?"

"Wait. Someone will be in touch." George paused. "One thing, though."

Jamie tensed. "What is it?"

"I've heard some rumors Amy Lynn has made herself a friend at school."

Damn and damn again.

"She has."

"She can't be friends with that girl."

Jamie winced. He should have seen this coming. He did, on some level. He just didn't want to. "But she's never really had any friends. You should see her. She's so happy."

"We'll find her other friends," George insisted.

"Oh, come on, George. They're just kids."

"It doesn't matter," George said. "You have to think about appearances, Jamie. Now if it were up to me, it wouldn't be an issue, but it's not. Amy Lynn can't be friends with the little colored girl. I'm sorry."

Jamie sighed. "Fine. I'll see what I can do."

He hung up the phone. He didn't have any intention of telling Amy Lynn she couldn't be friends with Ellie. He couldn't break her heart like that. There had to be a way they could stay friends. They could hide it somehow. But deep down he knew he was fooling himself again.

———

JAMIE TOLD Ginny it was an emergency. A cousin of his Ginny had met once before—and was never likely to meet again—needed his help. Ten years sober, he'd fallen into a bottle of whisky and couldn't get out. He lived in Dalzell, about an hour away, so Jamie would probably be pretty late getting home.

Another lie to add to the list.

At about half past eleven, he pulled into the driveway of the abandoned house near where Addie lived. She had told him to meet her there, but he didn't see any sign of her. As he waited, he let his gaze wander to the empty house, its outline stark against the surrounding trees in the moonlight. After dark, he could understand why Addie and her sister thought it was haunted. During the day, the house had seemed a little sad, but at night it took on some more sinister qualities.

The more Jamie stared, the more he imagined faint whispers, the words barely too soft to make out. Something inside the house moved, something darker than the darkness. When Addie's face appeared at his window, she scared him nearly out of his skin.

"Sorry about that," she said as she climbed into the passenger seat of the truck with her bag. She glanced toward the house. "What were you looking at?"

"Nothing," Jamie replied. "Just lost in thought."

He put the truck in gear and pulled out onto the main road. Addie directed him where to go. It seemed as if they were taking turns at random, but Addie acted like she knew where they were going, so Jamie didn't question. Soon, the houses gave way to farmland, and then the farmland gave way to woods and pastures. The dark night grew thick around the truck. They didn't pass another single car on the road the whole time. Eventually, Addie told him to stop at a crossroads.

Jamie couldn't see anything in the beams of his headlights except trees all the way around. "Are we lost?"

Addie slung her bag over her shoulder and opened her door. "Not at all."

Jamie joined her outside the pickup. "What are we doing way out here?"

"Hopefully, we're getting help."

Jamie wasn't sure he wanted help from anyone they might meet there. "Okay, how, exactly?"

Addie walked to the middle of the intersection. "We're going to ask nicely."

"Is there anything I can do?"

"Right now, stay out of the way. I may need more help if things go wrong."

"Like they did at the plantation?"

She glared. "That spell didn't go wrong. It just didn't go right either."

Addie took a piece of chalk from her bag and dragged it over the crumbling asphalt, etching out two intersecting triangles. Where the lines crossed, she drew symbols Jamie had never seen before. Then she set up six white candles at the points of the triangles and placed three pennies in the center. Next, she produced a glass and a bottle of dark rum. She filled the glass and put it in the center of the triangles with the pennies. Once she had set everything up, she opened her Bible and read aloud from the Psalms.

Jamie closed his eyes and listened to her voice. It seemed like the whole world stopped to listen, too. For a moment, Jamie forgot about the Klan, forgot about the werewolf even. For a moment, everything seemed right with the universe. When Addie closed the Bible, it sounded like a gunshot. Jamie stumbled backwards as reality crashed into him.

"Now what?" he asked when she joined him by the truck.

"Now we wait," Addie replied.

Jamie looked at the six dancing points of light in the middle of the crossroads. "For what?"

"For the Black Man of the Crossroads."

Every hair Jamie had stood on end as it all suddenly snapped into place—the candles, the pennies, the chalk symbols, the crossroads at midnight. "Wait, we're literally making a deal with the Devil at a crossroads?"

Addie shook her head. "He's not the Devil. He's just who he is, but he does have the power to make people really good at doing things, like playing the guitar. You go to the crossroads for nine nights in a row and perform the thing you want to be good at. On the ninth night he's supposed to show up and grant you the skill you want."

"You mean we have to do this for nine nights in a row?" Jamie didn't have that many cousins.

"Hopefully not. We don't have that long. And sometimes he shows up sooner. Also, I think I've stacked the deck in our favor. Since the skill I want to be better at is working my grandmother's spells, I worked one tonight for calling on spirits. Maybe it will call him." She leaned against the hood of Jamie's pickup and crossed her arms. "I just hope my parents never find out I went to the liquor store and bought a bottle of rum."

Jamie checked his watch. A few minutes after midnight. He was about to say something else when a black crow flew down and landed in the middle of the crossroads. It strutted around Addie's offering a few times before it looked directly at Addie and Jamie with one beady eye. It cawed and then flew away.

Jamie leaned toward Addie. "Is that supposed to happen?"

"I don't know," she said.

Jamie fiddled with another rock he'd found in his pocket earlier. Like the first one, this one was worn smooth, with a circular hole in the middle. The only difference was the color. This one was white. With each minute that passed, he grew more and more restless. Something about that place made him feel like they weren't welcome, like they were intruding.

He took in a sharp breath when a shadow detached from the underbrush across the street and formed itself into a black cat. It slinked toward the offering, twisting and turning its lean body around the lit candles. Jamie was sure it would catch its tail on fire, but it didn't.

When it finished inspecting the things Addie had left, it approached them. Jamie's instinct was to back away, but Addie's hand on his elbow told him to hold his ground. The cat rubbed its side against Addie's legs before it sprinted across the road again, back to where it came from.

Jamie let out the breath he'd been holding. "I hope that was a good sign."

Addie nodded. "Me too."

Jamie checked his watch again. Fifteen after midnight. "How long do we have to wait?"

"If it's going to happen tonight, it won't be long now." There was a little tremor in Addie's voice, though, like she was trying to convince herself as much as Jamie.

As if on cue, a rustling in the trees across the street drew their attention. A shape emerged from the woods, large and on four legs. Jamie and Addie both froze. A giant dog with a coat the color of midnight, easily the size of a Great Dane, stepped onto the road. It, too, lumbered over to inspect the offering.

It stepped carefully over the candles and sniffed at the glass of rum before taking its massive tongue and slurping up the brown liquid. When all the rum was gone, it approached Jamie and Addie, much like the cat had. It stopped when it was about three feet away and sat on its haunches. It stared at them, mouth open, sharp teeth gleaming in the moonlight. Then the black dog did something Jamie never expected.

It laughed.

A human laugh. And as it laughed, it changed, growing even bigger, front paws lifting off the ground, toes growing longer and thinner. Muzzle flattening, fur vanishing, until there was no longer a dog standing in front of them, but a man dressed in a completely black suit, as if he were headed to a funeral. His dark features weren't exactly handsome, but there was something striking about them. He reminded Jamie of the black preacher who'd come into his shop needing his car fixed.

Still smiling, he pointed a finger at Addie. "Oh, you've got some real gumption there, doing what you did, coming out here and calling on me, just expecting me to show up."

"But you did show up," Addie said.

"Well, of course I did. I had to meet the person who would be so reckless."

"Why do you say I'm reckless?" Addie asked.

"Because the rules are there for a reason, my dear." The Black Man cocked his head to the side and looked her up and down. "You think you're special and shouldn't have to wait nine nights like everyone else?"

Addie didn't flinch from his gaze. "Well, rules are made to be broken, right? I need your help, and I don't have time to wait nine nights."

Jamie wondered if Addie was as at ease as she appeared or if she was scared and just that good an actress. At the moment, he was terrified.

The Black Man laughed again. "Well, ain't this a pickle then."

Addie frowned. "What?"

"You asking me for help," the Black Man answered.

"I did what I was supposed to do. I performed the thing I need help to master. Now that you've showed up, you're supposed to help me." Addie balled her hands into fists. "Give me the skill to conjure like my grandmother could. You have to."

He let out a dry chuckle. "I don't *have* to do anything, my dear. Let's get that straight."

"Are you saying you won't help me?" Whatever confidence Addie had, or at least pretended to, was gone.

"What I'm saying is that you don't need my help," the Black Man elaborated, as if talking to a child. "You already know everything to be as good at conjuring as your grandmother."

Addie glared. "How is that possible? I've only had her book for a few weeks."

"And yet you were able to call on me after only one night when it should have taken nine. Not a whole lot of workers can do that. Then again, not a lot are stupid enough to try." His smile widened, revealing a huge set of canine teeth in his still human mouth. "You best be careful, though. Your magic has a reach to it, and other things you might meet at a crossroads aren't as nice as me."

He changed shape again, shrinking down until the big black dog sat in front of them once more. With a short bark, he trotted off.

"What did he mean by that last part?" Jamie asked.

Addie threw up her hands. "That's what I can't get anyone to explain. If my grandmother were here to teach me, I'm sure she'd show me what I'm doing wrong. She could tell me why my magic is 'spilling over' whenever I do a spell, but she's not here."

"Is that why the boo hags attacked you at the plantation?"

Addie nodded. "I suppose they were attracted to the spell I cast."

Jamie was suddenly aware again of all the things he couldn't see in the dark. "So, what did he mean about other things we might meet at a crossroads?"

"There are all kinds of spirits that dwell at crossroads," Addie explained. "He probably meant one of them."

"So, can we get going before one of these other spirits decides to make friends?" He already had a hand on the door handle of his truck.

Addie sighed. "I suppose there's no use hanging around."

She took a step toward the offering in the road, but at that moment, the trees rustled again, and something crashed through the underbrush.

"I don't guess the Black Man's changed his mind, has he?" Jamie reached toward her, urging her to come back to the truck, all the while keeping his eyes on the trees.

Addie also had her gaze fixed on the woods. "That would be a little out of character for him, I would think."

All of a sudden, a man on horseback emerged onto the road dressed in the white robes and hood of a Klansman. The horse he rode was solid black. He lifted the piece of cloth covering his face to reveal only a grinning skull. Two pinpoints of red light glowed where his eyes should have been.

"Addie, get in the truck," Jamie yelled.

But she seemed frozen at the sight of the apparition.

Jamie, despite the terror he felt, willed himself to move. He sprinted toward Addie, grabbed her by the arm, and pulled her to the truck. As they were getting in, the horse reared up and set off toward them. Jamie stabbed the key into the ignition and put the truck in gear. He dug the tires into the dirt getting away. The rider pursued them.

"I know I'm beginning to sound like a broken record here," Jamie said, "but what the hell is that?"

Addie frantically searched through her grandmother's spell book. "My best guess is some kind of crossroads demon."

"But we're not in the crossroads anymore, and it's still chasing us. Do you have something in that book that will stop it?"

Addie groaned in frustration. "There are spells for making amulets or mojo bags, but that's something you do ahead of time. I can't exactly set up a ritual in your truck."

"Then what do you suggest we do?"

"Right now, keep driving. I'll think of something."

Jamie glanced in the rearview mirror. The thing was still behind them, the white, bare skull of the rider gleaming in the moonlight, and it was gaining on them.

"You might want to hurry with your thinking."

Addie rummaged through her bag and pulled out her Bible. She flipped the pages until she found whatever verse she was looking for. She took a deep breath and read. "The Lord is my shepherd; I shall not want. He maketh me to lie down in green pastures: he leadeth me beside the still waters. He restoreth my soul: he leadeth me in the paths of righteousness for his name's sake. Yea, though I walk through the valley of the shadow of death, I will fear no evil: for thou art with me; thy rod and thy staff they comfort me."

The demon rider screamed, a sound that threatened to tear Jamie into pieces. He glanced over his shoulder to find it had fallen back.

"Whatever you're doing it's working," he said. "Keep it up."

But rather than read any more, Addie screamed and threw the Bible to the floorboard. Smoke rose from the pages. The smell of sulfur filled the cabin of the truck.

She cradled her hands in her lap. "It burned."

Another check of the rearview mirror confirmed the rider had closed the gap again. If they didn't do something soon it would catch up to them, and Jamie really didn't want to see what a demon horse would do to his truck. For the first time, he took stock of his surroundings, and to his surprise, he realized he knew where they were. He thought he was choosing roads at random, but maybe some benevolent spirit had influenced his steering wheel.

"I've got an idea. Hold on." He put his foot down on the gas, apologizing silently to the truck.

"I'm not sure I have much of a choice," Addie replied.

When they got to Dry Creek Road, Jamie nearly took the turn on two wheels.

"I'm going to stop the car, soon," he told her. "When I do, get out and run as fast as you can."

"Are you crazy? We can't outrun that thing."

"Hopefully we won't have to."

The demon rider was almost on top of them when Jamie pulled the truck onto the driveway leading up to the Jordan farmhouse. He brought the pickup skidding to a halt right in front.

"Now," he shouted.

He and Addie both jumped out of the truck and ran for the house. He looked back over his shoulder expecting the rider to be right on them, but the demon remained on the road. The horse snorted and pawed at the ground but didn't even put so much as a hoof on the Jordan property.

As soon as he and Addie hit the steps of the front porch, the door opened. Sarah Jordan stood framed by the light from inside. She didn't seem at all surprised to see them. They ran inside past her. Sarah lingered in the doorway. She peered out into the night and glared at the demon, the way a parent might glare at a misbehaving child. The demon vanished.

"I see you got into a little bit of trouble out there," she said after she shut the door.

"Were you expecting us?" Jamie asked, not quite sure what just happened.

Sarah turned to Addie. "I felt your magic, Addie Prichard. I felt it go wild. That's what drew out the demon."

Addie shot Sarah a puzzled look. "I'm sorry. I don't believe we've met."

"No, not in this world. My name's Sarah Jordan. Some people think I'm crazy." She laughed. "Please come in and sit."

She showed them into the small sitting room Jamie had seen on his last visit.

"How did you make the demon go away, Sarah?" Jamie asked.

"Demons know they're not welcome here. Simple as that." She didn't seem inclined to offer any other explanation. "Now tell me, what magic were you doing that got you in so much trouble?"

Addie explained about calling the Black Man.

When she was done, Sarah clapped and giggled. "You have some gumption all right. And you actually got him to show up. That's exciting."

"But he didn't help," Addie protested. "I need to know how to contain my magic so it doesn't spill over and do things like it did tonight."

Sarah picked up a deck of cards off the table next to her chair. Jamie was certain it hadn't been there a minute before. She idly shuffled it. "Can you contain lightning? Or the ocean tides? You can't contain magic."

"I don't understand," Addie said.

Sara laid out three cards on the table in front of her face down in a row. "You act like you can keep your magic in a box. It doesn't work that way. You're powerful, Addie Prichard, but you're holding back. You're not pouring all you have into the spells. That leftover magic you don't use, it goes wild."

Addie buried her face in her hands. "But I don't know how to do that."

"Well, you need to figure it out, because I'm not sure you have much time left." Sarah turned over the cards one by one.

They weren't the normal diamonds and hearts and spades Jamie was used to. These cards had strange pictures on them and names he'd never heard of before. The Knight of Swords. The High Priestess. The Hanged Man. Sarah pulled a fourth card from the deck and placed it underneath the others before she turned it over.

The Devil.

Jamie suddenly didn't want to be there anymore. "It's awfully late.

We thank you for your hospitality, but we should probably be on our way."

A knowing smile spread across Sarah's face. "You should be safe now."

As they left, Jamie couldn't help but glance at the family Bible in the entryway. It was open to Psalms 23.

17

SUNDAY, SEPTEMBER 2, 1962

J amie pulled up to the house with barely enough time to splash his face with water, comb his hair, and pull on his church clothes. He'd spent a restless night in his office at the garage, boo hags and crossroads demons running through his dreams. The last thing he wanted to do was spend the day with his father-in-law, but God forbid he skip church.

Ginny, thankfully, didn't ask too many questions about his night with his cousin. Jamie assured her he was in safe hands and everything was okay, and she seemed to accept his story, but he still felt horrible for lying to her.

When she climbed into the truck, squeezing Amy Lynn between them, Jamie eyed the foil-covered casserole dish in her lap.

"What's that for?" he asked.

"It's a green bean casserole for the social after church," she replied.

Jamie frowned. "What social?"

She glanced sidelong at him. "The end-of-summer social. The one we have every year? The one Reverend Griggs has been announcing every Sunday for a month? The one that's been printed in the church bulletin for just as long?"

Jamie gritted his teeth. "Oh, that one."

If there was one thing Jamie dreaded more in that moment than spending time with his father-in-law, it was spending time with the whole damn church congregation. He sat through the service underneath a dark cloud while Reverend Griggs droned on about sin and true repentance. By the time he dismissed the congregation after the final prayer, the knot in Jamie's stomach was easily the size of a basketball.

They set up folding tables on the lawn outside the church and put out all kinds of food—fried chicken, coleslaw, potato salad, ham biscuits, deviled eggs, and fifteen different casseroles—not to mention every dessert imaginable. Jamie fixed himself a plate and found a tree to stand under a little distance away from most everyone, hoping to avoid having to make small talk. Ginny chatted with some of the other ladies while Amy Lynn made flower chains in a patch of clover nearby.

Jamie's hopes were dashed when he spotted Sarah Jordan and her brothers approaching him. Nonetheless, he put on a smile. "Sarah, nice to see you out and about."

Sarah nodded. "Nice to see you, too, after the night you had."

Jamie glanced around, afraid someone might overhear. "Do you think you might be able to keep what happened last night to yourself? It would be a little hard to explain to the little old church ladies."

Sarah laughed. "Oh, we've all run from a demon at one time or another. It's just that most of the time they're not the kind you can see."

Jamie maintained his smile, with some effort. "I suppose it's true when you put it that way. Still, can you keep a secret?"

His question brought a chuckle from Calvin and the rest of Sarah's brothers.

"Of course," she said. "Keeping secrets is all I do."

"Thank you."

"One thing, though, Jamie." She leaned in close and whispered in his ear. "In sacrifice, abundance, in surrender, victory."

"What—"

But she was already walking away, surrounded by her brothers. Jamie stared at her, a deviled egg poised in his hand, wishing someone would just speak plainly for once.

"Nice day for a picnic, huh? Couldn't ask for better weather."

Jamie turned to find Jasper Cordell standing next to him. "Afternoon, Jasper. Sure, I suppose so."

Jasper pointed to Jamie's plate. "I'd be careful of that potato salad if I were you. It's a little suspect."

Jamie didn't care about the potato salad. He watched Sarah and her brothers as they milled about. "Thanks for the heads-up."

"Potato salad took out a whole Free Will Baptist church in Roscoe a few years back, you know. True story. I usually skip over it and go straight to the pecan pie, just in case."

"Not a bad idea." Jamie absentmindedly popped the deviled egg in his mouth.

Jasper followed Jamie's gaze. "Sarah Jordan. She's an odd one all right, isn't she?"

"I don't know. I think a lot of people misunderstand her. She sees things differently from the rest of us is all."

Jasper didn't seem too convinced. "So, how do you account for her brothers? And don't you find it strange no one's seen their parents in a while? I think it's been a couple of years since I've seen either one of them."

"That has occurred to me, yes." Jamie dug into a slice of Marguerite Carmichael's seven-layer chocolate cake, the one and only saving grace of having to endure a church social, in his opinion.

"Maybe they're dead."

Jamie nearly choked. "Jasper, that's a terrible thing to say."

Jasper rolled his eyes. "Oh, come on now. No one's around to overhear. Besides, you can't tell me the thought hasn't crossed your mind."

"Well, maybe it has," Jamie admitted.

"Lots of odd stuff going on in this town, you ever notice that?"

"What do you mean? Like all the stories about the Bray Plantation being haunted?"

"No, I mean really weird." Jasper's eyes got big. "Like have you ever walked into a room and turned on the light, only to have the darkness linger in a corner just a little too long? Happens in the store all the time. Or have you ever driven a road at night and sworn it follows a different path than it does during the day? Sam Murphy has a list of roads he won't drive at night, afraid he'll wind up ... somewhere else."

Jamie made a drinking motion with his hand. "Sam Murphy shouldn't be driving at all."

"He's not the only one who says that. You'd be shocked what people tell me. You ever felt like you're being followed, but if you just get inside your house, you'll be okay? Lots of houses around here, especially the older ones, have protections signs carved above the front door. We pride ourselves on being modern, but we're all just the same superstitious lot we always were. And who knows? Maybe we should be."

Jamie chuckled a little nervously. "Sounds like you got a little too much time on your hands, there, Jasper. All I do is fix cars. I don't have time to think about things like that."

Jasper was silent for a moment, and then he burst out laughing, too. "You're probably right. Maybe I do spend too much time thinking, but I've got to pass the time somehow when things are slow at the store. Speaking of which, I think I might get me some of that pecan pie before it's gone. Nice talking with you Jamie, as always."

"You, too, Jasper."

"You still need to bring Amy Lynn by," Jasper called as he walked away.

"Soon," Jamie said. "I promise."

———

GINNY DIDN'T SLEEP the night before, and it had nothing to do with Jamie being gone. Truth be told, she preferred it when she couldn't sleep.

If she didn't sleep, she didn't dream.

She'd worried Jamie wouldn't be back for church, but he rolled in with just enough time to spare. He didn't give many details about his night looking after his cousin, and she didn't press. She wasn't sure he'd tell her the truth anyway.

She only half listened as Harriet Page went on about some scandal at the last Junior League meeting. Her gaze kept darting to Jamie standing by himself underneath a big maple tree, plate piled up with more desserts than anything else. He was talking with Sarah Jordan and her brothers.

Ginny hadn't given much thought to Sarah since her incident at the church service a few weeks earlier. She showed up with her brothers the next Sunday like nothing ever happened, and everyone was too polite to say anything about it.

Ginny thought Jamie was simply being polite until Sarah leaned in and said something close to his ear. Jamie frowned and went white as a sheet, staring at Sarah as she walked away. A snippet of one of Ginny's recent dreams came to her. Jamie, his hands tied with rope, hanging upside-down from the maple tree, tears of blood streaming from his eyes. She shook her head to banish the image.

"Are you okay, Ginny?" Harriet asked. "You look like you just saw a ghost."

Ginny glanced quickly back at Jamie. He was talking with Jasper Cordell, now, and they were laughing about something. "Oh, no, I'm okay. I felt a little light-headed there for a second. Probably just the heat."

"Do you need to sit?" Harriet took her by the hand. "Come with me, we'll get you into the shade. Do you want a glass of tea?"

Ginny waved her off. "Oh, no, that's all right. You don't need to do that. I'll be fine."

"Oh, nonsense. It's not any trouble," Harriet insisted.

Ginny found herself being led to a folding chair. A cold glass was placed in her hands. As she sat and sipped the tea, she though back on her dream, one of many she didn't understand. In all of them Jamie was in some sort of horrible danger. She hoped she could do enough to protect him.

18

MONDAY, SEPTEMBER 3, 1962

Addie's heart sank when she heard a knock at the door. It was the Labor Day holiday, and all she wanted to do was spend her day off in peace. She was alone in the house, again. Her parents were out visiting another elderly aunt or cousin. There never seemed to be a shortage of shut-in relatives. Like with Rose, her instinct was to stay quiet until whoever was there went away, but then a familiar voice called out to her.

"I know you're home, Miss Prichard. You might as well answer."

When she reluctantly opened the door, she found David Ben-Ari waiting. He looked like he had made an attempt to put himself together, but he didn't quite succeed. His shirt was still rumpled, even if he had tucked it in, and his hair didn't seem to want to stay put.

He flashed her a smile she had only seen before on door-to-door vacuum cleaner salesmen. "Good morning! I hate to bother you, but I was wondering if I might have a word?"

"What are you doing here?" Addie barked. "No one can see you here. People will talk."

David waved a hand dismissively. "If anyone says anything, you can tell them I was trying to share the Good News about Jesus Christ with you, and you didn't want to be rude by cutting me off."

Addie fumed. That could actually happen. "My parents are going to be back soon."

He gave her that annoying smirk. "Your parents left at 9:36 this morning. They're visiting your mother's eighty-four-year-old second cousin, Ida Mae Henry, who lives in Olanta, like they do every month. They're not coming back until late this afternoon."

Addie sighed. "Okay, then. You have a few minutes. Go ahead and tell me about Jesus."

"I want to show you something, first." From behind his back, he produced a book and handed it to her.

When she touched it, a tingle of electricity passed into her hand. The book was small, not much bigger than her palm, and old, with a worn leather cover and a silver clasp crusted over with years of tarnish. Addie opened it, taking care as she leafed through the yellowed pages full of diagrams and drawings and cramped Hebrew handwriting.

"It's a spell book," David explained, "kind of like yours. It belonged to my father, and his father before that, and his father before that. You're also reading it backwards."

Addie turned the book over, though of course the writing was still incomprehensible to her. "You said you used to know magic."

David nodded. "I did."

"Why 'used to'?"

He got that far-away look in his eyes again. "That's a long story. The spells in that book, they don't work for me anymore. Let's leave it at that. Which brings me to why I'm really here. I thought I might ask you a favor."

Addie looked at him warily. "What would that be?"

"Surely you know a finding spell or two."

Given how the last finding spell resulted in nightly hauntings, Addie wasn't really eager to try another one. "What do you need found?"

"The documents Jamie told you about, the ones he found in the car that were stolen from his desk. They could lead us to the werewolf."

Addie grimaced. "That would be a long shot. You need a clear picture in your head of what you're looking for when you perform a spell like that, and I've never seen these documents you're talking about."

David took the spell book back from her. He opened it to the back cover and took out a folded sheet of paper. "Will this work?"

Addie took the sheet of paper from him. At the top, were the words *Unternehmen Werwolf*. She assumed it was German. David had filled the whole page with descriptions of what information might be in the missing documents. She glanced up at David's eager face. There were a few different finding spells in her grandmother's book. Maybe if she tried a different one, things wouldn't go so haywire.

"I'll see what I can do, but no promises."

David's lopsided grin returned. It could be endearing, at least a little, Addie decided. "That's all I can ask."

She pointed to his car. "Now you better go. You've had enough time to tell me about Jesus' saving grace."

She watched him get into his car and pull out of their driveway. As she shut the door, a flicker of movement in her neighbor's window caught her attention, and she wondered who else was watching.

———

JAMIE DID a double-take at the Harley parked on the street outside the five and dime. He'd seen it before, outside of McGill's Bar. He figured it belonged to the big biker who tried to pick a fight with Hank and Wade. Mack said he was in town "on business" for a few days. Guess his business wasn't finished yet. Sure enough, a few seconds later, the biker exited the five and dime and walked up the street, away from Jamie.

That might have been the end of it had he not spotted one of the tattoos on this man's arm. It was the symbol David had shown him, the line hooked at each end with a slash through the middle, the *Wolfsangel*, used by the Nazi guerrillas who called themselves Were-wolves. He knew he'd seen it before, and now he knew where. The biker crossed the street, and before Jamie even realized what he was doing, he crossed, too, his errands for Ginny all but forgotten.

Jamie stayed what he thought was a good distance away, following the man past the Tick-Tock Diner and the Drug Store. When the biker got to MacNeil's Hardware, he went inside. Jamie stood frozen, unsure of what to do—if he should follow him into the hardware store, if he should wait outside, or if he should do the smart thing and go on with his day. He was still deliberating when the biker came back out a few minutes later, a scowl on his face. He stalked down the street. Fortunately, he didn't look back in Jamie's direction.

Jamie stayed on his heels. When the biker reached the corner of Assembly and Independence, he turned left, and once he rounded the corner, Jamie lost sight of him. He came to the intersection not even a minute later, but the biker had disappeared. Puzzled, Jamie glanced around. There wasn't really anywhere for him to go. He literally vanished.

"What's wrong? You look like you just saw a ghost."

Startled, Jamie spun around to find Jasper grinning at him.

"No, I was just— I mean I thought— There was someone—" he sputtered.

Jasper cocked an eyebrow.

Jamie sighed and tried again. "Did you ever see someone walking on the street, and you thought it was someone you knew, and you were about to say something to them, but when you got up close, you realized it was a completely different person?"

Jasper chuckled. "Happens to all of us at one time or another, I suspect."

Jamie felt rather pleased with himself for concocting that lie on the spot. "I was coming into the five and dime to pick up some things. Think you can help me? Ginny's got a list."

Jasper laughed again. "I know all about those kinds of lists. Sure. Come on."

Jamie followed Jasper back toward the five and dime, but he couldn't shake the image of the tattoo on the biker's arm or help but wonder what "business" brought him to town.

THE PLAIN, white envelope waited on the porch for Jamie when he got home, his name scrawled across the front. He ripped it open to find a note from Rhett MacNeil congratulating him on his choice to join a "noble organization" with a "long and honorable history" of "maintaining peace and order." The note instructed Jamie to be at the Avalon First Baptist Church the following night at seven o'clock. When he finished reading it, he looked up to find Ginny standing in the door looking back at him.

"You coming in the house?" she asked with a hand on her hip.

Jamie fumbled to get the note back in the envelope. "Oh, yeah, sure."

She frowned. "What's that?"

"Nothing," he said, maybe a little too quickly. "Did you see anyone come by and drop this off?"

Ginny shook her head. "No, but I might have been upstairs folding clothes when they did. Everything okay?"

"Yeah, everything's fine."

She eyed him. "Well, come on in. Dinner's getting cold."

He hesitated. "It's just that ... it's a Chamber of Commerce thing. There's a special meeting tomorrow night. I'm going to be late again."

Ginny grimaced. "Again? You've had a lot of late nights lately."

He leaned in and kissed her on the forehead. "Yeah, I know. I'm sorry. It won't be like this much longer. I promise."

She nodded and turned away. She didn't believe him, he could tell, and it felt like a knife in his heart. He crumpled up the envelope and shoved it in his pocket. He'd make it up to her.

Somehow.

ONCE AGAIN, Addie waited for everyone else to go to sleep. She sat down at the writing desk in her room, the materials she needed laid out before her, ready to perform the finding spell for David's missing documents. She didn't plan to use the same spell she'd used to find her sister. This one involved praying to Saint Anthony, the patron saint of lost things.

Among her grandmother's supplies, she'd found a candle with a picture of a man in a monk's robe labeled "Saint Anthony of Padua" and some old sticks of incense. Following the instruction in her grandmother's spell book, she lit the candle and placed a glass of water, a pinch of salt, and a piece of bread in front of it. Then she lit one stick of incense, saying a small thank you it still worked and hoping the smell wouldn't wake up her parents.

In both hands, she held the piece of paper with David's description of the missing documents, closed her eyes, and recited the prayer to Saint Anthony, asking him for their return. She was supposed to say the prayer a total of nine times, and as the words of the prayer slipped through her lips, she focused on what Sarah Jordan had told her, about letting go and using all her magic so nothing was left over.

Addie was about halfway through reciting the prayer for the third time when a familiar melody tickled her ears—her grandmother's song. The wordless tune was so subtle at first, she couldn't even be sure she really heard it. She tried not to pay any heed to it, to finish reciting the prayer to Saint Anthony, but the song would not be ignored. It enticed her to get up from the desk.

Addie carefully opened her door. She crept down the hall, past her parents' room, through the living room, and out the front door. Outside the night air was still hot and sticky, but it didn't bother her. She followed the song down the street. Very clearly now someone was humming. When Addie neared the old abandoned house, she knew she was getting close to the source of the melody. She didn't notice the figure occupying one of the rocking chairs on the front porch until the chair moved, causing the old boards to creak. She jumped and let out a yelp.

The figure chuckled. "Now Addie, I know you're not that big of a chicken."

Addie caught her breath. It had been a long time since she'd heard that voice. "Grandma Zee? Is that really you?"

"It is if you think it is." Her grandmother beckoned her closer and gestured to the empty rocking chair next to her. "Come on now. Have a seat. We don't have a lot of time."

Addie came closer, until she could make out the kind face of her grandmother in the pale moonlight. Tears welled up in her eyes as she sat down. "Grandma, I have so many questions I want to ask."

Her grandmother nodded. "I know, and I'm sorry I haven't been here to help you, but you've done so much in so little time. I'm very proud of you."

Addie shook her head. "I've made some mistakes. Some bad ones."

At that, her grandmother let out a deep, throaty laugh that nearly broke Addie's heart to hear again. "Honey, if you knew half the things I did when I was starting out. Let's just say I'm lucky to have lived as long as I did."

Addie smiled, despite herself. "But every time I cast a spell, the magic goes wild. What do you do to control it?"

She looked at Addie the same way she looked when Addie was little and got caught sneaking candy out of her purse. "Magic isn't something you control, Addie. That's pride talking. You let it work through you. You're doing a good job, but you're resisting. You have to give yourself up to it."

"But what if I lose myself?"

Her grandmother smiled. "You can't lose yourself as long as you know who you are."

"That's what I'm afraid of. I'm not sure I know exactly who I am."

Grandma Zee leaned forward and took her hand. Her fingers were calloused, the way Addie remembered, and her skin was warm. "You are Addie Prichard, and you are my granddaughter, and that is enough. Now you had best be getting on. Your spell's almost finished."

Addie blinked, and her grandmother was gone, but Addie still wasn't alone. Something moved in the abandoned house, accompanied by a groan of old floorboards and a low-pitched growl. Addie jumped to her feet and leapt off the porch. She didn't dare look back as she ran home, back to her room, back to where her body sat, repeating the prayer to Saint Anthony. The candle had almost burned out.

Addie finished up the last repetition, she blew out the candle. Then she snuffed out the incense and cleaned up the offering. If the spell worked, the documents would be returned to David within a few days. When she finally climbed into bed, she cried herself to sleep again.

19

WEDNESDAY, SEPTEMBER 5, 1962

I t was Addie's favorite time of day, those quiet minutes in her empty classroom before the children arrived. Not that she didn't love every one of them, but there were so few calm moments.

The ghosts also didn't bother her there.

A knock at her door jolted her out of her reverie. Mr. Deakins stood in the doorway, a grim look on his face. She expected him to ask her about the progress on the storybook pageant she was supposed to plan, thanks to Rose. She didn't know what to tell him. She honestly hadn't made any progress, but blaming ghosts and werewolves wasn't going to work with the school principal.

Addie mustered as much of a smile as she could. "Mr. Deakins, what brings you by this morning?"

"I've got some bad news, Addie. I wanted you to hear it from me before you heard it from the gossip mill." He gestured with his head down the hall toward Cassandra's and Carol's classrooms. "Rose was taken to the hospital last night."

The news hit Addie like a slap in the face. "What happened?"

"No one knows for sure. Her sister said she complained about her stomach hurting after dinner, and then a few hours later, they found her unconscious in the bathroom. Last I heard she hasn't woken up, and they still haven't figured out what's wrong with her."

Addie's own stomach churned as her mind went to the lemon in the vinegar jar currently buried underneath her mother's camellia bush. "That's terrible."

"Hopefully it's nothing serious. Hopefully the doctors will figure out what's wrong, and she'll be home in a few days."

"Hopefully," Addie echoed.

Mr. Deakins stood silent for a moment. It seemed to Addie he wanted to say something else, but he just heaved a weary sigh. "Well, the kids are going to be here any minute. I'd best leave you to it."

Stunned, Addie stared at the empty doorway. She hadn't meant to do anything bad. All she wanted was to stop Rose from telling anyone about her meeting with Jamie. Addie didn't want to hurt her.

Of course you wanted to hurt her. You knew what the words you were saying meant. Every last one of them. You knew, and you did it anyway.

The hoarse voice was familiar to Addie. It had spoken to her before, the last time she performed a spell directed at Rose. But it lied. What it said wasn't true. She didn't know something this bad would happen.

You're the one who's lying. Someday you'll have to face the truth. You did this, Addie Prichard.

Her magic must have gone wild again. This wasn't a result of the original spell.

The voice chuckled. *Not this time. This time you poured everything you had into it, and it worked exactly as it was supposed to. You have a talent. Don't deny your power. You can do great and terrible things. Just think, of all the ways you've been wronged. Now you can do something about it. Those people who never cared once about whether you lived or died. You can make them care.*

Great and terrible things. Addie truly didn't mean to do what she did to Rose. As soon as she got home, she was going to dig up that jar with the lemon in it and hope it would reverse the spell against Rose. But after that, maybe—just maybe—she could make a few little fixes.

Bobby didn't show up for work. He'd asked to take off the Tuesday after Labor Day, wanting to get one last fishing trip in before the weather turned, and Jamie didn't see any reason not to let him. Bobby was always the reliable one, the one Jamie could depend on to keep the garage from going up in flames when he wasn't there.

Except for that one time, but that really wasn't Bobby's fault.

At first Jamie tried not to think too much of it. Bobby was just a little late. Maybe he'd had one too many beers out on the lake and needed to sleep off the consequences. He'd be in any minute.

But by mid-morning with no sign and no word, Jamie knew something was wrong. They were busy, though, and being a man down, he couldn't leave. Maybe Bobby had run into his own car trouble trying to get back to town. Maybe he'd call once he got to a phone.

After lunch, when Bobby still hadn't shown up, Jamie decided to go by his house, to make sure things were okay. Reluctantly, he left Eddie in charge, with strict instructions not to set anything on fire.

Bobby lived next door to his parents in a little house south of downtown, in a neighborhood full of very similar little houses. Bobby's was white with dark blue trim. He wasn't much of a green thumb, but the yard was neat at least. Jamie's heart sank when he saw Bobby's Pennant Blue Corvette in his driveway. So much for the theory about car trouble.

Jamie parked his pickup behind Bobby's car and made his way to the front door, scanning for any sign of movement in the windows. There wasn't any. The stagnant afternoon air lay like a heavy blanket, smothering the neighborhood in still silence.

Jamie knocked and waited but didn't get an answer. He knocked again, louder, but still no one came to the door. He turned the doorknob and pushed the door open a crack. From somewhere inside a radio was playing, Elvis Presley singing "Can't Help Falling in Love."

"Bobby, it's Jamie," he called. "Just checking in. You didn't show up for work. I wanted to make sure you're okay."

Nothing. Jamie opened the door all the way and literally nearly stumbled into a complete disaster. The front hallway was stacked waist-high with newspapers and cardboard boxes. Jamie had to step over what looked like the innards of an old radio to even get inside. Car engine parts sat in pools of oil, and everywhere there were piles of clothes.

Jamie couldn't make sense of what he saw. At work Bobby was the neatest person he'd ever met. They all teased him because he could spend an entire day underneath one car or another and not get a spot of grease on his clothes. Jamie had always considered Bobby a friend, but he realized he'd never actually been inside Bobby's house before. When he really thought about it, he didn't know all that much about Bobby's life outside the garage.

Jamie ventured farther into the house, stepping around the clutter as best he could. Between his fingers he rubbed the Mercury dime he'd found on his visit to Rhett MacNeil's house. He fallen into the habit of carrying it with him. Something about the feel of the worn coin in his hand reassured him, made him feel safe.

He counted parts from half a dozen different cars, plus two broken televisions and a busted Electrolux vacuum cleaner. As he passed the door to the kitchen, the music got louder. It took him a moment to spot the radio on the kitchen table, surrounded by news-papers, old mail, and general trash. If it weren't for the lack of whisky bottles, Jamie would have suspected Bobby and David were somehow related. Jamie was about to move on when something caught his eye.

A hand.

He'd almost mistaken the body for another pile of clothes. Jamie rushed into the room and knelt down beside Bobby's sprawled form. He was dead, there was no question of that. His neck jutted out at an unnatural angle, and his head lay in a pool of sticky, red-brown blood. His feet were tangled up in the cord of a broken toaster. It looked like he'd tripped and fallen and banged his head on the counter hard enough to crack his skull.

Jamie should have left then. He should have turned around and walked out and gone straight to the sheriff and told him what he found, but he didn't. It all *seemed* like a freak accident, but Jamie wasn't inclined to believe in accidents at the moment. He stood up and scanned the kitchen. He didn't know what he was looking for. Something, anything that would help him make sense of what happened there.

Elvis faded out, and the deejay started talking. Jamie reached over to the kitchen table and switched the radio off. He hated it when they talked, a stupid thing to be annoyed at right about then.

He was still scolding himself when his gaze fell upon a familiar tattered envelope nestled among all the trash on the table. He snatched it up and reached inside with a jittery hand, hoping he wouldn't find the documents he already knew were there. All the same, the giant swastika on the very top page hit him like a right hook. These were the documents from the silver Chrysler. Bobby must have been the one who stole them from his office.

Jamie swore. He trusted Bobby. He'd taken him under his wing. Bobby reminded Jamie a lot of himself when he was younger, and he even looked to the day when Bobby might take over the garage. How could he have misjudged him so badly?

A small leather-bound book and a ball-point pen also lay on the table. Jamie picked up the book and leafed through it, finding page after page full of Bobby's own handwriting. He'd been keeping a journal for a while it seemed. Jamie flipped to the front. The first entry was on June 23, 1959, a little more than a month after Bobby came to work for Jamie, but it wasn't what Jamie expected.

Betty Lowell gets undressed with the windows open and all the lights on. I think she does it on purpose.

Betty Lowell lived two doors down from Bobby. He'd talked about her before, even admitting he had a little crush on her, but he certainly never said anything to Jamie about what he wrote. He read the next couple of entries.

Every Tuesday a man in a blue car visits Annie Hayward's house while her husband is at work.

Ed Studdard stumbled home at one in the morning. He was so drunk he almost didn't make it through his door.

All the entries were the same.

So, Bobby's secret hobby was spying on his neighbors. That nagging voice in the back of Jamie's head told him he needed to put the book down and go. But he stayed put, letting his curiosity get the better of him. There were a few mentions of the garage here and there, mostly what Bobby really thought about some of their customers. In most cases, Jamie had to agree with what he wrote. Nothing else really jumped out at him until a series of entries starting at the beginning of the summer.

June 4, 1962. A man named Ted Sargent came to the meeting tonight. Brought some big bona fides with him. Rhett vouched for him, too. Said he'd just moved to the area and wanted to get involved. I don't know. He was awfully eager to be there. Something about him seems off.

Jamie didn't know any Ted Sargent, but as for the meeting in question, he had an idea, and he was tired of hoping he was wrong.

August 2, 1962. Saw Ted Sargent snooping around Boyd Parker's place. Tried to follow him, but I lost him.

August 6, 1962. Saw Ted Sargent again. This time he was poking around Jasper Cordell's house. Followed him for a few blocks till I lost him again. Not sure what he's up to.

August 9, 1962. Ted Sargent was looking over Bennett Blake's place today. Followed him until he got into that souped-up silver Chrysler of his. I think I should say something to someone.

Jamie froze. Silver Chrysler. Ted Sargent was Jeff DiCarlo. He must have been undercover or something, like David said. More importantly, though, Bobby knew who that damn car belonged to all along, and he never said anything. Jamie skimmed the journal until he got to the day the car showed up at his garage. Sure enough, there was an entry.

August 15, 1962. Ted Sargent's car showed up at the garage today. No one seems to know who it belongs to. Jamie talked to Rick for a long time. Looks like it got into some sort of accident, but I'm not sure what happened to Ted. Will ask around.

And then a few days later.

August 20, 1962. No one's seen Ted for a few days. There's definitely something fishy going on. I think Jamie found something in the car today, but he hid it when I walked in. Will have to see about that later.

And the next day.

August 21, 1962. Picked the lock on Jamie's office. Found what he took out of the Chrysler. They're a bunch of papers with some Nazi symbols on them, all in German. Wondering if Ted took them from someone else. Still no sign of him anywhere.

The next entry was the last one, dated the Friday before.

August 31, 1962. Going to the tent revival on Friday night. Got word Ted's been there a few times, but not because he wants to find Jesus. He's definitely up to something. I just want to figure out what. I tried to talk to Rhett about it. He laughed and told me I was being paranoid, but I'm going to get myself proof.

Tucked into the journal was a folded piece of paper. Jamie opened it to find one of the fliers for the Reverend Ewell Holt's tent revival. Now he should really leave, right? He should turn around and walk out the door and go to the sheriff.

But he didn't.

Still clutching the Nazi papers, he left the kitchen and moved farther into the house. Everywhere he looked, he saw the same story. Every single room was so full of junk walking was close to impossible.

Jamie didn't find anything different in Bobby's bedroom, except for the bed. It was pristine. The covers were made perfectly, hospital corners and all. And on top, neatly laid out, were Klan robes and a hood. Jamie was supposed to be inducted into the Klan the next night. He wondered if Bobby had known about that.

Jamie left the way he came. He could have walked out the door to his truck. He could've gone to his garage and called someone from there. But he didn't. He went to the kitchen, picked up the phone and dialed the sheriff's office.

"Hi, I'm at 541 Webb Street," he said when someone finally picked up. "I need a sheriff's deputy over here. There's been an accident."

Get out.

Get out.

Get out.

Behind him the radio came on. There was no chattering deejay or crooning singer this time, only static. Underneath the crackling and buzzing, though, Jamie could hear a low, raspy voice, laughing.

———

JAMIE TOSSED the Nazi documents down on David's kitchen table. They hit with a loud smack. "Here's your papers. You got a spot picked out for them on your wall yet?"

David stared down at them, a cigarette dangling limply from his mouth. "Where'd you get these?"

"Off a dead man," Jamie said.

David laughed. "No, really, where'd you get them?"

After spending an hour and a half with a sheriff's deputy going over in painful detail exactly how he'd found Bobby's body, Jamie didn't feel like being witty. "I'm not lying."

He told David the entire story, about nearly tripping over his best mechanic dead in a house full of junk, the victim of a freak accident, and then finding the Nazi papers stolen from his office sitting right there in plain sight.

David picked up the papers and thumbed through them. "Well, I guess Addie's spell worked."

Jamie frowned. "What spell?"

"I asked Addie to do a finding spell, to try to get the documents back," David explained. "Not the way I figured it would happen, but I guess they got found."

Jamie slammed his hands down on the table. "Dammit, David, you understand a man died, right? I don't think she meant for that to happen."

David shrugged. "You said it was an accident."

In what was becoming a common occurrence, Jamie fought the urge to punch him. "Do you honestly believe that? If Bobby hadn't missed work, I wouldn't have gone to his house, and I wouldn't have found these there."

"Still, you can't exactly call it her fault he died."

Jamie thought back to Addie pleading with the Black Man and then with Sarah Jordan to help her learn how to keep her magic in check. He'd heard the desperation in her voice and saw the disappointment on her face when they said they couldn't help. "I'm not sure she'll see it that way."

David sighed. "Look, I wouldn't have asked her if I didn't think there was any other way. If I could have, I would've done it myself."

"So why can't you?" Jamie asked. "You told Addie you used to do magic. What did you mean by that? Why did you stop?"

David's gaze shifted away. "It wasn't a choice."

"What changed?"

David didn't say anything for a moment. When he did speak, his words were deliberate. "Magic is about belief. You have to believe in what you're doing, or at least the possibility of it. You have to have hope, faith. No hope, no faith, no magic."

Jamie regarded him a little skeptically. "You don't believe in God anymore? Is that what you're saying? That's a little hard to swallow, given everything we've seen. I mean come on, God has to exist, right?"

"Oh, no, it's not that. I believe in God." David drew his mouth into a grim line. "I just don't believe He cares."

"Why is that?" Jamie asked.

David clenched his jaw. "Because He took someone away from me."

At least Jamie knew what that was like. "Who?"

David paused to pour himself another glass of bourbon. "This Jeff DiCarlo, you said you were close?"

"Like brothers."

"Then you'll understand. I had a friend. His name was Jakob. We were ... more than brothers. I ... let me back up a little. My last name wasn't always Ben-Ari. Once upon a time, it was De Leeuw. Before I was Israeli. Before there was an Israel, my family lived in Amsterdam. Jakob's family lived next door. There was never a time in my life that he wasn't in it.

"When the Nazis took over, Jakob and I escape to England with the help of a local priest," David continued. "Our families weren't so lucky. After the war, with the help of that same priest, we relocated to Israel. Jakob and I went through army training together. We both wound up joining ... the government. They made us partners. We were there for each other, always. In every way. I loved him."

"What happened to him?"

David's gaze became distant, as if he was watching a scene from a movie play for the thousandth time. "Shot in the back. My fault. He was in the wrong place at the wrong time. I wish it had been me. We were hunting another escaped Nazi hiding out in this rundown villa outside Mexico City. We had him cornered, or so we thought. I wanted to go in after him. Jakob said we needed to wait for backup. We had a fight over it. I insisted we go in. I was convinced if we waited he might get away. So, we went."

"Was this Nazi a werewolf, too?"

The corners of David's mouth quirked ever so slightly. "No, this one was a vampire."

Jamie eyed him. "For real?"

"No, he was just your average-run-of-the-mill Nazi war criminal." David's lopsided grin slinked across his face. "Everyone knows there's no such thing as vampires."

"A month ago, I would have said the same thing about were-wolves," Jamie muttered.

The grin faded and the distant look in David's eyes returned. "We thought he was alone. He wasn't. The whole mission went to Hell in less than two minutes. There wasn't even any sound. Jakob just ... crumpled to the ground, and he was gone. Five months later, I tracked the bastard to El Paso and returned the favor. That helped ... for a while."

A lot of things suddenly made a lot more sense to Jamie. "So now you're punishing yourself."

David scowled. "I'm not punishing myself. I'm doing my job."

Jamie swept his arm around the disaster of a shack. "David, I just came from a house that looked exactly like this. The junk literally killed a man. I don't know what was going on with Bobby, but after seeing the inside of that house, I sure as hell know he wasn't right in the head. So, what's wrong with you? Are you trying to get yourself killed?"

"So, what if I am?" David snarled. "It's my business."

"It's not just your business anymore," Jamie snapped. "It's my business, too, and it's Addie's. You're the professional here. You're supposed to be making sure none of us get killed."

"I didn't ask you to get involved," David said, raising his voice. "I gave you both a way out. Do you know how many Nazis I've personally escorted off this planet? I don't need your help."

Jamie slammed his fist down on the table, hard enough to make David's drink slosh over. "And how many of those other Nazis have been actual werewolves? You know damn well and good Addie and I can't walk away. As soon as I found out Jeff was killed by this monster, as soon as Addie's sister disappeared, we were caught up in this whether you like it or not. Whatever's out there is going to come for us all eventually, and it's going to take all three of us to stop it."

David glared. "I'm still the one who's going to put a silver bullet in his brain when we find him."

"That's all well and good, but we have to find him first." Jamie tossed Bobby's journal down on the table next to the papers. "Jeff DiCarlo was going by the name Ted Sargent. Don't know if that helps at all, but there you go. There's some other interesting stuff in that diary. You might want to take a look."

David glanced at the journal. "Duly noted."

"So, what now?"

David gathered up the papers in one hand while clutching what was left of his cigarette and his glass of bourbon in the other. "I'm going to read these documents and hope they give us some sort of clue who Heinrich Albrecht has been hiding as all these years. And why he's here, of all places. No offense."

Jamie held up a hand. "None taken. I've had the same thought."

David gestured toward the empty chair at the table. "Care to join me?"

"I should probably be heading home." Jamie pointed to the door. "Ginny's going to get worried, and word of what happened to Bobby is probably already getting around. The next couple of days are going to be ... interesting. Besides, I don't know any German."

"It's not that hard. You take all the pretty parts of English and remove them."

Jamie actually laughed at that.

David put on his serious face again. "You be careful tomorrow, Jamie."

Jamie gave a small salute before he turned to leave. "Will do."

The Knight of Swords. The Hanged Man. The High Priestess. Those were the cards Sarah turned over. Killing the werewolf was going to take all three of them. But which one was he? All told, he'd rather be carrying a sword, but he worried he might end up being the one hanged.

20

THURSDAY, SEPTEMBER 6, 1962

They were going to assassinate the mayors of Berlin, Hamburg, Bremen, Munich, Cologne, Regensburg, Leipzig, and a dozen other cities. They were going to attack the American military bases in Ansbach, Bamberg, and Garmisch Partenkirchen.

The Nazis had very detailed, horrific plans for revenge after the end of the War, but thankfully those plans never came to be. Operation Werewolf, for all the hype, was a failure.

David already knew all of that, though, which was why at eight in the morning, he pitched the papers across the room in a fit of frustration. He'd spent a sleepless night reading, fueled on whisky and cigarettes and coffee, only to come up empty-handed. Nothing. Nothing on Heinrich Albrecht himself, what his agenda was, which friendly face he was hiding under.

At the sound of tires on the gravel driveway, David holstered his Glock and darted to the window where he peered through the closed blinds. A pickup truck pulled up into the yard. He'd only caught a glimpse of it, but he swore it was the same one that had nearly run him off the road the week before. Billy MacNeil climbed out and stomped up onto the porch, every footstep rattling the shack. He banged on the door.

David waited almost a full minute to answer before he opened the door to a scowling, red-faced MacNeil brother. "Can I help you?" he asked smiling.

"David Ben-Ari? Is that you?"

"It is," he replied. "I don't believe we've been formally introduced. Who are you?"

Of course, they'd met when Billy followed David from the diner, but Billy couldn't admit that.

His scowl deepened. "I'm Billy MacNeil. You know ... uh ... like MacNeil Hardware, and MacNeil Road, and MacNeil Park." He glanced around at the shack, wrinkling his nose as he did. "This is where you're staying?"

"It is," repeated David.

Billy squinted. "Don't look like much. My brothers said ... ah ... said you told them you were fixing it up."

"I started on the inside." David took a step back. "Care to see?"

"No thanks," Billy said, shaking his head a little too vigorously. "I ... uh ... I just came to deliver a message."

Sweat dripped down his face. He was trying to be tough, but his fidgeting and stammering told another story. David almost felt sorry for him. No doubt his brothers had put him up to this.

"Well, then, by all means deliver your message," David said with a slight bow and a flourish.

"We'd ... ah ... we'd all like it if you'd finish up whatever business you have here and move on." Billy's words all came out at once. "We're going to give you a week."

David crossed his arms. "Who's 'we'? You and your brothers? The proud citizens of this town?"

Billy frowned. The question threw him. "It's just ... a bunch of us who think you should leave."

"Why? What am I doing to disturb anyone?"

"It's not that you're disturbing anyone. It's just that—"

"Then why should I leave?" asked David.

"Well, it's that we like our town a certain way, and ... ah ... you don't necessarily fit in with the rest of our community." By then Billy was in serious need of a handkerchief to wipe the sweat off his face. David could have offered one if he'd felt like being charitable.

David didn't feel like being charitable.

"How don't I fit in?"

He knew, of course. He didn't fit in because he was Jewish, but he was going to make Billy say it.

Billy turned even redder. "Look ... uh ... for the most part, this town is full of simple, God-fearing people. It ... uh ... it makes some people suspicious, knowing someone doesn't go to church on Sundays."

David rolled his eyes. That was probably as good as he was going to get. "Why don't you go back and tell your brothers that I have no intention of leaving until my business is done here, however long that takes?"

Billy stuck a meaty finger in David's face. "Now you listen here—"

David didn't flinch. "This isn't an argument, Billy. I'm not leaving yet."

"You will if you know what's good for you."

"Why? What are you going to do?"

"We'll ... uh ... make you sorry you didn't go," Billy spouted.

David couldn't keep the corners of his mouth from creeping upward. He liked this game. "How?"

Billy balled his fists up in aggravation. "Look, if you'll just go, things don't have to get so complicated."

David shook his head. "I'm not leaving, no matter how 'complicated' things get."

Billy glared at him for a moment, a vein on his forehead throbbing. A couple of times he looked like he might try to say something else, but without another word, he turned and stormed off the porch.

"Wait, there's one other thing before you go," David called after him.

Billy hesitated.

"I've been trying to get in touch with an old friend," David continued, "but I haven't had much success. Heinrich Albrecht? Maybe you know him? If you do, tell him I've been looking for him."

Billy shot him a puzzled look before stomping off to his truck. David shut the door.

Now the waiting began.

———

JAMIE PULLED up alongside Addie as she walked home from school. When she looked up, her eyes were swollen. She'd been crying.

"Hey," he said. "I think we need to talk."

She nodded. After glancing over her shoulder, she climbed into his pickup. He turned into the driveway of the abandoned house and parked the truck where it couldn't be seen from the road.

Addie wouldn't look at him. Instead, she stared at her hands resting in her lap. "I'm sorry about your friend."

Jamie shook his head. "It's not your fault."

"But it is," she protested. "He's dead because of what I did."

"You didn't kill him, not really."

She let out a dry chuckle. "Didn't I, though? If I had been driving and took my eyes off the road for a second, and I hit him with my car because I wasn't paying attention, it still would have been my fault even if I didn't mean it. People go to jail all the time for things like that. How is this any different?"

"Addie, look at me." He waited until she did. "You couldn't have known what was going to happen. He tripped over the cord of a broken toaster for God's sake."

"I should have known," she snapped. "It was only a matter of time before someone got killed. And this isn't just about him. Someone else got hurt because of a spell I did. I didn't mean for that to happen either. I can't do magic anymore."

"You don't mean that."

"I do mean it. Who else is going to get hurt? What if it's one of my parents next time? Or you or someone you love. Do you want to take that chance?"

Jamie's thoughts immediately went to Amy Lynn and Ginny. "No, I suppose not."

She reached into her bag and pulled out a red flannel sack tied with a length of black ribbon. "This is it. This is the last piece of magic I'm doing." She handed the sack to him. "You saved me the trouble of figuring out how to get this to you before tonight. I made you a mojo bag."

Jamie turned it over in his hands. The bag was heavier than it looked. "A what?"

"A mojo bag, to protect you tonight. There are herbs, a bit of dirt, and ... some other things inside."

He held it up to his nose and immediately wished he hadn't. "What do I do with it?"

"Him."

He shot her a look. "Excuse me?"

"The mojo bag is the physical embodiment of a spiritual ally, not an inanimate object," Addie explained. "And his name is Edward."

Jamie eyed the bag dubiously. "The bag's name is Edward?"

"Yes," she replied, "and you need to address him as such. Otherwise he won't help you."

Jamie was about to make a joke, but the dead serious expression on Addie's face convinced him not to. "Well, the whole rest of the world seems turned upside down, so why not? What do I do with Edward?"

"You wear him under your clothes, and he'll protect you from any evil forces you come across tonight."

"You mean like evil spirits? Demons and shit like that?"

Addie cocked her head to one side. She seemed amused ... almost. "It's the Klan. All that concentrated hate. You don't think the 'demons and shit' are going to pass up on the opportunity to have their fill?"

Jamie shivered despite the heat of the day. "I guess I never thought about it."

He expected the danger to come from flesh-and-bone men, not spirits he couldn't see.

"You shouldn't have to worry, though, as long as you have Edward close."

But Jamie did worry. He began to think joining the Klan was a bad idea all the way around. "Are you sure you can't do any more magic? Another finding spell, maybe? Something to tell us who the original owner of those papers is?"

"It's not like a mail-order catalog. You can't call up and ask for whatever you want. It's more like a negotiation with the spirit world. There's a back-and-forth. You ask nicely for something, offer up a gift or two, and maybe the spirits oblige you." She twisted her mouth into a scowl. "Or maybe they kill someone by making them trip over a toaster."

"Addie—"

She held up a hand. "Don't ask me again. Please."

Jamie sighed. "David's not going to be happy."

"David can do his own magic," Addie spat.

"He says he can't."

"Well, then he needs to figure it out." She opened the door to the pickup. "Be careful tonight, Jamie. I mean that."

Jamie sat in his pickup for a minute or so after Addie left. He tried hard to avoid looking over at the abandoned house, afraid he might see something moving inside again.

"Well, Edward, I guess it's just you and me," he muttered, holding up the red flannel mojo bag.

Edward didn't reply.

———

ADDIE STALKED HOME, becoming more and more furious with each step. How could Jamie and David expect her to keep doing magic after they'd seen what had happened? How could they ignore the danger? Or maybe they didn't care about the danger. Maybe they didn't care who got hurt, so long as her spells got them what they wanted.

By the time she reached the house, she'd worked herself up into a lather. It didn't help she had to walk by her mother's camellia bush where she'd buried the lemon in the jar of vinegar. After she found out about Rose, she came home and dug it up as soon as she could, but from what she'd heard, Rose wasn't any better.

As soon as she walked in the door, her mother came out of the kitchen brandishing a wooden spoon. The smell of pot roast wafted in behind her.

"You're a little late today," she said. "Something happen?"

Addie shook her head. "No. Just needed a little time to catch up on my lesson plans."

Her mother raised an eyebrow. "Are you sure everything's okay? You seem upset."

"No, everything's fine." She forced a smile.

Her mother's hands went directly to her hips. "Adelaide Prichard. You tell me what's wrong."

While Addie could keep a lot from her mother, there were some things she'd never be able to hide.

Addie sighed. "You ever been in a situation where someone expects you to do all the work, without even understanding how much work there is?"

To Addie's surprise, her mother started laughing. "Of course, I have. It's called being a mother. Is this about something going on at school?"

"It's a little complicated," Addie said.

Her mother gave her a reassuring smile. "Well, whatever it is, I wouldn't let it get to you. You do what your heart tells you is the right thing, and the rest will sort itself out. Now I could really use your help in the kitchen with this pot roast. Your father is going to be home soon."

Addie went to her room to drop off her bag. She tossed it on her bed. It fell over, and her grandmother's red spell book tumbled out. She felt a pang of guilt. She couldn't imagine how this was going to sort itself out. Grandma Zee had obviously meant for her to have the book, for her to use it, but how could she after what happened? She clearly wasn't the right person to carry on her grandmother's legacy. Jamie and David were going to have to stay mad. She grabbed the book and shoved it in the drawer of her desk before she went to join her mother in the kitchen.

The shadow things whispered to one another after she left.

———

HE DABBED the sweat off his forehead with his handkerchief. The room was packed, the air thick and heavy from the heat of all the bodies. The low din of a dozen quiet conversations surrounded him. The meeting time was getting close. Most everyone had already arrived, as far as he could tell, though a few stragglers were still coming in.

No sign of the guest of honor, yet, though.

Curious.

He spotted Billy standing by himself in a corner with a look on his face that would wither a cactus. He grinned. No better opportunity was going to present itself. He pushed his way through the crowd toward the youngest MacNeil brother.

"Hey, Billy, why so glum?"

Billy glared at him. "None of your business."

He held up his hands. "Okay, fine. I'm just trying to make small talk."

"Maybe you should do that somewhere else," Billy growled. "I'm not much for talking right now."

He followed Billy's gaze over to where Rhett and Danny were having a serious discussion, no doubt regarding the whereabouts of their guest of honor. "I saw them yelling at you earlier. Why do you let them treat you that way?"

"I said it's none of your business."

He persisted. "They really shouldn't, you know—talk to you like that, I mean."

Billy shrugged. "That's the way brothers are."

He cocked his head to one side. "Is it, though?"

Billy shot him a look somewhere between *Why do you care?* and

Go away or my fist is going to meet your face. "You wouldn't understand. You don't have any brothers."

At the moment it didn't matter to him if Billy wanted him to go away. "How do you know I don't have any brothers? I understand enough to know I'd never call my brother an idiot. And I'd never let him call me one either."

Billy shook his head. "It's not like that. Sometimes Rhett gets mad. He doesn't really mean all the things he says. He can't help it."

"So, what's your excuse for Danny?" he asked.

"Danny just agrees with Rhett."

"Do you agree with him, Billy? Do you think you're an idiot? Do you think you're a screw-up?"

Billy shrugged. "Seems like I screw up more things than I get right."

"Sounds like a self-fulfilling prophecy to me."

"A what?"

"They don't give you a chance, Billy. That's the problem. If they'd only give you a chance, you'd show them what you could do."

Billy grunted. "And how do you know?"

"Because I've watched you. You're strong, and you're smart. If you stood up for yourself more, you could be the one in charge of this town."

"I'm not so sure about that."

He glanced around before leaning in. "Rhett and Danny are just afraid you'll find your voice," he said as he looked Billy in the eye. "That's why they put you down all the time."

Billy snorted. "Afraid? Rhett's not afraid of anything."

He chuckled. "Everyone's afraid of something, and it's really not hard to figure out what Rhett's afraid of. You can see it in his eyes every time he blows up at someone. He's afraid of losing control. He's got this whole town under his thumb. Danny and you, too. But he's terrified it will all go away. He's scared out of his pants he's going to wake up one day and no one is going to do what he says, just because he's Rhett MacNeil. So, he screams and swears and stomps his feet and turns red."

"You don't know Rhett at all if that's what you believe." Billy's voice lacked a certain amount of conviction, though.

From the front of the room a bell rang, a signal the meeting was about to start.

"Watch Rhett tonight, and think about what I said," he told Billy. "Then come find me after the meeting if you want to talk some more."

———

JAMIE STEPPED out of his pickup into the balmy evening. The steeple of the First Baptist Church, black against the purple-orange sky, cast a long shadow over the parking lot. Jamie counted more than a few cars he recognized from working on them at the shop. He didn't know how he was going to look some people in the eye anymore.

Not that there were any people to look in the eye currently. No one was there to meet him or show him where to go. He wandered around outside the church looking for any sign of a living person. After about five minutes trying every door he came across, he finally found one that was unlocked. He slipped inside to discover himself in a darkened hallway.

Still no sign of anyone.

"Hello," he called. "Anyone here?"

No answer, but muffled voices echoed from somewhere in the church.

Jamie placed a hand near his heart, closing over the lump beneath his shirt made by the mojo bag Addie had given him. "Okay, Edward, don't fail me now."

If he didn't know better, he would have sworn the bag pulsed under his fingers.

Jamie followed the voices down the hall, past one closed door after another, darkness spilling out underneath each one. He imagined the church on Sunday morning, full of people, full of noise and movement, full of light. Welcoming. Comforting. But in the deepening evening, the empty church unnerved him. Something wasn't right about the still, the quiet, the shadows. More than once, he stopped to listen, to make sure he was going in the right direction. The voices came from up ahead, he was almost certain, but there were whispers, too, coming from those dark rooms, tempting him to open the doors and come face-to-face with what was inside.

Ahead of him the hallway ended at a juncture, light spilling from around a corner. He practically ran the last few yards. There, he found a set of double doors and his father-in-law pacing back and forth. It was the first time Jamie had ever seen George wearing his Klan robes.

His stomach turned. He knew. Of course he knew, but a small part of him still lived in denial of the truth, still held onto a shred of hope he had somehow gotten everything all wrong. That part of him died.

George gave an exasperated sigh. "There you are. Where have you been?" Jamie opened his mouth to ask why no one had met him outside to show him where to go, but George cut him off. "Not now, we don't have time. Here, put this on."

He handed Jamie a white robe. Jamie struggled to pull it over his head and find the arm holes. George had to help him get it adjusted. When he looked down at himself, he had to fight to keep from retching.

"Now put your hands together in front of you," George ordered.

"Why?" Jamie asked.

"Dammit, Jamie, just do it."

Jamie did as he was told. George produced a length of rope and used it to tie his hands together. Panic rising, Jamie struggled against the bindings.

"Calm down. It's part of the ritual. I've got to blindfold you, too. Hold still."

He put a piece of cloth over Jamie's eyes and tied it tight around his head.

"When we go inside, I'm not your father-in-law anymore. Do whatever I tell you, and don't speak unless you're spoken to. Do you understand?"

Jamie nodded.

George gripped his arm. "I'll guide you. Now walk."

He led Jamie through the doors. The heat hit Jamie in the face as soon as he entered the room. How many other people were there Jamie couldn't tell, but it must have been packed. The voices he'd heard from outside died away, but the other voices didn't. The raspy whispers. The mocking laughter. Jamie tried to ignore them. They weren't real, just a product of his fear.

He hoped.

"Stop here," George whispered. "On your knees."

Jamie complied.

"Before we begin tonight," a voice boomed, "let us take a moment of silence to remember our brother Robert Rawlins, taken from this world tragically all too soon."

Rhett MacNeil.

The room became deathly still and quiet, except for those damned whispers. Like flies buzzing in his ears. He wanted to swat them away, but he couldn't move.

After what seemed like an eternity, Rhett spoke again. "Faithful Brother, you may now speak."

"Your Excellency," George said, in a tone of voice Jamie had never heard him use before, "I present to you James Fletcher, who, prompted by unselfish motives, desires a more noble life. In consequence, he has made the honorable decision to forsake the world of selfishness and fraternal alienation and emigrate to the delectable bounds of the Invisible Empire and become a citizen of the same."

"Do you deem this candidate worthy?" Rhett asked.

"Indeed, Your Excellency, he is most worthy," George replied.

The bile rose in Jamie's throat.

"Stand up, James Fletcher," Rhett ordered.

George helped Jamie to his feet. The ropes were untied from his hands, and the blindfold was pulled from his eyes. In a room lit only by candlelight, a circle of white-robed figures surrounded him. Some wore hoods covering their faces. Some didn't. Among those whose faces he could see were Bartholomew Avery, Boyd Parker, Danny and Billy MacNeil, and Fenton Graham, the pastor of the First Baptist Church.

Rhett stood directly in front of him. Unlike the others, he wore a blue cape draped over his shoulders. Between them was a makeshift "altar" draped with an American flag. On top rested a cross, a dagger, a Bible, and a large goblet.

Sweat beaded up on Jamie's forehead. His heart pounded. The mojo bag grew warm and thumped in time with the beating of his heart. Something else was in that room. Jamie could see the shadows dart back and forth out of the corner of his eye.

"Each of the following questions must be answered by a loud an emphatic, 'yes,'" Rhett said. "Do you understand?"

George elbowed Jamie in the ribs.

"Yes," Jamie replied.

"Is the motive prompting your ambition to be a Klansman serious and unselfish?" Rhett asked.

"Yes," Jamie answered.

The mojo bag got warmer. The thumping grew stronger. The whispers grew louder.

"Are you a native-born, white, gentle American citizen?"

"Yes."

Hotter even. Stronger even. Louder even.

"Are you absolutely free of and opposed to any allegiance of any nature to any cause, government, people, sect, or ruler that is foreign to the United States of America?"

"Yes."

It was getting hard to breathe. Jamie could barely hear Rhett over the thumping of the mojo bag and the raspy voice in his ear.

"Do you believe in the tenants of the Christian Religion?"

"Yes."

Thump. Thump. Thump. The sweat poured down Jamie's face and drenched his shirt under his robe.

"Do you believe in, and will you faithfully strive for the eternal maintenance of white supremacy?"

"Yes."

Thump. Thump. Thump. Laughter now. Horrible, malicious laughter. Shadows flying all around. Bat wings and claws and barbed tails. Why couldn't anyone else see them?

"Will you faithfully obey our constitution and laws and conform willingly to all our usages, requirements, and regulations?"

"Yes."

Thump. Thump. Thump. The mojo bag burned. Jamie didn't know if he could take it anymore. He was suffocating. How many more questions were there? How did he make the voices stop?

Rhett gave a subtle nod. "James Fletcher, you have duly qualified to journey in quest of citizenship in the Invisible Empire. You will now recite the Oath of the Klan. Place your left hand over your heart and raise your right hand up toward heaven."

Jamie positioned his hands as he was told and choked out the entire oath, repeating each line after Rhett. It tasted like vinegar and turpentine on his tongue.

"Mortal man cannot assume a more binding oath," Rhett proclaimed. "Character and courage alone will enable you to keep it. Always remember that to keep it means to you honor, happiness, and life, but to violate it means death, dishonor, and disgrace. Kneel, James Fletcher, so that you may be welcomed into the Invisible Empire."

Jamie went back down on his knees. Without warning, all the candles save for one were blown out. The shadow things surged forward and filled up the space. The smell of blood and grave dirt filled Jamie's nostrils. Rhett lifted the goblet and the dagger from the altar and walked up to Jamie.

He poured a small trickle of oil from the cup over Jamie's head, and then holding the cup and the dagger in the air, he shouted, "By the authority vested in me by our Emperor, I now declare and proclaim you a citizen of the Invisible Empire, Knights of the Ku Klux Klan and invest you with the title of Klansman, the most honorable title among men. Stand up, brother."

Jamie stood, and was presented with his hood, which George helped place on his head.

Rhett gave another subtle nod, and a chorus of voices rose up singing "Just As I Am." More hymns followed. "Onward Christian Soldiers." "Nothing But the Blood of Jesus."

What can wash away my sin?
Nothing but the blood of Jesus.
Nothing but the blood.
Blood.

Blood everywhere Jamie looked. Dripping down the walls, covering the faces of everyone else in the room. Staining his own white robe crimson red. Jamie's knees nearly gave out. He could barely think, could barely do anything other than listen and follow along with the harsh, raspy voice of the shadow telling him dark and horrible things. He would have believed it, would have given into it were it not for the throbbing of the mojo bag, reminding Jamie of the cadence of his own heart.

Someone was watching him. Jamie turned his head as far as he dared and met the gaze of one of the men in the circle. Only his piercing blue eyes were visible through the holes in his hood, but Jamie held his breath. He was looking into the eyes of Heinrich Albrecht. He looked back at Jamie like he *knew*. He knew why Jamie was there. Jamie was an imposter, a liar, a traitor. Nothing but death, dishonor, and disgrace for him.

After the words of the last hymn faded away, Rhett raised his arms. "Our Heavenly Father, we beseech thee that an overwhelming sense of dedication will embrace this man before thee. Look on that to which he aspires and bless him in that which he hopes to overcome. Through Christ, our Lord, we pray. Amen. You may now take our brother and educate him on our signs, grips, ways, and words."

George took Jamie by the arm and led him out of the room. He imparted to Jamie the secret handshakes and signs and code words the Klan used to do their business, but Jamie barely paid attention. He was just thankful the horrible, raspy voice was gone.

When Jamie got home, he wadded up the robe and the hood and

stuffed them both behind the seat of his truck. He'd figure out what to do with them later. Inside the house was dark. Ginny had already gone to bed. Jamie wasn't going to be able to sleep any time soon, so he went out to the back, to his other truck. He climbed into the bed and lit a cigarette.

"What have I done?" he asked the nighttime.

21

FRIDAY, SEPTEMBER 7, 1962

J amie pulled his cap down over his eyes as he entered the tent. Rows of folding chairs had been set up in front of a makeshift stage. An old, beat-up upright piano stood on one side of the stage. On the other side was an American flag. Jamie took a seat in the back, hoping to stay unnoticed. Overhead, the canvas tent billowed in the evening breeze, and strings of electric lights quietly hummed.

The tent was about half-full when he got there, but as the time to start got closer, the crowd swelled until all the chairs were filled and the overflow spilled outside. Jamie spotted more than a few familiar faces. Fred Peterson. Herbert and Harriet Page. Don and Betty Evans. Hank Porter. He wondered what Pastor Griggs would say if he was there.

At seven-thirty sharp, three women took to the stage. They all had the same bouffant hair-dos and wore matching dresses, except for the color—blue, yellow, and green. If it hadn't been for that, Jamie wouldn't have been able to tell them apart.

"How y'all doing this evening?" the blue one asked. "I'm Betty Powell, and these are my sisters Patty and Minnie, and together we're the Powell Sisters. Are y'all ready to make a joyful noise?"

A shout rose up from the crowd. The yellow one—Patty, Jamie thought—took a seat at the piano and banged out the first few bars of "I'll Fly Away." The sisters sang in three-part harmony, and the crowd joined in whenever they knew the words. After "I'll Fly Away," they moved on to "Will the Circle Be Unbroken?" then "Rock of Ages" and "The Lily in the Valley." People threw their hands up in the air and danced in the aisles. This wasn't like any church service Jamie had ever seen.

Eventually the Powell Sisters retreated from the stage, and a short, slight man wearing a pair of round glasses took their place. Surely this wasn't Ewell Holt, renowned orator, but when he spoke, his voice boomed through the tent and beyond.

"The Gospel says in Matthew 7:15, 'Beware of false prophets, which come to you in sheep's clothing, but inwardly they are ravening wolves.' I tell you this right now, you are following false prophets. 'Me?' You say, 'Surely not!' But I'm her to tell you it's true. Oh, it may not be so obvious nowadays. There's no golden calves to worship or temples dedicated to false gods, but our society is full of these wolves in sheep's clothing, ready to lead you into ruin through drink and gambling and the pleasures of the flesh."

The preacher's words wove a spell over the crowd. As he talked, he grew more and more agitated, and the crowd grew more and more frenzied, with people shouting out "Amen!" and "Hallelujah!" at anything and everything he said.

"And God is angry," he shouted. "He was angry in the Old Testament. Psalms 79:5 says, 'How long, Lord? Wilt thou be angry for ever? Shall thy jealousy burn like fire?' He was angry in the New Testament. Romans 1:18 says, 'For the wrath of God is revealed from heaven against all ungodliness and unrighteousness of men, who hold the truth in unrighteousness.' And he's angry today. He is calling on every single one of you to repent. Repent from your selfishness. Repent from your slothfulness. Repent from your covetousness. Repent and turn back to Him before it's too late. Who among you is ready today?"

The crowd roared.

Reverend Holt walked over to a box on the side of the stage. He lifted the lid and reached inside and Jamie watched in horror as he pulled out two giant rattlesnakes, one in each hand. He held them aloft above his head.

The Powell Sisters returned to the stage. The yellow one had a tambourine this time. The other two clapped and stomped their feet while she smacked the tambourine with her hand and the preacher danced in circles. The two snakes writhed and twisted around his arms.

Jamie had heard of snake-handlers before, but he'd never seen one in real life. He could barely watch. Reverend Holt was going to get himself bitten, but no one else seemed to care. Jamie scanned the crowd, looking for anyone else alarmed by what was going on, but all he saw were ecstatic faces.

The preacher dared anyone with faith enough in God to join him. An elderly woman in a pink dress with a small pillbox hat danced her way onto the stage. The preacher handed her one of the snakes. Then he reached into the box and took out a third. A young man who couldn't have been older than twenty-five came up on stage and the preacher handed him a snake as well. Seemingly in a trance, the three of them danced in a circle holding the twisting reptiles.

Finally, after several agonizing minutes, Ewell Holt took the snakes and placed them back in the box. The others left the stage, and the preacher led the congregation in a prayer. After that, the service was over. People stood to leave and headed out of the tent toward their cars, but Jamie still didn't have the answers he had come for. He looked at Reverend Holt, still on the stage, watching everyone as they left, scanning the congregation, as if he was looking for someone.

Jamie pushed against the crowd, making his way toward the stage.

"Excuse me," he called when he got to the edge of the stage, looking up at the preacher.

The preacher looked down at him, a little surprised. "Yes, what is it?"

"My name is Jamie Fletcher. I need to talk with you."

He smiled, but it didn't reach his eyes. "You don't need my help, whatever is troubling you. Whatever you have going on, you should give up to God. He alone is the one who can grant you peace."

"It's not like that. I need to talk to you about someone who attended your service maybe a few weeks ago. His name was Ted Sargent."

The smile melted. "I talk to a lot of people, Mr. Fletcher, and you understand anything they tell me must be kept in confidence."

"I understand. I really do, but you see Ted Sargent wasn't his real name. It was Jeffrey DiCarlo, and he was murdered. In any event, I don't think he was coming to you for spiritual counseling."

A small crack opened in the preacher's façade. "Isn't that something best left for the police?"

"The police aren't going to be much help in this case."

"I don't understand what you think I can do." He scanned the thinning crowd again.

"Are you looking for someone?" Janie asked. "Maybe Bobby Rawlins? He wasn't able to make it tonight, since he's dead, too."

For the first time, the preacher looked Jamie directly in the eye. "I can give you a few minutes if you'll wait."

Jamie waited until everyone else had left except for Reverend Holt, the Powell Sisters, and the small crew taking up the folding chairs and stacking them in a corner. The preacher motioned for Jamie to come with him. He led Jamie to a small trailer behind the tent. He opened the door and beckoned for Jamie to join him inside.

There was barely enough room for the two of them. Jamie sat on a wooden stool near the door. The preacher took a seat on what appeared to be his bed. At the foot of the bed was a coffee pot and a hot pad and a box, but as far as Jamie could tell, that was it.

"Do you know why Mr. Sargent came to see me?" Reverend Holt asked.

"I don't have the first clue," Jamie answered, "but I know there's something going on in this town, and I know he was killed because of it."

"When Bobby Rawlins contacted me, he only told me it was

about Mr. Sargent and that it was important. How was he mixed up in whatever you're talking about?"

"He was snooping around in things he shouldn't have."

Reverend Holt cocked an eyebrow. "Like you?"

Jamie twisted his mouth into a grimace. "I wasn't given a choice."

Reverend Holt nodded solemnly. "Well, in that case, Mr. Sargent was an FBI agent, Mr. Fletcher. He was sent to Avalon to keep an eye on the Klan, to make sure things didn't get too out of hand when the black kids started going to the white schools."

"But why did he want to talk to you? Unless you're more than just a snake-handling preacher."

Reverend Holt chuckled. "No, I am just a snake-handling preacher. God put me on this path a long time ago, and I go where He tells me. I have put my faith in Him. Tell me, where is your faith?"

Jamie eyed the preacher warily. "I have faith enough. I don't need to prove it by picking up a rattlesnake."

"Is that what you think I'm trying to do? To prove my own faith?"

"It's not?"

The box next to the bed moved. Jamie's heart skipped a beat. Reverend Holt reached down and casually lifted the lid. He put his hand inside and pulled out a rattlesnake, not a fully grown one like he had on stage, but big enough. "When I pick up serpents, I'm showing everyone the goodness of God."

Paralyzed, Jamie watched the snake coil around the preacher's arm. "And what about the others, the ones that come up on stage from the congregation. What are they showing?"

"If they feel compelled by God to participate, it's not my place to stop them." He extended the arm with the writhing reptile toward Jamie. "Would you like to take it up, Mr. Fletcher?"

Jamie backed away as far as he could in the cramped space. "No, thank you. Maybe another day."

The preacher grinned. "Maybe."

Jamie didn't take his eyes off the snake. "So, if you're 'just a snake-handling preacher,' why did Ted Sargent come to you?"

"Because of who I was before." The preacher shifted so the snake could crawl over his shoulders to his other arm. "During the Second World War, I worked for the OSS, the Office of Strategic Services."

"You were a spy."

Reverend Holt winced. "If you want to put it that way. The truth is you never can quite leave that line of work behind. I still find myself having to lend my knowledge and expertise from time to time. Ted Sargent was given my name as someone he could reach out to if things got hairy for him, which they did."

Hairy. An interesting choice of words.

Jamie's gaze followed the snake's head bobbing up and down, its tongue flicking in and out of its mouth. "Did he tell you exactly how things got 'hairy'?"

Ewell shook his head. "He didn't give me all the details, but he said he had proof a Nazi war criminal was living here in disguise."

"Why didn't he go to his bosses at the FBI?"

"Because he didn't think they would handle the situation right." Reverend Holt splayed his fingers to give the snake purchase as it explored its surroundings. "Mr. Sargent and I both agreed they wouldn't properly bring him to justice. They'd likely insist on arresting him and putting him on trial."

"That's not properly bringing him to justice?"

"For what he is? No. He deserves to die." For a moment the glint in the preacher's eye matched the glint in the snake's.

"You know more than you're saying."

"That's how the game is played, Mr. Fletcher." The preacher gently bent his arm so the snake's head was level with his face. "How badly do you want the information?"

"You don't mean ..."

The snake doubled back, twisting its body into a loop like a noose. Jamie's heart pounded. Words caught in his throat as the preacher stared at him expectantly, a benign smile on his face.

Then he laughed. "Don't worry, Mr. Fletcher. I'm not going to make you handle a serpent if you're not called to do so. That wouldn't be right. Your promise to keep everything I've told you a secret is enough for me. Can you give me that?"

Still unable to speak, Jamie nodded.

"There's a village in southern Bavaria named Obersalzburg. The Bavarian Alps were riddled with Nazi bases—secret bunkers, prison camps, research facilities. After the War was over, I was attached to an army unit charged with clearing the area of resistance fighters."

"Werewolves," Jamie whispered.

"Yes, that's what they called themselves. Rather dramatic, don't you think? But if there's one thing the Nazis were good at, it was putting on a show." The snake dangled off Reverend Holt's arm, threatening to fall to the floor. Before it could, he took it in his other hand. "In any event, one day we stumbled upon a Nazi base underneath an old hunting lodge up in the mountains over the village. It seemed abandoned, the staff having done a half-assed job of trying to destroy the records of whatever they were doing there."

"*Seemed* abandoned?"

"Am I giving away the ending? Let me not get ahead of myself. In the main building we found a room full of strange objects. Daggers, stone carvings, jewelry. We would have thought they were merely artifacts collected by the owner of the house were it not for the voices and the moving shadows. It was ... unnerving."

Jamie flashed back to the voices and the shadows at the Klan induction.

"Below the house, carved into the mountain itself, was where we found the cells," the preacher continued, "a whole row, each with a heavy steel door. The locks were all mangled and broken. Blood covered the walls. At the end of the hallway, there was a circular room with strange symbols written all over the floor. I've never seen anything like it. Whatever they were, they were not of God. We came across it there."

"It?"

"An abomination," Reverend Holt replied. "A creature. I don't know how to describe it. In the darkness I didn't get a good look, and after it ripped apart the lieutenant, I didn't have any interest in what it looked like. All I can remember are claws and fangs, the putrid smell, and a howl that drove the reason right out of me."

"Of the ten of us, only three made it out of that house. To this day, I don't know how I survived, except by the grace of God. When we got back, we were ordered by the higher-ups not to say anything about what we saw. It never happened. That lodge didn't exist."

"But you told Ted Sargent, and you're telling me."

"I had to. He had a right to know what he was up against, just like you. I can't have any more lives on my conscience than I already do. And I gave him the name of someone who might be able to help him. Someone who works for the State of Israel. Beyond that, I told him I couldn't do anything save pray for him. And now that I've told you my story, I don't think I can do anything more for you either."

"You've helped a lot. Trust me."

He held out his arm one more time. The snake perched on it seemed to regard Jamie with an appraising eye. "Are you sure you don't want to show your faith in God's goodness?"

"I'm pretty sure," Jamie replied.

"Pity. It's a powerful feeling." He lowered his arm into the box, and the snake slithered back in.

Jamie stood, taking care not to bang his head. "I shouldn't take any more of your time. Thank you for speaking with me, Reverend Holt."

"I'll pray for you, too, Mr. Fletcher," he said as Jamie left.

———

DAVID LEANED back in his chair and closed his eyes. The Nazi papers lay scattered across the table, along with his grandfather's spell book, a copy of the Torah, and a notebook filled with line after line of letters and numbers. He was getting a headache. He wished he could light some herbs on fire and call it a day.

If Addie's magic was like a negotiation with the spirit world, his was more like breaking a code. The Torah and the rest of the Jewish sacred texts were full of hidden messages waiting to be found— magical formulae, special knowledge, glimpses of the underpinning of Creation itself.

But he was being unfair to Addie. She used her Bible. And he'd had his share of deliberations with angels and demons and everything in between. So, maybe they weren't all that far apart after all.

At the end of the day, it didn't really matter, though, because nothing was working. He had always been able to feel the magic gathering whenever he recited a spell, but ever since Jakob died, he felt nothing. He didn't even know why he tried, other than out of sheer desperation.

He dug his hand into his shirt pocket for another cigarette as the front door of the shack blew off its hinges. Easily seven feet tall with a broad muscular body covered in thick, brown hair, the werewolf crouched in the opening it made and glowered at him.

Intelligence lived behind its yellow eyes. Anyone assuming a werewolf was only a mindless killing machine made a deadly mistake. It retained its human intelligence, even during the full moon when the urge to kill was impossible to resist.

"Hello, Heinrich," David said.

He—for the monster was without a doubt male—bared his teeth and flexed his claws before he lunged at David. David threw the table up on its side. The werewolf slammed into it, splintering it into a thousand pieces, but not before David was able to scramble away. He swore at himself for not having his gun. It sat on his bed on the other side of the shack. His chances of getting to it without being shredded to ribbons were slim to none.

And Slim just got run over by a truck.

David picked up an empty bottle of whisky from the floor and threw it at the werewolf. The bottle shattered against the monster's chest, shards of glass embedding themselves in his pelt. He barely slowed down.

David uttered a phrase he'd heard his grandfather say a few times when he was upset or frustrated. David used to think it was some old Yiddish curse, but as he got older, he wasn't so sure. He never heard anyone else say it. He figured the phrase was just a verbal quirk his grandfather had, until the werewolf halted in his tracks and yelped as if he had been smacked across the muzzle.

He glared at David, but there was confusion in his eyes. David was perplexed, too. He wasn't sure what he'd done. The werewolf snarled and lunged. David blurted out his grandfather's curse again, and like before, the werewolf stopped and yowled.

Before the creature could recover, David sprinted across the shack and snatched the gun up from his bed. With a roar, the werewolf leapt at him. David fired. The silver bullets slammed into the werewolf's shoulder, and he crashed to the ground, screaming and pawing at the wound.

Finally, he struggled to his feet. His arm hung useless at his side. With one last glare at David, the werewolf vaulted through the hole he had made and retreated into the night.

David strode across the floor to where his grandfather's spell book lay face down. He picked it up. The pages were crumpled, but it was otherwise in one piece. It felt warm in his hands.

"Thanks, Zeyde," he whispered to his grandfather.

———

MARCUS JONES PULLED on his jacket as he exited Coach's office and stepped into the dark and empty locker room. His footsteps echoed on the hard concrete floor. All his teammates had left already. They'd probably picked a spot out in the woods somewhere to get drunk and celebrate another win. Without him. Even though he'd thrown the pass that led to the winning touchdown.

Again.

He should have been mad about it, and he had been, for a little while. Forced to use Coach's private shower because no one would share a locker room with him. Pretty much left out any time the team got together. But now he didn't care. He was marking time until he could get out of there anyway. Join the army, go anywhere in the world that wasn't Avalon, South Carolina. His mom didn't like that plan, but he was going to be eighteen soon, and she wouldn't be able to tell him what to do anyway.

Besides, she hadn't asked him if he wanted to leave Ezekiel's Mill.

and go to Avalon High School, if he wanted to be spit on, threatened, and called names. All that stopped when they figured out he was good at winning football games. But he saw past their cheers and their fake smiles and their high-fives in the hallway. He still wasn't good enough and never would be. They'd already shown their true colors. He wasn't going to forget.

He stepped outside into the balmy night. A slight breeze took the edge off the heat, which seemed to want to stick around that year. The parking lot was deserted. His uncle was supposed to pick him up. Must have forgotten again. Nothing to do but wait. His mom would get it sorted out.

"Great game tonight, Marcus."

He nearly jumped out of his skin at the sound of the voice. He scanned the parking lot for the speaker, but no one was there. "Who said that?"

"Just a fan." Something about the low, rough voice didn't sound quite right.

Marcus spun in a circle, trying to figure out what direction the voice was coming from. "This better not be another joke, 'cause it ain't funny. Guys? Where are you?"

"A joke? Why would you think that? Who would play a joke on Avalon High School's star quarterback?"

Something shifted in the shadows where the lights didn't reach.

"You're kidding, right? That's not me."

The hidden speaker grunted. "Sure seems that way. Must be proud of yourself, putting that Cole Carter in his place."

Marcus frowned. He was liking this conversation less and less. He wished his uncle would show up. "What? I haven't done anything to Cole."

"Haven't you? Cole was King of the Hill till you came along and knocked him off," whoever was there in the shadows practically growled.

This was definitely some kind of joke. Now Marcus was annoyed. "Look, whoever you are, all I do is show up and play when Coach tells me to play. I don't have anything against Cole. If he's mad at me, he can come talk to me."

Out of the shadows stepped a coal-black wolf, the largest one Marcus had ever seen. Except it wasn't a wolf. Marcus watched in horror as it reared up on its hind legs and stood like a man. It had the muscled body of an athlete, but with fur and claws. Its yellow eyes shone with malice.

It curled its mouth up in a sort of grin, baring rows of sharp teeth, and spoke again, somehow, in that same unearthly, gravelly voice. "Let's see how fast you can really run."

———

SARAH PUT AWAY THE CARDS. There was no use doing another reading. The outcome would be the same. She blew out the candle, leaving her room in near-darkness. The pale light of the quarter-moon cast faint shadows across the walls. The sheer curtains danced in the breeze coming in through the open window. Outside the frogs and the crickets sang and the owls called.

She ran her hands over the quilt on her bed and traced the stitches with her fingers. Her grandmother had made it. The last thing she wanted was for something to happen to it. She gently, almost reverently, folded it up and set it to one side. Then she sat at the foot of the bed. Briefly, she thought she might read her Bible, but there was nothing in there that could help her now. All that was left to do was wait.

Sarah wished she had time to talk to her brothers. They had always been so good to her. They had always tried to protect her. They never understood she didn't need protecting as much as they did. Except for maybe Calvin. He understood more than the rest, which was why she trusted him to take care of certain things in case something were to happen.

Before long, the frogs and the crickets and the owls fell silent. Sarah willed herself to stay calm as a dark shape loomed on the other side of her window. Two clawed hands grasped the casing, and the monster heaved itself into the room, its massive feet landing with a thud on the wooden floor. It smelled like the forest—damp earth and leaves, lichen and moss, and blood. Its near-white fur glistened in the moonlight. It eyed her hungrily but warily, its long tongue emerging from its lupine mouth to lick its sharp fangs. It was right to be cautious, but Sarah had read her future. No matter what she did, she wouldn't overcome this demon.

She locked gazes with the monster. "My, what big teeth you have."

22

SATURDAY, SEPTEMBER 8, 1962

Marjorie Evans sang "The Sweet By-and-By" as the pall bearers placed Bobby's casket down gently next to a freshly dug hole in the Rawlins family plot. As the last note of the hymn faded away, the pastor from the Avalon First Presbyterian Church stepped forward to speak.

Jamie couldn't remember his name. He was young and new, and he kept stumbling over his words. Somewhere around the third time he said Bobby was in a "better place," Jamie stopped listening. He glanced around at all the somber faces.

The day was overcast and a little wet, but a good portion of the town still turned out for the funeral. Bobby's family sat closest to the casket in folding chairs set out for them. His mother leaned into his father. He had both arms wrapped around her as she sobbed. Jamie couldn't imagine what it felt like to be them. At the same time, he had to wonder what they thought the first time they saw the inside of Bobby's house, or if they had known the state of it beforehand. At least he'd taken Bobby's journal, so they didn't discover his "hobby."

After the service was over, everyone milled about for a few minutes. Conversations drifted, as they do, to the weather, the news, last night's football game. Nobody wants to dwell on the dead for too long, even in the middle of a cemetery. Jamie spotted Billy MacNeil talking to Caleb Murray, who was waving his hands around like a crazy person. No doubt Caleb was telling Billy all about his essential work helping the police blow up underground moonshine stills. He almost felt sorry for Billy. Almost.

A hand came to rest on his shoulder. Jamie turned to see Calvin Jordan. He wore the same suit he'd worn to Jamie's garage when he came to tell Jamie Sarah wanted to meet with him. Always on the thin side, today he looked positively skeletal, pale with hollow eyes. When they shook hands, Calvin's trembled.

"Calvin, it's good to see you again, in spite of the circumstances. Hope everything's going well. How are your brothers and Sarah?"

Jamie was surprised Calvin even showed up. As far as he knew Calvin had never exchanged more than two words with Bobby. He didn't see Sarah, or any of their brothers, or their parents.

Calvin glanced down at his shoes. "That's what I wanted to tell you. Sarah died last night."

Yet another punch in the face. "What? Oh, God, Calvin, I'm so sorry. What happened?"

"She was taken by the shadows."

His answer took Jamie aback. "I'm sorry, she was what?"

"She was taken by the shadows. It happened close on midnight. We heard her scream. We all ran to her room, but the door was locked. By the time we were able to break in, it was too late. She was gone. All we saw was a set of bloody handprints by her open window." Calvin reached into his pocket and pulled out a small envelope with Jamie's name on it. "She told me that if anything happened to her, I should give this to you."

Jamie took the envelope. "Any idea what's inside?"

Calvin shook his head. "No, it's personal to you."

Jamie glanced around to make sure no one else was paying attention to them. "Calvin, if you didn't find her, how do you know she's dead? She could have been kidnapped by someone. Shouldn't you be going to the police?"

He shook his head, "No, she's dead. We all felt it when it happened. The police can't do anything to help her where she is." He paused and took a deep breath. "I'd best be going. As you can imagine, there's a lot to be done."

"Well, if there's anything I can do, you let me know, okay?"

Calvin nodded. "Okay, I will."

Jamie stared down at the envelope in his hands, angry at himself. They'd all been stupid. They thought they had until the next full moon, still a week away, but they didn't. All their talk. All their scheming. For nothing. He tore open the envelope from Sarah. Inside there was a tarot card—the Hanged Man. That must be him.

The man dangled upside-down from a T-shaped tree, tied by one ankle. His hands appeared to be tied behind his back. Strangely, he had a halo around his head, but the oddest thing of all was the smile on his face, almost peaceful.

There was one more thing in the envelope, a piece of paper with Sarah's neat handwriting.

In sacrifice abundance, in surrender, victory.

Sarah had written several Bible verses underneath. Psalm 79:5, "How long, Lord? Wilt thou be angry for ever? Shall thy jealousy burn like fire?" Romans 1:18, "For the wrath of God is revealed from heaven against all ungodliness and unrighteousness of men, who hold the truth in unrighteousness." And finally, Matthew 7:15, "Beware of false prophets, which come to you in sheep's clothing, but inwardly they are ravening wolves." All the same verses Reverend Ewell Holt had used in his sermon.

He crammed everything back into the envelope and shoved it down in his pocket. He needed to talk to David, to let him know time wasn't running out.

It was already too late.

———

GINNY WAS DOING the dinner dishes when Jamie walked into the kitchen later that night. She handed him a pot to dry. "I talked to Harriet Paige at the funeral today."

Jamie grabbed the dishrag. Had he been paying closer attention he might have noticed the odd tone of her voice. "Yeah, how is she?"

"She's fine ... but she did say something interesting. I mentioned you were out at a Chamber of Commerce meeting on Thursday night. She said Herbert was home with her on Thursday and never said anything about a Chamber of Commerce meeting to her."

Jamie froze for a second. His brain whirred as he tried to come up with something to say. "Oh, well, it was a subcommittee meeting, not the full Chamber."

Ginny raised an eyebrow, but otherwise her expression didn't change. "Who else was there?"

"Bartholomew Avery. The MacNeil Brothers. Pastor Graham from the Baptist Church, a few others."

At least that part wasn't a lie.

Any hope Ginny would drop the subject died with the next question, though. "And what was the subcommittee for?"

"What to do with the school integration issue, you know if the media comes back, how to keep them from painting our town in a bad light like they did before." The answer rolled off Jamie's tongue a lot easier than he expected.

Ginny aggressively scrubbed at the plate in her hand. "I see."

Jamie sighed. No use avoiding the elephant in the room. "There's something else wrong, isn't there?"

Ginny put the plate down and glanced sidelong at him. "About time you noticed."

"You want to tell me what it is?"

She looked away. "It's just that you've been gone a lot lately. Night meetings. Working late at the garage. Bailing cousins out of jail you've barely spoken to in ten years. And when you are here, you're not really *here*. I miss you. Your daughter misses you. And she really needs you right now."

Jamie wrapped his arms around Ginny and squeezed. "I'm sorry. There's a lot going on at the garage. And all this business with Bobby. I guess it's got me rattled. I promise to be better, okay."

It was a tiny gesture, barely noticeable, but she pushed back against his embrace.

23

MONDAY, SEPTEMBER 10, 1962

J amie tried more than once on Sunday to reach David, but he never picked up at the phone number he gave. Jamie didn't want to think too hard about what that might mean. He spent all day going through the motions—church, then dinner with his in-laws—aware of Ginny's gaze, aware of the distance, however small, that had opened up between them. He didn't want to admit it, but on Monday morning he was relieved to go to work.

He was the first one at the garage that day. He unlocked his office, but as soon as he stepped inside, he was aware he wasn't alone. A man sat at his desk. The blade of a knife flashed as he flipped it over in his hand.

"Shut the door," the man said.

"How did you get in here?" Jamie asked.

The man leaned forward. "How do you think?"

Jamie's heart leapt into his chest. It was the biker from McGill's, the one he had followed down Assembly Street, the one with the *Wolfsangel* tattoo.

"I know you," was all Jamie could manage to stammer out.

"You know, I asked around about you." The man stood and walked around the desk. "Everyone seems to think you're an all-around decent guy and a pretty good mechanic, so I had to ask myself, why would you be following me, an innocent visitor to your town?"

"Are you an innocent visitor, though?" Jamie asked.

"What makes you think I'm not?"

"The tattoo."

The man glanced down at his arms. "I have a lot of those. Which one are you talking about?"

"The one on your left forearm. The *Wolfsangel*."

The man cocked an eyebrow. "What about it?"

"Where'd you get it? Do you know what it means?"

"Why do you care so much? Are you one of those special dirtbags hung up on Nazi history?"

"So, you do know where it comes from."

"Yeah, I know. I got it when I was in the Klan."

"Was? Does that mean you're not anymore?"

The man grimaced. "Things change. Now I use assholes like you as punching bags."

Before Jamie could react, the biker grabbed him and slammed him against the wall, pinning him there, the knife ready to slash his throat.

"Wait," Jamie pleaded, "you've got it all wrong. I'm not ... one of them."

The biker pressed him harder into the wall. "You're not, are you? Well, if that's so, what were you doing last Thursday night getting yourself inducted into the High Exalted Order of the Knights of the Ku Klux Klan? You don't do that for fun. And you still haven't explained why you were following me. Did the MacNeils send you?"

"The MacNeils? No. Why would the MacNeils send me after you?"

"Let's say I'm not their favorite person right now." He held the knife so close Jamie could barely breathe. "I need you to listen to me. You stay out of my way. I see your face again, I won't be so kind as to leave it intact. Do you understand?"

He backed away, but he kept the knife in view.

Jamie rubbed his neck. "Look, you can believe whatever you want. I don't agree with anything the Klan stands for, but something's ... wrong. They've gotten violent. People have died. And more people are going to die. I thought ... I thought if I joined, I could stop them."

The biker laughed. "You're going to stop them? That's probably the dumbest thing I've ever heard."

"Yeah, well, no one ever accused me of being smart."

The biker turned serious again. "I really don't care what you believe. What I said stands. You stay out of my way."

"Why? What are you planning to do?"

Other than getting yourself killed.

"My brother is still in," the biker explained. "I want to get him out. After that, well that's my business, although I suspect you'll hear about it."

"Who's your brother?" Jamie asked.

"Everett Gordon."

Jamie knew Everett. He went to the same church. He moved to Avalon about ten years before. Perfect timing, Jamie realized, for when Heinrich Albrecht probably showed up in town. "Funny, he's never mentioned having a brother."

"He wouldn't. We had a falling out when I left the Klan. We haven't spoken since."

Jamie eyed the blade of the knife still in the man's hand. "I don't believe I've had the pleasure of learning your name."

The biker headed for the door, leaning in close as he passed by Jamie. "It's Clint. Clint Gordon. Remember what I said. I mean to handle things my way."

"You should reconsider whatever you're planning, Clint," Jamie called after him as he left. "You're putting yourself in danger."

Clint paused. "Thanks, but I know what I'm doing."

Jamie locked gazes with him. Briefly—just briefly—he considered telling Clint about the werewolf, but he didn't see any point. "I hope more people aren't going to get hurt."

Clint's mouth twisted into a crooked grin. "Nobody innocent anyway."

He turned and walked out of the garage. Moments later, a motorcycle revved up and sped off.

————

JAMIE DECIDED to pick up Amy Lynn from school that afternoon. They put her bike in the bed of his truck and drove into town. He took her to the five-and-dime where they found Jasper behind the counter. Amy watched with rapt attention as he made her a root beer float. As he promised, he put two cherries on top for her, and she clapped as he slid the big, frosty glass toward her. She sat on one of the big stools and delightedly slurped the float down while Jamie and Jasper talked.

"So, how have things been?" Jasper asked.

Jamie shrugged. "They've been okay, I guess."

Jasper's expression grew serious. "No, I mean, really. How are you holding up with everything? Outside of Bobby's family, you're probably the one who spent the most time with him. It's got to be hard, especially since you're the one who found him."

Jasper was right. Jamie spent more time with Bobby than anyone else did, probably.

And yet Jamie barely even knew him.

"I'll admit. There have been a lot of times I've turned around and expected him to be standing beside me or started to say something to him before remembering he wasn't there. And people have been coming by the garage, saying how much they're going to miss him. I know they mean well, but it makes it hard to get any work done."

For a moment, Jasper got a far-away look in his eye. "Grieving is a process. These things take time, for all of us."

Jamie studied the other man. What in Jasper's past had given him insight into grieving? "Yeah, I suppose you're right."

Jasper cocked an eyebrow. "Something else is bothering you, though, isn't it?"

An understatement, if there ever was one.

"It's just, the way he died," Jamie said. "It seems so ... arbitrary.

Makes you wonder what the point of it all is if a person can go out that way."

Jasper clasped Jamie's shoulder. "We all only have so much time. Seems like all we can do is make sure someone remembers our name."

Amy Lynn announced with a loud slurp she had reached the bottom of her root beer float. Jasper laughed while Jamie shot her a reproachful look.

As he and Amy Lynn were leaving the five-and-dime, they ran into Wade Tucker coming from the feed and seed with two gallons of diesel fuel. Jamie waved at him.

Wade nodded back. "How you doing, Jamie?" He eyed Amy Lynn, a sly grin on his face. "Did you stop by Jasper's for a root beer float by any chance?"

Amy Lynn giggled.

"We might have done just that," Jamie replied. "How are you, Wade?"

He shook his head. "Can't complain. Didn't see you over at McGill's on Friday."

"I had some things I needed to take care of. Maybe this coming Friday."

Wade chuckled. "*This* Friday? You might have the whole bar to yourself. Everyone's going to be at the football game."

Jamie frowned. "Why is that?"

Wade looked up and down the street and leaned in a little. "Didn't you hear? One of them kids from Ezekiel's Mill is missing, that boy they got on the football team. He disappeared Friday night."

Friday night. The same night Sarah was killed. "What do you mean by that?"

Wade shrugged. "I mean, no one's seen him since. He's vanished."

"People don't just vanish." Not without a reason anyway. Jamie knew very well what the reason probably was. He only needed Wade to keep talking.

"Well, he apparently did. The last anyone saw him was right after the game. Of course, everyone's upset. He was a good quarterback. Looked like we might be going to the state championship this year."

And there it was. No one would have cared if he wasn't winning football games for the high school. But the timing bothered Jamie. If Wade was right, the Ezekiel's Mill boy disappeared about the same time Sarah Jordan was "taken by the shadows," as Calvin put it. Supernatural creature or not, a werewolf couldn't be in two places at once.

Jamie did his best to push down his growing unease. "Well, now. That's a shame. Hopefully he'll turn up soon."

Wade shrugged. "We'll see."

"You have a good rest of your day, now, you hear."

"You, too, Jamie."

He waved to Wade, who continued down the street lugging his cans of fuel. On the way home, Amy Lynn told him all about the new book she was reading. Jamie nodded and gave affirmative grunts, but he didn't pay much attention. He needed to talk to David. The werewolf wasn't killing off a random victim every full moon anymore. Something more sinister than that was happening, and Jamie had the sinking feeling they weren't anywhere close to being prepared.

———

ADDIE WAS PACKING up to leave for the day when she heard a knock on her classroom door. She looked up to find Mr. Deakins standing in the doorway.

"Can I come in for a second?" he asked. "I know you're about to head out. This won't take long. I promise."

"Sure," she said. "What is it?"

"I just got off the phone with someone from the state Department of Education," he began. "They're talking about coming in and integrating more of the children next year."

"That'll be a good thing for the children, right? I mean it'll give them better opportunities."

Mr. Deakins frowned. "It means they'll probably close this school down. They might reopen it, but it won't be as an elementary school. I don't know what's in store for all our teachers, but there are probably going to be a lot of layoffs."

"They'll find places for us, or as many of us as they can." Addie wanted to believe it anyway.

Mr. Deakins shook his head. "You know that's not going to happen."

"Why are you telling me this?"

"Because you're one of the best teachers I have. You've got a good shot at finding something somewhere else. I want to give you a head start."

"What about you?"

"Me?" He chuckled. "I've been thinking about retiring for a few years now. I might take my chance while I have it." He took a step back. "Think about what I've said, and I'll keep my ears open. If I hear of any job openings anywhere, I'll let you know."

His words echoed in Addie's head on her walk home. She could hardly conceive of the school being closed. It was the elementary school she had gone to. Still, she hated how there were never enough books or pencils or paper or anything else for everyone. She hated how the roof leaked and how the carpet was torn up or how the plumbing didn't always work. The white kids didn't have to deal with any of that at their schools.

She was still thinking about what Mr. Deakins said as she unlocked the front door. She didn't notice how quiet the house was at first. Only after a minute or so did she realize she should have heard her dad watching television or her mother in the kitchen starting on dinner. She looked for them but couldn't find either of them.

"Mom? Dad?" she called.

The air in the house seemed different, too. Thicker, heavier.

"They ain't here," a voice behind her said.

Addie spun around to find the Black Man smiling at her, showing his gleaming white teeth. He was dressed in a black three-piece suit again, like a preacher on Sunday morning.

"What did you do to them?" she asked.

The Black Man held up his hands. "I didn't do anything to them."

"Then where are they?" Addie demanded.

"At home."

Addie's blood ran cold. "Then where am I?"

"A place in between," the Black Man replied.

"Why did you bring me here?"

"I want to help you."

Addie glared at him. "What's it going to cost me?"

He laughed. "You learn quickly. But this one is going to be free."

"And why should I believe that?"

"Let's say you're already doing us a favor by removing a problem."

"You mean the werewolf."

"It's dark magic that made him, the darkest. Full of hate and malice. It's got no place here. You're going to stop it."

She shook her head. "I'm done with that. I can't. I've hurt people. I killed someone."

He looked at her like she'd just said the sky was green. "Is that what you believe? That boy was gonna die anyway. What does it matter if your spell was the cause?"

"It matters to me," she whispered.

"What about the ones who visit you at night? You still keep a list of their names?"

Addie glanced at the drawer of her desk. She wrote down every name. Every person killed by the werewolf. That way at least someone would remember them. "How do you know about that?"

"Who do you think I am?" he bellowed. "You have power, Adelaide Prichard. It would be a shame not to use it. Do it for them."

"But I don't know how to keep the magic from going wild," she protested. "I can't control it."

Unless I'm actually trying to hurt someone, she added silently.

The Black Man pulled a card seemingly out of nowhere and handed it to her. A tarot card, the High Priestess, the same as Sarah Jenkins had pulled. "Do you know what it means?"

Addie turned the card over in her hand. "Not exactly."

"It's an invitation to trust your intuition," the Black Man

explained, "to embrace the mystery of the universe, to immerse yourself in your own inner wisdom."

Addie twisted her mouth into a smirk. "Oh, is that all I have to do?"

The Black Man held up a finger. "There is one other thing."

"And what is that?" Addie asked.

"You should be angry."

He snapped his fingers, and suddenly Addie was in her house, her real house. The television droned from the living room, and pots clanged in the kitchen. In her hand she still held the tarot card.

———

JAMIE LAY in the bed of his pickup truck in the back yard, staring up at the inky sky. The stars sparkled, and the waxing moon dusted everything in silvery light. The night was quiet. Normally Jamie found peace in the darkness, in the solitude, but the partially shaded face of the Man in the Moon looked down on him with a mocking grin. Less than a week until the full moon. Less than a week to stop whatever awful thing was coming.

When the shadow loomed over him, Jamie wasn't surprised.

"Got a light?" David asked.

Jamie sat up and tossed him his lighter. "I thought you might show up."

"I didn't know if I'd find you here or not," David said as he lit his cigarette.

Jamie grunted. "You have a pretty good chance these days."

"Nightmares?"

"Always."

David took a long drag. "Yeah, I know a little bit about those."

"What do you do to get rid of them?"

David stared off toward the tree line. "I kill things."

"I was afraid you were going to answer something like that."

David leaned against the side of the truck. "We need to talk."

Jamie hopped out of the truck bed. "Yes, we do. I've been trying to get hold of you for two days now. Where have you been?"

"Finding a new place to stay, seeing as how my door got busted in Friday night."

"What do you mean?"

"Just your friendly neighborhood Nazi werewolf."

Jamie swore. "What happened?"

As he listened to David tell him about his fight with the werewolf, Jamie thought he was going to be sick.

"And you say this was about midnight?" he asked when David was done.

"Yeah, why?"

"What would you say if I told you there were two other werewolf attacks Friday night at about the same time?"

David shot him a dirty look. "I'd say that's not a very funny joke."

"Not a joke. Just ask Sarah Jordan and Marcus Jones, except you can't, because they're missing."

"Who are they, exactly?"

"Sarah Jordan's family has a farm on Dry Creek Road," Jamie explained, "directly across from where Jeff crashed his car. To hear most people say it, she was a little touched in the head. I'm not so sure. I think she saw things the rest of us can't."

David scrunched up his face. "And the other one?"

"A high school student, one of the kids they let into Avalon High from Ezekiel's Mill."

"You're sure they were both attacked by werewolves?"

Jamie held up his hands. "What else could they be?"

David forcefully exhaled a cloud of smoke. "Three werewolves."

"So, does that mean more Nazis?"

"Worse." David paused and took another long drag. "Those are your neighbors."

———

THE RUMORS GOING around the school about Marcus were crazy. Some people said he ran off because he got a girl at his old school pregnant. Other people said he got caught trying to break into someone's house and was hiding from the police. Still others claimed he'd made a pass at one of the cheerleaders and her boyfriend didn't take too kindly to it. Mick didn't believe any of those stories.

Mick knew Marcus was dead.

He'd found Marcus' ripped-up, bloody letterman's jacket under the bleachers when he ditched biology class to go have a smoke. It wasn't even hidden that well, like someone wanted it to be found. He stuffed it as far down under the bleachers as he could, deep in the shadows where no one was likely to spot it.

After school, he thought about going back for the jacket, but figured someone would probably find him with it and accuse him of doing something to Marcus. His own parents would probably turn him into the cops. They sure as hell didn't care what happened to him. They'd probably be happy to have him away.

He was in the cemetery that night because his dad kicked him out of the house again. Another stupid fight over something he didn't do right. He didn't really even know what he fucked up. As soon as his dad started yelling, he'd tuned out.

So, he'd come there, to the cemetery. Most days he felt closer to dead than alive anyway. It was quiet, and he didn't mind the ghosts.

He leaned against the cold, stone walls of the MacNeil mausoleum and closed his eyes for a moment. He could almost hear the whispers of the spirits in their graves. He imagined them calling him to join them. Would it be so bad? What did he have to look forward to?

Maybe he could do what David said. Steal some money, buy a ticket on a Greyhound to New York. See the Statue of Liberty and the Empire State Building. And then what? Get a job? Work until he died? He could do that right where he was.

He took a last drag on his cigarette before he tossed the butt on the ground and stamped it out. Straightaway he went to light another one. Out of the corner of his eye, he caught the profile of a carved angel, seeming to reprimand him with its dead eyes.

"You got a problem?" he asked the stone statue.

"Littering is a crime," a gravelly voice said.

Mick looked up but didn't see anything except the black roofline of the mausoleum against the night sky, that is, until one of the angels moved. Two glowing yellow eyes glared down at him. He stood frozen in place. This wasn't a ghost. The creature loped across the roof of the mausoleum and leapt down to the ground in front of Mick as easily as someone hopping off a curb. Now he could see what it was. A giant coal-black wolf, but with the body of a man.

"You should show more respect for the dead." The wolf "talked" somehow, though its mouth didn't move.

"I'm sorry," Mick stammered. "I'll pick up all the butts and promise to never do it again."

He was seeing and hearing things. He wasn't really talking to a werewolf. Surely not.

The wolf let out a raspy chuckle. "It's not that easy, Mick. We have some business to take care of."

Mick's heart pounded outside his chest. He could try to run, but he knew it wouldn't do any good. "What sort of business?"

The wolf cocked his head to the side, ears pointed forward. "Weird Mick. Always alone. Eating lunch in the corner. Sneaking off to have a smoke under the bleachers. Finding things you shouldn't."

The jacket.

"What happened to Marcus?" Mick asked, his voice trembling.

"I put Marcus in his place." The wolf bared his teeth in a sneer.

"Why? What did he do?"

The wolf stepped closer, his movements like smoke. Mick could smell his rancid breath. "What's it like, Mick, always being on the outside? No friends. Never invited to the parties. Do you like it? Do you like watching? I actually think you do. You're always lurking, always snooping, sticking your nose in where it doesn't belong. Don't think people haven't noticed you talking with that Jew, telling him things that aren't any of his business."

What was it in the movies that hurt werewolves? Silver, wasn't it? Silver bullets. Mick didn't have any of those on him. But he did have something else. The silver lighter that used to belong to his grandfather.

"Here, catch," he said as he threw it at the wolf.

Instinctively, the wolf reached out with a giant clawed hand and caught the lighter. Immediately he shrieked as the metal seared his skin. Mick turned and ran as fast as his legs would carry him. If he could get out of the cemetery. If he could get to the Episcopal Church across the street. Maybe he'd be safe there, but the growls and snarls behind him told him there wasn't any hope. The wolf scrambled over the graves after him, closing the ground between them in mere seconds. As his claws raked across his back and the blood soaked his clothes, he realized he'd be joining the spirits in the graveyard sooner than he thought.

24

TUESDAY, SEPTEMBER 11, 1962

David's lungs ached. His heart beat so fast he thought it might explode. Tree branches smacked him in the face as he ran, and the slick, wet leaves covering the ground threatened to take his feet out from under him, but he didn't dare slow down. They were right behind him, and they were gaining, growling and huffing and yowling. If he stopped running, he died.

He raced headlong through the woods, not really paying attention to where he was going, only trying to get *away*, until suddenly he came upon a fast-moving stream blocking his path. The things would be on him any second. His only choice was to cross. He'd walk on water if he had to.

He never expected Jakob to be waiting on the other side. His partner looked exactly as he did the day he died—slicked-back, dirty blond hair, dark suit, polished loafers, and Browning pistol in the holster at his side.

He smiled at David, blue eyes gleaming in the mottled sunlight, but right before David leapt off the bank of the stream, a gunshot rang out. A spray of blood erupted from Jakob's head, and he collapsed to the ground. Stunned, David stumbled and fell. He didn't even have time to scream before the pack of wolves pounced on him and tore him to pieces.

David opened his eyes. Overhead the lopsided ceiling fan creaked and hummed as it spun. For a moment he forgot where he was, but bit by bit, the details came back. The rough, threadbare bedsheets, the smell of stale cigarettes and mold, the ripped wallpaper. He was in a motel room in Roscoe, the next town over from Avalon. Not ideal, but the best he could find at such short notice, not to mention what he could afford.

Light seeped into the room from around the edges of the curtain. He glanced at the clock on the nightstand next to the table. Nine-thirty. Uttering a string of swear words, he untangled himself from the sheets and rummaged around for his clothes. He was going to need coffee—and lots of it—before he could figure out his next move.

Roscoe didn't have a fancy diner like the Tick-Tock, and David missed the rapport he'd developed with Peggy the waitress, wherein he made witty comments and she ignored him, but the food and the coffee were both serviceable. After he downed his third cup, the cobwebs in David's brain began to clear, and a plan took shape.

Yet, all the coffee in the world couldn't banish the black thoughts in his head. And why would it, when the whisky didn't help either? No matter what he did, the sight of Jakob lying dead in a dark puddle of his own blood haunted David. On the drive back to Avalon even the weather mirrored his dark mood. They were in for a storm.

It was already almost noon when he pulled into the driveway of the Jordan house on Dry Creek Road. The house itself sat on top of a small rise and commanded a bit of a view of the surrounding area. Farmland and pastures stretched out toward the horizon, dotted here and there with patches of woods. One of those patches of woods was directly across the street, the place where Jamie said his army buddy's car was run off the road. Anyone looking out the window that night would have had a front-row seat for the show.

Walking up to the front door, David rehearsed everything he was going to say, but he didn't get a chance to say any of it. As he was about to knock, the door opened to reveal a tall, lanky man. His hair was light, almost white, and he had the palest blue eyes Jamie had ever seen.

"You shouldn't be here," the man said.

David took a step back. "Excuse me?"

"You shouldn't be here," the man repeated. "They're hunting for you."

David looked askance at him. "I'm sorry, but I'm pretty sure we've never met before. Who are you?"

"I'm Calvin, Calvin Jordan." He extended his hand.

Despite his unease, David shook with him. "How do you know who I am?"

"You're the Knight of Swords," Calvin replied as if it were the most obvious thing on earth.

David frowned. "The what?"

Calvin reached into his pocket and pulled out a folded and creased playing card. He handed it to David. "Sarah told us all about you before she ... went away. She said to give this to you if you ever came by the house."

David glanced at the card. It wasn't and ordinary playing card. It came from a tarot deck. The image was a knight on horseback, sword held high, rushing into battle.

"I don't understand."

"The Knight of Swords meets the fight without a second thought. He is single-minded in his pursuit of his ordained mission." Calvin spoke as if he were reciting lines from a play. "Sarah said you'd understand when you were ready."

This conversation was getting stranger by the minute. "About Sarah. I'm sorry for your loss."

Calvin shrugged. "It was her time. Besides, she's not gone. Not completely."

"But do you have any idea why she was ... targeted, I guess?" David asked.

Calvin was silent for a moment. "Sarah knew things. Spirits from the other side of the Veil talked to her. I think her visitor that night wanted to know about something she'd been told. And she wouldn't tell him."

"Did she ever share with you the things she'd been told?"

Calvin nodded. "Sometimes."

"Do you know what this 'visitor' wanted?"

"Not exactly, but I'm pretty sure it was about you. And about the others. The Hanged Man and the High Priestess."

David had about had it with the cryptic bullshit. "The Hanged Man and the High Priestess? Who the hell are they?"

Calvin wrinkled his nose. "There's no need for language like that. I think you know who they are already."

David did. Of course he did. *Jamie and Addie.*

"Sorry," David said. "One more question. Who's hunting for me?"

Calvin glanced back over his shoulder, as if there were someone standing behind him. "I can't tell you anymore right now. You should go."

And with that he shut the door.

David walked back to his car, wary of every sound, every moving shadow, but no werewolf ambushed him. Once in his car, he tossed the tarot card onto the passenger's seat. The Jordans were strange, Jamie had been right about that, but it didn't mean they were crazy. He didn't doubt Sarah Jordan knew things, but unlike her, they didn't have a direct pipeline to the supernatural. They had to figure out things on their own and hope it wasn't too late.

David's next stop was Avalon High School. He parked his car behind the school by the football field. There wasn't anyone around as far as he could tell. Still, he didn't want to be there any longer than he needed. School was in session, and he didn't want to get caught out there without a good explanation.

Fortunately, it didn't take him too long to find what he was looking for—prints in the dirt. They looked like they had been made by a giant dog. He followed them in the direction of the football field, but when they got close, they took a turn toward the bleachers. Here he came upon a jumble of other footprints, and for a second, David was afraid he'd lost the trail, but he picked it up again after scanning the ground for a few minutes. The paw prints led underneath the bleachers.

The shadows were thick there, and brambles and vines covered the ground. Dark clouds had taken over the sky, and even though it was only a little after noon, it seemed like twilight. The trees swayed in the wind, but underneath the bleachers, the air was still. It weighed down on David like a heavy blanket.

A foul smell filled the air, and the feeling that he shouldn't be there overcame David. He needed to leave. At the same time, he knew for some reason he couldn't, not until he found ... something. He scanned from side to side, stepping his way carefully through the overgrown weeds. Eventually he reached the point where the bleachers overhead were low enough he had to duck.

There, nestled among the weeds and cigarette butts and empty liquor bottles, he found what he didn't know he was looking for, a bloody and torn jacket in bright blue and gold—the school colors—with the name Jones embroidered on the left front. David picked it up, and something tumbled out. A head, without the body attached. Mick's head, his eyes frozen over in terror.

————

ADDIE WALKED into a silent house for the second day in a row, but today at least it wasn't because of any uninvited supernatural guests. Her father was working second shift for the rest of the week, and her mother was out visiting one of her aunts. So when the phone rang, it nearly startled her out of her skin.

She picked up. "Hello?"

"Is this Addie Prichard?" a man's voice asked on the other end.

Immediately, Addie's guard went up. "Yes, this is she. To whom am I speaking?"

"My name is Harlan Elder," the man replied. "I was a friend of your grandmother."

"I don't recall her ever talking about someone by that name."

"Well, she might not have. I run the drug store over on North-brook Drive right beside the old Simpson's Grocery Store."

The building that used to be the Simpson's Grocery Store had been vacant and abandoned ever since Addie could remember. They passed by it every Sunday on the way to church, and Addie didn't recall a drug store there.

"What is it that you need to speak to me about? My grandmother's been gone for a few years now." If this "Harlan" was trying to play a trick on Addie, she certainly wasn't in the mood.

"Your grandmother came to me for certain ... hard to find ingredients she needed," Harlan said, "and I thought you might be running low on some things yourself, like sulfur powder and High John the Conqueror root. You should come by and pick some more up."

A peculiar feeling came over Addie, like if she turned around, she'd see him standing behind her. "How did you know I was out of those things?"

Harlan chuckled. "Your grandmother was always going through those ingredients. I told her she needed to be a little more judicious in their use, but she always said the recipe called for what the recipe called for. Now are you coming down to get some more or what?"

"You mean today?"

"You got a better time?"

The logical part of Addie's brain practically screamed at her. She didn't know anything about this man, not even if he was really who he said he was. She didn't know what he wanted, if he could be trusted, if he meant to do her harm in some way. But another part of her wanted desperately to learn more about her grandmother's secret life, and maybe why her grandmother had deliberately kept it hidden from her.

She took a deep breath. "I'll be there as soon as I can."

"Great! I'll be looking for you." He hung up without saying another word.

Addie ran next door to their neighbor Mrs. Beauchamp. She was a widow who rarely ever left her house. The Pontiac out in front sat unused since her husband died. Addie's mother had borrowed the car a few times when she needed one and her dad was at work. Mrs. Beauchamp looked at her a little sideways when she asked to use it, saying she needed to take something to her mother, but she nodded and gave Addie the keys. Addie just hoped Mrs. Beauchamp never mentioned anything to her mother about it.

As she neared the Simpson's Grocery Store, she started to have doubts again. Someone was playing a joke on her. A pretty nasty joke. And only if she was lucky. The smart thing would have been to turn around, go back home, and pretend nothing ever happened, but she couldn't do that, not without the answers to the questions she had about her grandmother.

She pulled into the cracked and weed-strewn parking lot of the abandoned store, and sure enough, there was a small building next door, set back from the road a little and hard to see unless you were right up on it. She wondered why she'd never noticed it before. A sign out front said, "Elder's Drug Store," and the word *Open* flashed in neon letters in the window.

Addie got out of her car and approached the store warily, navigating the puddles in the parking lot. Thankfully the storm had blown through quickly, leaving as abruptly as it had come up. Though there seemed to be a spark of electricity lingering in the air.

She stopped at the door, still debating whether she should go in. The front window had the types of things you might expect from a drug store—cigarettes, cigars, candy, antacids, headache powder—no sulfur powder or High John the Conqueror root. She almost lost her nerve when the door opened, and an elderly man stepped out.

He was big. His skin was almost as dark as the Black Man, but his hair was cotton white. Smells of old leather, mothballs, and tobacco wafted out the door with him.

He looked at her expectantly. "Well, what are you waiting for, Miss Prichard? Are you coming in or not?"

Addie's face felt flush. She couldn't speak for a moment, and when she did, all the words came out at once. "I'm sorry. I ... I've never been here before, and I never even knew this place existed, and I'm sure my grandmother would have brought me here before, and you seem to know an awful lot about me, but I don't know anything about you."

The man laughed, a rich, warm sound that put Addie at ease, at least a little. "I'm not going to bite. We'll start there."

He stepped aside to let Addie through. The inside didn't look like any drug store Addie had ever seen. The light from the front window didn't seem to reach very far. Among the candy and the antacids, bottles and jars crowded the dim, wooden shelves, some with labels, some without. Some of them held different colored liquids. Some held what looked like dried herbs. A few held other things, including a jar Addie would have sworn was full of bones.

Harlan led her farther into the store. "Now about those ingredients you said you needed ..."

"I never said I needed them," Addie corrected. "How long did you know my grandmother?"

Harlan scooped a jar of something off a shelf as he passed by. "Oh, a very long time, a very long time indeed."

"Where did you meet her?" Addie persisted.

"I met her right here in this very store. She was a lot like you then, a little nervous. A little unsure of herself. She learned." He frowned, like he was doing mental calculations, and then he took another jar off the shelf beside him.

"She never talked to me about her ... recipes. I mean, we talked about sweet potato pie and biscuits and collard greens, not the ones that required these ingredients. I didn't know anything about this part of her life."

Harlan stopped and looked at her. "That's a shame. You have so much talent. She wanted to teach you. I guess she never got the chance."

"She talked about me?"

"All the time. She was so proud of you." Harlan grabbed a few more things and carried everything he had collected up to the counter where an old-fashioned cash register sat. He rang up each item one at a time, naming them off. "Sulfur powder and High John the Conqueror root, like we talked about. And I'm throwing in some other things you're probably going to need, too. Some sandalwood oil and some hyssop, since that's a little hard to find around here. Also, you can't ever have too much bluing." He picked up a shiny black rock. "And this piece of schorl might come in handy."

"But I'm not doing magic anymore," Addie protested. "I can't control it."

Harlan waved a hand. "Nonsense. You don't control the magic. You let it work through you. It will do what it wants."

"I don't want to hurt anyone."

He stopped ringing up her purchases and regarded her with a kindly look on his face. "When you do a spell, do you think about it, or do you feel it?"

Addie stared down at her feet. How was she supposed to "feel" a spell when she'd never done one before? When she didn't even know what half the ingredients were and had to rummage through her grandmother's cigar box of supplies, trying to read the faded hand-written labels on the jars? When she had to read the instructions over and over to make sure she was doing everything right?

The only times it all seemed to come natural were the spells she'd directed at Rose. All that anger and resentment, and jealousy. She let her emotions lead her. And the spells had worked.

"Your grandmother loved her family and loved her community," Harlan continued. "When she worked her magic, she always did it to help someone or protect someone. That didn't mean shying away from bad emotions. Sometimes she poured her sorrow into her spells, or her anger, even her fear, but regardless, she always poured everything she had in, because of the people she cared for. Now this'll all be a dollar fifty. Are you going to take it?"

Before she could talk herself out of it, Addie pulled her money purse out of her handbag.

Harlan put everything in a paper bag for her and handed it over with a smile. "Now you don't go using it up all at once. Some of this stuff is hard to get, like I said."

Addie thanked him and left, his words still running through her head. As she pulled out of the parking lot, she glanced in the rearview mirror. Harlan Elder's drug store wasn't there anymore.

———

It was close to closing time, and Jamie was the last one left at the garage. He sat in his office and studied the peculiar collection on his desk—three river rocks, four Mercury dimes, two Indian Head pennies, and a silver dollar. All found in the pocket of his pants or in his shoe. He would have assumed Ginny was putting them there for some reason, but after the first couple, he started checking his pockets as soon as he put on his pants. Nothing was ever there, until later in the day a coin or a rock appeared by magic. And that didn't give him great comfort.

The ringing phone jolted him out of his thoughts. He sighed and rolled his eyes. Probably someone with an "emergency" who needed their car fixed right then on the spot. Never in Jamie's experience had there ever been an emergency that couldn't wait until the next day. So he was surprised to hear his father-in-law's voice on the other end when he picked up.

"Jamie, there's a meeting tonight. Seven-thirty at the Baptist church."

He hung up before Jamie could even open his mouth to ask a question, but George didn't have to tell him what kind of meeting. Another evening out. Another lie for Ginny. He hated it. All of it. He wished he'd never found those damn papers.

With a heavy sigh, he called Ginny to say he'd be late. She started to argue with him, but he told her he didn't have time to talk about it. Fortunately, he still had his robe and hood in his truck, so at least he didn't have to sneak that past her.

A little before seven-thirty, he pulled into the parking lot of the Avalon First Baptist Church. It was already full. He couldn't help but wonder what someone driving by thought was going on there on a Tuesday night, but then again, most people probably pretended it was only a men's Bible study, even if they knew the truth. Everything was easier that way.

Before he got out of his truck, he patted the place where Edward, the mojo bag, hid under his shirt. The bag gave off a reassuring warmth against his skin. Even if Addie had sworn off magic, Jamie was at least grateful for Edward.

He entered through the same door as the last time and followed the voices again to the fellowship hall where his induction ceremony had taken place. Everyone was chatting while they put on their robes, making small talk and laughing like they were out at a church social. Jamie spotted his father-in-law, but George didn't come over to greet him. He only nodded, a grim expression on his face. While Jamie pulled on his robes, he scanned the room for the man with the piercing blue eyes. He failed to find him.

A few minutes later, the doors opened, and Rhett MacNeil strode into the room in full regalia. If anything, his robes seemed fancier than the night of Jamie's induction. "Okay, boys, let's go," he bellowed.

All Jamie could do was follow the stream of his fellow Klansmen out of the fellowship hall. Outside several pickup trucks sat waiting. One of them, a blue Ford, belonged to Oliver Grant. He had brought it to Jamie's shop a week before for a tune-up. Wendell Grayson was there with his Chevy, too, and Roy MacBride's shiny black restored 1946 Ford brought up the rear. Jamie clambered up into the back of Oliver's truck alongside his father-in-law.

"What's going on?" he asked in a low voice.

George shook his head. "I can't tell you. You're going to have to see."

By then it was getting dark. They took backroads out of town, avoiding any of the main streets. Jamie's heart sank when he realized where they were going.

Ezekiel's Mill.

He wondered what the people living there thought as they watched from inside their homes the trucks full ghostly figures in white hoods drive through their neighborhood. Actually, he didn't have to wonder at all. He knew all the things the Klan had done.

They hoped as they peered through their closed curtains the Klan would pass them by that night, that they wouldn't be singled out, that the Angel of Death would spare them that evening.

Terror. That was the Klan's goal. They wanted everyone who saw them to be afraid. To hide. Don't speak up. Don't make waves. Don't call attention to yourself, because maybe those hooded men were bluffing, but maybe they weren't.

When they pulled up into the clearing across the street from Ellie Morris' house, Jamie's panic rose. Why did it have to be her? If they tried to hurt her or her family, could he do anything to stop them? What would happen to his family if he tried? His mind raced even as another truck came into the clearing. Several of the men unloaded supplies from the back, including what looked like two big beams of wood. They fit the beams together and nailed them in place. Jamie fought to keep down the bile that came up in his throat.

They had made a cross.

Someone painted the cross with pitch while others dug a hole in the ground. Then they erected the cross and made sure it was secure before piling kindling all around the base.

A torch burst to life. Then another and another. The light cast dancing shadows across the clearing, making them all look like the ghouls they were.

George approached Jamie with a torch and held it toward him. "Go on. You've got to be the one to do it."

Jamie glanced around to find everyone looking at them. "What? Why me?"

George lowered his voice. "I told you when you agreed to join, Amy Lynn couldn't be friends with that girl anymore, but I'm still hearing things about them spending time together. People are talking, Jamie. You're making me look bad, and you're not doing yourself any favors. You need to do this, to prove your loyalty."

Jamie thought desperately for a way out. "Why does Amy Lynn need to be dragged into all of this? She's just happy she has a friend."

"And I told you we'll get her new friends." He did little to hide the scorn in his voice.

The two men had had their disagreements over the years, but this was different. Jamie didn't even recognize the man standing in front of him. "George, she's your granddaughter. You know it's not that easy for her."

"She'll get over it." George shoved the torch at Jamie. "This is more important."

So that was it, then. Without any other options, Jamie took the torch and turned around to face the cross. The others had cleared a path for him. They started singing, low at first, but rising in volume. They sang hymns, ones Jamie had grown up with but would never hear the same again.

Nothing but the Blood of Jesus.
Nothing but the Blood.
Blood.

When Jamie reached the base of the pitch-covered cross, their voices echoed across the clearing. He touched his torch to the kindling. It caught quickly. The flames climbed up the cross and clawed at the night sky.

And the demons were unleashed.

The mojo bag burned so hot Jamie was sure it scorched his skin. He saw them, demons filling the air, feeding off the hate and the fear. Shadowy creatures with claws and teeth and leathery wings. He heard their laughter over the singing. These men called themselves Christian, but the fire burning that cross was hellfire. God had nothing to do with what they were doing.

The *thump thump thump* of a drum reverberated through the air, and they all fell in line, marching in time counterclockwise around the cross. Widdershins his grandmother would have called it. Unlucky. Evil. Did they know? Did they care? Or was it by design?

Across the street, the front door of the house opened, and Isaac Morris' face peered out. Behind him, the faces of his wife Josephine and Ellie appeared briefly before Isaac pushed them back and shut the door. For as long as he lived, Jamie would never forget the terrified look in the girl's eyes.

Thump. Thump. Thump. They marched and sang, and the demons fed. Jamie lost track of time, of where he was, what he was doing. All he could hear was the *thump thump thump* of the drum. Or was that the beating of his heart?

Sirens wailing in the distance broke the spell. Someone had called the police or the fire department or both. The drum stopped. The singing ended. The cross was doused with water. Everyone loaded back up in the trucks and left the authorities to find only the smoldering cross.

As Jamie drove home, he kept his eyes on the road directly ahead of him. If he listened, he could still hear the *thump thump thump* of the drum, and he knew if he looked behind him, he'd see the demons following him.

25

WEDNESDAY, SEPTEMBER 12, 1962

All anyone could talk about was the cross burning. By midmorning Jamie was already sick of it. Everyone who came into the garage had their opinions and their theories, their gossip and their conspiracies. That afternoon, they brought in stories of reporters in town from as far away as Columbia and Charleston, there to talk to people about what had happened. Thankfully none of those reporters made their way out to his garage. He wasn't sure what he would have told them.

When he got home that evening, he found Amy Lynn and Ginny together in the kitchen getting dinner ready.

He paused in the doorway. "Come here, Amy Lynn. I need to talk to you for a minute."

Amy Lynn looked to her mother, who nodded. She came to where he was standing. "Am I in trouble?"

He knelt down so they were eye-level with one another and took her hands in his. "No, not at all. It's just ... Was Ellie at school today?"

Amy Lynn shook her head. "No, she wasn't."

"Do you know why she wasn't?" he asked.

She scrunched her face up into a frown. "Some of the boys were talking. I didn't really understand all of it. Some people went and ... did something to her house, to try to scare her."

The image of the terrified girl's face came unbidden to him. "You remember last year how there were police everywhere when she and her friends came to your school? You know those police were there to protect them so they didn't get hurt, right?"

Amy Lynn nodded. "Ellie told me about it. She said she was really scared when she started school. A lot of people yelled at her and called her names because they didn't want her there. Some of the kids are still mean to her, but mostly they leave her alone."

"Except for you."

A cautious smile spread across her face. "Except for me."

"Are the other kids mean to you?"

"No. They don't really pay attention to me, either, but no one ever does, so I'm used to it."

Jamie winced. All he wanted was for Amy Lynn to be happy. He didn't realize how lonely she must have felt. "Do you know why they don't want her at your school?"

"Because she's black," Amy Lynn whispered.

"And there are some people who think they're better than her because of the color of her skin."

"Do you think that?"

"No, no I don't. We should let people live their lives. That's what I've always believed." Jamie took a deep breath. He didn't know doing this was going to be so difficult. "I need you to do something for me, and I know it's going to be hard, but I need you to stop spending time with her. It's not safe."

Amy Lynn jerked her hands away. "But that's not fair. She didn't do anything wrong."

"You're right. It's not fair at all, but your mother and I don't want you to get hurt."

Tears welled up in Amy Lynn's eyes. "But she's my best friend. You can't make me stop talking to her."

"Amy Lynn, listen—"

"No, I won't do it," she yelled. "You can't take my friend away from me."

Crying, she ran away upstairs.

Jamie threw himself into a chair at the kitchen table. Ginny sat down next to him and covered his hand with hers.

"I'm just trying to keep her from getting hurt," he said.

Ginny squeezed his hand. "Maybe this is something we should have discussed first."

He met her gaze. "But you agree with me. It's not safe for Amy Lynn to be around her right now. What if they decide to get more violent and Amy Lynn happens to be in the way?"

"No, I do agree with you, but maybe there was a better way to approach that?"

"Like what?"

Ginny pursed her lips. "I could have talked to her instead."

Jamie frowned. "What's that supposed to mean?"

"It means your delivery was pretty bad. I could have talked to her about what it means to be safe, about what her friend is doing to be safe. Something a little more diplomatic."

"Are you saying I don't know how to do that?"

"I'm saying we all have different strengths."

Jamie glanced toward the stairs. "Do you think you could go talk to her now?"

"She needs some time to calm down. Then I will. I promise." Ginny smiled, a real smile, one that said they'd get through this together. "Now I need to get dinner finished or we're never going to eat."

All the guilt from lying to her came down on Jamie like a ton of bricks. For the hundredth time, he wanted to tell her the truth. He even started to, but he couldn't get the words to come out of his mouth. There's no way she'd ever believe him.

He felt like a traitor as he intertwined his fingers with hers. "Thanks. I don't know what I'd do without you."

———

As Clint parked his bike, he wondered about Emmett's choice of a meeting place—the high school football field—well after school was over. Friday night, the lights would be on, and the bleachers would be full of people, cheering on the home team, either reliving glory days they'd never get back or experiencing them, not realizing they'd be over soon. Nothing ahead but a whole life in this small town with nowhere to go.

But right now, the field was empty, and there were no lights save for the glow of the nearly full moon. He had a knife in his boot and another hidden in his vest—just in case—and the gun in the holster at his side was pretty hard to miss.

Emmett stood waiting for him at the fifty-yard line.

"Hell of an inconvenient place to meet up, Emmet," Clint said. "We couldn't go get a beer at a bar or something?"

"It wouldn't be good if we were seen talking to one another," Emmet replied.

"And why exactly is that? We're brothers, remember? I thought family was supposed to be the cornerstone of the Klan."

"Usually, but there are some things more important than family."

"Like what, exactly?"

"Loyalty. Honesty. Trust."

Clint laughed. "You think you're getting any of those from the Klan?"

"I'm getting more than I ever got from you."

"Look, Emmett, I know I haven't always been there for you, but they don't care about you. They will chew you up and spit you out as soon as they think they don't need you anymore. You are nothing more than a useful idiot."

Clint expected Emmet to blow up at him, to start yelling, probably throw a fist or two. Wouldn't be the first fight they'd ever had, but Clint knew once Emmett got it out of his system, he'd be easier to reason with.

Except Emmett didn't do any of those things. He just stood there. And when he spoke, there was no emotion in his voice except for cold, hard malice. "He told me you'd say those things."

Clint frowned. "He? Who's he?"

Emmett didn't answer his question. "You're wrong, Clint. The Klan has always been there for me. These men, they are my brothers. Not you. They're fighting for this country. They're fighting for the good."

"It's a lie, Emmett. They're fighting for themselves. They're fighting for power and money. That's all they care about."

"No, you're the one lying," Emmett yelled.

Finally, a raised voice. "Emmett, listen to me. You know I'm not. This is going to sound crazy, but something's going on with the Klan. Something big, something not exactly of this world. Think about your 'brothers' in the Klan. Haven't you seen some weird stuff lately? People not acting themselves? More violent. Quicker to anger. More impulsive. Haven't you noticed it at the meetings, like there's a presence in the room?"

Emmett smiled. It was not at all pleasant. "Of course I have. Everyone has."

"Doesn't it bother you?"

"Should it?"

"Your mechanic friend said something about the Klan being involved in killings here. Is that true? Are you okay with that too?"

Emmett knit his brows together in confusion. "My mechanic friend? You mean Jamie Fletcher? You talked to him?"

"I had him pinned to a wall most of the time, but yes."

"And he told you that?"

"Among other things."

Emmett shook his head. "Sometimes people just need to die, Clint. Good-bye. Hope you can make it back to your bike."

He turned and walked away.

"Emmett, what are you talking about?" Clint called after him. "Emmett, come back and talk to me."

Emmett didn't turn around. "Run, Clint. You don't have a lot of time."

Clint started to follow him when a low growl came from behind. By the time he spun around, his gun was already in his hand. He fired three times. Two of the bullets went astray but the third hit the giant wolf in the shoulder. The creature yelped in pain. Clint dashed across the field for his bike. The creature took off after him, but the silver bullet slowed it down.

Ten years. Ten years it had taken him to track down the werewolf that had attacked him that desolate night when he was on his way home from some bar or another. It came out of nowhere, all claws and fangs. There was blood and pain and then nothing. He woke up in the hospital. Two people he'd never met before stared down at him. They were both black. They told him what happened to him. He'd been mauled pretty badly, but he was alive. They'd scared off the monster.

Their names were Frederick and Marilou. They were brother and sister. At least one of them visited him every day in the hospital while he recovered. Usually both of them. They read him the newspaper and smuggled in food he wasn't supposed to have. They had to know he was a Klansman. They could see his tattoos as easily as everyone else, but it didn't seem to matter. From their kindness he learned the things the Klan told him were lies. From them he also learned about the Klan's dark connection to the werewolves.

Tonight, he was going to finish it off. He reached his bike and hopped on, spinning around to avoid the claws of the monster. He took aim with his gun again, but never got the chance to fire.

Clint never expected the second werewolf to barrel into him, knocking him off his bike. He skidded across the ground for what seemed like forever, and when he finally stopped, he couldn't move. He lay in the dirt, gasping for air, struggling to stand again, but he couldn't get his legs to work. His head swam, and his ears rang. He tasted blood in his mouth. The growls came closer. There would be no one saving him that night.

————

LYING IN BED, Addie knew better than to investigate the noise outside her bedroom window. It was a subtle sound, a low moan, barely audible against her father's television, but she heard it clearly every few minutes.

After several hours without any sleep, she'd had enough. She threw the covers off and stalked to the window. She half expected to see the inhuman face of another ghost staring back at her, and she was fully prepared to tell them that if they wanted to talk to her, they were welcome to come inside her bedroom, but there was no way in hell she was going outside. When she yanked the curtains aside, though, she didn't see anything except the black night. She went back to bed and pulled the covers up as far as they would go.

Then it called her name.

Addie.

She tried to ignore it, but it called again.

Addie.

She covered her head with her pillow, but still the voice called.

Addie.

She stormed over to the window again. Still, nothing but the darkness, and with a huff she went back to bed again. Mercifully, the voice stopped.

But then the front door opened and closed, and footsteps made their way down the hall. They paused briefly outside her bedroom door before it creaked gently as it opened. The footsteps came into her bedroom and stopped at the foot of her bed. Addie lay paralyzed, too terrified to look anymore.

Addie.

The voice came again, from nowhere and everywhere all at once.

Addie, get up out of bed. It's time to go. We have to hurry.

The voice, a woman's voice, seemed familiar somehow, but Addie couldn't place it. She felt the weight of someone sitting on her bed and a hand gently brushing her leg.

Addie, enough hiding. You must know the truth.

Slowly, Addie pulled down the sheet to see the woman who had brought Jamie to the Bray Plantation looking back at her. She wore the same purple, green, and gold dress and headwrap as before.

"Who are you?" Addie asked.

"The answer to that question is always changing, but for now you may call me Grandmother Sorrow." The woman held out her hand. "Now come with me. It is time for you to find out the truth and to decide."

Despite her doubts, Addie took Grandmother Sorrow's hand. The spirit led her out of the house and into the night, through the garden and down the street. Despite walking barefoot, the rough dirt road didn't hurt her. The night air felt slightly cool as they went along. At the end of the street, instead of turning to go toward the elementary school, Grandmother Sorrow led her off the road into the woods.

The underbrush became thicker the farther they went from the road, but the roots and the branches seemed to move out of their way. The ground was wet. Addie's feet sank into the mix of decaying leaves and dirt.

Deeper and deeper they went. Addie didn't remember the woods being this big. These were the same woods she and her sister played in when they were kids. They should have come upon more houses by now. The trees grew bigger, their trunks so wide Addie didn't think she could get her arms even halfway around, and up above, the canopy blotted out the moon and the stars.

Finally, they came to a small clearing in the shape of a perfect circle. A figure stood in the center in a shaft of moonlight, a man, completely naked. Out of his head a pair of antlers grew. He faced away from them.

"Go ahead," Grandmother Sorrow said, "ask him the question that has been weighing on your heart."

She pushed Addie into the clearing. The man turned around, seeming to notice her for the first time. He smiled, not the least bit embarrassed.

"Sir," she said trying hard not to stare at his manhood, "whoever you are, I'm sorry to disturb you, but I hope you can be the one to finally answer my questions."

He laughed. "I can, but only if you ask them."

"Who am I?"

"You are Addie Prichard, daughter of Marie and Arnold Prichard, granddaughter of Zora Garland. You are the High Priestess."

"But what does that mean? All I have is a notebook from my grandmother, a few colored candles, and some old jars of powder."

Before her eyes, the man changed, the antlers disappeared. He grew to at least ten feet tall, and thick green fur appeared all over his body. When he spoke, it sounded like a falling tree.

"That's not all you have," the man said. "Magic is far grander than what's in that notebook. There is a whole world out there you don't see. Your grandmother understood that. You have her music. Remember when you hummed it and conjured up the wind? You didn't need a ritual or a candle for that."

"Why don't you sing her song now?" Grandmother Sorrow asked.

Addie turned back toward her. She had changed as well. Now instead of one woman, there were three, each one identical, except one held a torch, one a key, and one a dagger.

"I don't know if I can."

"Close your eyes. Don't think. Just feel."

Addie did as she was told. She closed her eyes and tried to remember her grandmother and all the feelings her memories brought. She hummed, searching for the tune again, and then she sung out a single note, followed by another and another. Something about the song was wrong, though. It wasn't the pleasant melody she had hummed on that hot afternoon.

No sooner did she stop than a wind rushed into the clearing, nothing like the cool breeze that had come up before. It shook the tree branches and swirled around in an angry circle.

"You're mad. That's good," the man, or whatever he was, said.

Addie shook her head. "But that's not what I was trying to do."

"You were trying to force pleasant, happy feelings, but that's not what's in your heart right now. It's not what should be in your heart. You will need that anger for what is coming."

He changed again, the green fur becoming leaves, his skin turning brown and rough like bark.

"What's coming?"

"A fight," the tree-man replied.

"Don't listen to him." Another figure stepped into the clearing, a black man dressed in suit pants and a coat, but without a shirt. He wore a top hat, and his face was painted to look like a skull. "There's a fight coming, all right, but they want you to play by their rules. Come with me and I'll show you all the things magic can truly do."

"Who are you?"

"A friend."

"You are not a part of this conversation. You should leave now," Grandmother Sorrow said. Only she had changed again. There were still three, but they weren't identical anymore. One was a young girl. One was a grown woman, stomach swollen with a baby. The third was an old, stooped crone. She was the one who spoke.

The man in the top hat ignored her. "When you hexed that woman, how did you feel?"

"It was a stupid thing to do."

"But it made you feel powerful, didn't it? It felt good."

He wasn't wrong.

He changed, the same as the others. He became a woman in a head covering, but the skull face paint remained. "I can show you how to feel that way all the time. I can show you how to make sure no one ever hurts you or the people you love again." She stabbed a bony figure at the tree-man. "They only want to use you for their own ends. The choice is yours. Ask them."

She looked to the tree-man.

"It's true," he said. "The choice is yours. You can follow a different path, if you'd rather. It depends on the price you want to pay."

Part of her wanted to follow that different path. She could help her family. None of them would have to struggle again. But what if the price was her soul?

She shook her head. "No, I know who you are. You're Death. I can't follow you."

The specter changed again. This time turning into a man dressed all in black, with a grinning face. He reached up and placed a hand on either side of his head. Then he slowly and gently lifted his head off his neck and tucked it under one arm.

"If you know who I am," he said, "then you know you can't escape me forever. I may be Death, but I'm your Brother. I'll wait for you, should you change your mind, and if you don't come to me, I'll come for you, Addie Marie Prichard. Maybe soon."

She stood up as tall as she could and stuck out her chin. "And when my time comes to leave this world, I'll go with you, but my time is not today."

The smile grew wider if possible. "You have a lot left to learn. You'd better hope you have time."

He vanished, evaporating into the shadows.

"I knew you'd make the right decision," the tree-man said, smiling.

She held up a hand. "Now listen, Brother Death had a point. I'm not your pawn. In this fight that's coming, it's going to be for those people who are dead, and for the ones yet to come. I don't care about your magic being off kilter or whatever the Black Man said. I'm doing this for all of them, not you. Do you understand?"

The smile didn't fade. "I understand perfectly."

He reached his arms up in the air. They grew longer and longer, his fingers stretching into branches. His body gained in girth until it became a solid trunk. In his place an oak tree stood.

"Come," the woman said, "I'll lead you back. The path is not easy to see, and there are things in the woods you wouldn't want to meet."

It didn't surprise Addie to see she had changed once more. The triple figures were gone. She had returned to a single body, but now her dark skin was a light tan. She wore a red dress, and she had four arms. She was silent as she led Addie through the forest again. Addie couldn't help but look into the gloom surrounding her, wondering what those things in the woods were. Once she thought she heard something calling her name.

"Don't look," Grandmother Sorrow said, taking her hand. "Close your eyes, I'll lead you."

They emerged on the road a few minutes later.

"I trust you can make it to your house from here. Get some rest. The fight has almost arrived." And with that she retreated into the woods.

26

THURSDAY, SEPTEMBER 13, 1962

J amie knew something wasn't right when he came home and found Ginny sitting in the living room by herself. She didn't look at him. He sat down on the couch next to her and tried to put his arm around her, but she shied away.

"Ginny, what's wrong?" he asked.

She held out her fist and opened it up. In her palm rested the pin Rhett MacNeil had given him. He'd forgotten all about it. "I found this in the pocket of one of your pairs of pants. I pricked my finger on it."

"That's just a button I found," he said.

She narrowed her eyes. "I know what this is, Jamie, and I know you don't 'find' buttons like this. Where did you get this?"

Jamie rubbed his hands across his face. No point in lying anymore. "Look, it's a long story. I got the button from Rhett MacNeil, but I only met with him because your father wanted me to. He's a Klansman. He wanted me to join. I'm sorry. I'd hoped you wouldn't find out."

Ginny set her jaw. "Jamie, I've known my dad was a Klansman since I was twelve."

She may as well have slapped him. "You've known?"

"One night I got out of bed to get a glass of water," she explained, "and I accidentally saw him when he came home wearing his robes."

"Why didn't you ever tell me?"

"Because it's not something I'm proud of," Ginny replied, "and it didn't seem important. But now. You'd only have this pin if you joined, too. Did you?"

Jamie hesitated.

She shook her head. "Oh, Jamie …"

"It's not for the reason you think," he said quickly.

She stood. "Jamie, no."

"Listen—"

She balled her hands into fists. "No, you're going to tell me you joined for business reasons, because they'd make things bad for you at the garage if you didn't."

"Well, they did imply that, but that's not the reason either."

"Then what is it?"

How much could he tell her, without her thinking he was crazy? "You know that car they brought in after the accident on Dry Creek Road? It had a hidden compartment, and I found some documents in it, documents people were willing to kill the driver for. Something's going on with the Klan. Something bad. More people are going to get killed. I'm just trying to stop it."

Angry tears came up in her eyes. "You said you'd leave it to the sheriff. You promised. Joining the Klan isn't something you do lightly, and certainly not something you do so you can play amateur detective. What else are you lying about?"

"I'm not lying about anything else. I told you it was complicated."

"I don't want to hear anymore."

"Ginny—"

"No. I said I don't want to hear it."

He sighed. "Fine. I'm going, then. I'm getting a drink. Don't wait up for me."

If looks could kill, Jamie would've been a dead man. "I won't. I've gotten used to you being gone."

Jamie drove to McGill's, mad at himself for leaving that pin in his pocket. He walked in and sat at his usual place at the bar. He flagged down Mack and ordered a beer, but when Mack brought it to him, he didn't really want it. He and Ginny rarely fought. On the one or two occasions they'd really had a major disagreement, the whole world seemed off center until they made up. He didn't know how he was going to fix this one, though. A bunch of daisies wasn't going to cut it, and he couldn't think of any way to explain to her what was going on that didn't make him sound like a complete madman.

It wasn't long before Billy MacNeil came in with Hank and Wade. They waved. He waved back halfheartedly. The last thing Jamie wanted was company, but he couldn't exactly tell them all to go away when they took the seats beside him. They seemed to be in a festive mood.

"So, what brought you here tonight, Jamie?" Billy asked, slapping him on the back. "You're not usually out here on a week night."

Jamie shrugged. "Been a long day. Thought I'd unwind a little before I headed home. How about you?"

They all looked at one another with a conspiratorial look in their eyes.

"We're celebrating," Billy said.

Jamie eyed him. *Something's not right.* "Celebrating what?"

"Celebrating people finally getting what they deserve," Hank elaborated with a wicked grin.

Jamie laughed nervously. "What's that supposed to mean?"

Billy leaned toward Jamie and lowered his voice. "It means after tonight, there won't be any more talk of letting those kids into our schools anymore."

Clarity came to Jamie like a bullet to the head. Hank and Wade both worked at the chemical plant. They weren't farmers. Hank didn't need fertilizer. Wade didn't need diesel fuel for a tractor. And when Billy was talking to Caleb Murray at Bobby's funeral, he wasn't listening to Caleb tell war stories. Jamie learned a lot of things from his time in the army, and he knew fertilizer, diesel fuel, and dynamite were the ingredients for a bomb.

They had planted a bomb.

And it wasn't hard to figure out who their target was.

Jamie finished his beer in several quick gulps, tossed some money on the bar, and stood, trying not to make it obvious he was in a hurry. "Well, it's been good to talk to y'all, but I'd best be going now."

He forced himself to walk to the door, but as soon as he was outside, he ran to his truck. He spun the tires getting out of the parking lot and sped down the road faster than he had ever driven before. When he got home, he ran into the house. Ginny was still sitting in the living room, her eyes red and puffy from crying.

"Jamie, I—"

He threw up a hand. "I'm sorry, Ginny, not now. This is an emergency."

He dashed for the telephone and dialed a number scribbled on the pad next to it. A busy signal. He hung up and tried again, only to get the same.

Frustrated, he slammed the phone down. "Damnit. I've got to go over there. I've got to warn them."

"What are you talking about, Jamie?" Ginny pleaded. "You're not making any sense."

Jamie was already halfway to the door. "I've got to get to the Morris' house."

She caught him by the arm. "Why? What's so urgent?"

He pulled free of her grip. "The Klan planted a bomb. They're in danger."

Ginny covered her mouth. Fear crept into her eyes. "A bomb? Are you sure? You should call the police."

Jamie shook his head. "I can't trust them to make it there in time. You call, but I've got to get over there."

"I should go with you."

"No, you stay here with Amy Lynn."

"I don't want you hurt." Her voice trembled.

He wrapped his arms around her and squeezed tight. "I'll be careful. I promise."

Jamie raced to Ezekiel's Mill as fast as he could, praying the whole time he wasn't too late. He felt no small amount of relief when he

pulled onto the street where the Morrises lived and didn't find everything on fire, but that could change at any second.

He jumped out of his truck and leapt up onto the porch. He
banged on the door until Isaac Morris answered.

Isaac looked him up and down. "Jamie? What's going on?"

"Please," Jamie said. "I know you're going to think I'm crazy, but I
don't really give a shit anymore who thinks that. Someone's planted a
bomb at your house. I don't know where, and I don't know when it's
supposed to go off, but you and your family need to get out now."

He called for his wife and for Ellie. Jamie ticked off the seconds in
agony as they spoke in hushed tones with their backs to him, willing
them to hurry up. Finally, they moved, grabbing a few pictures, some
books, and a suitcase. They ran out of the house and over to the
neighbors to warn them about the bomb. They did the same with the
neighbors on the other side. All told about twenty people gathered in
the field across the street where the cross burning had happened.

"The police should be on their way," Jamie told Isaac. "Then
maybe we can get to the bottom of what's going on." He glanced
down at the suitcase by Isaac's side.

"We had an idea something like this could happen," Isaac
explained. "We put a plan together in case we had to leave the house
in a hurry."

A sheriff's car pulled up to the front of the house. The door
opened and Rick climbed out. Jamie waved to him. He started across
the street toward the gathered group.

"What's going on—"

He didn't have a chance to finish. The explosion blew open the
front of the house and turned his patrol car on its side. Jamie and the
others threw themselves to the ground, but fortunately they were far
enough away to avoid the worst of it.

Rick wasn't.

When the smoke cleared, he lay face down in the middle of the
road, not moving. The entire front of the house—and Jamie's truck—
were gone. Everything was on fire. People panicked, crying and
yelling and running in every direction. Some of them had cuts and

bruises from flying debris, but everyone seemed to be at least conscious, except for Rick.

Jamie made his way over to the sheriff's deputy. Thankfully he was still breathing, although his breath was shallow and raspy. His clothes were all torn up and bloody.

Jamie gently placed a hand on his arm. "Don't worry. Help's coming."

Sirens screamed in the distance. The firetruck arrived a lot faster than the night of the cross burning. Firemen scrambled to take care of the blaze. A swarm of sheriff's deputies showed up not even a minute later, along with a couple of ambulances. Jamie stood by as they loaded Rick into one and watched it go on its way, lights flashing and siren howling.

Isaac came up alongside him. "Thank you," he said. "You saved our lives. I don't know how I could ever repay you."

Jamie held up a hand. "Don't. I did what any other decent person would have done."

Isaac sighed. "I wish I could believe that."

Jamie decided he wanted to change the subject. "Do you have a place to go for tonight?"

"My mother lives up by the AME church on Jordan Road. We'll go stay with her."

Jamie shook his head. "Man, if I were in your shoes, I'd get as far away from here as I possibly could. Maybe never come back."

Isaac clinched his jaw. "That's what they want us to do. They want us to run and hide. I'm not giving them the satisfaction."

Jamie didn't know how to reply to that, but as it turned out, he didn't have to. A sheriff's deputy called to him, a pudgy guy maybe a decade younger. Jamie seemed to recall he was the nephew of Beulah Martin, one of the old ladies in the church choir. For the next several hours, the deputies took turns questioning Jamie about everything. They asked him how he knew about the bomb, when he knew it, why he knew it. He told the truth and didn't waiver, no matter how many times they repeated their questions.

Finally, around two in the morning, they let him go. Ginny was waiting up for him when he got home.

Jamie took her in his arms and hugged her tight again. "Ginny, I'm sorry. Things are going to get a little strange for a little while. I never meant it to get like this. I'll tell you every little detail, no matter how insane it sounds."

She put a finger to his lips. "You can tell me after we've both had some sleep, but I promise I won't think you're crazy."

———

LONG BEFORE ADDIE knew anything about fertilizer bombs, she stood at the edge, in the space between the road where her house sat and the woods where magic lurked. She didn't have a guide this time, and she didn't know what was waiting for her among the trees, but she was there nonetheless, poised to cross the threshold.

With a deep breath, she stepped into the trees. Nothing changed. The woods were still the everyday woods they always were. A glance over her shoulder confirmed her house and the street were still there. She took a few more steps. Still nothing. She feared she'd never find her way back to the clearing and the tree-man. Twenty feet in, she almost turned around, but a crow cawed in a tree above her. It looked at her with its black eyes, head bobbing from side to side, before it spread its wings and flew off, deeper into the woods.

Rosemary, the mojo bag Addie had made for herself, hummed softly in the pocket of her skirt. Her skin prickled. The air crackled, and the whole forest fell silent. When she glanced behind her, she couldn't see the road anymore. The woods had closed in, the way blocked by a thicket of bushes. In front of her, a neat path through the woods opened up, following the flight of the crow.

She had no choice but to go forward, it seemed.

As she walked, the woods grew darker. The trees took on bent and twisted forms, reaching out with gnarly roots and branches. Something in the shadows called her name, but she didn't dare reply.

Things darted among the trees at the edges of her vision. If she stayed on the path, she'd be safe, she told herself. At least she hoped.

Finally, she came upon the clearing where she had been the night before. The oak tree stood tall and majestic in the center. She approached it hesitantly.

"I've come back," she said.

There was no answer.

"I have more questions," she continued. "I've read my grandmother's spell book cover to cover, but I still don't understand. How do I fight the werewolf? I can make mojo bags. I can make amulets. I can draw circles of protection. I can defend. But how do I fight?"

The tree still didn't respond.

"You're not asking the right question."

Addie spun around at the voice.

Brother Death stepped out of the shadows once again, back in his top hat and skull face.

"I told you I'm not following you," Addie said flatly.

"And I'm not here to persuade you otherwise, although I'd be delighted to have your company." He gave her a wide toothy grin. Then the smile faded. "No, today I am merely a messenger. Tell me, what's really the question you came today to ask the Green Man of the Wood?"

Her gaze went back to the tree. "How do I use my grandmother's song?"

Brother Death shook his head. "I'm afraid he can't answer that question."

"But he said—"

Brother Death silenced her with a hand. "He can't do that because it's not your grandmother's song. It's your song. It has to come from your heart. No one else can sing it but you."

Addie's heart sank. "I don't even know how to begin."

"Start singing."

Without any other choice, Addie closed her eyes and took a deep breath. She sang, the sound of her voice tentative and halting at first. She sang her grandmother's melody, but somewhere along the way, it changed. Her voice grew stronger, louder. She let the magic flow through her for the first time, and poured in all of herself, all her fear and her anger and her frustration, but also all her hope her joy and her love.

The wind stirred. Addie opened her eyes. This was not a simple breeze or an uncontrollable gust. It spun and twirled and danced, picking up leaves and making patterns. It was alive. Addie couldn't help but smile.

Brother Death shook his head slowly, a disappointed expression on his painted face. "A shame. You would have been powerful by my side. A queen. You have too much of your grandmother in you."

Addie looked Death in the eye. "I'm not supposed to be the queen. I'm supposed to be the High Priestess."

Brother death wrinkled his nose and twisted his mouth into a sneer. "If that is the destiny you seek to fulfill."

A noise like an explosion rumbled through the clearing.

"Learn quickly, though," he continued as he faded into the shadows, "because it's a destiny closer than you think."

27

FRIDAY, SEPTEMBER 14, 1962

A my Lynn didn't go to school the next day. Jamie and Ginny let her stay in her room and read her books while downstairs in the living room Jamie went over with Ginny everything that had happened, step by step, from finding the papers in the silver Chrysler to figuring out Hank, Wade, and Billy had planted a bomb at the Morris' house. He didn't leave out anything, not the boo hags or the werewolves or Sarah Jordan's tarot cards, or the flying demons at the cross burning.

When he was done, Ginny sat quietly for a moment, her hands folded in her lap, gaze toward the floor, lips drawn into a thin line.

"You didn't have to lie to me," she said finally.

"All I wanted to do was protect you and Amy Lynn." Jamie ran his fingers through his disheveled hair. "I figured the less you knew the better."

Anger flashed in Ginny's eyes. "The better for what? So, you go off and get yourself killed and I never know why? Or worse yet, you disappear and no one ever finds you? I could have helped. You didn't give me the option."

"Helped? How?"

"Where do you think all the rocks and coins you've been finding came from?"

"You? I don't understand."

"Your friend Addie isn't the only one whose grandmother taught her a little magic." Ginny hesitated, chewing her lip. "The truth is, I have dreams, about things that haven't happened yet, and I've had a lot of them lately, about you. They ... don't have happy endings."

"Why didn't you ever tell me about this?" Jamie asked.

"Would you have believed me? Before the last month, I mean. When I was little, I told my parents. They laughed it off as an active imagination. My Grandmother Owens, though, she believed me. She taught me how to make little charms to protect myself from ... whatever is out there in the dark." Ginny closed her hand, and when she opened it up again, she held another Mercury dime. "That's what I did. I made little charms for you. They were supposed to show up when you needed them."

Jamie was about to reply when the telephone startled both of them. When he answered, his father-in-law gruffly asked to speak to Ginny. Jamie passed the phone to her. He didn't stick around for the conversation, but based on what he overheard, he didn't think it was a pleasant one. She spoke in hushed, clipped phrases.

"What was that about?" he asked when she hung up.

"Dad wants me and Amy Lynn to come stay at their house," she said.

"What did you tell him?"

"I said no, of course."

"Maybe you should listen to him."

She looked at him like he had suddenly grown three heads. "What do you mean? We're a family. We stay together."

Jamie could barely believe what he was saying either. "You're right. We are a family, and that's not going to change, but things are going to get really dicey over the next few weeks. If you go stay with your parents, maybe they won't come after you."

"You don't honestly think someone's going to try to hurt *us*, do you?"

"Ginny, they've already killed innocent people. They're absolutely capable of hurting you and Amy Lynn."

And tonight is a full moon.

The phone rang again, and again Jamie answered.

"Jamie, this is Rhett MacNeil." His voice dripped with menace. "I'd like to discuss your recent talk with the police concerning the unfortunate explosion. In person."

The last thing Jamie wanted was another meeting with Rhett MacNeil, especially one he wasn't sure he'd return from. "Rhett, I'm sorry, but it's not a good time right now."

"I'm not asking. My house. This evening. Seven-thirty. Don't be late." He hung up.

All day long the telephone rang. Bartholomew Avery, Boyd Parker, Bennett Blake among others, all telling him he'd made a mistake for giving Hank and Wade and Billy away to the police. He shouldn't have used their names. He should have lied about how he knew about the bomb. Or worse yet, he should have left it alone completely. He shouldn't have stuck his nose in. It wasn't any of his business what happened to anyone in Ezekiel's Mill.

Jamie listened to every one of them without replying. What was there to argue about? He couldn't go back and undo anything. And he'd do it all over again. He couldn't live with those lives on his conscience.

Toward evening, the calls finally slowed down. Jamie was about to go upstairs to check on Amy Lynn and tell her to get ready for dinner when the phone rang one more time.

"Yes, what is it?" Jamie answered, letting all of his irritation come out in his voice.

"Jamie? This is Isaac Morris. Is ... is, ah, Ellie there with Amy Lynn?"

Jamie frowned. "No. Why do you ask?"

"She's not here. She snuck out, and her bike is gone. I didn't know if maybe she made it there." Isaac was obviously trying to stay calm, but the panic in his voice was impossible to miss.

"No, Amy Lynn's up in her room."

Ginny shot Jamie a confused look. He motioned upstairs toward Amy Lynn's room and watched as Ginny went up, a sudden feeling of dread overcoming him.

"Maybe you could ask her if she knows where Ellie might have gone?" Isaac asked.

"Sure, sure. No problem." Jamie's gaze remained fixed on the stairs.

Isaac said something else, but Jamie wasn't paying attention to him anymore. Ginny should have been talking to Amy Lynn.

Why didn't he hear them talking?

Why didn't he hear his daughter's voice?

Ginny came rushing back down the stairs, her face stark white. "Amy Lynn's gone."

"What?" Jamie shouted. "What do you mean she's gone?"

"What's going on?" Isaac's frantic voice came from the receiver.

"I thought she'd be in her bed reading one of her books, but she's not." Ginny clutched the railing of the stairs. "Her window's open. It looks like she tied bedsheets together to get to the ground. It's a wonder she didn't kill herself."

If anyone would know how to tie knots, it would be Amy Lynn.

"Amy Lynn snuck out, too," Jamie told Isaac.

Ginny lowered herself onto one of the steps. "She's never done anything like this before."

"We've never been through anything like this before." Jamie glanced outside. The days were getting shorter. It was already starting to get dark. The moon would be up soon. "Where could they have gone?"

"I think I might know the place," Isaac said. "The Bray Plantation. Ellie's gone there before. I overheard her telling Amy Lynn about it when they had their sleepover. We've told her she's not allowed to go there. It's dangerous, but you know how kids are."

"Okay. Ginny and I will meet you there as fast as we can." Jamie hung up and turned to Ginny. "We need to get to the Bray Plantation. Isaac thinks the girls may have gone there."

"How? You don't have a truck anymore, remember?"

Jamie's pickup was a twisted and burned hunk of metal. One of the sheriff's deputies had dropped him off at home the night before.

"I can get us there," he said. "I just need to make a phone call."

About half an hour later, David's Ford Fairlane pulled up in front of the house. He had picked up Addie along the way. Jamie made quick introductions before they all jumped into the car and headed for the abandoned plantation.

Isaac and his wife Josephine were already there.

"We can't find their bikes anywhere," Isaac said. "We've covered a lot of the grounds, all the way over to the old slave's quarters."

At the mention of the slave's quarters, Jamie shivered. "Did you look in the house yet?"

"Surely, they wouldn't have gone in there, would they?" Ginny asked.

Isaac shook his head. "Not yet. We were waiting for you to get here."

They found the girls' bikes behind an overgrown bush next to the house, deliberately hidden.

"Looks like this is the place." Jamie sprinted up onto the porch. "Watch your step."

Inside, Jamie, David, and Isaac swept flashlights all around the entrance. A few old chairs and a table—broken, rotten and moldy— lay strewn about the room. The remnants of wallpaper still clung to the walls in tatters, the pattern long faded away. In the back a sweeping staircase led upward to the second story. Half the boards in the floor were rotten out.

They called the girls' names as they carefully stepped around the broken furniture and the crumbling floorboards. A muffled reply came almost immediately.

Jamie pointed toward the second floor. "Upstairs."

They all rushed toward the staircase.

"Wait," called David. "That's not going to hold all of us at once. We need to go up one at a time."

"I'm first," Jamie and Isaac both said over one another.

They locked eyes for a moment. All the fear and anxiety Jamie felt he saw reflected in Isaac's face. They were both just fathers who wanted their little girls to be safe. He motioned for Isaac to go first. He went up next. David and Addie took the rear.

They continued to call out. The girls' cries grew louder as they climbed.

When they all reached the top, Jamie pointed down a hallway to the right. "I think it's coming from this way."

They went down the hallway single-file, past half a dozen closed doors until they reached one that was open. Inside they found a bedroom with a collapsed four-poster bed, and Amy Lynn crouched over Ellie, whose leg was stuck in a hole in the floor.

"She fell and hurt her leg," Amy Lynn said through her tears.

Ellie's father rushed over to her. "Can you walk, sweetie?"

Ellie, crying too, shook her head. "I don't think so."

Isaac ran a gentle hand over her hair. "You won't have to. I can carry you."

Amy Lynn wrapped her arms around Jamie and squeezed. "Daddy, I'm sorry. I didn't mean to do anything bad. We just wanted to see each other one more time. We came up with a plan to meet here, in case anything bad ever happened."

"Why did you think something bad might happen?" But as soon as the question left Jamie's mouth, he remembered the suitcase Isaac and Josephine had packed. He hugged Amy Lynn back. "It's okay, Amy Lynn. We'll worry about all that later. I'm just so glad you're safe."

Isaac knelt down and carefully lifted Ellie up. Ginny took Amy Lynn by the hand and led her out. They went single file again, back the way they had come, but as they reached the top of the staircase, the howl of a wolf rose up. Moments later, a second howl joined the first.

No one said anything, but as one they all ran. They barely made it two steps down the staircase before the front door burst off its hinges. Two monsters charged through the opening. Over seven feet tall, covered in fur and heavily muscled, with long muzzles showing rows of gleaming teeth, they growled and snarled and snapped their jaws.

The one on front had brown fur and was larger and stockier. The other one was pitch black and had the lithe body of an athlete. It would have blended into the darkness but for its yellow eyes gleaming with murder. They fanned out in the entryway.

"Everyone back," Jamie said.

The brown werewolf turned to them and grunted something resembling a laugh. He charged at the stairs but staggered backwards when David fired his gun. Howling in pain and clutching at his leg, he collapsed to the floor, which partially caved in under his weight.

The black werewolf leapt over him, taking the stairs five or six at a time. David fired again, but the shot went wide. The werewolf was almost on top of them when he seemed to hit an invisible barrier and tumbled back down the stairs. Jamie noticed Addie, her eyes closed, clutching the necklace she wore and muttering something under her breath.

Almost immediately, though, the black werewolf pushed himself up from the floor and readied for another attack.

David waved to Jamie. "Go see if you can find another way out. A servant's stairs or something. Addie and I will hold them off as long as we can."

Jamie eyed the snarling monsters down below. "Are you sure?"

"We both have some tricks up our sleeves." David brandished his gun. "This is a fairer fight than it looks. Now go."

Jamie herded everyone back down the hallway. His flashlight swept over the decaying floor, looking for weak spots. All the time he wondered if he was leading everyone to a dead end, in more ways than one. David had slipped him a gun before they arrived at the plantation. He told him it was loaded with silver bullets. Now he fished it out of his pocket.

Finally, they came to a back staircase like David had said. They all hurried down. At the bottom they found themselves in the derelict kitchen. Jamie silently motioned for everyone else to stay back while he checked the door. Once he saw everything was all clear, he beckoned for them all to follow him.

On the other side was a short hallway ending in a door. Moonlight shining through a broken window lay in a rectangle on the floor, beckoning them, but as they approached, a shadow blocked the light, and a low growl reverberated through the darkness.

———

GHOSTS of the former slaves who worked the plantation swirled in the air around David and Addie. Whole families. Generations. Only Addie could see them. Translucent and ephemeral, but not without their own power. The black werewolf leapt at her and David again, snarling and baring its teeth, and again it hit the barrier the ghosts made.

"How are you doing that?" David asked.

"The ghosts are helping me," Addie said.

"But you didn't call them. Don't you have to do some sort of ritual first?"

Addie clutched the amulet she had made from the supplies Mr. Elder gave her. Suspiciously, exactly the things she needed. "I did call them, just in a different way. The ghosts are part of this place. All I have to do is reach out beyond myself a little, and I can see them. I can see their lives, their hopes, their desires. I can feel their pain."

"Maybe you can direct some of that pain at these guys."

The brown werewolf was working his way out of the hole he had made in the floor, and the silver bullet in his leg wasn't going to keep him from shredding them to bits if he got the chance. Addie's ghostly shield could hold off one werewolf, but she didn't know how long they could keep two at bay before using up what strength they had. She and David needed to do more.

She thought back to what the ghosts had said about killing a werewolf, apart from silver bullets, and she formulated a plan.

"Can we get to the first floor?"

David eyed her dubiously. "You want to go toward them?"

"I do. Trust me, and duck when I tell you."

"Okay. I'll make a path."

He fired off two more shots at the black werewolf. The monster dodged the bullets, but the extra few seconds allowed David and Addie to get down the stairs. The black werewolf charged at them.

"Now what?" asked David.

Addie's gaze remained on the wolf barreling toward them. "Remember what I said about ducking?"

"Yeah."

"Do it now."

The stairs exploded, throwing splintered wood, plaster, and old iron nails in the air. Not strictly by chance, two of those iron nails impaled the black werewolf through his hands and pinned him to the wall opposite. The werewolf let out a howl of pain, which ended in an all too human cry. The ghosts had told Addie piercing the palms of a werewolf with iron would turn it back into a human. In the wolf's place now was a man, a boy, really, with jet black hair. He couldn't have been much older than eighteen.

His head hung down at an impossible angle. His neck was broken. He was dead. Forced to become human, he couldn't heal from his injuries.

"He's only a high school kid," David said. "What a shame."

"Marcus Jones was only a high school kid," Addie retorted. "His parents live down the street from me."

"You think ..."

Addie shrugged. "It stands to reason. He looks like an athlete. Probably played football. I wouldn't waste too many tears on him."

David eyed her. "Wait, did you—"

"Did I break his neck? No. He must have broken it when he slammed into the wall."

She almost convinced herself she was telling the truth.

"He's obviously not your Nazi, though," she continued.

The brown werewolf roared as he threw off the rubble and debris that had landed on top of him. He eyed them with a hatred so deep it was a wonder they didn't both drop dead on the spot.

"Got any more ideas?" David asked.

Behind the stairs, or rather where the stairs used to be, there was a door to another room, a parlor maybe. Addie thought she spotted something moving but realized quickly she was seeing their reflection in a giant mirror.

"Lead it back here," she directed.

David watched the brown werewolf push itself up. "I don't think that's going to be a problem."

The two of them raced toward the room with the werewolf in pursuit. It turned out to be smaller than it looked—and a dead end. If this didn't work, things were going to go badly very quickly. The werewolf charged in growling and snarling, obviously thinking it had them trapped.

David took aim at the monster. "I hope you know what you're doing."

"So do I." Addie closed her eyes and reached out to the ghosts. The giant mirror lifted off the wall and smashed into the werewolf, flattening him to the floor and shattering into pieces. A claw reached out from under the wreckage of the giant frame and morphed into a human hand before it fell, unmoving.

"Old mirrors are backed with real silver." David knelt over the ruined mirror. "Death by a thousand cuts. Clever."

He and Addie lifted up the smashed frame to reveal the man underneath.

David took a step back, the lines of his face hard. "Billy MacNeil."

The youngest MacNeil brother was covered in blood. Shards of the mirror dug into his body, including a large piece slicing his neck.

Glaring, he managed to croak out three words. "I hate you."

David knelt over him. "I know, and I'm sorry that's all you have left."

Billy sputtered and coughed up blood. Then he closed his eyes and breathed his last breath.

"He's not your Nazi, either," said Addie.

David set his jaw and drew his mouth into a grim line. "Jamie was right. There are three."

———

THE WOLF ADVANCED TOWARD THEM. Hulking and muscular, like the others, its yellow eyes held the same evil intelligence. The only difference was its tawny-colored coat. Jamie panicked and fired off three shots from his gun. Amy Lynn screamed and grabbed her mother. Two of the shots went wide, but the third one hit the werewolf in the arm. He howled and jerked back, but he didn't move from their path. Instead, he dug a clawed finger into the bullet hole and fished the bullet out.

They could turn and run, but they'd never make it.

"You ruined everything for me," a voice said. "Years of planning. All gone in the blink of an eye. You're too smart for your own good, Jamie Fletcher."

The werewolf was talking somehow, despite not having the mouth for it.

"All those years grooming the right people," he continued, "making sure all the pieces were in place at the right time. Do you know how hard I worked to keep things from exploding last year when they sent the kids from Ezekiel's Mill to the schools in Avalon?"

Jamie glanced around frantically, looking for any way out. "Why? Why here? Why now?"

"The war has to start somewhere. Avalon was going to be the spark that started the blaze. But the timing had to be right. Wet kindling doesn't catch. And I've been oh so patient pretending to care about all your petty problems, about who won the Friday night high school football game, what the preacher said in his sermon Sunday morning, whose marriage is in trouble, whose kid is on the wrong side of the law." He paused and licked his teeth with his long, pointed tongue. "Or who likes two cherries on their root beer float."

Jamie gasped. "Jasper? Jasper Cordell? But you're from here. Your parents grew up in Roscoe. You have an aunt and uncle and a couple of cousins in Walton. You went to Walton High School and community college in Sumter."

"When did I ever tell you those things?" The wolf was close enough now Jamie could smell his putrid breath. "All I ever said was that I have family in Roscoe and Walton. That's all it took. You all filled in the rest for me. Gossip is such an underestimated weapon."

Jamie shook his head. *A minute more. Just figure out a way to survive a minute more.* "You don't have to do this, Jasper."

The wolf laughed, a horrible sound. "You know that's not my name. You've ruined things for me, so now you're going to watch everyone you love die."

"No," Jamie said. "I won't let you."

"How are you going to stop me?"

"Because I'm not alone. And I have more bullets."

The wolf sneered. "Your bullets can't hurt me."

According to Sarah Jordan, Jamie was the Hanged Man, the one who binds himself in order to free himself, the one who surrenders in order to be the victor. Maybe that meant he couldn't win with a direct attack, but he could get creative. "They can if they bring the ceiling down."

Jamie raised his gun and fired into the exposed beam above the werewolf's head. With a bang that echoed the gunshot, the beam cracked. Chucks of wood and plaster came crashing down on top of the werewolf.

Jamie held up an arm to shield against the dust and debris and turned back to everyone. "Run. Now."

They all did as they were told, but the wreckage didn't keep Jasper down as long as Jamie hoped. The werewolf burst through the rubble, and a clawed hand dug into Jamie's side. He was vaguely aware of Ginny and Amy Lynn screaming as the wolf's teeth sunk into his shoulder. He closed his eyes against the pain, waiting on the darkness to come for him.

———

DAVID AND ADDIE followed the sounds of gunfire through the maze of rooms in the old house until they came to the kitchen. Gunshots echoed from the other side of the door, followed by a loud crash. They rushed through the door and nearly collided with Isaac Morris carrying Ellie. Ginny Fletcher and Amy Lynn were there, too, along with Josephine Morris. They watched in horror as a blond-colored werewolf sank its fangs into Jamie's shoulder.

David raised his gun and fired. The bullet hit the wolf in the side. He howled and let go of Jamie, throwing him down like a rag doll. But the wolf didn't go down. Instead, he reached into the bullet hole and extracted the bullet with the flick of a claw.

"You'll have to do better than that, Jew," the monster said.

"So I will," replied David.

He used his grandfather's spoken talisman, the one that had driven Billy MacNeil away, together with the other names of God his book of spells said could be used to fight demons. Wounds opened up on the wolf's arms and side as if David had unleashed a dozen knives. The wolf cried in pain, but as quickly as the wounds opened up, they healed over.

"How dare you use your magic on me!" the wolf screamed. "I'll make you pay for that."

"You're welcome to try, you bastard." David recited the names again, and again the invisible knives slashed open the wolf's hide.

"What has been put in motion cannot be stopped. Even if you manage to kill me, there are others out there doing their part. The world as you know it is about to come to an end. You can't stop us all."

"Maybe I can't, but there are others like me out there, too. I don't have to stop all of you by myself, and there are more of us than there are of you."

Enraged, the monster lunged. David fired his last bullet, hoping to hit the wolf's heart, but the shot went wide. The monster kept coming. David unsheathed his silver dagger. The werewolf's claws missed him by a hair's breadth. He surged forward and embedded the knife in the monster's side. Unfortunately, the sheer force of the were-wolf in motion wrenched the handle of the dagger out of his hand and threw him into the wall, knocking his breath out.

Dazed, he could only watch as the wolf came at him, a frenzy of fangs and claws.

———

ADDIE CALLED on the ghosts to stop the wolf baring down on David, but they could only deflect his attack. They couldn't repel him completely like they had the black wolf. He was too powerful. With the werewolf wheeling around for another try, Addie was out of options. She asked the ghosts silently if they would give their assent for what she was about to do. They did. All of them.

She sang her song, and as she did, she named off the ghosts that had visited her, starting with her sister. Cora. Minerva. Mae. Cynthia. Agnes. A dozen more. She sang for every last one of them. For every life cut short, for every missed birthday, every missed holiday, every missed smile and laugh and kiss and heartbeat. Her voice grew stronger, gathering up the magic like winding up a thread, but Addie didn't conjure up a wind this time.

She thought of fire.

The flame leapt from her outstretched palm and inscribed a fiery circle around the werewolf. He screamed in frustration as the fire grew higher, but soon those screams changed to howls of pain. The fire spread fast in the tinderbox of a plantation house, and soon the heat and the smoke became unbearable. Addie let her song trail off. She stared at the wolf writhing in agony, knowing the souls of his victims were finally free.

David's voice brought her back to reality. "Addie. We've got to get out of here."

He heaved Jamie up over his shoulders like a sack of potatoes, and together they all raced out of the house, even as it fell apart around them.

———

THEY WEREN'T twenty feet away from the house before the whole structure collapsed in on itself, but they didn't stop running until they made it back to the entry gate where they had left their cars. David put Jamie down in the damp grass.

He opened up Jamie's shirt to take a look at the bite. "It's not as bad as it looks. We can get you mended."

Jamie, breathing hard, struggled against him. "No, it's too late. I feel it inside me. You might as well kill me too. I'm going to change soon."

He convulsed, and his eyes, normally a deep blue, changed to shimmering yellow.

Ginny screamed. "Please, help him."

Addie knelt beside him and placed a hand on his shoulder. The act seemed to calm him, but his breathing was still heavy. Words and images came to her. Wulver. Faoladh. Vilkacis. Okuriokami, Kurtadam, the Hounds of God.

"There are other legends of werewolves besides the evil these men brought into the world," she said. "In some places, the werewolf is the protector of the vulnerable and the lost. In some places, the werewolf is generous and kind. I can't take the curse away, but I can take away the hate and the evil. You can choose which legend to follow. You don't have to be a monster. Do you understand?"

Jamie nodded.

Addie closed her eyes and dug the fingers of her left hand into the earth while she placed her right hand over Jamie's heart. She called to the Green Man of the Forest to help her.

The power flowed up through her, a tingling that started in her fingers and passed up into her chest, then moved out her other arm into Jamie. At first it seemed to work. He stopped writhing, and his breathing slowed.

But then he jerked and cried out. Whatever evil, demonic thing was inside him wasn't going to give up so easily. It pushed back against Addie's magic, clawing and tearing, growling and snarling. Addie almost let go of Jamie, but she knew she couldn't.

Jamie reached into the pocket of his pants and pulled out a silver coin. He held it toward Addie even as it seared his skin. "Here. Give this back to Ginny. Let me go. Tell her I'm sorry. Tell her I know she tried. Tell her it's not her fault. Tell her I love her."

The coin, a Mercury dime, was charmed. A protection spell.

Made with love and determination. Magic stronger than it seemed. The werewolf in Jamie recoiled from it.

"No," Addie said. "Keep it. Hold onto it, no matter how much it hurts. Focus on it. Focus on Ginny and Amy Lynn."

Jamie nodded and clutched the coin. Addie closed her eyes and called on the Green Man again, and Grandmother Sorrow, even Brother Death. She called on her own grandmother, too. She sang her song and poured her magic into the dime, amplifying its power. Gradually, slowly, the demon inside Jamie retreated and shrank until it was nearly gone.

Addie turned to Ginny. "You may want to take your daughter away. I don't want to scare her. He'll be okay. You'll see him tomorrow. I promise."

Ginny hesitated for a moment before taking Amy Lynn by the hand and leading her to David's car. She opened the door and made the girl climb in the back.

"Shut your eyes and cover your ears and don't look no matter what," she told her daughter.

Isaac and Josephine retreated with Ellie as well. Only David stayed with Addie.

Addie faced Jamie again. "Don't fight it any more. The turning will just be that much more painful. You won't harm any innocent soul tonight. I promise."

Jamie spasmed again and tore off the remnants of his clothes. He screamed, but midway through, his cry turned into a howl. The man was gone, an animal in his place. Unlike the others, though, he didn't appear to be a monster at all, just a larger than normal wolf with a sandy brown coat. He barked once at Addie and David and took off into the night.

28

SATURDAY, SEPTEMBER 15 1962

When they finally got home, Ginny carried Amy Lynn, who had passed out from sheer exhaustion, up the stairs and tucked her into bed. She lay down next to her daughter. Ginny watched Amy Lynn's chest rise and fall with each breath and stroked her hair. Everyone always said Amy Lynn looked everything like her and nothing like Jamie, but Ginny always saw Jamie in her, the way she thrust her chin out when she was being stubborn, the way her eyes got big when she talked about something she was excited about, even the way she put her hand on her hip when she was thinking really hard about something. Ginny prayed she wouldn't only have those things to remember Jamie by.

About five in the morning, she heard the door open. She went downstairs to find Jamie sprawled unconscious on the couch, not a stitch of clothing on him. She covered him up with a blanket. There would be time to talk later. For now, she'd let him sleep.

Around ten o-clock the phone rang. Ginny answered to find her father on the other end of the line. The day before he'd asked her to bring Amy Lynn to come stay with them. Now he was telling her.

"We're not coming to stay with you, Dad," Ginny told him, glancing over at Jamie still asleep on the couch. "In fact, I think maybe we won't be coming over for Sunday dinner anymore, and you know why."

She hung up without giving him a chance to reply.

———

RHETT MACNEIL SWORE. Everything was going to shit. The state police were swarming all over because of the bombing. He'd told Billy it was about the dumbest idea he'd ever heard, not to even think about it. Rhett wasn't above violence when it was called for, but there wasn't any need to go down that road yet. For some reason, Billy disobeyed him.

And now it seemed Billy had disappeared.

Everything was that Jamie Fletcher's fault. He didn't know what kind of game that mechanic was playing, but Rhett was certainly comfortable with a little violence where he was concerned. Jamie wouldn't ever repair so much as a toaster again when Rhett was through with him.

Rhett poured himself a glass of bourbon and went to his study to smoke a cigar. When he turned on the lights, he was startled to find someone already sitting in the chair at his desk.

David Ben-Ari, the Jew.

"What the hell are you doing here?" he asked.

David stood and came around to the front of the desk. "I thought we might have a little conversation."

"You give me one good reason why I shouldn't call the cops."

"Because they won't come." David leaned against the desk and crossed his arms. "I've spoken to your sheriff. We've come to an understanding."

"Why you son of a bitch," Rhett snarled.

He put the bourbon down and rushed at David, fully prepared to beat the Jew senseless, but he quickly found himself pinned face-down on the floor with his arm wrenched behind his back.

"You ready to hear me out?" David asked.

Rhett wanted to kill him in that moment, but all he could do was nod.

"We need to talk about my friend Jamie Fletcher," David continued. "I understand you've got reason to be upset with him, more than you even realize. A few other people in this town might be grinding an ax as well. I wanted to let you know that if you or anyone else dare to lay a finger on him or his family, I'll be on you like white on rice. Did I use that phrase right?" He smashed Rhett's face farther into the carpet. "I will take away everything from you. Your business, your money, your house, all your precious influence. Gone in the blink of an eye. Nod if you understand."

Rhett nodded while letting out every expletive he could think of.

David laughed. "Good. I'm glad we could have a productive conversation."

The force holding Rhett down vanished. He jumped to his feet, but by then David was already gone. He screamed and threw his glass of bourbon across the room. It exploded in a million pieces against the wall.

———

ON A SUNNY DAY in the middle of September, the Knight of Swords, the High Priestess, and the Hanged Man all stood facing one another outside an abandoned house on a quiet street in Ezekiel's Mill.

"I don't think we're going to get another chance to talk," David said. "I wanted to let you both know I'm headed out of town today. I've got no reason to be here anymore, and there are other Nazis out there that need their clocks cleaned."

David had cleaned up himself. He'd shaved and his hair was combed and all the buttons in his shirt were in the right holes.

Jamie, on the other hand, felt like death and knew he didn't look much better. The things running through his head didn't make a whole lot of sense to him, and all he knew for certain was that his whole world got turned upside-down. "Jasper Cordell. How did I miss it? Surely there were signs, clues, something. He was always so nice.

Never had a bad word to say about anyone. He made Amy Lynn laugh with stupid jokes. And he did know how to make a good root beer float."

David shook his head. "Don't beat yourself up about it. Hitler himself loved dogs and kissed babies. That didn't make him any less of a monster. None of us got it right."

"Any idea where you're headed next?" Addie asked.

David shrugged. "Wherever they send me."

"Wherever that is, I wish you better luck than you had here," Jamie said. "I'm sure you're probably eager to get out."

"I wouldn't say eager," objected David, "but my people have a lot of work to do. We're searching Jasper's house top to bottom. We have leads now on Nazis we've been looking for for years, but we also have some idea of their plans, too. Things in this country are going to get a lot darker in the next several years, I'm afraid."

Jamie grunted. "Things here aren't going back to the way they used to be anytime soon. That's for sure."

"How's your cop friend doing, by the way?" David asked.

"You mean Rick? From what I hear he's going to make it, but he's got a long road ahead of him. There's a good chance he may never be able to walk again." Jamie scowled. "And some people are even blaming me for that. If I hadn't told Ginny to call the police, he wouldn't have been there when the bomb went off."

David spat on the ground. "That's bullshit, and you know it. Look, it's a shame either of you had to be involved in what went down here, but I've seen agents absolutely crumble in situations that were a ride on a merry-go-round compared to what the two of you went through. I'd choose you any day of the week to watch my back."

Jamie let out a rueful chuckle. "You hiring? I might need a job after everything I did. I'm not sure I can show my face here anymore."

"I think you might be surprised." A sly grin spread across David's face. "I had a little talk with the sheriff and with Rhett MacNeil. I don't think you need to worry about them anymore."

Jamie looked askance at him. "You had a talk? That's all it took?"

David smugly tapped his chest with his thumb. "I can be very persuasive. Besides, from what I gather, you're a hell of a mechanic. People might be mad now, but we'll see how long they stay mad when they get stranded on the side of the road. You can go back to fixing cars until your heart's content."

Jamie fought back the sudden tears. "Thank you. That's all I've ever wanted. That and to raise my family in peace. Maybe I can still. I just have to take monthly 'camping trips' now." He turned to Addie. "And thank you. I know you couldn't stop what happened, but you at least showed me another way."

Addie held up her hands. "I did what I had to."

Jamie gestured toward David. "You could have let David put me down."

She met his gaze with a look somehow stern and gentle at the same time. "You didn't deserve that."

Jamie wished he could one hundred percent agree, but he decided it would be best not to argue. "What about you? What are you going to do now?"

"The same thing I've always done," Addie said. "Teach kids."

David cocked an eyebrow. "What about your magic? Are you putting your grandmother's cookbook away?"

A sudden cold breeze made Jamie shiver. "Not likely," Addie replied, a glint in her eyes. "Someone needs to look out for this community. Seems like that has to be me."

"Well, between the two of you, I think I'm leaving this place in good hands at least." David glanced at his watch. "Listen, I'm really bad at good-byes, so let's call this 'until we meet again,' okay?"

The others agreed. The Knight of Swords, the High Priestess, and the Hanged Man parted ways, returning to their normal lives as best they could, but of course, some doors, once they're opened, can't be closed again.

———

"ROSE, DEAR, YOU HAVE A VISITOR."

The figure in the bed slowly turned her head. Addie barely recognized her. She didn't look anything like the Rose Ellison Addie knew. She wasn't wearing any make-up. Didn't have her hair done. Wasn't wearing any designer clothes. She was too thin. Too frail. Too vulnerable.

She smiled. "Addie, so nice of you to come by."

Unlike so many times before, her smile seemed genuine.

Addie willed herself to approach the bed. "I wanted to stop by to see how you're doing, Rose. We all miss you."

Addie had never been in Rose's house before. She had to admit it was nice. Nicer than her parents' with their mostly hand-me-down furniture. But something about it was almost too perfect. Obsessive. Anxious.

"Well, you know I'd be there tomorrow if I could. I just can't shake this ... affliction." Her smile faded. "I can't even make it two steps out of bed these days."

"Doesn't stop you from trying, though," came the voice of Rose's mother from the other room. "Look at what happened yesterday. You're lucky I was there to catch you."

Rose winced, and for the first time Addie came close to understanding her. "Oh, Rose, I'm so sorry."

"Sorry for what? It's not your fault."

If she knew, though. "I just feel bad you're having to go through this. That's all."

Rose sighed. "Well, if it's God's will, I'll endure. Surely He has a plan."

Addie took Rose's hand and slipped a small bag into it. A mojo for healing. "I'm sure He does. And I have a feeling you'll be better in no time. I'm going to go now so you can get some rest. You hang in there, Rose."

29

SATURDAY, OCTOBER 13, 1962

T he orange moon hung low on the horizon like a giant pumpkin, barely clearing the nearly bare trees. A chill permeated the air. What was it Amy Lynn called the October full moon? The Hunter's Moon? That made sense to Jamie as he darted in and out of the shadows, sniffing the air and following trails no human could ever find.

In the month since they'd gone up against Jasper Cordell, life had gotten back to normal, or as normal as it could be at any rate. Amy Lynn and Ellie both went back to school. Thanks to David's kindly influence, no one dared bully them. The community even pitched in to help the Morrises find a new place to live. They helped Jamie get a new truck as well—new to him at least—much to Ginny's consternation. She'd hoped Jamie would finally have a reason to fix up the '33 Chevy in the back yard, but that project would have to wait a little longer.

David was right about the garage. Business hadn't suffered really. Sure, there were those who still refused to speak to him, but they were the exception rather than the rule.

All of that receded into the background, though, as the sandy brown wolf moved like flowing water through the woods and across the open fields. Jamie reveled in his new form and wondered at the sharpness of his senses. Only the inky black sky mattered, only the cold night air, only the sounds of the calling owls and chirping crickets, only the dozens of heartbeats all around him belonging to the frightened animals hoping he would pass them by.

Only the lingering ghosts.

Only the spirits.

Only the demons.

A great many things lurked in the dark, but Jamie was sworn to protect the place where he lived, and those things that hid in the shadows dared not harm anyone that night.

When Jamie emerged from the woods onto Dry Creek Road, he caught a familiar scent. Lilac perfume. He tracked the scent to the Jordan farm. He hadn't been there since the night the crossroads demon chased him and Addie.

All of the windows in the house were dark. Nothing stirred inside, living or otherwise. He skirted around and went to the back. There, set some distance away from the house under the branches of an old oak tree, he found a family burial plot.

The gravestones went back more than a century, to before the Civil War, but there were two off to the side, newer than the rest. Lila and Beauregard Jordan, both passed away in 1960. That explained why no one had seen Calvin and Sarah's parents recently. Another small marker stood nearby, a memorial for Sarah since no one ever found her body. The Lilac perfume was strongest there.

As Jamie sniffed at the marker, a hand ran through the fur on the top of his head. Jamie looked up to find Sarah standing beside him, gazing down with a smile. The edges of her body were fuzzy, though, and Jamie could see through her to the black outline of the farmhouse behind her.

"Come on, wolf," she said. "The cards don't lie. Something dark is coming soon. We've got a lot of work to do if we want to save this town."

ACKNOWLEDGMENTS

Thanks as always to my wife Lara for her help and advice as well as her love and support. Thanks to Melissa MacArthur for her superb editing skills. Thanks finally to the German professor in college who showed us the movie *Europa* and gave me this weird little idea.

ABOUT THE AUTHOR

J. Matthew Saunders is the author of the Daughters of Shadow and Blood trilogy inspired by the Brides of Dracula, the Dreadful Penny occult detective series, and numerous published fantasy and horror short stories. He is a member of the Horror Writers Association.

A native of Greenville, South Carolina, He received a B.A. in history from Vanderbilt University and a master's degree from the School of Journalism at the University of South Carolina. He received his law degree in California and practiced there as an attorney for several years.

Matthew is an unapologetic European history geek, enjoys the Celtic fiddle, and makes a mean sun-dried tomato-basil pesto. He currently lives near Charlotte, North Carolina with his wife and two children. To find out more or to sign up for his newsletter, visit www.jmsaunders.com.

ALSO BY J. MATTHEW SAUNDERS

Daughters of Shadow and Blood

Book I: Yasmin

Book II: Elena

Book III: Elizabeth

Dreadful Penny

Dreadful Penny

Unsettled Spirits

Local Haunts

Legend Trip

Dreadful Penny Compilations

Dreadful Penny: Haunted Past (Novellas 1-4)

The Serbian Bureau of Strange Occurrences

Wolf's Tooth

A Peculiar Reading

The Ghost Lights of Dragutinski Monastery

Nothing but the Blood